A VERY PROPER THIEF

A VERY PROPER THIEF

"4 Stars...A delightful Regency tale."

—*Tara Manderino*
Scribe's World

"Lovers of traditional Regencies will appreciate this book."

—*Debra Bent*
Romantic Times

...As Lord Courtlea rested his arm on the mantel and stared into the fire's sullen flames, Daphne bit her lip, wanting to scream at him to berate her how he would, and have done with it.

"So," he murmured, "to recover this bauble, you became Flora, who offered to stir my fire."

Daphne closed her eyes, feeling again that rush of heat, those conflicting desires that had so shocked her. "Yes," she whispered, "to my everlasting shame."

"Oh, I would not say that! Your performance was masterful. I would swear I held a warm, willing maid in my arms, as eager for love-play as I."

Her eyes flew open. What mercy or understanding could she expect from a man who considered his own wants and pleasures above all else?

Besides, part of what he said was true.

"What, no words of defense or protest?" The earl raised his brows as if surprised. "Come, Miss Summerhayes, you glibly attacked my character. What of your character?"

"I told you why," Daphne protested. "If you were a gentleman—"

"Oh, 'tis all my fault?"

He smiled, his eyes hooded, and a shiver ran down Daphne's spine. Her breath seemed stopped in her throat. 'Twas the smile of the wolf at the helpless rabbit.

"As for you not being a wanton..." he murmured with wicked promise.

Deliberately he walked toward her...

ALSO BY PATRICIA HARRISON

Lord Compton's Folly

A VERY PROPER THIEF

BY

PATRICIA HARRISON

AMBER QUILL PRESS, LLC
http://www.amberquill.com

A VERY PROPER THIEF
AN AMBER QUILL PRESS BOOK

This book is a work of fiction. All names, characters, locations, and incidents are products of the author's imagination, or have been used fictitiously. Any resemblance to actual persons living or dead, locales, or events is entirely coincidental.

Amber Quill Press, LLC
http://www.amberquill.com

All rights reserved.
No portion of this book may be transmitted or reproduced in any form, or by any means, without permission in writing from the publisher, with the exception of brief excerpts used for the purposes of review.

Copyright © 2004 by Patricia Harrison
ISBN 1-59279-859-4
Cover Art © 2004 Trace Edward Zaber

Layout and Formatting provided by: ElementalAlchemy.com

PUBLISHED IN THE UNITED STATES OF AMERICA

*With love and thanks to Bill, Stephanie and Valerie,
and to the Golden Horseshoe Group for their
often-vociferous help and encouragement.*

CHAPTER 1

The disappointment was too much for her to bear with calm decorum. Seizing the first cloak that came to hand, Miss Daphne Summerhayes threw it about her shoulders and stormed from the elegant manor house into the cold January morning. Too overset to wait for the carriage to be brought around, Miss Summerhayes sped through the park and briskly climbed over the stile into Seven-Acre Field. In the gleaned field, under heavy winter skies and with only noisy sparrows to witness, she let loose the temper that matched her bright auburn hair.

"'Tis unfair!" she cried, stamping across the frost-crisped barley stubble. "'Tis completely and excessively unfair! And all for a come-out!"

No voice answered; even the sparrows stilled as Daphne plunged into Howey Wood. She strode along the narrow, twisting path, her half-boots crunching through an occasional thin patch of snow, her gloom deepened by the moan of the wind in the tree tops. For the first time in her life she was blind to the beauty of ruby-red hawthorn berries and bare beech trees gray as smoke among the conifers.

'Twas prodigious unfair, but, as her papa said, what could one do in the face of family duty?

"I am of a dutiful and accommodating nature," Daphne stated aloud, choking back tears of frustration and disappointment. Had she not happily and capably supervised Weldern Manor for her papa and brother since her mama's death nine years previous? Was she not always sensible and helpful?

"But must I always oblige?"

A rook cawed derisively from a tree branch just above her head.

"'Tis not that I begrudge Sophie her come-out," Daphne assured the sooty-feathered bird, "for I most assuredly do not."

Far from it. 'Twas a most thrilling time in a young girl's life, and Daphne was not so long in the tooth as to forget the fun and excitement, the flirtations—

Cold as the winter wind came recollection of her own come-out at seventeen and Sir George Sowerby, to whom she had been introduced at a masked ball at Vauxhall Gardens. Devilishly handsome, smooth of speech, adept at poems comparing Daphne's eyes to rare emeralds and her skin to rose petals, by the end of her Season he had quite turned her inexperienced head and almost won her young heart. All to render another lady jealous enough to accept his suit!

She was sure that Sir George's betrayal had not soured her disposition nor turned her nature at all cynical. If her innocent trust was bruised, the damage was of short duration. Although, she admitted, maturity had brought a more skeptical angle to her eye. She would never again be so easily bammed by a gentleman's winsome words.

Mayhap that was why, with her twenty-fourth birthday fast approaching, she was yet unmarried. Her friends knew her single state was by choice. Those less charitable claimed it was because she was too hard to please or too witheringly direct for any gentleman's taste. Then, too, her papa, happy with her competent management and fond of his comfort, was only too glad to have her remain unwed.

The rook cocked an impudent eye and flew off, and Daphne continued her march and glum thoughts. She was delighted to visit London, for the pain of Sir George's defection had long since passed, and she quite loved the city. 'Twas a pleasant change from her quiet though busy life in the shadows of the Chiltern Hills.

"But not this year!"

Beyond Howey Wood, the full force of the wind tugged at her cloak as though to tear it from her shoulders. Her hood blew back, letting the cold wind flow down her neck.

"Blast!" she muttered, pulling the hood up and fumbling for its ties with hands chilled to the bone. One tie was missing, and Daphne realized that in her haste not only had she forgotten her fur-lined gloves but she had blindly thrown on the old red woolen cloak she used for such tasks as overseeing the gardening or gathering apples.

"Oh, blast twice over!"

No matter, her indignation kept her warm, and she knew that Julia Todhunter, her dearest friend, would not be offput by her attire. Julia would be as overset at this catastrophe as Daphne.

Daphne hurried on, almost losing a boot in a ditch's muddy bottom. The mired hems of cloak and gown flapped wetly about her ankles when at last she reached the hedge bordering the road. Opposite the hedge was the entrance to Todhunter Park.

The hedge appeared a solid, interwoven mass, towering seven feet in height, but Daphne and Julia had, over years of visiting back and forth, created their own secret passage. Impatiently, Daphne pulled aside some branches, bent low through a tunnel-like aperture, and burst out on the road.

Wrapped in misery as much as in her cloak, Daphne heard, too late, the crunch of carriage wheels and the drumming of hooves. A woman screamed, and a man's deep voice shouted a single, sharp curse. Startled, Daphne looked up, but the horses were upon her, neighing frantically. The off-sider, a big bay, reared high.

Daphne cried out, arching back and throwing up her arms in frail defense from the bay's flailing hooves. The animal's eye, white-ringed, rolled wildly. Suddenly, the horse's head was wrenched aside. Foam flew from the bit as the great beast swung away. Its shoulder struck Daphne, knocking the breath from her body and sending her spinning hard to the ground. A wheel scraped past, barely missing her leg but tearing a great rent in her cloak.

Daphne raised her head, tasting dirt on her lips, and caught a fleeting glance of the curricle's occupants. A white-faced young lady, her mouth agape as if frozen in a scream, stared down at her with dark, terrified eyes. Her companion, leaning forward, his profile stark against the opposite hedge, had eyes only for his team as he handled the ribbons.

The sharp veer sent the little vehicle teetering dangerously on one wheel. For a heart-stopping moment, Daphne feared that it would overturn. In saving her, the passengers faced their own deaths. She had neither breath or time to scream. Winded, helpless, she watched the driver swing his team hard, righting the little two-wheeled vehicle, and then halt the frantic animals in the center of the road.

The sudden, terrifying encounter safely over, Daphne turned icy cold and began to tremble. Her heart pounded as if to leap from her breast. But for the driver's great skill she might now lie dead, or the carriage overturned, leaving horses and bodies in a frightful, broken tangle. And, she thought with a rush of guilt, such carnage would have been her fault.

The driver vaulted from the curricle, his cinnamon-colored greatcoat a bright show in the wintry landscape. With the briefest of glances in Daphne's direction, he tossed the ribbons to his fair companion in lieu of a tiger, and strode to the horses' heads.

"Now, then, my good boys, 'tis naught. There, there, all is well, Pharaoh."

Daphne clearly heard the murmur of his deep voice quieting the pair, and wished her agitation could be calmed as easily. Her abundant hair had escaped from its knot, and the bitter wind whipped her loose tresses wildly about her face and shoulders. With some absurd notion of propriety, on hands and knees she groped blindly about in the dirt and gravel for her hairpins.

Suddenly a pair of shining black boots appeared, stopping inches from her grubby fingers. She sank back on her heels and raised her head.

From her lowly position, the driver of the curricle appeared extraordinarily tall. His wide shoulders were made broader by an elegant, many-caped greatcoat she recognized as a "Garrick." A black, high-crowned beaver was pulled low over a pair of dark brows and the coldest, yet most furious pair of gray eyes Daphne ever had the misfortune to face. They seemed to pierce straight through her. She would have shuddered if she were not already shaking beyond control.

He loomed over her, fists on hips, ominous and silent, but fairly crackling with anger. "Are you hurt, girl?" he demanded at last in a tone suggesting that, if she were injured, it was no fault of his.

Daphne's heart had mercifully slowed to a mere gallop. She drew a deep, ragged breath. "I think not," she managed.

"Then up you get, girl," he demanded crisply, "and let me have a look at you."

Reaching down, he grasped her as though she were a common chit, and hauled her to her feet. Daphne gasped, affronted at such rough audacity. She pulled free, but to her dismay, her trembling limbs refused to support her. Her knees buckled, and she sagged forward.

"Ho! Steady on, there!" The driver roughly caught her in his arms, clasping her to him so snugly her toes barely touched the ground.

Never in the whole of Daphne's pampered, protected life had a man dared hold her thus. Moreover, even through his heavy coat she sensed a strong, hard-muscled masculine body. While such solidity might have been reassuring in someone sympathetic and gentle, with this gentleman 'twas more like cuddling with a stone wall.

"What the devil were you playing at, eh?" How harsh his tone to her, and what a gentle croon to his horses! He appeared to care not a whit for her pitiful state. "Come, speak up."

"Indeed, sir, I shall!" Indignantly, sharply, she brought her head up. "'Tis...oh!"

She had moved too fast. Her senses swam, her vision suddenly dimmed, and for a frightening moment Daphne feared she would swoon. All she could do was cling to the wide revers of his greatcoat and stare up at him through the curtain of her wind-tossed hair.

His eyes, the color of the clouds overhead and every bit as threatening, glared down at her. His supporting arms were as comforting as iron bands, yet he had an arrogant air as if clasping a trembling woman to him was a most natural action. That thought disconcerted Daphne even more.

"I—I am not hurt," she blurted through trembling lips, "but I have lost my pins—"

"Pins!" His glare became, if anything, more fierce. "You might well have lost your life, you lack-brain!" His arms tightened until she could scarce breathe. He gave her a hard little shake. "You might have been trampled to death, do you understand that? As it is, you terrified my team, and alarmed Miss Butler. Of all the fool, bird-witted pranks! What were you thinking of, popping out of that hedge like a cork from a bottle?"

Daphne reddened under his cold, cutting tone. Admittedly she was not without blame, but his total lack of sympathy or apology cleared her head and stiffened her limbs.

"I fear, sir, I was not thinking at all," she rejoined tartly. Nor could she think clearly now, held so crushingly in a man's powerful arms. "Pray release me. At once."

She braced her hands on his chest and pushed back against his hold. His eyes narrowed, and for a long moment Daphne feared he would not free her. His head bent closer until his grim face hovered mere inches away. She caught the pleasant, crisp scent of bergamot. His breath warmed her frost-chilled cheek.

Something flickered in his eyes' gray depths, something that sent a jolt shooting along Daphne's nerves. Not of fear exactly; rather a hot rush of excitement, and a warning of danger.

His lips softened a little from their grim line and parted slightly. His gaze locked with hers, and Daphne's heart, barely recovered from its terror, gave a strange leap. Trapped more by those eyes than by his arms, she was breathless, powerless to move. His stare seemed to probe into her deepest core. For what seemed an eternity, they stood crushed together, bonded by some unseen, unknown force.

The jingle of harness broke the spell. Daphne suddenly became all too aware of the stranger's strength and of her own helplessness.

"Sir, you must release me," she whispered through a dry throat.

At once his frown returned, masking the glow in his eyes. His lean features hardened, grew cold. Slackening his grip, he almost pushed her away from him and took a step back. 'Twas not far enough for Daphne's peace of mind. She retreated a few steps, noticing with a mix of guilt and satisfaction the marks her soiled fingers had left on his greatcoat.

"I am sorry—" she began stiffly, striving for dignity.

"'Sorry' is not enough, not by half."

Standing with booted feet spread wide, the curricle owner slowly raked her with that blazing stare from her straggling hair down the worn, bedraggled cloak to her mud-caked boots.

"What, has your mistress turned you out, and you thought to end your life? Or is this a game, a ploy to pretend hurt and thus cadge money from me? I assure you I am not that soft." He took a menacing step closer. "If I thought you had purposely leaped out at us, I would have—"

Daphne's chin came up, and her fists clenched. Oh, this was too much! She held her ground, glaring up into his threatening countenance, challenging the powerful aura of male authority he projected. "Naturally I did not leap out," she snapped. "I am not deranged, or turned out—"

"Hmm. Flushed and tart-tongued." He peered closer, and to Daphne's complete horror, tipped up her chin with one gloved hand. "Have you been tippling so early in the day?" he demanded. "Is that it? Are you foxed, by God, so drunk that—"

"Oh!" Miss Butler cried. "Make haste, I beg! I cannot hold them!"

Daphne jerked her chin from his hold. "How d-dare you," she spluttered, "d-dare to impugn…You, sir, are—are—"

He paid her no heed but looked over his shoulder at the horses, which were mouthing their bits and moving restlessly. Frowning, he swung back to Daphne. His glare raked her again.

"You are shaking like a leaf in a high wind. Where are you bound, girl?"

Frostily, Daphne indicated the drive's entrance across the road. "Not far. The Park. Miss Todhunter—"

"You are in no fit state to wander about the road. Come." He seized her arm as if he had every right in the world and urged her toward his little carriage.

"No! I shan't!" Daphne cried, pulling against his hold. Surely she, always in control of any situation, had suffered enough indignities at his hands.

"Devil take it!" His countenance darkened into grimness as he picked her up in his arms and strode toward the curricle. He carried her as though she were no burden at all.

Daphne gasped in mortification. Did this man's gall have no limit? "S-Stop!" she hissed, when she could speak. "Put me down, sir, at once!"

He paused, looking down at her as she lay cradled in his arms. Once again she saw that glimmer of speculation or promise in his eyes, and a shudder ran through her body.

"Do not press me, girl." It was a quiet, icy threat. Without a further word, he tossed her into the curricle and climbed in after her.

"Oh, no, my lord," protested Miss Butler, giving Daphne a disgusted look. Her pretty mouth took a sulky slant as she pulled her heavy, fur-trimmed pelisse closer around her. "There is no room."

"A squash, I grant," growled his lordship, "but 'twill take but a moment to deliver this addle-cove home. She is too demented to roam loose on the roads. Come here, girl."

Daphne found herself dragged on to his knees. She sat in a daze, too mortified and embarrassed to protest this latest insult. He took the reins, and with an arm on each side of her, skillfully turned his team. Daphne closed her eyes while trying hard to sit erect. 'Twas impossible, as the light carriage bounced on the rutted drive and she was thrown against him.

Surrendering for the moment, she sagged wearily against his chest, drained by her severe fright and the shocks to her sensibilities. His arms enclosed her, and his muscular thighs moved beneath her as he shifted his feet. Thank heavens for her thick cloak and his heavy greatcoat or her situation would have been too intimate to endure.

Daphne could not be sure, but leaning against him as she was, she thought she heard the rumbling of a chuckle deep in his chest. 'Twas the final insult: the cool, reserved, elegant Miss Summerhayes was a figure of fun. Resentment flared in her, then helplessly faded.

At the Todhunter's door Daphne was only too happy to scramble unaided to the ground. The driver leaned from the curricle, and with a curiously gentle gesture, cupped her cheek in his leather-clad hand.

"Brush your hair and wash that pretty face before your mistress sees you," he said softly, though his expression was as grim as ever. "Learn some sense, girl, and give up hoydenish ways, or Miss Todhunter will be needing another maid."

He leaned farther, and before Daphne could guess his intent, lightly kissed her on the lips. With that, he swung his team, and in a moment the little vehicle was going at a damn-my-neck speed down the drive.

Daphne stared after him in confusion, still feeling the cool firmness of his lips on hers. The hand she raised to her mouth trembled. A brash dancing partner had once kissed her when she was younger, and had been slapped for his liberty. Yet this light brush of a stranger's lips was different, though she could not say exactly how.

* * *

Not until a shocked Julia Todhunter had let her wash, and then set her by the fire in the Park's cheerful morning room, did Daphne's composure return. With a hot toddy in her hand, she recounted her frightening experience. Though she shared her deepest thoughts with Julia, for some reason Daphne did not tell how the bold curricle driver had disturbed her. Nor did she mention the kiss.

Sipping her toddy, Daphne sought to make light of her adventure. "He said, 'You terrified my team and alarmed Miss Butler.' Can you believe it, Julia? Poor Miss Butler, to come second to his horses, magnificent as they were."

"Oh, how unfeeling of him!" Strong censure from shy, gentle Julia! Distress showed in her large brown eyes as she shook her head with its neat ringlets of fine, light brown hair. "He sounds totally reprehensible. Have you no notion who he is?"

"Under the circumstances," Daphne answered dryly, "I did not feel the need for introductions. Miss Butler called him 'my lord.' Doubtless he is another self-absorbed, self-indulgent, arrogant gentleman like Sir George Sowerby, pursuing his own pleasures without a care for the hurt he causes those who stand in his way. Probably speeding back to London after New Year's revels in the country."

"Mayhap."

Julia sounded tentative, even for her timid nature, and Daphne looked quizzically at her. "Yes, Julia?"

Miss Todhunter blushed and twisted her handkerchief. "In truth, I cannot be sure, but Biggins caught a glimpse when he opened the door, and he thinks it may have been Lord Courtlea or Lord Bennington, one of Lord Dunston's guests. They all rode through yesterday, so he got a good look at them."

"Oh. I had thought him simply passing through." A stir, part excitement and part apprehension moved through Daphne. "Well, Julia," she said off-handedly, "if we meet again, I shall certainly tell him my opinion of Whips who speed along country roads without regard for others."

Mention of roads suddenly reminded Daphne of her errand. Amazingly, that frightening encounter with the disturbing, gray-eyed lord had quite driven it from her mind. She drew a deep breath.

"Julia, dear, I have the worst news." She paused, but could not keep the bitterness from her voice. "My cousin Sophie is to have her come-out this Season in London, and I must chaperon her. I cannot go to Italy with you and your parents in April. Instead of marveling at the glories of Rome and Florence, I shall be shepherding a shy country miss through the maze of a London Season."

"What are you saying, Dee? Not go to Italy?" Julia stared, her face drained of color. "Oh," she wailed, her large dark eyes brimming. "You cannot mean it! There must be someone else who may sponsor your cousin."

"I asked that, you may be sure," rejoined Daphne shortly, drawing back her feet a little from the blazing hearth. "Aunt Agnes, Sophie's mama, is a rattle-brain. She imagines herself ill and swoons with astonishing ease and frequency. Just thinking of her daughter's come-out sent her to bed with an attack of the vapors. And Sophie has no other family, save a great-aunt who is slightly mad." Daphne heaved a sigh and set down her empty beaker. "No, Julia, pray believe me, I exhausted all possibilities. I am the only choice."

"But why this year?" demanded Julia, mopping at her tears. "Why now, when all our plans are made? Cannot the wretched girl come out in her own circle? Why must she needs go to London?"

"Uncle Charles wants her presented, not at court, of course, but to as broad a spectrum of Society as possible. Mayhap the husband market is rather limited in Cornwall, and he expects better choice in Town."

"Oh, Dee, how can you bear it?" Julia mourned.

"Not easily, I assure you," Daphne answered with a grim laugh. "Oh, how I had dreamed of Italy! The paintings I would study, the magnificent buildings, the colors—" She stopped as a large lump rose in her throat.

"I shan't go to Italy either," Julia vowed, searching her handkerchief for a dry spot. "I should be too miserable without you. Mama and Papa must go without me."

"Fustian, Julia!" Daphne jumped to her feet and put her arm around her friend's thin shoulders. "With the Treaty of Amiens, the continent is again safe for travelers, but who knows for how long? No, you must not miss this chance. I shall visit Italy through your eyes, and I rely on you to report on every facet of your trip. Promise me you will go, and cheerfully."

Miss Todhunter tearfully promised, and a few hours later Daphne returned to Weldern Manor, not happier, but at least a little resigned to chaperoning her cousin. Unlike Mr. William Shakespeare, she had never been one to trouble deaf heaven with bootless cries, and although disappointment still stung, she resolved not to dwell on it.

But she could not so easily put aside her brush with the curricle and its blazing-eyed, haughty driver. Indeed, he had hovered in the back of her mind all the time she was with Julia.

Briggs, her abigail, clucked over her gown's muddy hem and muttered of hoydens. Daphne said nothing, recollecting with a little tremor how the beau's blazing gaze had taken in every feature of her dishevelment. Expertly, she might add, as though he were adept at assessing a woman's every aspect. In fact, she recalled little of his face save those fierce gray eyes and dark brows. Oh, and a mouth, of course, that wore an angry sneer, doubtless its habitual expression.

She did not want to recollect the feel of his arms tight about her trembling form, or that look flickering in his eyes, stirring the strangest responses from deep inside her. She closed her eyes, feeling again a feather-light touch on her lips.

This would not do! She had a household to run, and duties to see to. Rallying, striving to find her usual calm, unruffled self, Daphne briskly crossed the corridor to her brother's room. When her tap on the door received no answer, Daphne tapped again, more loudly. "William, I know you are there. Thomson told me you had returned. Answer me at once."

An indistinguishable mutter came to Daphne's ears. She opened the door and entered the room. No candles were lit, and the curtains still open, a shocking lapse on the servants' part, as Daphne insisted curtains be drawn in winter not later than five o'clock.

"William, this will not do. Why are you lurking in the dark?" Daphne took a spill from the fire and lit a branch of candles on the mantel. Turning, she saw her brother supine on his bed, one arm thrown over his eyes.

"Devil take it, Dee, can't a fellow have a bit of peace?" The words were muffled by his shirtsleeve, but the plaintive tone was clear.

As she carried the light to the bedside, Daphne bit her lip against a reprimand for his muddy boots on the counterpane. "What is amiss with you, William? Are you ailing?" she asked, setting the candelabrum on a small table.

A shake of his head was her only answer, and Daphne sighed. William had always been a merry boy, with an easy manner and natural grace that charmed all who met him. Until lately, Daphne and he had enjoyed a close bond, perhaps because of their mother's early death and their father's absorption in his work of cataloguing the flora found on the Chilterns.

"I wish to speak with you, William," Daphne said with a firmness she reserved for unpleasant subjects. "Your conduct over the holidays has distressed me. Why, you have hardly been at home, and I have heard tales of you racing your horse like a jinglebrains. Drinking overmuch, as well. Even gambling—"

A violent motion of his arm cut off her words. "Blast, Daphne, you are my sister, not my mother. Give off prosing at me, for pity's sake. When will you learn I am a man?"

The arm dropped again, but not before Daphne caught sight of a face white with misery. She sat down on the edge of the bed.

"Willy, dear, sit up, do, and tell me what is troubling you," she said in a softened tone. "I did not mean to prose. I forget sometimes that you are eighteen now, but surely that is not too old to tell me what is wrong, as you always used to?"

William slowly removed the shielding arm, peering at her as if suspicious that her gentle manner were a ruse, and that hot words would soon rain on his head. As slowly, he sat up, and his unhappy countenance sent a rush of sympathy through Daphne.

"There now, that is better," she said. "Can you tell me now what has you so blue-deviled? Nothing is so bad we cannot put it to rights together." Daphne bent forward and brushed from his brow the curling, golden-brown hair that refused to lie in the Brutus cut he so desired.

He scowled, but suffered her touch. Daphne knew he possessed a high intelligence, but a tendency to indolence prevented him from making full use of it. Since starting at Oxford University the previous year, he attended more to the pleasures of student life than to its duties.

"Can you not stop managing me, for pity's sake, Dee?" he said wearily. "You are such a manager, always thinking you know best. It gets a fellow down, I can tell you." Wrapping his arms around his bent knees, William shot an apprehensive glance at his sister. "What did Father say when I missed breakfast this morning?"

"He said nothing, for he did not know you had slept from home last night. He thought you still abed, and I did not enlighten him."

"Oh, what a brick you are, Dee." Gratitude warmed his hazel eyes, momentarily banishing their worry. "And he said nothing about—he said nothing else?"

"About what? Willy, dear, are you in some kind of trouble? You have been a bit wild, you know, and perhaps that happens quite naturally when a boy becomes a young man. But you have a good heart, and I cannot—will not—believe you are guilty of anything more than high spirits." She gently touched his arm. "You know, my dear, I shall always stand by you."

Her brother's face flushed, and he caught his lower lip between his teeth. "I know I have been somewhat of an ass, kicking up my heels and plunging a bit, and I'm sorry for worrying you, but I'll do better from now on. I was taught a sound lesson last night, and by a master."

Deep misery settled on his young face and he dropped his forehead to his knees, muttering something Daphne could not comprehend.

"You spent the day with Tim Franklin, did you not?" she probed gently. He nodded without raising his head. "Did the two of you get into some mischief?"

A shudder passed through his body as he looked up at her. "Tim's brother Stafford is home, with some friends from London."

Daphne managed not to shiver. "Yes, so I heard."

"I met them yesterday afternoon, out riding. Tim was trying out that new hunter of his, and I matched my Kingman jump for jump against him, and the London coves made bets... Then one of them said hedges and brush fences were one thing, but stone walls were another, so we went down to Squire Todhunter's sheepfold—"

"Willy! Not the drystone dyke! Why, 'tis taller than I, and broad into the bargain."

"Think I don't know that? I see it every blessed day—"

"Yes, of course. Go on, what happened?"

William swung his feet to the floor, not noticing, or ignoring, the streak of mud his boots left on the counterpane. "Tim was in a quake, but he went first, and his new galloper refused the leap."

"An exceptionally clever horse," Daphne observed. "He obviously has more sense than his master. Did Tim try again to clear the wall?"

"Oh, Tim had already cleared the wall. When Juniper refused, Tim went sailing over his head, neat as a diving duck, and landed belly-up on the other side."

"Oh, Lord, Willy! Was he hurt?"

Her question earned her a disgusted look. "'Course he was hurt. What do you think? He strained a wrist, was shaken to a jelly, and don't walk too well."

"Oh, poor Tim, the silly young gudgeon. Still," Daphne gave a sigh of relief, "that was the end of such foolishness."

William colored and lowered his eyes.

"William! You didn't!"

"Well, Juniper badly hurt his knees, and might have to be put down, and then all the swells looked at me... Tim had at least tried, you see, not defaulted, and...well, a fellow can't look a flat, or an out-and-out coward, can he?"

"A man should not have to prove himself to anyone, except perhaps himself. He—" Daphne stopped, caught by William's despairing eye. "So you jumped Kingman?" she asked quietly.

William swallowed hard. "He had already done prodigious well, Dee, clearing raspers we'd never attempted before. I told him he'd better act sharpish if he wanted his oats and bran that night, and he nuzzled me to scratch his poll, and I looked into his eyes, and he looked back, so trusting, you know how he does, and I—I turned hen-hearted, Dee. I couldn't risk killing him, so I cried off."

"Oh, Willy, how wonderful! I am excessively proud of you for showing such courage."

Her approval did little to lighten her brother's gloom. "No one else thought so. One fellow, Lord Bennington, had the cheek to call me a whey-faced poltroon. Then another cove, the Earl of Courtlea, called him off, and I thought he understood why I wouldn't jump, but then he said, lazy-like, what could one expect from rag-mannered country younglings in spatterdashes. Then I said I had as much nerve as the next man, and if he cared to try me, I was willing."

Daphne sat frozen. Lord Bennington and Lord Courtlea. One of them was her nemesis with the curricle, the man who had humiliated her and then dared to kiss her. One of them; but which lord?

"You said that?" she asked, forcing out the words. "Oh, he might have called you out, you foolish boy! You must learn to curb your temper, or—" Daphne's fingers flew to her lips and she stared in horror at her brother. "He—this Lord Courtlea—he did not call you out, did he?"

William squirmed uncomfortably and shook his head. "No, but it was a near thing. His eyes went all hard, like stones, but then he laughed. Said there was more than one way to prove your mettle than letting a horse do it. I almost hit him then, but Tim held me off, and Courtlea dared me to meet in the cardroom after dinner, if I could dress appropriately for an evening party. The blackguard!"

"He sounds utterly reprehensible," Daphne agreed. Was he the one with the fierce gray eyes and the fine hands with horses? "You played cards with him for money?"

"Of course for money! What do you think?"

"How much did you lose?"

"Dash it, you don't give a fellow much credit, do you?"

"How much, Willy?"

Her brother propped his elbows on his knees, and with a sigh that appeared to come from the bottom of his heart, dropped his head in his hands. "A monkey."

Daphne gasped. "Five hundred pounds! But you do not have near that amount. Oh, Willy, how could you lose so much?"

"Oh, 'twas easy! No trouble at all. Whenever I wanted to quit, that blasted Courtlea would look at me, just so, as though he weren't surprised to see me cut and run, and dash it all, I had to keep going."

"Truly, what an odious man this Lord Courtlea is! But how did you pay him off?" A second concern made Daphne grasp his arm and give it a shake. "Hilary term starts next week, does it not? How will you pay your college expenses? I have a little saved from my allowance, but nothing near that much. Oh, Willy, you will have to tell Papa."

Brother and sister stared at each other, both knowing that the Hon. James Summerhayes, although enjoying a comfortable income, was not of unlimited means. Five hundred pounds, while not a crippling amount, was still far more than a trifle for him.

"Oh, Dee," William moaned, "I would rather face that drystone dyke again than confront Father. Not when I've made such a cake of myself. You don't know…"

"I said I would stand by you, and I will." Daphne gave her brother's hand an encouraging pat. "Come, you and I will face Papa together. He is not a harsh man, you know."

"Yes, but I also know how he will look at me—bewildered disappointment, that's what, and hurt... No, Dee, it's all in hand. Tim made up the difference, and I can repay him from my allowance. Although," he added gloomily, "it may take ten years."

"Are you certain that is the course you intend to follow? If we tell Papa—"

"No!" He caught her by the arm as if she intended rushing away at that moment. "My way is best. As it is, Father may learn of my scrape soon enough." He looked so piteous that Daphne's heart was wrung. "Oh, Dee, I will never wager again as long as I live!"

In respect for his very real remorse, Daphne forbore to add that if he had indeed learned such a lesson, the cost was not too high. "There now," she said instead, "do you not feel better for having confided your trouble?"

The look he gave her was not as relieved as she had expected. Indeed, his misery appeared hardly lessened. Perhaps it was as well, she thought, for the stronger his repentance, the stronger would grow his aversion to gambling. Still, something prompted her to take her brother's chin in her hand and turn his face to meet her gaze.

"Is there something more, Willy? Something you have not told me?"

"More?" he exploded, jerking away from her hold. "Demme, what more would you need? I am in tick to Tim, disgraced as a coward and a dunce at cards, and a—" He broke off with a grimace. "Is that not enough?"

Daphne did not press him further, but got to her feet and shook out her skirts. "When you come down to dinner," she said briskly, "pray be as cheerful as may be, for Papa's sake. He is unhappy, as am I, that my trip to Italy is put off. Oh, and Cousin Sophie arrives tomorrow."

"What?" William stared blankly at her. "Oh, Dee, your heart was set on Italy! And why Sophie? Dash it, I don't recollect her in the slightest."

"No, for she was a mere child when last she visited. Uncle Charles asks that I—how did he put it in his letter?—instruct her in any small points of etiquette she may lack. To this end, she comes tomorrow, so as to be fully prepared by March to descend on London in my charge for her come-out."

Daphne's sigh found an echo in William's groan as he again dropped his head into his hands. She looked thoughtfully at his bent head, sure that despite his protests, her brother held something back. Something mayhap pertaining to the despicable Lord Courtlea, who so mercilessly had taken advantage of him. Had the lord cheated, or was he merely indifferent to the foolhardy pride of a green boy?

"Um—Willy, how would one recognize Lord Courtlea?"

William did not look up. "Full of his own importance. Mean, cool, and fast as an adder."

"That is not much help. Is he tall? Short? Fair? Dark?"

"Dark. Big. Nasty mean eyes, like stones."

"And Lord Bennington?"

He looked up, perplexed. "Why do you want to know that?"

Daphne gave a casual shrug. "Mere curiosity, brother mine. Is he tall and dark as well?"

"Well, he's fairish, about my height, and plump as a partridge. You'll see them both at the ball in two days time."

"Yes, I shall. I had forgotten that." Lord Courtlea. The name rang in her mind. Vaguely she nodded to her brother. "Pray be on time for dinner, William."

Daphne hurried from William's room. She had been keen to go to the ball, as she enjoyed dancing, and Eugenia, the Dunstons' daughter, was a close friend who shared Daphne's love of horses. Now Daphne wondered if she should attend. In her usual robust health, she could not cry off without raising questions. Besides, she was not one to run from difficulties.

On one hand, she yearned to upbraid Lord Courtlea for his reckless driving, and express her disgust at his treatment of her brother. Oh, discreetly and with subtlety, to be sure, but with such an edge his lordship would be fully aware of her contempt.

But on the other hand, suppose he recognized her as the girl he had treated so outrageously on the road? Her cool brain reminded her that he thought her a servant. He would not expect to meet a serving maid at Lady Dunston's ball.

Her heart was in too much excited turmoil to tell her anything.

CHAPTER 2

Victor Merritt, Earl of Courtlea, leaned negligently at the window and frowned at the rain-streaked pane. But for the downpour, he would have his team out for a run. "Bennington, I vow this country is criminally dull, with nothing to recommend it. I doubt even the shooting is decent, were it the season."

Arthur Norton, Viscount Bennington, dozing in an armchair before the fire, opened one bloodshot eye.

"You have the right of it, Courtlea," he agreed with a yawn, "but you must grant that the grub is first-rate, as Staff claimed it would be, and his mater and pater have turned themselves inside out to please you."

The other eye, equally reddened, opened in Lord Bennington's round face. "'Tis not often they snare such a rich prize in this country backwater," he added slyly. "They want to show you off, mayhap leg-shackle you to their daughter, Miss Thingummy."

Courtlea turned again to the desolate view of Dunston Hall's drenched, cold-nipped garden. "You talk such rot, Benny," he drawled, "even when you are not half-foxed from brandy. Miss Thingummy, in fact Miss Eugenia, has nothing to fear from me. She may be the apple of the Franklin family's collective eye, but she brays like Balaam's ass. My ears ring from her hilarity."

"Hah!" snorted the viscount. "Stop her mouth with a kiss or whatever comes to hand, and then you may find, be she ass or mare, she will give you a good ride."

He laughed uproariously, slapping his thigh, and Lord Courtlea, although no prude, grimaced at his coarseness. The reflection in the window pane grimaced back, and Courtlea, caught by the sullenness of the mouth, the indifference of the eyes, barely controlled the urge to smash his fist through the glass.

Boredom was the cause of his mood. He cursed the moment of cork-brained weakness in which he agreed to accompany Stafford, the eldest Franklin cub, to Buckinghamshire. He soon realized the Franklins had not invited Victor Merritt, breeder of fine carriage horses, and a man known for his keen interest in politics. No, they wanted the wealthy and influential Earl of Courtlea, exhibiting him like a prize won at a fair. Other invitations had been sent him with the same intent, but this situation rankled more than usual.

Doubtless the fact that he had ended his relationship with Miss Maryann Bisely had prompted him to accept the invitation. The affair had become tedious after the lovely Maryann showed signs of wanting a more permanent arrangement, namely marriage.

"Missing the charms of a fancy-piece?" continued Bennington. Rising, he wobbled to a drinks tray and poured himself a tot of brandy.

The near-accuracy of the surmise startled Courtlea into turning from the forlorn view and favoring his tipsy companion with a cold glare. Besides the obvious qualities necessary for a mistress, Maryann Bisely possessed the knack of keeping quiet. She did not yammer at a man, and Courtlea had, over the months of their amour, rewarded her well for those hours of peace. That her silence stemmed from a lack of wit rather than a desire to please did not signify in the slightest.

Impervious to Courtlea's displeasure, Bennington lurched back to his chair. "What bad luck that the Butler girl took fright of you and ran back to town with her brother." He gestured carelessly with his glass and some of the amber liquor sloshed over the rim. "Thought you had a good thing there."

"As Miss Butler's brother Tom is one of my best friends, I hardly think of her as a 'good thing.' She is, however, rather timid, and prefers Town to the wilds of the country."

Courtlea recollected with some heat how frightened poor Adele Butler had been yesterday when that red-headed harridan burst in front of the carriage. The episode had given him a worse turn than he had cared to admit, which was why his temper had utterly exploded on the maid's bare, wind-blown head. Nor had that feckless girl—a handsome piece despite her dirt-smeared face and untidy state—shown the slightest remorse. Stubborn, high-headed chit.

Still, there was something about her, something that had driven him to kiss her. Only a serving lass, yet she had an air, an appeal that kept her image constantly in his mind. He would like to see her with a clean face.

"Nev' mind." Bennington's slurred voice broke into his thoughts. "Tomorrow night the fairest of th' county will be here for th' ball. Sure to find some agreeable lass amongst the flock."

"You will be in fine fettle to tread a measure, I must say," Courtlea commented in disgust. "Have a care; some of these country noddies are quick to take offence. Pester their ladies and you may earn an invitation for pistols for two, breakfast for one."

"Hah, like that youngling t'other day, all primed to have at you." Bennington snuffled into his glass, scowling like a man with an injustice. "Should have let 'im, Courtlea. Teach 'im a lesson. 'Course you'd have snuffed 'im, but he deserved it, the pudding-heart."

Lord Courtlea shook his head. "The lad don't lack nerve, and I think he learned not to face up to his betters. Well, I am off for a walk, rain or no. Recollect my warning about taking care tomorrow. As for me, bucolic revels have never suited. I shall do the honors with my hostess and her daughter, and then withdraw."

Courtlea smiled wryly as he strode from the room. Doubtless he would enjoy the ball more if a certain serving maid were allowed to attend. Hah, what a to-do that would cause!

*　　*　　*

Sophie Summerhayes chattered from the moment she alighted from the carriage, repeatedly proclaiming how prodigious glad she was to have arrived. The friends of Sophie's papa seemed equally pleased to discharge their passenger, and declined refreshment, claiming lodgings bespoke farther on. As the coach rattled hastily away, Mr. Summerhayes retired to his study, and William silently slipped off, leaving Daphne with their guest.

Daphne had grimly wondered why her cousin must needs come at this time. Why could she not have waited a few days more, until Daphne had settled with Lord Courtlea? Still, 'twas not Sophie's fault.

"Oh, Cousin Daphne, I vow it is such a relief to get here!" Sophie exclaimed anew as Daphne conducted her to the stairs. Tyson, Sophie's abigail, a stolid, middle-aged woman, trailed behind, leaving two trunks and a large valise to the footman. "Such a beautiful house, and so sizable!" Sophie went on, tossing her fur muff to Tyson. "I vow, what

Mama said made you out to be rather the poor relations, but mayhap I misheard."

Daphne searched the pretty face framed by golden curls and a small-brimmed crimson velvet bonnet and found no malice in the sparkling blue eyes or gay smile. "Mayhap," Daphne agreed, starting up the stairs.

"Oh, Cousin Daphne, 'tis strange to hear you called 'Miss Summerhayes,' for, as I said to Papa, I am Miss Summerhayes too, am I not?" Sophie laughed, seemingly able to scamper up stairs and still chatter at full speed. "I vow, I near expired from vexation last year. Imagine getting the measles, and missing my come-out! Papa was furious, for I have three sisters waiting their turn, and he considers a girl of eighteen is past the best age."

"Indeed," agreed Daphne. "A girl has so few years of youth in which to snare a husband."

Sophie beamed, obviously missing the irony in Daphne's tone. "Oh, you have the right of it! Just think, Cousin Daphne, of the romps we shall have together. Oh, oh, when I think of the parties and the routs, I could die of excitement. Oh, I vow we will have a rare time!"

"Yes, Sophie, I hope we will rub along well together. And plain Daphne will do."

"Truly?" Sophie cocked her head. "Are you positive that will not be disrespectful? My mama told me to be respectful to my elders, and I mean to be. And you are so much older than I, are you not, Cousin?"

Without missing a step, Daphne started along the upper corridor toward the bedrooms. "You are younger than I by exactly five years and six months," she said evenly.

"Oh, that is a great difference, I vow! Not that you look aged, not at all. Perhaps the way you arrange your hair, all rolled up in that knot at the back of your head—very elegant, I vow, but... Or perhaps it is your manner. Very grand, I think, but then Mama said you have been tied to managing this lovely big house for ever so many years. I do so admire you, Cousin. Mama was quite loud in your praises, even though you have not managed to find a husband."

Daphne found no answer to that, but she could not take offense, either. Apparently, her cousin spoke without thought whatever came into her head, but her words seemed without guile or intent to wound.

"Our cousin has been let run wild," Daphne moaned to William that evening, "and encouraged to consider only her own desires. She has no more idea how to behave in London society than—than a pea-goose. I shall let her settle in, then attempt to instill some decorum into her." Daphne shook her head. "In any case, I have more than a month to instruct her."

At dinner, Daphne learned more of Sophie's determination to achieve her own wants when the subject arose of the ball which was to be given the next evening by Lord and Lady Dunston.

"Oh, a ball!" cried Sophie. "How I love dancing!"

"That may be, Cousin, but it is out of the question for you to attend," asserted Daphne. 'Twas enough for her to face Lord Courtlea without chaperoning Sophie as well. "Recollect you are not yet introduced to Society. The whole point of our going to London for your come-out—"

"Oh, bosh!" Giggling, Sophie dismissed such considerations with an airy wave of her hand. "Who cares if I go to a ball now, rather than waiting? Mama let me attend her parties and those of our friends, and no one was overset."

"I am sorry, Sophie, but I cannot allow it. The Franklins would be horrified at your breach of manners, and their London guests would be sure to carry the tale back with them."

Daphne desperately hoped the mention of people from Town would cow Sophie into submission, but the thought of meeting members of the haut ton only spurred the girl to stronger protest. Finally, James Summerhayes, proclaiming peace at any price, allowed that she might accompany her cousins to the ball.

"Oh, dear Uncle James, how prodigious kind you are!" Sophie clasped her hands in delight and beamed her thanks to Mr. Summerhayes. "Now, Daphne, I have the sweetest white muslin with the most fetching flounces edged with pink silk. Tell me, do, what gown you will wear to the ball. What is the color? Does it have elbow sleeves or those splendid little puffs? Oh, oh, does it have a train? Do you not agree that a train is the most elegant thing?"

Daphne signalled Thomson to serve the pudding. "Perhaps the most satisfactory way to answer such a blizzard of questions," she said resignedly, "is to show you the gown itself. Come to my room after dinner, if you like."

"Oh, I vow, such fun! But, pray tell me the color, just the color, or I shall never last until I see it! Is it white, like mine? Oh, but for your hair, we would be sisters!"

"'Tis of tawny silk. White does not suit me, and in any case, I prefer stronger colors." Daphne smiled and added, "We aged spinsters may do as we please."

Although Daphne enjoyed discussing fashion as well as any woman, her mind refused to dwell on anything but her confrontation with Lord Courtlea. Already butterflies tried their wings in her stomach, an unheard of sensation for the cool-headed Daphne.

The next day, however, a rumor reached Weldern Manor that brought Daphne tremendous relief. And, though she hated to admit it even to herself, more than a twinge of disappointment. In any case, her heart was lighter that evening as the cousins departed for Dunston Hall. The night was clear and crisp, not overly cold, although the hot bricks wrapped in straw felt welcome beneath Daphne's silk slippers.

"'Tis a pity the odious Lord Courtlea will not attend the ball tonight," Daphne commented to her brother, seated opposite. "I had anticipated the pleasure of expressing my disgust at his behavior toward you."

William regarded her with horror. "What! Take a peer to task for his nastiness to your little brother? Dash it all, Dee, you shan't, d'you hear? A fellow could never hold up his head again, he'd be such a laughing-stock. Leave it lie, for pity's sake." He shuddered. "'Tis a mercy Lord Courtlea and Miss Butler have returned to London."

Sophie's bright blue eyes had followed the exchange with interest. "Why, of what behavior do you speak, Cousins?"

"Naught that merits your concern," answered Daphne, a trifle curtly. She should be delighted at Lord Courtlea's absence, yet the evening ahead promised to be unusually flat. "And while we speak of such matters, pray hold your tongue unless you are addressed directly. Even then, I beg, answer simply and discreetly. Recollect you are here on sufferance."

Laughing gaily, Sophie leaned forward and kissed her cousin's cheek. "Oh, dear Daphne! My poor head is crammed with your caveats! Be assured I shall do my best to heed them all. You are the very best of teachers. Oh, we are there! Look, such grand livery on those footmen. And powdered wigs! Such elegance! Mama will be thrilled when I write her of this."

Daphne sighed, gathered her fur-lined cloak about her, and alighted from the carriage, wishing for leading strings to control her exuberant relative. Sophie was as frisky and as innocently affectionate as a kitten, and as incapable of thinking anyone would be offended by her antics.

Dunston Hall, erected a mere ninety years ago, thrust its stone walls four stories high. Its builder, perhaps dreaming of a marquisate or a dukedom, had planned for massive additions. Such advancement in rank had not followed, and Dunston Hall remained, four-square and solid, a rather grand irregularity in the countryside.

William touched his sister's arm as they surrendered their wraps to a footman. "Lord Courtlea may be gone, but the other coves—Lord Bennington and Sir Thomas Butler—are still here. Your promise, Dee, to say nothing, not one squeak, to anyone about—dash it all, you know perfectly well what I mean."

Touched by his wretched expression, matching so ill the elan with which he wore his dark brown coat, cream knee-breeches and dazzling white cravat, Daphne could do nothing else but promise. Her brother, much subdued, had rarely left his room. Indeed, his behavior had improved immeasurably since his humbling at the hands of Lord Courtlea, and although that in no way excused the earl's vile treatment, she was almost grateful for his lesson.

"Now, Sophie, I beg you try very hard to act with decorum," she whispered to her cousin as they mounted the sweeping staircase. "Stay at my side. When I dance, you will wait with Mrs. Todhunter. Oh, and it is not necessary to share with all and sundry the information that you are not yet out."

Sophie's nod set her golden curls dancing, but her head switched from side to side so energetically in her efforts to see every aspect of the grand house, that Daphne doubted her cousin heard. However, she coped splendidly with her introduction to Robert Franklin, Viscount Dunston, and his wife, and then rhapsodised to Daphne over Lady Dunston's elegance.

"Amaranthus is such a modish color, I vow, neither pink nor purple. Did you notice the vandyke hem? And the train! I vow I must have a dozen such gowns when we reach London. But do you not think, Daphne, that her parure of garnets and yellow sapphires was not the thing with her sallow skin? Oh, oh, look how the ballroom sparkles!"

Daphne knew not whether to scold or laugh, and then decided to cease fretting over her cousin's conduct. She must remain alert, lest Sophie bring disgrace or contempt on the Summerhayes family, but she would stop agonizing over the girl's every word.

The splendid ballroom, in crimson, blue and gold, ran the full width of the house, and boasted a minstrel gallery, where a group of musicians waited. Scores of the finest wax candles blazed in chandeliers and wall sconces, their light reflected and magnified in large gold-framed mirrors. Masses of shrubs, palms, and flowers plundered from the Hall's greenhouses added color and a softening touch of foliage.

The cream of county society, a hundred or more souls, conversed in knots about a room designed for five times their number. Daphne scanned their faces, all of them familiar. She sighed, she knew not why, and for Sophie's sake, tried to summon some enthusiasm for the party.

"Come, I see Miss Todhunter and her parents. William?"

But William had quite disappeared. Hoping he had not forgotten her order to lead out his cousin for her one dance, Daphne had barely presented Sophie to the Todhunters, when Tim Franklin, Viscount Dunston's younger son, appeared at her elbow. He showed no signs of his toss from Juniper as his dark eyes goggled in wonder at Sophie.

Daphne could not blame him; Sophie looked delectable in her white muslin trimmed with pink silk. Her golden hair was dressed in curls and adorned with a posy of silk flowers. While only a string of pearls circled her smooth young throat, her eyes sparkled brighter than any sapphires.

"Daphne—dash it, I mean—" Tim's open, guileless face, crowned with a shock of light brown hair, turned an embarrassed crimson. He cleared his throat. "Miss Summerhayes, pray introduce me to this charming lady. Your cousin, I believe?"

Daphne smiled at the young man, her brother's closest friend, and presented him to her cousin. Timothy bowed to Sophie's excited curtsy, and begged the honor of the first dance. Without so much as a glance at Daphne, Sophie accepted.

As she went off on Tim's arm, Daphne heard her exclaim: "Oh, your father is Viscount Dunston! But you are a younger son, are you not? How unfortunate for you! My grandpapa, and Daphne's too, naturally, was a baron, and now my uncle Alfred…"

Daphne exchanged a despairing glance with Julia, who, glancing over Daphne's shoulder, murmured, "Prepare yourself, Dee. Sir Reginald Forthtyne ogles you with a glare of purpose in his eye. Mayhap he has screwed up his courage and is at last determined to offer for you."

Daphne laughed. "I do not scorn to have a husband and family, but a portly widower with eight children is beyond even my enthusiasm. He—"

Daphne broke off as Lady Dunston, with the expression of a Grimalkin who has lapped all the cream, entered the ballroom on the arm of a tall, dark-haired gentleman whose handsome features were stiff with boredom. Behind her came her daughter, Eugenia, prettily gowned in white silk, with a stocky gentleman, undoubtedly Lord Bennington, whose fair hair gleamed with pomade. Lord Dunston in his purple velvet coat rather forlornly trailed in the rear behind his elder son, Stafford, who oozed self-satisfaction at snaring such beaux as his guests.

The dark gentleman, doubtless Sir Thomas Butler, raised his eyes to survey the company. His indifferent glance brushed Daphne's face, paused, and then moved on. As he led Lady Dunston out to begin the dancing, Daphne stared, rooted to the spot.

She recollected gray eyes blazing with fury beneath lowering, night-black brows. A mouth, tight-lipped and grim, yet touching hers with gentleness. Boredom had replaced the fury, elegant evening clothes the Garrick and topboots, but this was the same man. The man who had possessed her thoughts for days, horribly upsetting her calm, sensible nature—not Sir Thomas, but Lord Courtlea!

CHAPTER 3

Julia heard Daphne's intake of breath and touched her arm with concern. "Is aught amiss, Daphne?" she asked in a low tone.

"No, nothing, dear Julia," replied Daphne, a tremor she could not control in her voice. Her stomach clenched, and all the butterflies took wing.

Miss Todhunter appeared mystified, but delayed further questioning as plump Sir Reginald Forthtyne, he of the many children, appeared at Daphne's elbow.

"Would you honor me, I beg, with this dance, Miss Summerhayes?" he ventured, shifting from one foot to the other. The baronet's balding pate towered two inches above Daphne's curls, and his pale eyes, as if too nervous to meet her glance, stared at her hairline.

Daphne wrenched her mind back. Lord Courtlea was here, despite the rumor that he had left with Miss Butler. Daphne must gather her forces, and be ready to challenge him. Or, her quaking heart whispered, cut and run for home.

She managed a smile, and as Sir Reginald proudly led her out, Daphne's gaze met that of Lord Courtlea. Decorum and common sense demanded she look away, or lower her eyes, but the recollection burned through her of herself sprawled in the dirt at his feet. Worse still, the vision danced before her eyes of him holding her intimately in his arms, sparking strange, dangerous responses, even kissing her. Bruised pride bred indignation, and without dwelling on the wisdom of such an act, Daphne raised her chin and sent him a telling stare.

Cold indifference fled his features as his eye kindled in return. Quick as thought, Daphne read interest, assessment, and then agreement in his expression before he gave a slight nod. With an effort, she managed to break the bonds of his gaze, and turn away.

Oh, heavens, what had she done! He did not recognize her as his near-victim, and now he had mistaken her stare for bold invitation. And thinking her a flirt, or worse, he had accepted that invitation!

The music started, but Daphne's concentration was in tatters. Then, as the head couple began their figures, Daphne took herself to task. She was no missish ingénue to be flustered by a leering dark gallant. Lifting her head, Daphne gave her hand to her partner and herself to the dance.

Yet, as she turned in a circle round, she knew that Lord Courtlea watched her from the other set. Her back stiffened under the weight of his look, and she shot him her iciest glare. He answered with a lazy smile so suggestive that she missed a step and nearly brought the whole set to confusion.

Try as she might, she could not stop her glance from straying in his direction. Granted, he was well set up, with broad shoulders and an erect carriage. But, now that she was not trembling in shock, and had a clear view, Daphne thought his features ordinary. A lofty brow, narrow-bridged straight nose, a firm, rather square jaw, and a well-shaped mouth neither too large nor too small. Yet, Daphne noted with scorn, his face and figure attracted the eye of many of the ladies present. Doubtless they knew nothing of his reckless, dissolute nature.

"You appear abstracted this evening, Miss Summerhayes," commented her partner as they advanced and retreated. "All is well with your family, I trust?"

"Indeed, yes, Sir Reginald," answered Daphne, realizing with a start how badly she had ignored him. In atonement, she offered him her best smile. "You yourself, sir, and your sweet children, are all in good health and spirits, I hope?"

"How kind of you to inquire, Miss Summerhayes." The baronet blushed and twitched nervously. "Your attention is most edifying. One might say 'tis encouraging. Yes, Miss Summerhayes, one would say your concern is most encouraging."

"Oh, Sir Reginald," Daphne replied hastily, "Do not, I beg, overcredit my sensibilities. I assure you, I in no way intended to express any untoward curiosity or interest."

"Quite, quite. One understands how maidenly modesty must govern such discussions." He actually winked, his plump cheeks flushing anew from his audacity.

Daphne was shocked into silence. Encouraging Sir Reginald had never entered her mind. How had she so miscalculated? Obviously, had her thoughts not been concentrated on that—that rogue, she would have taken more care. But it was the outside of enough for the widower to find encouragement in a smile and a simple inquiry as to his family's health!

What a ridiculous situation in which to find oneself! Now two gallants, poles apart by any standard, perceived a promise of her favor. One, who pressed her gloved fingers with damp fervor, intended respectable matrimony. The other, who watched and waited like any beast of prey, intended— Daphne's cheeks grew hot.

The dance ended at last. Quickly and firmly excusing herself from Sir Reginald's company, Daphne scanned the room. Nearby, Lord Courtlea talked with Stafford Franklin, but she could not approach the earl, even if she wished to; as yet they had not been introduced. She gave a nervous little laugh. He had held her most intimately, even kissed her, but they could not speak at a social gathering until introduced.

Her gaze sharpened, swept the room more closely. Sophie was not to be seen, nor was William nor Tim. With an uneasy qualm, Daphne started off to search for her cousin. She had barely taken six steps across the floor when her way was blocked by Stafford Franklin. Beside him was Lord Courtlea.

He was elegance itself in a corbeau coat simply but beautifully cut, white knee-breeches, and silk stockings revealing well-shaped calves. His cravat fell in artful folds to a ruffled shirt and an embroidered white silk waistcoat. From his watch chain dangled a little gold seal and a fine emerald. A slight smile warmed his eyes, as though his thoughts had already progressed into the speculation Daphne had firmly repressed.

No, she was not ready for this, for the powerful allure he projected. And now, in her concern for Sophie's whereabouts, such a meeting was doubly unwelcome. Stiffening, Daphne acknowledged Stafford's presence with a cool nod. Then, though inwardly trembling, she set her features in what William called her "cold fish" look—an aspect that quieted rowdy children, cowed impudent servants, and intimidated obnoxious tradesmen. Any gentleman would immediately be cut by it.

The smile of the Great Gambler and Road Menace widened.

"Miss Summerhayes," said Stafford, nearly bursting with an

importance which doubtless blinded him to Daphne's coolness, "this gentleman begs to make your acquaintance. Miss Summerhayes, I have the honor to present my good friend Victor Merritt, Earl of Courtlea."

The moment had come. Curricle, Courtlea, cards, her promise to William—all whirled through her brain in a chaotic muddle. Caution warred with angry impulse, and, undermined by Daphne's wilfulness, lost the battle miserably. All else, including Sophie, was forgotten.

"The honor is mine, Miss Summerhayes," Courtlea murmured, bowing. Miss Summerhayes did not acknowledge his bow, and for a moment, he thought, with amazement, that she would refuse the introduction. Her pretty lips, so primly held, parted in a very kissable fashion, and her eyes, of the clearest green, widened, but in determination, not coyness.

Her coolness puzzled him, but he was willing to play the game of pursuit and capture if she so decreed. In her richly tinted gown, a welcome change from virginal white, she had caught his eye the moment he entered the room. The gown revealed enough of her figure to promise charms well warranting further exploration.

Perhaps the similarity of her coloring to the little maid had helped attract him. This lady's hair, however, was more burnished bronze, and she seemed taller.

A pretty piece, he had thought, no girl, but experience had not affected her freshness. Now, on closer inspection, he realized the lissome Miss Summerhayes offered more than a surface prettiness. He discerned poise and character in her noble brow and dainty chin, and in the queenly turn of her head. For once, the game promised to be worth the candle.

Miss Summerhayes lowered her gaze and curtsied, murmuring, "My lord," as if prompted by manners rather than intention. Courtlea flicked Stafford Franklin away with a glance.

"I have awaited this moment with mounting impatience," he murmured when Franklin was beyond earshot. "Will you join me for a stroll about this delightful room?"

He had noted several nooks, created with tubbed ferns and other greenery, at the end of the room farthest from the musicians. Intended for the use of the aged or weary, the alcoves could serve other purposes where privacy was desired.

Miss Summerhayes did not budge. "I fear, Lord Courtlea," she said, "that you suffer from a misapprehension, one for which I take full responsibility." He approved of her low, sweet voice, despite its firmness. Stridency, he felt, betrayed both bad manners and bad breeding.

"Indeed?" he drawled. "Rarely do I err in my convictions, Miss Summerhayes, and more rarely still, in my intentions."

She did not blush or coyly press him to reveal his purposes; instead, her chin rose the merest amount. "None the less," she said evenly, "my explanation will, I hope, alter both your convictions and intentions. When you entered the room—"

"Your lovely eyes flew to mine with a message that needed no words." He expected her to dimple enticingly, and was surprised by a flash of something akin to vexation.

"Sir, the message received was not the message sent. Will you hear me out, pray, my lord?"

He smiled winningly. "With pleasure, but we stand near the centre of the floor. We must dance or walk, or risk causing a noticeable obstruction. What is your wish, Miss Summerhayes?"

Her hesitation further increased his interest. He was familiar with all the tactics ladies employed, but this fascinating flame-haired miss did not have the air of a flirt. There were no meaningful glances or coquettish smiles behind her fan, no teasing words or subtle movements. Indeed, one might say she showed reluctance. Yet, deny it she may, she had stared into his eyes, openly and boldly, with a knowing look, one almost of recognition.

That look had pierced him with the force of an arrow.

"We should dance, sir," Miss Summerhayes stated in her delightful, low voice, "if only to avoid drawing further notice, but if we are to talk, dancing will not serve. Therefore, the choice is made for us. We must walk."

Ah, she, too, wished for privacy! Pleased, he offered his arm, and she laid her hand lightly on it. Lady Dunston frowned as they left the floor, but Courtlea ignored her. His own pleasures were of paramount importance to him, and he cared not a jot for the opinions of others. He was inured to attention, and dismissed the stares following him and Miss Summerhayes as they strolled the length of the room.

She moved easily and gracefully beside him, not speaking, yet her composed features betrayed no shyness. "Well, Miss Summerhayes," he said, glancing at her. "Have you nothing after all to say to me? Am I left with my original conclusions firmly fixed?"

"Oh, no, sir," she coolly protested. "In truth, I hardly know how to begin, there is so much churning in my mind. However, a promise given this night prevents me from saying all I would wish."

"What is this? A promise, regarding me? You intrigue me further, Miss Summerhayes, you do indeed. Pray be seated that we may discuss this promise in privacy." Smiling with anticipation, he gestured toward several chairs tucked into a secluded alcove.

Miss Summerhayes shook her head. "Thank you, my lord, but I prefer to continue walking." She went on a few paces, and Courtlea, barely concealing his annoyance, must perforce stroll at her side.

"I thought your lordship had left for London with Miss Butler," Miss Summerhayes began. "Hence my astonishment at your introduction. Indeed, had I known of your presence in the county, I would have warned our coachman to have a care when venturing out lest he find himself and the carriage in a ditch."

This unusual opening halted Courtlea in his tracks, wondering if he had heard aright. "My dear Miss Summerhayes, you speak in riddles," he protested, raising his brows. "Tom Butler took his sister home, and I remained. But what has your coachman to fear from me?"

She turned and faced him, her lovely bosom rising and falling most attractively. He felt a rush of desire to claim this beauty as soon as may be. She would be well worth the taking.

"What every soul who ventures out in the roads must fear," she replied warmly. "The peril of Whips, who think the roads are solely for their amusement, and who dash about the countryside at such speeds that all must get out of the way or risk life and limb."

"What put that bee in your bonnet, Miss Summerhayes?" Courtlea smiled, for he enjoyed the manner in which the heat of her argument caused her green eyes to flash, and brought a tint of rose to her alabaster cheek. He imagined that fiery, vibrant hair loose from its pins and curling about bare white shoulders—

"Good God!"

Candle flames brightening the curls piled atop her head, a lovely gown, elegant surroundings—'twas no wonder he had failed to recognize his ill-clad, dirty-faced serving girl.

Miss Summerhayes nodded with an air of triumph. "Yes, my lord, you may well stare. 'Twas I your lordship nearly ran down with your curricle and then treated my person in such an outrageous manner. Now perhaps you understand my concern for our coachman!"

For a moment Courtlea was held speechless. He saw with displeasure that she was perfectly serious. Few persons, and none since long before he had reached majority, had dared criticize his behavior.

Why, this sharp-tongued miss had made sport of him, pretending to be other than she was, and filling his head with the tenderest of notions! Fool that he was!

"One hesitates to gainsay a lady, Miss Summerhayes," he said coldly, "but any blame for your misadventure must lie squarely on your own shoulders. You burst upon the road with no regard for possible traffic."

"Had the traffic progressed within a reasonable speed," she retorted, "the misadventure would have been easily averted. Plump and plain, sir, you drive recklessly, and much too fast!"

"You speak nonsense, madam! I had my pair in complete control. Had I not, Miss Summerhayes, you might not be alive tonight to upbraid me so rudely. As to my outrageous treatment of you, mayhap I should have left you lying in the roadway, shaking as in a fit!"

"A gentleman would have ascertained my name and position, not taken it upon himself to be so forward."

"Demme, madam, I will not be criticized for an act of kindness."

"Oh, sir!" Miss Summerhayes actually smiled, while the light of battle blazed from her eyes. "How much more I would delight to say to you! But I see 'twould be in vain to continue. I hope merely that in future your conduct might be guided by my remarks, although you refuse utterly to accept responsibility in this instance."

"I!" Courtlea struggled for speech. The impudence of this upstart miss was far over the mark. "You dare cry me irresponsible, when you will not admit your own culpability! Were you a man, you would answer for that slur on my character, and at once, madam. That being impossible, I bid you adieu."

He turned on his heel and stalked away, so outraged a red haze overspread his vision.

CHAPTER 4

"Daphne?"

Daphne, watching Lord Courtlea's retreat with the fire of a conqueror burning in her bosom, grew aware of Julia Todhunter shaking her arm.

"Daphne, what are you about?" Julia whispered. "Come and sit down." Without ceremony, she dragged Daphne into the very alcove Lord Courtlea had eyed. "Are you mad to ring such a peal over his lordship's head?"

"Fustian!" Daphne seated herself on a little gilt chair while Julia nudged a potted fern nearer to shield them somewhat from curious eyes. "Lord Courtlea got not above half what I hoped to give him. Why, Julia, do not stare so at me! You are as pale as your gown. Surely you do not fear the wrath of the mighty Lord Courtlea? He is all bash and bluster. Shall I tell you what I said?"

Miss Todhunter shuddered. "There is no need. The end of your conversation was clearly audible to half the room. Oh, Dee! How could you talk so recklessly, and cause a scene? Lady Dunston will be furious. She is sure to complain to your papa."

"She may well do," Daphne declared with a proud lift of her head, "but I care not a fig. Papa will take little notice, especially when I recount how the lout dares to blame me for the mishap. I am not bamming you—he blames *me*. Can you credit that?"

"But, my dearest friend, recollect what you told me. Were you not just a little to blame? Did you not just…well, pop out on the road in front of his horses? Could not a carriage going much slower still have had difficulty missing you?"

Stung, Daphne sat bolt upright to face her friend. "Julia! Are you siding with that arrogant beast against me?"

Miss Todhunter's gentle doe eyes filled with distress. "I seek only fairness, Daphne. Justice, if you will. You know how strong-minded you are, once you are set on a course of action.Come now, I beg, think on it."

Julia's words acted as cold water on Daphne's overheated emotions. Her glow of victory cooled into an uneasy suspicion she had gone too far, allowing what some might call a mere incident to assume the proportions of a tragedy. Of course, they would not know the real reason for her attack: his treatment of William. And how that "mere incident" had shaken her to her soul.

"Yes, perhaps I did run with the bit between my teeth, but he deserved more. When I think of all—" She stopped, held by her own pride and her promise to her brother. "I cannot reveal, even to you, dear Julia, the source of my aversion to Lord Courtlea. I fear that my strong dislike of him may have driven me—no, I will admit it—has driven me to behave in a shockingly rude and reckless manner."

Daphne sighed, recollecting how, barely two days past, she had smugly bid young William learn to control his temper. How soon she had forgotten her own advice!

"Perhaps you have the right of it, Julia," she said. "At the time I felt somewhat in the wrong, so it seems I must share the blame after all."

"Oh, how good of you to admit it, Dee!" Julia's plain little face lit with delight. "Now, I beg, go to Lord Courtlea and tell him so. It will smooth matters, and restore harmony."

Her plea won a reluctant smile from Daphne. "'Blessed are the peacemakers,'" she quoted. "That is you to the life, Julia Todhunter." Rising, Daphne adjusted her shawl, a length of cream silk figured with gold thread. "I would rather face a French invasion than ask pardon of that gentleman, but for your sake, and the sake of justice, and so as not ruin Lady Dunston's ball, I shall apologize for my forwardness, if not for my sentiments."

Lord Courtlea had chosen not to dance but sat with his friend in a small corner bower formed by several tubs of plants and shrubs. Daphne approached, with Julia at her heels, and paused by a palm to gather her thoughts.

Fortunately, Lord Courtlea seemed unaware of how deeply his

cavalier handling had affected her. As she had disdainfully thought earlier, holding a pliant woman in his arms was too usual for him to take much notice of it. And what was a kiss to him? Nothing worth recollecting. Oh, how she despised him!

"Good God, Bennington," Daphne heard Lord Courtlea say, "never have I endured such a dull rout! All country dances, not a waltz among 'em. And look you, at the array of beauties assembled for our delectation. Harpies, the lot. Lady Eugenia brays while her mama poses. That pretty blonde piece has some charm, but her tongue rattles like seeds in a dry gourd, with as much sense."

Daphne gasped, but, as the friendly palm concealed her, and the music drowned her indignantly indrawn breath, Lord Courtlea remained unaware of her presence. She did not doubt the "blonde piece" to whom the earl referred was Sophie Summerhayes.

"I take it by your bad humor," drawled Lord Bennington, not bothering to conceal his smirk, "that you had no success with the red-haired beauty. Mayhap I shall try my luck."

Daphne had turned away, not wishing to eavesdrop, but Lord Bennington's words stopped her. Julia, overhearing the stout lord and seeing Daphne's eyes start to gleam, caught at her friend's arm.

"She will eat you whole, you poor sot, and spit out the bones," replied the earl to Bennington. "Pure vinegar and acid, she is, mixed with a large dose of impudence."

"Egad, Courtlea, but you protest overmuch. Pricked your pride, has she? Or are you like the fox who slanders the grapes as sour because they are out of reach?"

Daphne waited no longer, but shook off Julia's restraining hand and stepped into view. She noted with satisfaction how Lord Courtlea paled and then flushed red as he rose to his feet.

"My lords," she said sweetly, with a cool nod to Lord Bennington who had also risen, "pray excuse my impetuous interruption of your conversation, but I could no longer disregard the pangs of conscience. Lord Courtlea, forgive me, I beg, for the untoward fashion in which I earlier presented my opinion of your character and lack of responsibility. It was intolerably rude of me."

Allowing a tremulous smile to touch her lips, she lowered her eyes with exaggerated timidity. Her glance fastened on an emerald set in gold filigree on Lord Courtlea's watch chain. The stone shimmered as the earl took a step forward.

"Why, Miss Summerhayes..." With his color still high, his lordship appeared at a loss for words. "Miss Summerhayes," he continued with more firmness, "there is no need for you to search me out so. I vow I have already forgotten our little difference of opinions."

"How noble of you, my lord, to let my unkind remarks slip from your mind. Such rudeness as mine was without the slightest merit, as I am sure you will agree, sir, and such slanderous words, such brazen manners, were far from courtly."

His lordship's gray eyes flared, then focused more sharply on her face.

"In truth," Daphne continued, "anger and embarrassment clouded my judgment, and spurred me to deny my part in our encounter. The fault was mine, and I freely own up to it. Indeed, I own it as freely as I earlier berated your recklessness and disregard for others. If, my lord, you grant pardon for my forwardness, my heart will be considerably relieved."

With an air of contrition, Daphne bowed her head, as though meekly awaiting sentence from on high. The emerald again caught her eye and nudged her recollection, but before she could think why, Lord Courtlea spoke.

"Let us share the pardon as well as the blame, Miss Summerhayes. My pair have recovered from their fright, as has Miss Butler, so let us say no more on the subject."

His tone was dry, and Daphne, glancing up into his face, discerned a flicker of amusement there. That is to say, his mouth, which she conceded to be a rather handsome feature when it was not snarling, moved in the barest suggestion of a smile.

"Agreed, my lord. Now I leave you to the enjoyment of the music and the company." With a deep curtsy, Daphne withdrew to Julia, who waited wide-eyed behind the palm.

"Dee," Julia gasped as they moved away, "never have I heard such a mixture of insult and obsequiousness from anyone's lips."

"Truly, I rather enjoyed it. When I heard him laying waste to our friends, good people for the most part, who have gathered for his honor and delectation—Well, you heard."

"But to play thus on his names—Merritt and Courtlea—oh, I trembled! He quite terrifies me."

"I believe he has no merit, and for the other, was there ever such a misnomer?" Daphne stopped and glanced behind her. There was no sign of Lord Courtlea. The next dance was forming, and Lord Bennington, with apparent boredom, was leading Eugenia, all smiles, to the set.

"The earl twigged to my puns, I think," Daphne mused. "Could a sense of humor exist with all that arrogance and pride? In any case," she went on more briskly, "my apology has seemingly calmed the waters, as you wished, Julia, and now let us find Sophie, and hope she has acted with more decorum than her chaperon."

She turned, and could not restrain a gasp. Lord Courtlea stood at her elbow. He bowed, as expressionless as if nothing had ever passed between them.

"Miss Summerhayes, pray favor me with this dance."

Thoroughly taken aback, Daphne groped for words. "Why, Lord Courtlea, I—um—sir, I beg you to excuse me. A family matter requires my instant attention. My friend, Miss Todhunter, is free, and would be happy to oblige."

A tiny strangled sound came from Julia.

"An honor, Miss Todhunter, I assure you," Lord Courtlea said smoothly, "and one I hope to claim at another time. Miss Summerhayes and I, however, have matters to resolve." His gaze returned to Daphne, and she tensed at the steely glint of determination in his eyes.

"Oh, I quite understand," Julia assured him, blushing to the roots of her hair. "In any case, I must go and—and locate…"

She gave Daphne a flustered glance that her friend took as a promise to look for Sophie, and fled.

"Miss Summerhayes?"

The earl held out his hand. Short of causing another scene, and it seemed that every eye in the room was on them, she had no choice but to agree. Reluctantly she gave him her hand, and without a further word, he led her out.

Her anger against him had cooled, although her dislike had not. In silence she stood beside him, and although only her fingertips were held in his gloved hand, she was very aware of his strong masculine presence. Nonsense, she told herself, lifting her chin. He is but a man, and a despicable one at that.

The music began, and as they advanced, he inclined his head toward her. "You ran away, Miss Summerhayes," he murmured in a tone she deemed too intimate by half, "before I could properly respond to your gracious apology."

"On the contrary, sir, I did not flee," she replied briskly. "I considered our exchange quite ended." Daphne passed in front of him to turn with the next gentleman. 'Twas Sir Reginald, who gave her a reproachful look. She answered with an absent smile.

"Ended?" Lord Courtlea asked as she returned to him.

They balanced, face to face, coming a shade closer than necessary. Indeed, overeager swains had been known to steal a kiss from their blushing partners. Daphne stiffened, but Lord Courtlea moved back with the utmost correctness.

"I had rather hoped it was beginning, Miss Summerhayes, not ending." He did not smile; indeed, his expression was austere in the extreme but for his eyes.

When Daphne looked into their gray depths, clear as water, she felt again that strange tremor, half excitement and half a portent of danger. Her breath came a trifle faster, and though she brusquely ordered herself to recollect her dignity and position, the room seemed suddenly overly warm.

"I fear, my lord, your hopes must be dashed. What began on a country road now ends at a country ball." She turned under his raised hand to weave with the lady beside her. If this worldly earl thought she was eager for his interest and ultimate conquest, she must disabuse him at once. She would not fall into his hands like a ripe peach from the tree.

"Ah, then you are affianced, Miss Summerhayes," he continued as they met again. "Is the fortunate man among our number this evening? Perchance that well-fed personage whose eyes follow you like those of a doting spaniel?"

In spite of her dislike of him, she almost laughed. Sir Reginald's lovesick expression had always reminded her more of one of the rather jowly hounds than a spaniel, but she would never admit that to Lord Courtlea. Sir Reginald was one of her own people, and not to be ridiculed by any condescending outsider.

"Surely that is too delicate a subject for two strangers such as we to discuss," she chided him with an archness she did not know she possessed, and which she immediately deplored.

"My dear Miss Summerhayes," he murmured, his eyes lazily hooded, "one must ask if one is to learn."

Daphne turned out, and back, and decided to refrain from conversation entirely. 'Twas too easy to fence with him, which, in a detached way, she found stimulating but which he might consider encouraging. Had she met him tonight, with no previous knowledge, his admitted charm might have captivated her. Now it was too late. She knew and despised him too much.

Silently then, with no smile or glance, she raised her hands to shoulder height for the advance en promenade. A pretty step, one of her favorites, with right hands together and the gentleman's left arm stretched behind the lady's shoulders to grasp her left hand. Only the gloved hands touch, and Daphne had never considered the figure as sensual.

But then, she had never danced with Victor Merritt, Lord Courtlea. He infused every step, every movement, with subdued sensuality.

He moved faultlessly, with utter correctness, but his fingers curled around hers with added firmness and warmth. His arm seemed ready to scoop her up as he had on the road. She had only to lean back the slightest bit to let her head rest against his broad shoulder. And did she imagine it, or did his thumb gently rub against her knuckles? Her breath caught, and she knew the oddest impulse to let him bring his hands forward and so enclose her in his arms.

"How is it that a fair flower as yourself has remained so long in the single state?" he murmured, his lips so close his warm breath stirred the ringlets at her temple. "Are the swains hereabout so lacking in bottom that none has yet claimed you as his?"

She dared not glance at him and see in his eyes the mockery she heard in his voice. Nor could she speak, lest she deliver a spate of angry words. He was toying with her, she realized in a fury, mayhap paying her back for the wigging she had given him. The wretch! To twit her about not being married at her age! Thank mercy the dance was nearly ended.

"'Tis naught but my own choice to remain as I am," she said evenly. "I am not averse to marriage, but hope for a blending of hearts and minds instead of a mere union of bodies and incomes."

She heard his indrawn breath. "Gad, Miss Summerhayes, rarely if ever have I met such a direct lady." He gave a soft laugh. "But pray continue; you mentioned union of bodies?"

Daphne bit her lip. "Union only in holy matrimony," she continued firmly. "Furthermore, I believe that modern unmarried gentlemen, and especially those in Town, lack the intelligence, initiative, and plain good manners to be successful husbands."

"But that is too severe, I protest," Lord Courtlea said lightly as he bowed to end the dance. "You are overly harsh on my sex. Have you known so few unattached young gentlemen with the talents you list so glibly?"

Daphne sank into a deep curtsy. "I have known none, sir." She rose and faced him, noting how amusement or condescension glimmered in his eyes. All her reasons for disliking him rose in a flood. "Nor have I, up to the present moment," she added coldly, "met a gentleman with even one of those requirements."

Lord Courtlea stiffened and went very white. She turned from his dumbfounded expression and walked off the floor, leaving him standing alone. The earl would recollect that cut for a very long time, she hoped, and perhaps his pride would be a touch humbled. His humiliation at this moment was nothing to the humiliation he had heaped on her head.

A light hand on her arm stopped her.

"Oh, Mrs. Todhunter," Daphne said blankly, realizing she had walked right past Julia's mama without seeing her. "Is something amiss?"

Mrs. Todhunter's usually mild features bore a disapproving frown. "Daphne, pray come at once," she said from behind a discreetly-held fan. "Julia is tending Miss Summerhayes, your cousin, in the powder room. William awaits you as well."

"Is Sophie—oh, I hardly dare ask what has happened to the feckless girl! Pray tell me at once, Mrs. Todhunter."

"A few minutes ago, William came to me, saying his cousin was suffering from a severe chilling," Mrs. Todhunter explained as they hurried from the ballroom. "It seems that, after their dance, Tim and Miss Summerhayes foolishly stood out on the balcony for some time, then, with William, went to the stables—can you imagine, in a thin gown and slippers, with only a shawl, in January!—to see some horse. Of course the child was frozen to the bone. I have her well wrapped, but she still shivers. There is your brother."

Pale with concern and guilt, William rose from his chair outside the room originally set aside for freshening the powdered wigs of guests. Now, with powder obsolete, and periwigs declined in fashion, ladies used the room for primping, or waiting while a maid repaired a torn gown.

"I have ordered the coach brought around," said William quietly, "and sent a footman for our cloaks."

"You did well, William," said his sister. "Now go bid goodnight to Lord and Lady Dunston. Hurry, now! We will talk of this later."

William tore away, and in a remarkably short time the Summerhayes family was speeding toward home. Wrapped in blankets and William's cloak as well as her own, Sophie still shivered uncontrollably.

"Now, William, can you explain this piece of work?" Daphne asked, after ascertaining that all the hot bricks lay under the chilled girl's feet.

"Well, I went to claim my dance with Sophie—I was not going to go to ground because Courtlea was there—and she and Tim were coming in from the balcony, and Tim mentioned that Juniper's knees were healing. Then Sophie said she would as soon see a good horse as dance, so we went down to the stables, and led him out, and I guess we stayed too long..." William turned an admiring look on his cousin. "In any case, Sophie was a brick, not a peep of complaint, until I noticed her nose turning blue."

"Oh, D-Daphne, I am s-so s-sorry!" Sophie wailed through chattering teeth. "I have quite s-spoiled your f-fun, and m-made you miss s-supper, too. C-can you f-forgive me?"

"Hush. That don't signify, as I do not in the least mind leaving. But what possessed you to go out in the cold in such a state? You must learn to think—Oh, pray do not cry, dear!"

Daphne drew the sobbing, shivering girl into her arms. 'Twas perhaps just as well they had to leave, lest another scene erupt between Daphne and the earl. She would take care not to accept invitations if Lord Courtlea were to be present. The earl was doubtless of the same mind, wanting never again to set eyes on the saucy Miss Summerhayes.

She could still see those gray eyes, puzzled and shocked by her sharp words. Mayhap no one had ever taken him so smartly to task before. She did not regret doing it, as his proud lordship needed to be taken down a peg or two, but she could not repress a twinge of something like remorse. Had she been perhaps a bit too severe? Was she meanly paying him back for mortifying her so?

At Weldern Manor, after Sophie was hustled into a warmed bed with a hot lemon and honey drink, Daphne left her to Tyson's care and retired to her own room. Briggs came in at her heels.

"Now, isn't it just a shame Miss Sophie came down with a chill," she said, taking and folding Daphne's shawl, "and you and Master William had to come home early."

"A short stay, but an exciting one," sighed Daphne, stripping off her gloves.

"Better a good short time than a long boring one," Briggs stated, unfastening the pearl and diamond necklace around Daphne's throat. As the necklace, inherited from her mother, slid into her hand, Daphne suddenly recollected the emerald on Lord Courtlea's watch chain. A terrible suspicion formed in her mind. Without a word to her astounded abigail, Daphne ran from the room and rushed down to her father's study.

In a wall, hidden behind a shelf of books, was a safe box. Her father kept his most valuable papers there, with certain keepsakes and treasures. Daphne retrieved the key from its hiding place in the desk, opened the safe box, and withdrew a flat, velvet-covered jeweler's case.

"Oh, let me be wrong," she whispered. She knew its contents well—her mother's emerald necklace, earrings, bracelets, and brooch. The brooch was a single, large emerald, finely set in gold filigree. It was made in such a fashion that one could wear it as a pin, or add it to the necklace for a truly magnificent effect.

With trembling fingers she opened the case. In the candlelight, the stones of the necklace, bracelets, and earrings shimmered with green fire. The brooch was gone.

CHAPTER 5

Daphne rapped urgently on her brother's bedroom door. Hardly waiting for his response, she slipped inside quickly, easing the door closed behind her. Clad in a red plush dressing gown, William stood leaning on the mantel and staring into the fire.

"I do not want Papa to hear, or Briggs either," Daphne explained in a low tone. "William, what do you know of Mama's emerald brooch? Tonight I saw it, or its twin, on a certain lord's watch chain."

William's features clouded with an expression of shame that smote Daphne's heart even as it confirmed her suspicions. "Tell me all, William. The truth now!"

Squaring his shoulders, he turned to his sister with a certain air of relief. "I've been in a quake waiting for you or Father to find me out. Yes, I took the brooch that night I was to play cards with—at the Hall. I wanted to show some style, that we weren't all bumpkins without a bauble to our name. Oh, I know it was a ninnyhammer trick. Then, I lost it."

"Lost it, at Dunston Hall?" Daphne's heart sank. "Then Lord Courtlea must have found it, and being the man he is, said 'finder is keeper' and took it for his own." Her heart sank even farther. Of all men, why was it he who found the brooch? Just when she had thought him out of her life forever!

"Uh, well—"

"I can just see him," exclaimed Daphne, pacing the floor, her temper rising hotly at this fresh reason for grievance, "pocketing the brooch, not caring that someone might treasure it, not only for its cost, but as a keepsake. Oh, the bounder!"

"Dee, are you not rushing your fences regarding Lord Courtlea? He—"

"Not a bit. I read his shallow character the moment I clapped eyes on him. William, pray recollect I have seen more of the world than you, and you should be guided by my greater experience. Now, as Lord High-and-Mighty has no legal right to the brooch, we must reclaim it."

William groaned and dropped into a fireside chair. "Leave it, Dee, for mercy's sake! I know you think him a downy cove, and me a cork-brained nodcock, but I have it all in hand."

His sister stopped her pacing and faced him, arms akimbo. "In what fashion?" she demanded. "Why have you not already identified the brooch to him and demanded its return? You know how Papa treasures everything that belonged to Mama. Indeed, we all do. Oh," she cried, striking her palms together in frustration, "why did I not recognize that piece for what it was? Why, I would have faced him out then and there!"

William gestured in frustration. "Exactly. In your usual 'I know best' manner, you would have charged ahead. Demme, when will you stop managing all the world?"

Daphne stared in hurt surprise at her brother. "Why, Willy, are you quite fair? I hope my actions always stem from the purest of motives. Oh, why bring that up now? What are we going to do? The thought of facing that man again..." She shook her head and resumed her pacing, feeling utterly desperate.

"Why, what have you done?" demanded William. "You did not throw me in his face, did you?"

Any other time Daphne would have laughed at that imagery. Now she merely shook her head. "'Tis of no account. We must think how best—I have it!"

She hurried to William's writing table and drew out a sheet of paper. "I will write a letter to his lordship, explaining the matter and requesting the return of the brooch. Surely even he cannot ignore such a missive. You will not mind if I sign your name, Willy? He has cause not to welcome mine."

William sighed, but Daphne busied herself with her message, and in a few minutes it was done. "Let me convey the note," William said, "so we may be sure it goes directly into Lord Courtlea's hands."

"An excellent idea," Daphne agreed warmly. "Perhaps he will

deliver the brooch to you immediately." And I shall not have to face him again, she added silently with a little shiver.

Her brother did not answer, but tucked the folded paper carefully away in his dressing gown pocket.

* * *

William returned empty-handed. Daphne waited for two days for some sign from Lord Courtlea. She half feared, half hoped he himself would appear at the door with the gem. She decided to be coolly courteous, yet could not control a nervous flutter whenever Thomson announced a visitor.

William had little to say, outside of urging his sister to allow him management of the matter, but by the third morning after the ball, Daphne's nerves were stretched to breaking.

Sophie's chill had developed into a cold, confining her to bed and postponing the much-needed lessons on decorum. While Sophie snuffled and sneezed, Daphne got out brushes and paints, hoping a morning spent at her easel would take her mind from her troubles. A rendering in oils of Howey Wood, however, would not come right.

Images of Lord Courtlea insisted on intruding between her and her canvas. Smiling, furious, haughty, seductive, and abashed—she saw him reflect a whole gamut of expressions culled from their two meetings. Why, the stormy sky in her painting was the tint of his eyes. Even the smooth-barked, towering beech trunks reflected his strong, well-proportioned body and grace of movement.

Daphne grimaced. Could nothing drive that irritating earl from her mind? Would she never forget the strength of his arms about her, the appeal of his eyes smiling down at her? Such natural charms the man possessed, all blighted by a shallow, rude, overbearing nature! Sadly but truly, Victor Merritt, Earl of Courtlea, personified the wealthy, modern gentleman. There was much in him to condemn, little if anything to praise.

"He is little better than a thief," Daphne muttered to the canvas propped on her easel. "Nay, he is no better than a dastardly robber who comes in the night—"

She broke off, the brush forgotten in her hand, as she dwelt on a sudden, desperate notion. No, the plan was too hare-brained, too monstrous, too…perfect. Excitement gripped her. She flung down her brush and began to pace the red drugget carpet of her little studio.

Had she the courage? Yes. The right? Yes. And time pressed, for at any time James Summerhayes might detect the loss of the brooch, to his pain, or Lord Courtlea might depart the country.

Daphne said nothing of her plan to her brother, although she was hard put to conceal her excitement for the remainder of the day. Pleading the headache, she retired early, aided by a concerned Briggs, then lay in growing impatience and dread until the tallcase clock in the entry hall chimed midnight.

Swiftly she dressed in her darkest, warmest gown, and pulled a mob cap over her hair. The white cap was hidden by the hood of her black, fur-trimmed cloak as she slipped from the sleeping house. She resigned herself to shank's mare, as taking her horse chanced rousing Jem, the ostler, who slept above the stable. The moon played peek-a-boo with silver-rimmed clouds during her two-mile trudge over frosty fields, and disappeared completely as Daphne circled to the back of Dunston Hall. A gray lurcher, chained behind the house, let out a questioning growl, but catching Daphne's familiar scent, wagged its tail and curled back into sleep. Daphne had long known of a certain loose window off the scullery, used by Tim when he wished to slip in or out unobserved. In a frighteningly short time, Miss Summerhayes became an unlawful intruder, tiptoeing up three flights of stairs to the bedrooms.

She turned to the left, toward the guest rooms, her heart hammering in her breast. A lone night-light on a table served only to enhance the darkness, and pale faces peered at her from portraits on the walls. A floorboard creaked under her foot, and she froze, scarcely breathing. When no alarm was raised, she moved cautiously to the end room, the one most sumptuously furnished and with the finest views. Doubtless it was occupied by the most important guest.

Despite the chill in the corridor, Daphne's palms were wet as she tried the door. It yielded to her touch, and she breathed a prayer of thanks. At first, all seemed black as pitch inside, for the curtains were closed, and the fire a mere glow of coals. Slipping off her cloak, whose voluminous folds might hamper her search, she waited until her heartbeat calmed and her eyes adjusted to the meager light. Silent as a wraith, she moved to the bed whence came the sound of deep, regular breathing.

The sleeper lay on his back, arms thrown above his head, dark hair showing clear against the white pillows. Daphne bent over the figure, straining to make out the features. A wide forehead, straight nose, lips relaxed and slightly parted. Yes, it was he, exuding brandy fumes with each breath. Satisfied, she turned away to begin her search, when a gleam of some golden object on the dresser caught her eye.

It proved to be Lord Courtlea's watch hanging on its stand with the gold seal and the emerald brooch still dangling from the chain. The brooch's pin had been passed through one of the links; a snug fit, as Daphne discovered. She tugged gently, then gave a hard pull. The brooch came free, but the chain rattled against the wooden stand with a noise that seemed to her as loud as musket fire. Daphne glanced fearfully toward the bed as she pinned the brooch to her chemise, but except for a slight pause, Lord Courtlea's breathing remained steady.

Her impulse was to run like the wind, now the jewel was in her possession. She fought down the urge, and crept silently toward the door. Then, she stopped and turned toward the bed. All her senses cried out for her to leave, at once, but some other power drew her on to look once more at the detestable earl.

In truth, he hardly merited that epithet now, with his haughtiness drained away, his mouth sweet-lipped and gentled by sleep. His strong corded neck rose from the open collar of the ruffled nightshirt. The hollow at the base of his throat was shadowed and somehow vulnerable.

A strange, aching softness moved through Daphne as she gazed at the sleeping lord. Slowly her hand stole out, following but not touching the curve of his cheek. Heat from his skin warmed her palm.

Aghast, she snatched her hand back before it could smooth back the dark hair tumbled over his forehead. Was she mad, to linger like some moon-struck Bath miss ogling the object of her desires? Daphne desired only to be gone, and quickly.

She turned away, and had taken a few cautious steps when there was a rustling from the bed. Before she could move, two strong arms circled her waist. A scream rose in her throat, but mindful of her situation, she throttled the scream to a choked gurgle. She struggled to break free, pulling at the sinewy hands, frantic to escape before she was recognized. Although her captor reeled back a step, laughing, the arms about her tightened until she could scarce breathe.

"How now, mistress?" Lord Courtlea murmured in her ear. "Do not run away, not yet. Tell me who you are, come to cheer my cold, lonely hours."

His arms held her tight against him, her back pressing against his powerful chest. His breath fanned her neck like a warm caress, startling her into a delicious shiver. Horrified, she twisted her head away, but his warm lips sought her earlobe, nibbled at it, and then gently kissed a tender place just below her ear. Daphne gulped, jolted by a charge of heated sensation that flowed from the spot his lips touched right down to her toes. Even the deceitful Sir George Sowerby had never attempted more than to kiss her hand or discreetly touch her arm. And his touch had never affected her senses like this.

Outraged, Daphne gritted her teeth and fought against the unfamiliar sensual stirring, refusing to admit the frightening pleasure his kisses caused. Kisses that were much more potent than that light brush of his lips on hers that she recollected so clearly. She must get away.

Having tested his strength, she realized it was useless to struggle. He would simply tighten his grip. Her breath coming hard and fast, she forced herself to relax as if in submission.

"It be only Flora, my lord," she whispered, naming a non-existent servant, "followin' me orders to set the fires to rights, like, because of the cold. Let me go, please, my lord. I don't want no trouble."

She kept her face turned away to prevent recognition, but that position presented the slope of her neck to Lord Courtlea's attentions.

"Mmm, no more do I, dainty Flora." He kissed her neck, gently, lingeringly, as if tasting her skin. Despite her outrage, Daphne closed her eyes and swallowed a moan as waves of pleasure weakened her knees. She leaned back, tipping her head a little. His body thrust hard against her, and she bit her lip to keep from crying out.

His fingers stroked her nape, then pulled at the neck of her bodice to bare her shoulder. "Skin soft as rose petals," he murmured between kisses, "and sweet as violets. What other treasures does your lissome form hold?"

Keeping one hand clamped about her waist, the earl slid the other slowly down her side, over the curves of waist and hip to her thigh. Then, his hand as slowly moved up, higher still, to caress her breast. Daphne gasped as the heat of his hand penetrated her woolen gown and set her skin tingling. Startled, shocked by a sudden, intense desire, Daphne moaned aloud.

To this moment, she had feared only recognition followed by exposure as an intruder and a thief. Now, her apprehensions took a different course. A part of her was furious that he should dare try to seduce her, but another, hitherto hidden part quivered with excitement and not a little curiosity.

"How can I believe you came to see to the fire, little flower?" His lordship's voice held a smile, and its low, honeyed tone twined beguilingly through Daphne's mind. "You have not touched it. See how the hearth barely glows. And why tonight, when I have passed many nights under this roof without such a visitation? Is it because I leave tomorrow? Look at me, girl."

His hands moved up to her shoulders, but his hold was yet too firm for her to break away. Daphne allowed him to turn her around, but kept her head down as though overcome with shyness. In truth, she could not have looked at him under any circumstances after his intimate stroking.

"Come," he whispered, drawing her against him, "the bed is warm, and I will show you another, happier manner to tend my fires!"

Pressed against the long hard length of his body, her cheek resting on his broad chest, Daphne fought with the quite insane urge to simply become Flora, and surrender to the strange forces burning within her. But she was not Flora, and this was the odious Lord Courtlea. She would loathe herself if she surrendered to him. Keeping her face averted, she reached up and spread her hands on his chest. With an effort, she closed her mind to the warm firmness of his flesh beneath the thin linen nightshirt.

"Oh, your lordship does me too much honor," she whispered.

And pushed hard.

"Hey!"

Lord Courtlea fell back against the bed, catching the bed curtain as he went. The curtain tore from its rings, and Daphne seized the other end to flip it neatly over the earl. The counterpane went on top, further muffling his lordship's comments. Leaving him to fight his way out of the bundle, Daphne seized her cloak and ran as she had never run before.

As she dashed downstairs to the scullery window, she prayed that Lord Courtlea's pride would not allow him to rouse the house because of a put-down by a servant. Indeed, he had seemed half-foxed. Mayhap by morning, he would think it all a brandy dream.

The westering moon floated clear of clouds as Daphne hurried toward home with burning cheeks and her senses in such confusion she scarce noted her way. Now that she was far from his disturbing presence, she considered Lord Courtlea a libertine of the worst kind to take advantage of a servant girl. She shuddered, hating to recollect how his kisses, his closeness, his touch, had affected her so deeply.

Why did her hands still feel the heat of his body as he held her in his arms? Why did her whole body tingle, her breast burn? She despised the man, yet he had stirred her emotions in a way totally new to her; new, but exquisitely pleasurable, melting, and, because so powerful, not a little frightening. Such emotions made a girl lose her head, and mayhap lose more than her head.

The proper and sensible thing, Daphne decided, lifting her heated face to the wind, was to choose the right gentleman and marry him before allowing such exciting liberties to her person.

The right gentleman for her would in no manner resemble that dark, devilish rogue who doubtless already snored unconcernedly at Dunston Hall.

CHAPTER 6

Daphne's cool sanity had returned by the time she quietly let herself in to Weldern Manor. For the second time that night, she tiptoed up the stairs of a sleeping house. Too elated with the success of her plot to wait until morning, she lit a candle, shook her brother awake and held out the missing brooch.

"What flummery is this, Dee?" he asked, rubbing his eyes. Yawning, he sat upright. "Good God, the brooch! How...where..." Words failed him, and he stared blankly at his sister.

"Tonight I paid a visit to a certain bedroom in Dunston Hall," she said proudly. Swiftly she told the story, but omitted any mention of Lord Courtlea's awakening.

William's stare changed to one of pure horror. "Oh, my God! Dee, you gudgeon! Why did you not leave it to me? Do you know what you've done?"

"Hush, or Papa will wake! Why, William, are you not pleased? I merely took back our own property. I thought you would be delighted, and so proud of your sister."

"Proud!" came his hoarse whisper. "You and your everlasting meddling! Yes, I lost the brooch, but at cards. Lord Courtlea won it. You have just stolen a jewel that legally belongs to a confounded peer of the realm."

"Oh!" Daphne sank slowly to the edge of the bed. The emerald in her hand winked as if in glee at her discomfiture. "Oh, Willy, why did you not tell me?"

"Why did I not—? When did you ever listen to me? I tried to stop you, but no, off you went like a rocket, so sure you knew best. Dash it, Dee, will you ever learn? Will you ever—"

Daphne stared at her brother, stricken with remorse and guilt. William's tirade stopped in full flight. With a shake of his head, he reached out for her hand lying limply on the counterpane.

"Dee, forgive me. I should have made it plain that I lost the thing at cards. When you assumed otherwise, I hoped all might come right, without you learning what a beetle-headed flat I was. With the brass I get tomorrow from Squire Todhunter, I planned to redeem the brooch from Courtlea."

The quietly contrite tone in which he delivered his explanation only deepened Daphne's misery. "Oh, and I have made things worse!" she wailed. "But you cannot think to borrow money from the squire. However will you repay him?"

William paused. His lower lip trembled once, then firmed. "No need to pay it back. He is buying Kingman."

"You will sell Kingman? But he is your favourite mount. You raised him from a colt. Oh, my dearest, bravest boy!" Totally unnerved, Daphne threw her arms about her brother's neck and burst into tears.

"Oh, rubbish, Dee, don't take on so." Awkwardly he patted her shoulder. "Now, forget all else and think only how we may put this muddle to rights."

"Impossible!" Daphne gulped.

"But Dee, the servants will get blamed for the theft. D'you want that on your conscience? Why, all of 'em might lose their places." His comforting patting ceased, and he gave her arm a little shake. "Gad, didn't you think what would happen when Courtlea discovered his loss? Or were you hoping he simply wouldn't notice?"

"I thought only of reclaiming what was ours, and saving Papa from distress," Daphne admitted, terribly aware now that her impetuosity had plunged her into unforseen complications. "Courtlea found the jewel, so mayhap he will think it lost again…" She bit her lip and shook her head, miserably ashamed at her own blind stupidity.

"Give it me." William's voice held a new decisiveness. "I'll return it the way you took it, and he'll be none the wiser."

"You are brave to offer, but 'twould not be safe." Daphne sat up, wiping her eyes on a corner of the bed sheet. "Dawn is not far off, and the staff will be stirring soon. No, if suspicion falls on any of the servants, or indeed, on anyone else, I will return the brooch to Lord

Courtlea's hand, with due apology."

"You'll not face him alone, Dee. I stand with you."

Daphne managed a smile for her brother, but her heart quailed at the thought of facing the earl and telling him of her crime. Worse, he would know she was the woman he had grappled with in the darkness of his bedroom. Would he also be aware of the tumult of sensations he had stirred in her?

"If only he had acted the gentleman," she began resentfully, "and answered my note…" Her voice trailed off, and her blood seemed turned to ice. "The note," she whispered, staring in horror at William. "How could I have forgotten that wretched note? He knows the brooch is ours. Now he will know at once, will he not, that we…that I…?"

After all, she must not needs go to Dunston Hall to confront an irate earl, for he doubtless would be soon hammering at the manor door with the sheriff in tow, demanding her arrest.

"Don't be overset on that score," William assured her with a sheepish look. "Your note never left my pocket."

Although she was still on the hook to somehow return the brooch, Daphne knew a great warming surge of relief. "For once I am grateful you disobeyed me, you rascal."

"D'you mean I did something right for a change?" Amusement glimmered briefly in her brother's eyes. Then he sighed and scratched his tousled head. "What a rackety cockup! In any case, we can do nothing until daylight. Go to bed, Dee. You are worn to a nubbin."

"I will go," Daphne agreed, rising from the bed and taking her candle, "but I shan't sleep a wink. Goodnight. And thank you, brother mine, for not prosing more at me, although I deserve it."

He grinned, and Daphne quietly left his room, thinking how sensible and more commanding her baby brother had suddenly become. In her own room, she changed swiftly and then flung herself on her bed and buried her flaming face in the pillow. She was adept at thrusting unpleasant subjects from her mind, but she knew she could never forget this night. The Earl of Courtlea had burst into her life like a whirlwind, and she feared the storm was not yet over.

The next thing she knew, Briggs was opening curtains with more energy than seemed necessary. Heavy-eyed, she sat up to see rain streaking the windows. Her spirits drooped. Oh, a perfect day to witness her humiliation at Lord Courtlea's hands!

"Oh, Miss Daphne, what a to-do at Dunston Hall," said Briggs, handing her mistress a cup of chocolate. "The post told Mr. Thomson and Mr. Thomson told me. Oh, they all are in a fuss, I can tell you."

Daphne's heart plummeted to new depths. "What is the time, please, Briggs?"

"'Tis gone half eleven," answered the abigail, tucking a loose strand of gray hair under her cap. "I came in earlier, but you slept so soundly, I hated to rouse you. How is the headache?"

"The what? Oh, yes, the headache. Gone, I think."

Briggs frowned. "You are too pale, Miss Daphne, and dark 'neath the eyes. Are you sickening for something, child? Mayhap you have caught Miss Sophie's cold."

Daphne sipped her chocolate. "No, I am well, Briggs, just tired. Tell me of the excitement at the Hall." She hoped her tone held the right amount of innocent interest.

"Well, now," began the abigail with relish, "Lord Courtlea's man, Fleck, came down to the servants' hall, all in a dither because some bauble of the earl's had gone missing. His master was not overset, as nothing else was gone, but Fleck said it put a shadow on his reputation, and he insisted on an investigation.

"Lady Dunston was in a stew, I can tell you! She was all for sacking the servants on the spot, but Lord Courtlea wouldn't hear of it. He lined up all the maids, except, of course, Mrs. Bates the housekeeper, and the ladies' abigails. They were all weeping and trembling, as you might imagine, but his lordship asked them, as kind as may be, if a Flora was among them. They said not. Then Lord Courtlea questioned them, nicely, so I hear, but with his nose just inches from their faces. Gave them quite a turn, no doubt, being that close to such a handsome, wealthy young lord."

Briggs chuckled, her plump frame quivering with amusement, and took the empty cup from Daphne's nerveless fingers. "His lordship announced he was satisfied they were innocent—at least of the robbery, he added with a grin that had them all blushing and giggling—and sent them off.

"Then someone discovered an open window in the scullery, and marks on the ground outside. Lord Courtlea deduced that a thief had entered the house, taken the bauble, a brooch or some such, and was disturbed before he could make off with anything more. But, I ask you, what disturbed the blackguard, and why did he go to Lord Courtlea's room? Why did he not steal the plate, or try for Lady Dunston's jewels?"

"I have no idea." The lie came guiltily, if not easily, to Daphne's lips.

Briggs went on about Lady Dunston's hysterics and Lord Dunston organizing a search of the countryside, but Daphne barely heard. Lord Courtlea's actions puzzled her. Instead of stamping about and raging, as she might have expected him to do, he had behaved kindly toward the frightened servants. Then, although he well knew the gender of the intruder, he had diverted the search to a non-existent, masculine thief. In short, he had conducted himself in a most gentlemanly fashion.

She noticed her abigail looking at her with a questioning expression. "What was that, Briggs?"

"I said that it was a mite peculiar that Lord Courtlea queried only the maids, and none of the men servants. Surely one of them would be more like to act the robber."

"Oh, as to that, doubtless the discovery of the open window proved the thief was not of the household. Further questioning was unnecessary." Daphne threw back the covers and climbed from the bed to hide her blush. Dash it, she was turning into an accomplished deceiver!

But what to do now? As she washed, she toyed with the notion of doing nothing but simply returning the brooch to its case. Suspicion had not centered on any innocent person, and she was quite safe. Her brother need not sell Kingman, his beloved horse, and she could bend her energies on readying Sophie for her come-out. Yes, that would be best.

Daphne dressed, and then stood by her bedroom window staring out at the dripping landscape. Her thoughts swirled as darkly as the clouds blanketing the hills.

No, she could not keep the brooch. Her conscience would not allow it, despite her papa's distress. And what of William and his sense of honor? No gentleman reneged on a loss at cards. She could not ask her brother to bear such a stigma, even though no one but their two selves knew of it. Much as the thought stung, she knew she must find some manner of quietly returning the brooch, or face up to her foolish, impulsive action.

Before she could lose her nerve, and without telling William of her intention, she ordered the carriage and left at once for Dunston Hall.

The Hall suggested an overturned anthill. Gardeners and laborers searched the grounds, peering behind every tree and shrub. Lookouts marched briskly about the perimeter on the assumption, no doubt, that the thief would attempt a second foray, and that in daylight.

"Well," Daphne murmured to herself as her carriage drew up to the door, "in assuming that, they are not too wide of the mark. 'Tis day, and here I am."

Her grip tightened on her reticle in which lay the brooch, wrapped in a twist of paper. She wished her knees would stop their trembling. Suppose Lord Courtlea was the first person to greet her? Imagine his sharp glance reading her overset emotions and realizing the proper Miss Summerhayes to be the wanton, thieving Flora.

No, she could not bear it! Almost she gave the order to drive on; only the thought of William stayed her tongue. She must do this, and face whatever scorn, condemnation, or ridicule the earl might choose to heap on her head. Bracing herself, she alit from the carriage.

Daphne was greeted in an elaborate, Chinese-style sitting room by an excited Lady Eugenia. A swift glance showed her to be alone, and Daphne breathed a touch easier.

"Such a fuss, Dee, has never been! Poor Mama is prostrate with hysterics, and has ordered a pit dug in the cellars in which to hide the silver plate and our jewels. Papa is furious, because this happened to a guest, and has ridden off in all directions organizing search parties."

She laughed, and because she was comfortable with her visitor, it was a normal, if hearty sound. Only when she felt nervous, or otherwise ill at ease, did her laughter merit Lord Courtlea's unkind comparison to Balaam's ass.

"Sir Gerald sent word that he will be here directly, but how he heard so swiftly, I cannot imagine." Her mother's dark eyes, which were Eugenia's best feature with her father's strong nose and retiring chin, shone with shy affection.

"The post brought the news to us, and no doubt he continued spreading the word." Daphne spoke vaguely, as her mind dwelt on the possibility of slipping the emerald brooch back into the earl's room. "But why is Sir Gerald coming? To join in the search?"

Eugenia blushed, and she gave a little, excited bounce in her chair. "You know, Dee, that he has been—well, what shall I say—attentive? I thought he would never bring himself to the mark, but—"

"'Genia, he has offered for you! Oh, wonderful!"

"The night of the ball, he was disturbed, so he told me, by the sight of Lord Courtlea and Lord Bennington vying for my favor." Eugenia laughed again. "Of course they were doing no such thing, but Sir Gerald got into such a state of jealousy, that he came back yesterday to propose to me and make his formal offer to Papa. Oh, Daphne, I am so happy!"

"And I am happy for you, dear 'Genia." Daphne rose to hug her friend and kiss her flushed cheek. She was genuinely glad that Sir Gerald Thackett, Bart., had finally roused himself after three long years of the most dilatory courting.

"Oh, 'Genia, how dreadful to have everyone so overset at such a time," Daphne exclaimed, stung by guilt. "I am truly sorry. Shall I stay with you for a day or two, and help settle down the household?"

"Thank you, Dee, but I do believe Mama and Papa are reacting too strongly. Lord Courtlea did not fly into a pelter over it. No, indeed, he rather laughed it off. 'The bauble is hardly cause for the fuss, being worth only a trifling amount,' he said." Eugenia shrugged and drew her shawl closer around her shoulders, Dunston Hall being noted for its draughts. "I do not recollect ever seeing the thing, so I cannot say whether he were being truthful or just kind."

Daphne had her own notions as to the earl's kindness, but she forbore to mention them. "Does Lord Courtlea plan to remain until the thief is caught? Oh, perhaps he is at this moment out with your papa, seeking the miscreant?"

Hope rose that she might not have to face those discerning eyes after all. Mayhap, with some excuse, she might reach his bedchamber, and then—

"Not a bit of it. He and Lord Bennington—" Miss Franklin cocked her head, doubtless listening for the footstep of her beloved. Daphne, her nerves thinly stretched, bit her lip at the interruption.

"Yes?" she prodded. Really, she had no taste for this secret, prying work!

"Oh, I beg pardon, Dee. I thought I heard… What was I saying? Oh, yes, about Lord Courtle and Lord Bennington. Well, they have gone back to Town."

"What?" Daphne stared at her friend. "Gone?"

Words stirred in her recollection, words to which she had been too flustered last night to heed. Something about leaving?

"Yes, truly. They left not two minutes before you arrived. Why, whatever is the matter, Dee? You have gone quite green."

Somehow Daphne turned Miss Franklin's concern into other channels, and soon took her leave. Back in her room at Weldern Manor, she unwrapped the brooch and balefully stared at it. The lovely green gem sparkled in her palm.

She dare not entrust the thing to the mails, even if she knew where to send it, and she, a maiden lady, could not simply ask for a bachelor's address. All sorts of surprised, probing questions would fall on her head, especially after the display she and the earl had put on at the ball. Scandal spread by eager tongues would surely reach the ears of her papa. Then the fat would truly be in the fire!

"Oh, why did that man choose to come here?" she muttered. Then, with a sigh, and knowing her papa to be out on the Chilterns, she returned the brooch to the safe box.

CHAPTER 7

The rain slowed to a drizzle as the towers of Dunston Hall sank behind the trees, and Lord Courtlea wished he had opted to drive his curricle, rather than share Bennington's coach-and-four. Courtlea trusted his groom to bring the horses safely to London, and he would have spared himself a tiresome companion.

Lord Bennington, unused to contending with the light of day before noon, had fortified himself with generous portions of brandy and hot rum punch. The coach interior reeked like a distillery. Sitting opposite him, with his back to the team, Courtlea let down the window to stir the air.

"Demme if I know why we had to fly off in such a rush," the viscount complained for the tenth time. "Demmed short visit."

Courtlea scowled. "You need not have left at all, but, as I have explained more than once, I have appointments in town that I may not miss. Do you not recollect insisting on leaving with me?"

"But what if they catch the bounder, eh? Wanted to see the fun. Give 'im a hemp neckpiece, I say, and let the fellow dance. Now you ain't a beggar's chance of getting your watch back."

"My watch is safely in my pocket," sighed the earl. "Now leave it be, for pity's sake."

"What, not the watch? Then why all the halloo?" Bennington peered at Courtlea with eyes more than a little out of focus. His lips pursed with an air of intense concentration. "Wait, I recollect...'Twas a jewel, eh? Yes, demme, an emerald brooch. And," he ended triumphantly, "'twas on your watch-chain."

"Your reconstructive powers are amazing," Courtlea drawled.

His dry tone was lost on the viscount, whose fair brows creased in befuddlement. "Why on the chain? Not a usual spot, not for a brooch. Don't recollect it, in any case. Sure you had it when we came down?"

Lord Courtlea passed a hand across his eyes. "Benny, you will drive me to distraction. I won the plaguey thing at cards, at the Hall, and must have stuck it on the chain for the moment. When it was wagered, and by whom, is lost in brandy vapors."

He grimaced in distaste at having his senses so fuddled. Mentally he damned the boredom that had driven him to drink far more than his wont.

Bennington smacked his thigh and gave a great whoop of laughter. "You mean you were foxed?" he shouted. "The great Courtlea bosky? One can't tell, you know. You always look cool and mean. Hah! Wait 'til I tell 'em at White's!"

"Are you certain you want to do that, Bennington?"

Courtlea did not raise his voice above its usual quiet tone. Lord Bennington sent one startled look at his companion's calm but set expression, and flushed scarlet.

"Just bammin', that's all." He wriggled uncomfortably. "Just a jape, no need to fly into a pelter."

"Just so. I assumed that was your intent. Now I suggest you recapture some of your lost sleep."

"Wide awake now. Demme, don't see why we had to tear away so early…"

Lord Courtlea groaned, tilted his hat down and stretched out his long legs. Folding his arms comfortably across his chest, he settled back and closed his eyes. Feigning sleep seemed the only escape from Bennington's repetitive muttering.

Immediately the phantom Flora sprang to mind. Even the most charitable of men must believe she had made off with the jewel, and while Courtlea was benevolent on occasion, he was not gullible. He had not been dreaming when he looked up with slitted eyes to see her shadowed face and white cap bending over him.

Why had she taken only the emerald? It was valuable, of course, but so was his watch, the chain, and the gold seal. Why not take all?

Courtlea frowned. Which of those vague faces at the gaming table had wagered the stone? Had the owner hired the girl to reclaim it? If so, he was a dishonorable cur who should not be allowed in a gentleman's game.

As for the girl, a quick-witted little baggage, Courtlea recollected with pleasure the warm softness of her slim young body in his arms, the velvet skin, the breathlessness in her whispered, uncultured voice. There was a moment when, crushed against his ready body, she had seemed willing. He would not have forced her. Indeed, he was amazed at himself and a little ashamed; dalliance with maidservants, however willing, was not his style.

But Flora was not, after all, a servant, but an accomplished thief. She had inflamed his senses to a degree he never attained without instant satisfaction. Then she had neatly outwitted him, leaving him to recover as best he might.

In all, Courtlea was content to leave Buckinghamshire. He detested sycophants. The only person who had dared do aught but toady and simper was that red-headed Miss Summerhayes—an intriguing chit, though appallingly rude. She spoke her mind with a vengeance, and he did not take kindly to such treatment from anyone, man or woman. What a termagant! And for why?

The question nagged at him. Something more than that curricle episode lay behind her aversion, he was sure. Yes, he had offended her modesty and dismissed her with a light buss. Surely, at her age, those rosy lips had received more passionate kisses than that!

Her words rankled, unless she simply disliked men, and spoke so to all. A shrew, in fact. No wonder she was yet unmarried! A picture sprang to his mind of her tamed of shrewishness by a brave Petruchio, and given a babe or two of her own to nurse at those lush, tempting breasts.

'Twas a pity duty recalled him to London. He relished a challenge, if the prize were worthy, and given time, he might himself have undertaken the taming and bedding of Daphne Summerhayes. 'Twould not be a dull undertaking, for a certainty!

Lord Bennington, his own eyes grown heavy, wondered what the deuce Courtlea was dreaming about, to bring such a saturnine smile to his features.

* * *

The next afternoon, Courtlea presented himself at a small but elegant house on Brook Street, and was shown into a first floor sitting room. The furnishings, he noted with a wry twist of his lips, were not only in the best of feminine taste, but were both expensive and new.

That was to say recently purchased, for a mahogany French

escritoire, with magnificent inlay, was not a year later than Louis XIV. Heavy damask curtains of crimson and gold framed the windows, while an Indian silk carpet in rich tints glowed on the polished floor. The earl shook his head, then rose as the door opened and a slim, dark-haired woman garbed in deep sapphire blue swayed gracefully into the room.

"Victor, what a pleasant surprise!"

"How are you, Mother?" He kissed the cool, pale cheek presented to him. Even at close range, her carefully powdered skin showed few wrinkles, although frost touched the dark hair at her temples. "How went Christmas with Aunt Gwendolyn?"

Lady Felicia, Countess of Courtlea, shrugged with a faintly resigned air. "Oh, frightfully dull, as usual, but you know Gwenny. Roasting chestnuts in the grate is high excitement. It was, however, preferable to sitting alone at my own hearth. Come now, my dear boy, you will have luncheon with me. We shall make it a party to liven my quiet days." She moved to a cream brocade sofa and patted the space beside her in mute invitation. "I so miss your company, Victor, as well as your good advice."

Victor shook his head as he sat down in an arm chair facing the sofa. "My thanks, but I must decline luncheon, as I am due at my tailor's in an hour's time."

His mother smiled gently with such sweet resignation that Courtlea braced himself against a rush of guilt. He quickly recollected her nature, and his guilt as swiftly died.

Although ten years a widow, Felicia still affected somber colors. The dark blues, grays, and lavenders in silk and satin gowns made in the highest kick of fashion, emphasized her fine complexion and slim figure. They also lent her an air of wistful fragility that gentlemen found beguiling. Victor, however, knew exactly the depth of her grief.

"Burnley tells me you are again overdrawn on your allowance," he said abruptly. "This time by near four hundred pounds."

Lady Felicia's mouth hardened, and for an instant she looked every year of her age. "Oh, Burnley!" she snapped. "What does a stodgy solicitor like Burnley know of a lady's needs!"

She met her son's steady eye, and her petulance fled. Her lips curved in a smile and her eyes glowed like dewy violets.

"I am but a lonely widow, dearest," she said with a tragic dip of her head, "struggling to live without the guidance of a strong mind and hand such as yours. Had you been here to advise me—but no, I must not upbraid you for neglect. Many mothers, I know, hardly see their sons from one year's end to the next. Truly I am grateful for the little time every few weeks you spare me from your busy life."

Victor's teeth clenched as a familiar tension knotted in his middle. He rose abruptly, startling his mother, but when he strode to a small oak cellaret and lifted the sherry decanter, she recovered and nodded acquiescence. Swiftly he poured out two glasses, tossed off half of his, and handed the other to Felicia.

"Burnley has the bills for all this," he gestured at the room, "and for furs, hats, boots, and a dozen gowns. But on what else did you spend the money?"

With her free hand she touched her throat in a dainty gesture of helplessness. "Victor, you are most cruel to bait me in this way. How may I, a frail woman, recollect such matters?"

"Pray try, madam."

"Now you are angry." Swiftly Felicia put down the sherry glass and clasped her hands together. "Oh, I deserve it. I am the worst of mothers. Yet I have always—"

"The four hundred pounds, if you please. Plus your allowance. Why, a dozen of my tenant families could live on that for a year."

"Oh, you cannot wish me to live in a cottage on one of your farms! Tucked away in the country…" Her voice trailed wistfully, but when he showed not the least response, she shrugged with a slight lift of her shoulders. "Very well, I shall attempt to account for every farthing, although I am sure the amount was far less than four hundred pounds."

Felicia sipped daintily at her sherry, giving him a glance from under lowered lids. "Are you sure your Mr. Burnley is trustworthy? Mayhap he lines his pocket and lays the amount to my charge. Have you considered that, Victor?"

"Never, because John Burnley's integrity is above reproach."

The earl refilled his glass, and went to stand by the fire. The wine shimmered a liquid ruby as he set the glass on the carved travertine mantel.

"Mother, is not your allowance generous enough to cover all your personal needs as well as the costs of this house?"

His mother pressed her fingertips to her temple, her brows knitting as though in pain. "Oh, pray cease this inquisition at once. My poor head is quite muddled."

"I do not wish to victimize you, Mother, in regards to monies." He spoke gently, but he was determined to reach the end of the matter. "Indeed, your allowance has been twice increased in the past year. Fair enough, but not when you throw money away with both hands to your— friends."

Her head lifted, and the color left her cheeks. She stared warily, as if daring him to continue, while hoping he would not.

"Last month young Tomlinson purchased his colors into the Horse Guards," Victor said quietly, looking into the fire, "and lately Baron Roszinsky returned to Poland with a sumptuous new wardrobe. We both know from whose hand the money came. I shall not deny you your escapades, but you must employ more discretion. Otherwise, you will find your funds sharply curtailed."

He turned and faced Felicia, his features as hard and implacable as the marble mantel behind him. "Sly tongues will not make a mockery of my father's name."

He half-expected an angry outcry, a furious denial, but as he looked stonily into his mother's lovely face, he recollected that confrontation was not her way. Indeed, under his gaze, her expression softened into resignation, and her coral lips quivered as though with a brave attempt to staunch tears.

"'Tis because I am lonely, my dear, living on my own like this." She rose and came to him, putting her hand gently on his arm. "Let me come to Courtlea House," she begged with a pretty pout. "I will be your hostess, and what fine times we may have! Dinner parties, dances, musicales, all the best people—"

"I think not." Then, because his heart was softened despite his resolve, he added gently, "I keep bachelor's hall, Mother, with no allowance for feminine fol-de-rol. You are always welcome at Mordaine Knowe."

Her nose wrinkled in distaste and she gave a delicate shudder. "Yes, the country." She half-turned, releasing his arm, then suddenly brightened with new eagerness. "Mayhap Edgar will come and live with me here. A mother should have at least one son at her side."

"Edgar seems happy enough with me." Victor shrugged, aware that, as usual, his mother thought only of her own convenience. "I will ask him, if you wish," he offered, knowing full well what his younger brother's choice would be.

Courtlea soon took his leave, and walking briskly down Brook Street he drew in great draughts of air. After even a half hour in his mother's presence he felt smothered by her selfishness. How those violet eyes entreated, oh, so tenderly, and pulled at his will until he felt the veriest brute in denying her!

As always after being with his mother, he thought of his father, a quiet man who had been shyly inept in relating to his own children. Only once had he given Victor advice.

Reared by a tyrannical, widowed mother, and marrying a woman who was just as ruthless in her own sweet, smothering manner, the earl sought to warn his young son. "When you look for a wife, my boy, avoid an opinionated, headstrong woman like the plague. She will contest your every wish, and strive always for control. Also, beware a sweet, pliant miss who will cling like a limpet and drain you of your will."

"But sir," Victor had asked, "how may one safely judge the right balance of humors?"

"Ah, I will tell you," answered his father with a bitter smile. "Marry at forty, not before. Choose a young filly, the Nonpareil of the Season, for your own enjoyment and so your heirs may be comely. Get her with child at once, and keep her occupied with babes until you tire of her. Then take a mistress. Keep your own life separate, Victor, do you hear? 'Tis the only way a man may have any peace and happiness."

Victor had been seventeen at that time, but he never forgot his father's words. Now, twelve years later, he still considered the advice sound, and had every intention of following it. Enjoying the favors of pretty women for as long as they pleased him was one thing—marriage was another, and far in the future. Too, just as Miss Daphne had not yet found any gentleman who met her standards for marriage, no lady as yet appealed to him as a desired mate.

* * *

As the dusty coach jostled its way down North Audley Street, Daphne Summerhayes eagerly leaned forward. "Through the Square and then to Upper Grosvenor Street! We are nearly there, Sophie."

Sophie, who had hung half-way out the window since the coach entered London, gave a deep sigh. "Oh, Dee, all those wonderful shops! Oh, 'tis heaven! How prodigious kind of Lady Wentford to have us come at once, instead of waiting for March. I vow, 'tis a pity those lessons you intended went by the board, but I will do my best to behave as a proper lady. As you do, dear Cousin. Behave, I mean. Oh, you know what I mean."

"Yes, of course," murmured Daphne, feeling a total fraud. Did a lady scold a peer? Or sneak into a gentleman's bedroom and steal his belongings? Did a lady throb with conflicting desires, to flee, to stay, when in the arms of—

She must be mad to let her imagination loose like that! While Sophie exclaimed over Grosvenor Square, Daphne dabbed her heated brow with her handkerchief. Then, at Sophie's inquiring glance, she flicked off a speck of soot from her new yellow pelisse. Even with the windows tight shut, soot from the countless hearth fires found its way into the coach.

At last the coach stopped on Upper Grosvenor Street at Wentford House, a handsome mansion with stately pillars and a stone facade. Daphne's Aunt Elizabeth Burstone, Countess of Wentford, met them in the spacious, elegant hall with a wide smile and her hands outstretched.

"Bless you, my dears, you are here at last. Daphne, my darling child, you grow more lovely every year." She enfolded her younger sister's daughter in a close embrace.

"Oh, dearest Aunt," Daphne cried, returning the kiss. "It warms my heart to see you looking so well." A few grey strands threaded Lady Wentford's thick auburn tresses, her graceful figure was a shade less trim, but the same love shone in her warm brown eyes.

The countess greeted Sophie in the same affectionate manner, bidding her think of Wentford House as home for as long as she wished.

With her eyes large as saucers, Sophie managed a smile. "Thank you, my lady," she murmured, curtsying. Then her smile broadened. "Oh, I vow you are the kindest, most generous of ladies to welcome me so."

Lady Wentford laughed, and patted Sophie's blushing cheek. "Dear child! Pray think of me as your Aunt Elizabeth. One cannot have too many lovely nieces. Oh, such plans I have! Such routs and assemblies and dances and balls to attend! But first, my dears, let us go shopping! In London, one may purchase almost every item known to man."

"Dear Aunt," said Daphne with a laugh. "We are more interested in purchasing every item known to woman!"

* * *

Lady Wentford was as good as her word, leading "her girls" into a whirl of shopping at all the best places in Oxford Street, Bond Street, and Piccadilly. Daphne, knowing the detestable Lord Courtlea lurked somewhere in town, and she must find a way to return the brooch so she could breathe freely again, had to force herself to concentrate on her purchases. Sophie's father had entrusted monies to her for gowns, hats, and any fripperies Daphne deemed necessary. The amount was neither niggardly nor generous, but was adequate, if some caution were observed.

"And caution," Daphne murmured ruefully to herself, "is not strong in my nature." Sophie was excitedly showing her new bonnets to Tyson when Daphne was called to Lady Wentford's sitting room. Daphne found her seated with her embroidery before a crackling fire.

"Now, my dear," Lady Wentford said briskly, "pray allow me to interfere a little with your plans. I know Sophie's come-out was intended as a mild affair, allowing little fuss, but would she not enjoy making her curtsy to the queen, as you did?"

"Oh, Aunt, she would indeed!" Daphne cried, with a warm rush of gratitude. With Aunt Elizabeth, a former lady-in-waiting to Queen Charlotte, as her sponsor, Sophie's acceptance was assured. "Uncle Charles will be delighted, as he did not expect such a course. But must not Sophie's name be proposed and accepted before such presentation?"

Lady Wentford laid aside her tambor frame and smiled guiltily. "'Tis all in hand. I sent in her name the moment your father's letter arrived. Queen Charlotte will graciously receive Sophie at her next Drawing Room, in four weeks' time."

"So soon!" Daphne shuddered, a frightful picture flitting through her mind of Sophie Summerhayes galloping into St. James's Palace while chattering like a magpie.

"Exactly so. And you, my dear, must have a new gown for Sophie's party. Oh, did I not say? On the Friday after the presentation I am giving a ball in Sophie's honor."

Daphne dropped into the companion chair beside the hearth. "A court presentation and a ball! Oh, Sophie will be top of the tree! But Aunt, I am sure Uncle Charles did not expect you should trouble—"

"Trouble! La, I have not enjoyed myself so much since your own come-out. 'Twould do you good too, miss, to kick up your heels a bit, to forget there is such a word as responsibility, and recollect you are yet a young woman."

"In truth, I do not think of myself as old," Daphne replied absently, spreading her new green shawl across her knees. Was she indeed becoming a stodgy, dry-stick provincial, slipping all too easily into old-maidenhood?

She forced her mind back to Sophie. "Sophie is warm-hearted and intelligent, and if she acts on impulse occasionally, why, she intends no harm, and is still young enough to learn better."

"Just so." Lady Wentford said dryly. "As for Sophie's intelligence, mayhap 'tis best not to broadcast that. Most men do not consider good sense a virtue."

They exchanged understanding smiles, and then Lady Wentford stared for a moment into the dancing flames. "We must do well by her, my dear, and find a suitable husband. I have several eligible gentlemen in mind. Lord Hamper, Lord Launten, and Mr. Sutton, for three. Then there is Victor Merritt, Earl of Courtlea. He is—did you speak, my dear?"

"Um—no, Aunt. A sudden cough." Daphne swiftly decided to say nothing of the earl. Her aunt would surely include him in their circle if she knew of a connection. Daphne shuddered, imagining him constantly invited to Wentford House.

"As I was saying," Lady Wentford went on, "Victor is sought after by almost every mama with a marriageable daughter. He is a prize worth setting a cap for." She smiled. "I cannot imagine how he has eluded the parson's mousetrap for so long."

Knowing the earl's poor opinion of Sophie, Daphne shook her head. "I know aught of the other gentlemen, but that last, Lord Courtlea, sounds too high in the instep for Sophie's taste. Mayhap he would think our Sophie too—too playful, too enthusiastic?"

"Hmm. You may have the right of it," agreed Lady Wentford, nodding, and Daphne breathed a sigh of relief. Then she read speculation in her aunt's look. Daphne smiled.

"Aunt, are you perhaps thinking of a double wedding, when you may launch me, as well as Sophie, on the sea of matrimony?"

"Why ever not?" the countess demanded with raised brows. "I admit to certain dreams, but you, of course, must decide for yourself." She leaned forward, stretching her hands out to the fire. "Pray tell me, Daphne, but only if you wish, whether any gentleman you consider suitable has yet presented himself?"

Daphne laughed, appreciating the tactful phrasing. "Our corner of the world is not without respectable swains, and one or two have hinted at a closer relationship than friendship. None, however, awakened any stirring of affection or offered a happier situation than my present one.

"I am completely content as mistress of Weldern Manor. Papa gives me a free hand in the running of the house, and Mama's bequest will keep me comfortably in my old age. Why, Aunt, I have a household of my own, few restraints, any thing I might desire, and all without the bother of a husband. Who would not be happy?"

She listened to the echo of her words, and a queer emptiness settled around her heart. Unbidden recollections flooded her mind; a chamber at Dunston Hall, lips pressed hotly against her skin, hands intimately stroking, rousing strange, weakening desires in her. Lord Courtlea was everything she disliked in a gentleman, but she could not deny his devastating effect on her senses. Would she never know the like again, never share passionate, complete love with a husband, never cuddle her own babe in her arms?

In the short silence, the fire flared as a lump of coal fell deeper into the grate. Daphne looked across at her aunt.

"Do I protest too much?" she asked quietly.

Aunt Elizabeth smiled but did not answer. When she at last broke the thoughtful silence, it was to inquire after Daphne's plans for the morrow. She nodded approval of introducing Sophie to the works at the Royal Academy, but begged off going herself.

"If Sophie has decided which hat to wear," she said, rising, "let us get on with our morning calls. We will first present our protegee to my good friends, Lady Silversby and Lady Mary Burgess, Countess of Daly. You recollect them, of course? They will not be overcritical if Sophie happens to put a foot wrong."

Daphne agreed, rather absently, for suddenly her perfect life seemed not so perfect. She shrugged off the feeling and went to fetch her cloak. Still, she was filled with disquietude about Lord Courtlea's acquaintance with the Wentfords until she reflected that her aunt and uncle knew virtually everyone in the ton. At least tomorrow was secure; Lady Silversby and Lady Daly were hardly ladies on whom Lord Courtlea would call, and the Royal Academy was doubtless the last place a man like him would frequent.

* * *

As Lady Wentford's carriage stopped at the Strand Block of Somerset House, Daphne finished explaining something of the Royal Academy and its Academicians.

"Pray attend, Sophie," Daphne said sharply, alighting to the pavement. "Ladies must converse with gentlemen about topical and interesting subjects, and art is one of the best."

"But I have never been troubled about what to say to gentlemen," protested Sophie, her cheeks pink in the brisk wind. "I open my mouth and words simply come."

Daphne sighed, but stubbornly continued her lecture as they entered the building. "The summer exhibition is the great event, but there is much to see. Sculpture, etchings, architectural drawings, models—"

"Oh, Dee, I vow I can never hold all that in my head at once," Sophie wailed, a sudden fear in her eyes.

Sophie's dismay stopped Daphne in mid-step. Young Miss Summerhayes, fresh from the wilds of Cornwall, had acquitted herself reasonably well on the morning calls the previous day. She had even elicited a laugh when she asked a duchess visiting Lady Silversby why a duke, a duchess, and an archbishop were all addressed as "Your Grace."

"Would it not be simpler," Sophie had queried, "to call the latter 'Your Archness' or something similar?"

Only when they had returned home did Sophie reveal how she had trembled from nerves, lest she embarrass or humiliate her family. Now Daphne gave her cousin's arm a reassuring squeeze.

"Pray forgive me," Daphne said gently, "for sounding like a stuffy headmistress attempting a complete education in a single day. Come," she continued recklessly, "we shall simply enjoy ourselves and be as silly as may be."

The magnificent portraits showing elegant gowns and robes caught Sophie's attention, but she found most pleasure in the landscapes. Marveling, she bent near a rural scene by a senior student of the Academy, Mr. John Constable.

"Oh!" Sophie exclaimed, clapping her gloved hands. "See the cows in the river. So real! Why, I vow I can see my reflection in the water. What say you to a swim, Cousin?"

With a loud, excited giggle, she bounced up and down, making a diving motion that set her reticle swinging. Daphne burst into laughter, and Sophie laughed harder, the sound ringing throughout the gallery. Still chuckling, Daphne glanced about, hoping their hilarity had not jarred the sober air of the Academy too badly.

Two gentlemen, elegant in caped greatcoats and wide-brimmed beaver hats, stood before a painting farther down the gallery. The taller, with a graceful gesture, was pointing out some feature of the picture.

Daphne looked again, and gasped in dismay. She knew those broad shoulders, the arrogant tilt of the head, and the long-fingered out-flung hand. Her blood ran cold, then flaming hot, and for the life of her she could neither speak nor flee.

CHAPTER 8

Edgar Merritt withdrew his watch for the third time in as many minutes and gloomily wondered if the hands were glued in place. "Victor, are you certain we shall be in time for the sale at Tatt's? I should hate you to lose that chestnut gelding."

"Demme, Edgar, attend! Even you must see that the fellow did a first-rate job, worth every penny of the brass I paid him. He caught the—"

A burst of gay laughter rang out like gold and silver chimes, overwhelming his words. "—the look of—"

He paused, annoyed and yet charmed by the unseemly interruption, then turned to look down the gallery. Few people had braved the raw day to visit the Academy, and he saw them at once—two slender, well-dressed young ladies, quite unattended, halfway down the gallery.

Their backs were to him, but the taller of the two, in a modish yellow pelisse trimmed with dark green braid, appeared anxious to leave. The other, protesting, turned to gesture at the paintings, and Courtlea saw her face. Obviously she wished to examine the rest of the works on display, but it was not her zeal for art that narrowed Courtlea's eyes.

Yellow hair, blue eyes, unrestrained laughter, pretty face framed by a pink, feather-trimmed bonnet. Now where the devil had he seen her before?

Her companion, in stressing her wishes, allowed the merest glimpse of her profile, but it was enough. Courtlea forgot painting, brother,

Academy—indeed, forgot all in the sudden need to face the bold-tongued virago, Daphne Summerhayes. Her insults at the close of that delightful but disastrous dance had rung in his ears since. This time he would not come off second best. Besides which, he had never been one to resist a challenge.

"But all those pinkish clouds," Edgar complained, studying the painting. "They—egad, Victor, where are you off to?"

Courtlea did not bother to answer, but strode toward the two misses. Perhaps Daphne Summerhayes had already seen him, and, hoity-toity, chose not to face him.

As he neared the pair, the younger Miss Summerhayes met his gaze. "Why, look, Daphne," she said in a most natural, pleased manner, "'tis Lord Courtlea. Good day, my lord."

He gave a nod, barely polite, his gaze on the averted head covered by a smart brown velvet bonnet bound with yellow ribbons. Daphne Summerhayes turned slowly, her face pale, and despite her calmness, he knew at once she had been aware of his presence. Something in her eyes, green as summer grass, and the slight tuck in one corner of her mouth betrayed her as she made a brief curtsy.

So she *had* tried to elude me, he thought in triumph.

"My lord."

"An unexpected pleasure, Miss Summerhayes," Courtlea said, bowing. "Will it reassure you to know my curricle is safely in the mews, and you may brave the streets without danger from me?"

Her gaze flickered, and whatever he had seen—dismay, embarrassment—disappeared from her expression. She stiffened, and one brow rose a trifle. The effect both charmed and warned him.

"That is indeed heartening, my lord," she said, with a straight look, "although I must confess that the worry of a second encounter with that vehicle had never entered my mind. London is much too large."

"And yet, here we are," he murmured with a deprecating smile, and saw color tinge her cheeks. She looked away, dark copper lashes veiling her eyes.

"I believe, sir, you are acquainted with my cousin," she said stiffly.

He spared her cousin a single glance. "Indeed yes. Miss Summerhayes and I shared a dance set."

Sophie nodded energetically. "Oh, to be sure! I vow it was prodigiously delightful! A prime romp, was it not?"

Her bouncing speech and beaming smile recalled his original impression of her as a chattering ninnyhammer. Had the elder Miss

Summerhayes overheard him express that opinion to Bennington? Had that unguarded comment pricked her family pride deeply enough to attack him so roundly, denouncing him as unmannerly and lacking in wit?

"You are unescorted, ladies?" The question was hardly polite, the answer obvious, but he thought to put Daphne Summerhayes on the defensive.

"My aunt's carriage awaits us," she answered, cool as the winter wind. "Indeed, we are on the point of leaving, sir."

"May I inquire as to the identity of your aunt? Mayhap we share acquaintance."

He cared not who her relation was, but since she so obviously wished to escape him, he perversely intended to prevent her. Antagonism fairly sparked from her, but coldly, and he was intrigued. Then, too, he enjoyed watching the play of emotions on her lovely face, even the shadow of consternation, almost of alarm, that flickered across her features at his question.

"The Countess of Wentford is my late mother's sister. Sophie and I are lodging with her on Upper Grosvenor Street." Her rosy lips closed primly, as though they had revealed too much.

Courtlea hid his surprise. The countess wielded great influence in Society, was active in various charities, and had connections with St. James's. He was about to comment further when a nudge reminded him he was not alone.

"Ladies, pray allow me to present my brother, Edgar Merritt."

The young man bowed, with an easy smile, murmuring his delight. Daphne estimated his years at about twenty, and although his handsome features resembled those of Lord Courtlea, young Edgar's expression differed greatly from that of his brother. He exuded a warm cheerfulness instead of reserved hauteur. His clear gray eyes, lacking Courtlea's cool wariness, looked eagerly on the world. Daphne wondered if the earl had once been like this boy, and, if so, what might have changed him.

Edgar Merritt's gaze swung to Sophie with the alacrity of a compass needle finding north. "I trust you are enjoying your visit to London, Miss Summerhayes?"

"Oh, indeed, Mr. Merritt. I vow it is a wondrous place, and quite overwhelming. My cousin is teaching me a prodigious amount, as I know so little of Society." She smiled in innocent candor.

"We share an interest in Mr. Constable's work," Daphne said

hastily, hoping to divert Lord Courtlea's scorn of Sophie's self-deprecation, "and were admiring his considerable talent."

She smiled at Edgar, but all her senses centered on the man who stood silent and forbidding at her side. She could not forget the knowing smile that had shaken her. Did he somehow suspect her involvement with the emerald? No, 'twas impossible, just as he could not know how her senses swam, recollecting Flora moaning in delight in his near-naked clasp. Her breast tingled in remembrance of his stroking fingers. With an effort, she returned to the conversation.

"Indeed?" Lord Courtlea's raised brow expressed skepticism, but whether to the shared interest or to the choice of artists, Daphne was unsure. "To the exclusion of all others?" he went on.

"Oh, not at all. Sir Joshua Reynolds, of course, and Mr. Gainsborough, and Mr. Joseph Turner—"

Daphne stopped, no longer able to continue with light chatter. Her nerves screamed for her to flee, lest her guilt show in some word or expression. Besides, she could not think at all clearly when the earl hovered so near. And why had Lord Courtlea bothered to approach them, if his intent was merely to mock their provincialism?

"Just so." With an infuriatingly patronizing air, the earl gestured with his cane toward the painting he and his brother had been studying. "Perhaps you would enjoy one of Mr. Turner's works which I have lent for exhibition. Your opinion of it will be valued, I assure you."

"And your opinion as well, Miss Summerhayes," exclaimed Edgar to Sophie even as Daphne opened her lips to refuse. He beamed into Sophie's sparkling eyes. "The painting is of my brother's country seat, Mordaine Knowe. Would it please you to examine it?"

"Oh, I vow it would, Mr. Merritt," Sophie agreed eagerly, missing Daphne's warning frown, "but truly, I know little of art."

"You amaze us, Miss Summerhayes," Lord Courtlea murmured, as his brother and Sophie moved away. Sophie, however, heard his comment. Her smile faltered, and she glanced uncertainly back at the earl before Edgar Merritt again claimed her full attention.

Daphne's hands clenched inside her quilted velvet muff as she fought the urge to box the arrogant lord's ears. Such insufferable sarcasm was the outside of enough. And Aunt Elizabeth had counted him as a suitor for Sophie!

"Every one of us has something to learn, my lord," she said through stiff lips, "even those with the benefit of a superior education. I think it rather fine that my cousin realizes her lack, and, in the best of humor, seeks betterment."

"Then you suggest we all need improvement, whether we acknowledge the fact or not?" Lord Courtlea drawled, his smile ironic. "My state satisfies me completely, but I shall, if you wish it, hear those improvements you desire to make in your own character."

Daphne drew in a deep breath. Oh, if he knew! "I would not dream of so taxing your patience, my lord, which is famed for being in short supply. I say only, as regards Sophie, that innocence should not be taken as stupidity."

With one cold glance into his lordship's handsome, mocking face, Daphne turned her back and followed Sophie and Edgar down the gallery. Her lips tightened; she would not bandy words with the earl. The least said, the better.

In two long strides Lord Courtlea was beside her. His looming presence, the determined way he matched steps with her, made Daphne feel like the prey of a stalking animal. Fustion! She would not play the goat to his tiger, or the mouse to his cat. Daphne resolved to glance at the painting of Lord Courtlea's home, then seize Sophie by the arm, if necessary, and depart.

"You may have the right of it," the earl continued without a trace of rancor, "although announcing one's lack to the world may raise doubts as to the depth of one's intelligence, if not the quality of one's character."

"Words are trifles," Daphne retorted, drawn despite her vow of silence, "and may be thoughtlessly spoken. As to indicating character, surely actions speak more clearly than any words."

Appalled, Daphne bit her lip, hoping that the brim of her bonnet hid her expression from Lord Courtlea. Indeed, if certain actions revealed her character, she was branded a thief, a liar, and a wanton.

"And yet a gentleman's given word is not a trifle, but is binding on his honor," the earl persisted. "Perhaps ladies do not agree with that premise, or—I speak solely for the purpose of discussion—ladies have their own perception of honor."

Daphne could not allow that challenge to go unanswered. "It has been said that words were given us to hide our thoughts," she said quietly. "I find that observation cynical in the extreme. As to honoring one's given word, I hope I may always do so."

Lord Courtlea chuckled. "The trick, Miss Summerhayes, may be in obtaining your promise in the first place. You fence with great skill; 'tis my good luck you choose words over blades. I could, however, suggest other weapons."

Her eyes flashed up at him, only to meet the full, sensual force of his deep gaze. His mouth quirked into a teasing smile. Daphne swallowed, determinedly ignoring the subtle insinuation in the earl's murmured words.

"If you prefer pistols at dawn, sir, know that long ago I learned how to handle such weapons. I consider that every lady should know something of defense."

He laughed, showing even, white teeth. "A meeting at dawn suits me, Miss Summerhayes, but not to raise a pistol against you. No, not a pistol."

Daphne jerked her head around, but she could not hide her flushed cheeks. Oh, how she hated the man, and wished he would vanish from the earth! Yet she was doing his bidding, trotting beside him like the meekest miss!

"A blush, Miss Summerhayes? I thought you delighted in plain speaking."

Daphne heard his quiet chuckle, but did not answer, as they were nearing Sophie and Edgar. Sophie, her spirits quite restored, was excitedly exclaiming over the painting.

"Oh, Daphne, do see," she implored, drawing back to allow a clear view. "Is not this the most prodigiously handsome place you have ever seen? Why, I vow it is not a house, but a palace!"

The canvas depicted a magnificent stone building crowning a broad hill, with soaring, turreted roofs, and sheer walls pierced by long, many-paned windows. Sunlight warmed the stone, while pink-tinged clouds built layer by layer behind it. A treed park with a glimmering pond enhanced the scene without detracting from the splendid edifice. Daphne gazed in awe, not of the residence, but of the genius that captured its likeness.

She thought of Weldern Manor, snuggled in its cosy hollow, with trees drawn about its ears and bushes warming its feet. This vast—dare one call it a home?—thrust boldly, contemptuously, above the world. Although beautiful in grace and symmetry, the great house radiated pride, strength, and power.

As does its owner, Daphne thought.

"Well, Miss Summerhayes, what is your opinion of Mordaine Knowe?" asked Lord Courtlea, his casual tone not quite concealing the complacency in his voice.

"As a painting, it is superb," Daphne answered feelingly. "Mr.

Turner expresses light so magnificently, he enhances every subject. See how the structure appears almost to float, despite the solidity of the stone."

"Egad, Miss Summerhayes!" exclaimed Edgar, peering over her shoulder. "I never noticed that."

"My cousin is herself an accomplished painter, Mr. Merritt," commented Sophie proudly, "and is never happier than with her oils or water colors. I vow she captures any scene to a nicety."

"Hush, Sophie," begged Daphne, her cheeks warming as she glanced back at her cousin. "Pray do not boast of my small talent in *these* halls."

"Yet you have an excellent eye, Miss Summerhayes," Lord Courtlea said quietly. "Many look at art, but fail to see it. Pray continue."

A new note in his voice so closely resembled respect that Daphne forgot her reserve and looked up at him. The mocking, insinuating light was gone from his eyes as he gazed at her. A small, warm smile played about his lips. Indeed, she had not seen the earl's features so unguarded, so free from condescension, save once.

Recollecting that time, when he lay asleep and she hovered yearningly over him, Daphne colored afresh and wrenched her gaze from his to return to the painting. She did not see it, however. All her energies were directed to recovering her composure.

"Mordaine Knowe is magnificent, Lord Courtlea," she managed despite her breathlessness. "One can well believe it to be yours."

"Indeed?"

She heard his surprise, but gave him no opportunity to query her further. "Now we must be off," she said briskly. "Good afternoon, Lord Courtlea. Come, Sophie. Sophie?"

Daphne spun about. Sophie had quite deserted her, and was drifting toward the door, chatting animatedly with Edgar Merritt. Daphne gritted her teeth in frustration, but there was nothing for it but to retrace the length of the gallery as calmly as possible beside the earl. Lord Courtlea did not offer his arm, for which she was thankful, but his steps slowed after a few paces.

"Pray tell me, Miss Summerhayes," he asked, and Daphne was relieved that his quiet tone was free from suggestive teasing. "why, at our last meeting, you ran away from me. Why did you not stay longer?"

Daphne stopped dead, her mouth suddenly dry, and stared up at him. "What do you mean, sir?"

Lord Courtlea halted, doubtless somewhat taken aback at her intensity. "Your leaving the Dunston ball so precipitously, of course," he said, raising his brows. "You gave me no chance to defend myself against your attack. Why, Cinderella herself could not have flown away so quickly. I would have continued our discourse."

"Oh, the ball," she said, relieved.

Really, a guilty conscience was an uncomfortable thing, making one suspicious of the most innocent remark. Then the earl's obvious puzzlement at her relief warned her to have a care. Lest he ask when since they had met, she hurried on.

"I assure you, my lord, 'twas not on your account that I left the party. Nor was my brother William attempting to avoid your company. Our cousin Sophie took ill, quite unexpectedly, and we at once conveyed her home."

As she hoped, Lord Courtlea was diverted. "Your brother? I do not recollect him. Why should he avoid me?"

Astonishment robbed her of speech. Was he so hardened in his own self-interest that the encounters with young William Summerhayes— the wagers on the horses, the near-challenge, the losses at cards—were too trivial to recall? She warmed with indignation at the memory of William's anguish, and of her own involvement, and opened her lips to recount the earl's injustices. Discretion seized the reins of her runaway temper, however, in time to pull her up short. Lord Courtlea's lack of recollection might be in her favor.

She shrugged slightly and continued walking. "'Tis of no matter, sir." The doorway and escape were near. She saw Sophie and Edgar lingering in the hall, talking animatedly, apparently unaware of visitors to the Academy having to walk around them.

"A moment, pray." Lord Courtlea lightly touched her arm to halt her, and she almost flinched. "I admit to a certain vagueness surrounding that time, but nothing occurred to cause anyone…"

He frowned at the floor, absently tapping his cane against his boot. In a moment his piercing gaze swung back to her, his eyes flaring in triumph. "Ah, now I have it! Something with horses, was it not?"

Daphne dared not meet his eyes, but pretended to study the painting before which they stood.

"Just so," Lord Courtlea said, and laughed. "So that young jackanapes who was ready to call me out was your brother. 'Twould seem confrontation is a trait in the Summerhayes family."

Daphne's head came up. "Only when we are in the right, my lord," she retorted, glaring at him.

He smiled tightly, but with some satisfaction. "I believe you have answered a question troubling me. Did that mild contretemps—and you must admit I let the lad off easily—bear on your attack of my character? Did it, perhaps, add warmth and color to your denunciation?"

"Perhaps," she snapped. "Your cavalier treatment of him—" Daphne stopped. He had made no mention of winning the brooch from Edgar. Had he forgotten that as well? "One cannot help but be protective of a younger sib," she went on more quietly, glancing at Sophie and Edgar. "Can you refute that?"

Lord Courtlea followed her look, and sighed. God knew he was hard put sometimes, acting as father as well as brother to Edgar. "No, Miss Summerhayes, I cannot, but at some point, the young must stand on their own feet. Do you expect to manage your brother his whole life?"

That shot told, for her eyes widened, and the look she gave him showed consternation. She said nothing, however, but turned and walked swiftly to her cousin. Courtlea followed her slim, straight back, not yet ready to let the strong-minded Miss Summerhayes escape.

She gave him no chance. With scant farewells, she linked arms with Sophie, and hurried from the building.

Edgar regarded his brother with reproachful eyes. "Egad, Victor, what did you do to drive Miss Summerhayes off? She was quite tiffed."

"Mayhap I accidentally put a flea in her ear. If good comes from it, her brother may thank me some day." Courtlea set his gray beaver more firmly on his head before facing the outdoors. His interest in the Academy had vanished with his last glimpse of the yellow pelisse.

"But, I say, Victor." Edgar appeared rooted to the spot, as if entranced by a vision. "Such splendid hair! And such glorious eyes! Why, they shoot right through a man. Have you ever seen the like?"

The question may have been a rhetorical one, but Courtlea was caught in a sudden vision of his hands revelling in the richness of that Titian hair, its silken softness slipping through his fingers. Those eyes, jade-green with surrender and passion; those lips full and luscious under his own, opening to him—

Courtlea drew a shaking breath. His brow was damp, his palms wet in the leather gloves. God above, if imagining such an encounter stirred him so, what would a real tryst with her do to him?

He had never lost himself in a woman, surrendering control to her, and the thought of giving such power into a woman's hands sent a chill through him. No, he must be mad to consider Daphne Summerhayes as a lover. Why, she was exactly the type of woman he swore to avoid. Opinionated, out-spoken, independent—

"And such a ready wit, too," Edgar went on, oblivious to his brother's reaction. "I vow I could listen for hours to her sweet voice."

"Have you taken leave of your senses?"

Courtlea impelled his brother out to the busy Strand traffic. A brisk wind swirled about, fluttering ribbons and feathers on ladies' bonnets and threatening to carry off gentlemen's hats.

"Breathe deeply, you young paperskull, and clear your wits! Of all the females in London— nay, I am wrong!—in all England, Miss Daphne Summerhayes is the least to merit your attentions. She needs a stronger hand than yours, my lad." With an air of having spoken the last word, he stepped to the curb and signalled his coachman.

Edgar stopped dead, like a rock in midstream, forcing other pedestrians to flow around him. "Miss Daphne! Have you a screw loose, Victor? Who spoke of Miss Daphne? It is her cousin, sweet Miss Sophie, who has quite dazzled me."

"What!" The earl whirled, seized Edgar's arm and dragged him out of the way. "Good God, Edgar!"

For a moment Courtlea stared speechlessly at his brother. He grew aware that his carriage had drawn up, and said no more until he had pushed his brother within and the carriage was once again moving.

"Has a pretty face quite overcome your good sense?" Courtlea demanded. "Why, I knew the moment I clapped eyes on the girl that she has not a brain in her head. Her chatter would soon drive any man around the bend. Sophie Summerhayes!"

Edgar's features set in a stubborn frown. "See here, don't talk down Miss Sophie. She's the most fetching miss I've seen, more than passing fair, and with sweet, taking ways."

"Just so, you have hit on it!" Lord Courtlea thumped his cane on the carriage floor in agreement. "'Take' is what she will do, in abundance, given half a chance. She is a silly, brainless chit who would ruin your life. Do you want your children to be lack-wits? In any case, you are too young to consider marriage, and her family would never accept any other arrangement."

He looked coldly on his brother's grim expression. "Edgar, I warn you; be guided by me in this. Forget Sophie Summerhayes."

"You seemed willing enough to approach them," Edgar protested, "and more than willing to keep Miss Daphne's company. Does your interest lie in her direction?"

"Demme, sir, mind your impudent tongue!" Courtlea exploded. "What man in his right mind would take that saucy, stubborn lady for his own?"

Edgar looked unconvinced, but Courtlea forbore further protests, and pretended interest beyond the window. His thoughts, however, were not so easily diverted. Daphne Summerhayes had not been far from his mind ever since he had returned to London, but now he would think of her no more.

She had a vixen's temper and a man's logic, a fierce loyalty to those she loved, and more courage than discretion. She both repelled and attracted him. On one hand, he wished to seize her, shake her, and see her humbled. On the other, he wanted to seize her and kiss that challenging mouth until she melted in his arms. He grunted, and a grin tugged at his lips. He had held her in his arms, that wintry afternoon when she nearly ran into his curricle. She had clung to him, too, even sat on his knees, but the experience was sadly spoiled by his thick greatcoat and her heavy cloak. Next time he would make sure there was less between them—

"Damnation!"

He shifted impatiently against the leather squabs, ignoring Edgar's startled look. Next time? He would make sure there was no next time. Damn the woman!

CHAPTER 9

Daphne rounded on her cousin the moment they were seated in the Wentford carriage. "Sophie, pray recollect that you are in my charge, and must stay by me at all times! I was horrified to find you had wandered off with Mr. Merritt, a gentleman to whom you had just that minute been introduced. Your conduct was unforgivable."

"Oh, Daphne, I vow I did not think it was wrong!" Sophie's countenance registered bewilderment as well as repentance. "At home, Mama would think nothing of such—"

"You are not home, Sophie, and I cannot impress that fact too deeply in your mind."

As her cousin's cheeks flushed pink, Daphne reflected bitterly on Agnes Summerhayes's lack of discipline in the raising of her daughters. Daphne believed her aunt's ill health nothing more than self-indulgence leavened with a generous dollop of laziness. Her vapors and swooning fits afforded the perfect excuse to avoid her family responsibilities. It was no little miracle that Sophie was of a sunny, wholesome disposition and not pettish and spoiled, responding sullenly to correction.

"A lady's reputation is a priceless, but fragile thing," Daphne went on, "especially for a young girl entering Society for the first time. All eyes assess her behavior, and a whisper here, a murmur of disapproval there, a breath of condemnation—all may have the most frightful result. She may not be received by the ton, and I assure you, Sophie, one must avoid such a situation at all costs."

Her wigging delivered, Daphne guiltily wondered if she were venting her extreme vexation with Lord Courtlea on Sophie's unprotected head. No, truly, the girl needed to be made aware ere she found herself in the briers.

"Yes, Daphne," rejoined Sophie, with unusual meekness. "I vow, I thought only to allow you peace to converse with Lord Courtlea. You two seemed to rub along quite well together."

"Oh, fustian, Sophie! I cannot abide the man. He is—" Daphne shot a suspicious glance at her cousin. "No, my girl, you cannot draw me off on a false trail. We are speaking of your behavior, not mine."

Sophie responded with a grin that quite belied her humble manner. "But what did you think of Mr. Merritt? I vow, he is prodigiously agreeable. Why, we had a fine coze, like the best of friends. He is not as severe as his brother, I think."

"Nor as above himself, I dare say," added Daphne. "Still, to be fair, he does not bear the responsibilities of the title, as Lord Courtlea does." She paused, amazed to hear herself defending the man she thought of as "that odious earl." With a shake of her head, she returned to the issue at hand. "In any case," she ended mildly, "if, by any chance, you again encounter Mr. Merritt, I expect you to behave with more decorum."

As Daphne sank back on the plush squabs, the steady advance of the carriage abruptly ceased and the noise of the streets reached a new crescendo.

"Charing Cross," Daphne commented, looking out to where traffic from the Strand and Whitehall met with that from the Haymarket and Pall Mall.

Drays, farm carts, and carriages of all types competed for the right of way. Drivers exchanged shouted insults. Horses neighed, hoofs clattered, sending yelling street sweepers scrambling. Hucksters shouted or sang their wares, adding to the nerve-jangling, ear-splitting, glorious din that to Daphne personified the vitality of London. She heard her own coachman shout, the crack of a whip, and the carriage moved slowly on.

Daphne turned from the lively scene to surprise a cloud on her cousin's usually open expression. "Does something puzzle you?" she asked. "Speak, Sophie, dear. Although I may ring a peal over your head occasionally for your good, I do not enjoy doing so. You know, I hope, that you may ask me about anything troubling you, and I will do my best to help."

"Oh, I know. You are most patient, and I do appreciate your

attention more than I can say." Sophie picked up the little muff she had thrown on the seat and absently began stroking the soft fur. "But you said if I should happen to encounter..." She glanced up. "Well, I shall encounter Mr. Merritt on Thursday afternoon, when he takes me for a drive in the park."

Daphne stared speechlessly at her cousin. With an effort she repressed the urge to shake Sophie until her teeth rattled. "You were wrong to accept his invitation," she said as evenly as possible, "and Mr. Merritt was wrong to invite you without first asking my permission."

"D'you mean that I am not fully out in Society yet, and so cannot accept such invitations?" demanded Sophie. "Dash it! I vow this coming-out is a slow process! Did my being received by the Marchioness of Silversby and the Countess of Daly count for nothing? How much farther out must I come?"

Sophie's indignation and choice of words were too much for Daphne. Envisioning her cousin as a shy winkle venturing timidly from its shell, she burst into laughter, and reached across to clasp Sophie's hand. "Oh, dear Coz, you enliven my life, and no mistake! But, while here in London under my care, you must resign yourself to chaperonage."

Sophie met that news with the expression of one receiving a life sentence to Newgate. "Not to walk, or ride, or—or— Oh, may I dance alone with a gentleman, or must we do a three- hands round?"

"Did you not dance at Dunston Hall?" Daphne demanded. "And recollect, pray, what happened when you slipped away with Tim Franklin. Fortunately for you, Tim is a good sort, but not all gentlemen are so trustworthy. For your own protection, Sophie, as well as my peace of mind, you must pay more heed."

Recollection came of a totally untrustworthy gentleman, whose insufferable arrogance had just caused her to flee the Academy. Dash it! Must every instance remind her of Lord Courtlea?

"Sophie, did you know that Lady Silversby expressed concern over my position as chaperon?"

"Oh, no, I did not!" Sophie gave an indignant sniff. "'Tis surely not her concern in any case. I vow she is an old dragon. A thin, hawk-faced harpy. What did she say?"

"'Unmarried, much too young, and hardly a dowdy frump,'" Daphne promptly quoted, mimicking the marchioness's blunt manner. "'Who guards the guards, and who chaperons the chaperons, eh?'

"Fortunately," Daphne continued, "Aunt Elizabeth spoke warmly in my favor, but you see, Sophie, why we must be doubly watchful. My reputation as well as yours is in the balance."

Sophie nodded, her large blue eyes serious. "Oh, dearest Daphne," she said, clasping her hands together, "I vow, I would never wish to cause harm to anyone, least of all to you."

Daphne believed her, but consistency was not Sophie's long suit. Until Sophie's sense of decorum greatly improved, Daphne must still act the watchdog. Meanwhile, the problem remained of Lord Courtlea's brother.

"Mr. Merritt deserves a sharp put-down, you know," Daphne said. "I would send a note to him, crying off from Thursday, if I knew where he lodged. As it is, you will simply not be home to him when he calls."

"Oh, must you? Must I?" Sophie cried, near to tears. "Oh, Daphne, why do you dislike him so? Is he not Lord Courtlea's brother? I vow, Mr. Merritt is the most trustworthy of gentlemen. Can you not arrange things in some manner? Do, I beg, dearest cousin."

The depth of Sophie's distress surprised Daphne. She did not answer her cousin's entreaty at once as she searched for the most tactful words.

"Mr. Merritt appeared pleasant," she said at last, "but he is the first gentleman to whom you have been introduced, and that introduction was a trifle backhanded. You will meet many fine young men during the Season. Why, Aunt Elizabeth has mentioned several eligible bachelors, whose characters, backgrounds, and expectations are all known to her. Come now, Sophie, you will have many a drive in the park, and in better weather than this."

Sophie bravely attempted a smile, but remained quiet for the rest of the drive. Meanwhile, Daphne determined to learn what she could about young Mr. Merritt. She had realized at once that Sophie had presented her with a possibility to discover Lord Courtlea's address. Not that Daphne would use her cousin to serve her own ends, but when Fate handed one a shovel, why not dig?

She found her aunt at her writing desk, folding and sealing her last letter. She greeted her niece with a smile as Daphne settled into a ladderback chair beside the desk.

"Aunt, will you tell me, pray, what you know of the Merritt family, especially young Edgar Merritt?"

"Indeed, I shall," Lady Wentford answered agreeably, "but why your interest?"

Daphne related the encounter at the Royal Academy, and its result.

"Sophie is overset, I fear, but what else might I do?"

"Naught else," answered Lady Wentford, shaking her head, "and now you must decide whether to allow this acquaintance or nip it in the bud. Well, as to the Merritts, I knew the previous earl, a shy, quiet man, not too much backbone, I would say, but certainly of good moral character. He died when Edgar was about ten years old. Victor took Edgar to live with him and saw to the boy's schooling."

"Not with his mother, or is she also deceased?" inquired Daphne, hanging on every word.

"When not in the country, he is at Victor's house somewhere on Green Street. His mother leads a...busy life, quite separate from her sons. The arrangement is not an unusual one, of course, and it suits all concerned."

Daphne cocked an eye at her aunt. "Aunt, I know you too well. Your tone tells more than your words. What is it about Lady Courtlea that you are not saying?"

Lady Wentford shrugged. "Felicia is a handsome piece, young enough to marry again, but she flirts with danger." She gave a short laugh. "As well as with every presentable male she encounters. So far, her amours have been discreetly hidden, but she grows careless, and, without the protection of a husband's name, may find scandal of the worst kind breaking over her head."

"Oh, how foolish of her! Do you think her—her activities are known to her sons?"

"To Victor, of a certainty, but he would shelter Edgar, I think, from any shameful revelations. He is fond of the boy, and 'tis said he steers him clear of undesirable influences."

Daphne wondered if she had heard aright. "You amaze me, Aunt. I pegged Lord Courtlea himself as an undesirable influence. Dissolute, proud, cruel, contemptuous of his inferiors, a gambler, a libertine—"

As Daphne paused for breath, Lady Wentford gave her an odd look. "Why, I had no notion you were so knowledgeable about Victor's character," she commented.

"We—we met in Buckinghamshire, and he impressed me as being thoroughly disagreeable."

"Oh? You did not mention this meeting when I listed Victor as a possible match for Sophie." Lady Wentford's voice held no censure, only mild interest.

Daphne shifted uncomfortably in her chair. "It seemed unimportant. I knew he thought little of her, and would not consider her for a moment."

"I see." Lady Wentford closed the silver-mounted inkwell and returned the wafers and stationery to their places. "You are too harsh, my dear," she said with a smile that took any sting from her words. "Victor has his faults, no doubt, what gentleman does not? But he is active in the House, pushing for agricultural reform, and has the reputation of a caring landlord. Perhaps you saw only one side of his nature."

Lady Wentford gathered up her letters and rose to her feet. Leaning forward, she laid her hand gently on her niece's shoulder.

"None of us is without fault. Some judge too quickly, and never alter their opinion. Others lay blame everywhere but at their own door. Still others must control, not only their own affairs, but those of everyone else. We are all an odd mixture, my dear, but when we love, or are loved, flaws cease to matter."

She patted Daphne's shoulder, and left the sitting room, leaving her niece to a maelstrom of emotions and doubts.

Daphne had never considered herself perfect, but neither had she deeply questioned her character. Was she really as hidebound, as inflexible, as Aunt Elizabeth implied? William had accused his sister of managing his life, and Lord Courtlea had intimated the same thing. When did loving care become meddling?

If William had only told her the truth about that wretched brooch, she would never have interfered. Oh, dash it, now she blamed William for her own impulsive behavior, as she had heaped blame on Lord Courtlea merely for having come to Buckinghamshire! Spurred by thorns of self-revelation, Daphne sprang from her chair. With hands behind her back, she paced the floor, wishing for Golden Sovereign and a gallop across the fields to clear her mind. But Goldie was in the stable at Weldern Manor, and her uncle kept no saddle horses. In any case, what was past was beyond mending.

Had she been quite fair to Lord Courtlea? Could one wonder at his cynicism, with such a mother and without a father's guidance? He must have been younger than Edgar's age now when he attained the title and became guardian of his young brother. And see how sunny-natured and guileless Edgar was, under his tutelage. Mayhap the earl had some redeeming qualities after all.

The room had grown chill. Daphne wrapped her green shawl more closely around herself as she stopped at the window. Soon a maid would be in to draw the drapes and build up the fire, but for the moment all was quiet as Daphne looked down on the high-walled rear yard.

The yard was larger and deeper than most, with room enough for a garden which already bloomed with crocus and early jonquils. A curtain wall separated the garden from the cobblestone path leading to a gate which opened on a mews. Oh, if only Golden Sovereign were stabled there, so near to hand! What she would not give to ride away from her troubles!

Daphne sighed. She must rid herself of the emerald soonest, and mayhap rid her mind of the earl at the same time. "Mr. Merritt may have his drive," she muttered, turning from the window. "Surely I can ferret Lord Courtlea's address from him without causing comment. And I shall be prepared."

She pulled the bell rope. "Oh, Clapham," she said to the butler when he entered the room. "I have need of some string, paper, and a small box. Can you oblige?"

"Indeed, miss. How small a box is required?"

"About so, I think." Daphne held her fingers a few inches apart.

"Perhaps a pill box would prove satisfactory, miss."

"Excellent. Bring them to my room. And Clapham, do you know of a messenger service, one that might deliver packages?"

"There are movers, of course, miss, for large items. For messages and such, Lady Wentford sends one of the footmen, or myself, if greater care is desired. May I be of service, miss?"

"Perhaps. Thank you, Clapham."

The butler bowed out, unaware that while he solved one problem for Miss Summerhayes, he had presented her with another. Simply, how to return the brooch without leaving a trail that led back to Wentford House. The footmen had Lord Wentford's coat of arms stamped on their buttons. Clapham was doubtless a familiar in the brotherhood of butlers. Nonetheless, when a maid brought the desired items, Daphne wrapped the brooch up well, to be ready when chance presented itself, and hid it in the back of her bottom bureau drawer. Oh, if only Thursday were tomorrow!

It was not, however, and in the afternoon Daphne rather gloomily listened as Sophie chattered on the way to Lord and Lady Silversby's home near Richmond. As their carriage, one of a long procession, moved slowly up the winding drive, Daphne decided to forget plans and plots until Thursday. After that—

One step at a time, she reminded herself with a sigh.

Daphne fell in love with the beautiful Palladian mansion at first sight, with its simple yet elegant lines, soft colors and white-and-gilt trim. She expressed her delight to Lady Silversby, carelessly elegant in primrose yellow taffeta.

"His lordship," Lady Silversby confided, referring to the marquis, as she showed the Misses Summerhayes through the lovely reception rooms, "was sure he would hate it, but I stuck fast, and now he takes full credit for the place." She glanced about the room, already crowded with beautifully-dressed ladies and gentlemen. "But where are the Wentfords? Are they coming later?"

"Aunt asks your forgiveness, but there was a mix-up of dates," Daphne explained. "She and Uncle Valentine must attend a charity fair at the Assembly Rooms. She apologizes most heartily. She was so looking forward to greeting Mr. and Mrs. Manley."

"Yes, Elizabeth has known Esther from a child. Esther is my goddaughter, you know, and now that she and Charles have returned from their wedding trip, I thought it amusing to reintroduce them as a married couple."

She lifted the quizzing glass fastened by a ribbon to her bodice and openly examined Sophie's gown of peach cambric daintily trimmed with inserts of white lace. Daphne could not help but stiffen as the marchioness next scanned her deep amber gown with the same intensity. Daphne did not consider old age or high rank excused rudeness.

"You both look a treat, as usual," Lady Silversby commented, dropping the quizzing glass. "Doubtless you will catch the eye of every man here. Not the bridegroom, though. A more besotted man I have yet to see. Come and meet the happy pair."

Daphne sensed utter happiness radiating from the newly-married couple as she offered her congratulations. Mr. Charles Manley seemed puffed with pride, the fine, fair hair falling aslant his brow giving him a boyish air. Adoration shone in his blue eyes whenever he looked at his wife.

Esther Manley's sweet smile lit her pretty, heart-shaped face with a serene contentment. Her gown of green moiré silk befitted her status as a married woman, and set off her white skin and lustrous brown eyes.

"Miss Summerhayes," she said to Sophie, "you must meet my cousins. They have spent several summers in Cornwall, and mayhap they share some friends with you. Excuse us, pray, dear Lady Silversby." She slipped her arm through that of Sophie, and led her away, both chattering like old friends.

"And excuse me, too, I beg. Your ladyship, Miss Summerhayes." With a brief bow, Charles trailed after them.

Daphne watched while Sophie and the Manleys joined a laughing group of young people. She relaxed, gratified, when they received Sophie eagerly and with evident pleasure. "Mr. and Mrs. Manley seem an ideal couple," she commented, accepting a glass of cordial from a footman.

"Naturally." Lady Silversby impatiently waved the footman away. "I hand-picked them."

Daphne choked on her drink, and Lady Silversby snorted in delight at her reaction.

"You heard aright, my girl," the marchioness said with relish. "Something as important as marriage cannot be left to the whims of younglings. Charles was the man I wanted for Esther, and I made sure they met. I knew they would hit it off, and of course they did."

"But if they had not hit it off, Lady Silversby, what then?" Daphne asked.

The marchioness looked at her as though she had lost her senses. "But I knew they would, dear child, do you not see? They are perfect for each other in every way. I am never wrong." she added comfortably, a complacent expression on her thin, sharp-featured face. "'Tis the duty of parents, or godparents, to arrange the happiest of connections for their children. Do you not agree?"

"Miss Summerhayes has decided views on marriage, Lady Silversby, and does not hesitate to share them."

Daphne started at the deep, mocking voice, nearly spilling her cordial. Slowly she turned her head. Lord Courtlea stood beside her, a sardonic smile on his lips, his gray eyes glinting with amusement. Her heart leaped with the oddest mixture of alarm, aversion, and pleasure.

Lady Silversby lightly struck his maroon sleeve with her fan. "You scamp, Victor! Eavesdropping is a disgusting habit, quite the outside of enough."

"Indeed, I agree, and I fear my skill at it will never equal yours, sweet lady." His smile widened, and he bent forward to kiss Lady Silversby's cheek.

Daphne goggled in surprise. The marchioness cackled with laughter, looking archly pleased. "Your tricks don't strike sparks with me, rascal. Oh, what is it now?"

She turned sharply to an anxious-faced footman hovering nearby.

As he spoke hurriedly for Lady Silversby's ear, Daphne took a sip of her cordial. It might have been plain water for all her noticing.

"Have a care, Miss Summerhayes, your hand is trembling," Lord Courtlea murmured, his voice like warm honey. "Shall I find you a chair, lest you swoon?"

"I am in no danger of swooning," she retorted, stung that he should notice her reaction. Nevertheless, she set down her glass on a nearby table and took a deep breath before facing him. "You startled me, my lord, with your abruptness. Not to mention your comment on my opinions."

He cocked a brow, but forbore to answer as Lady Silversby rejoined them.

"I must be off." Her heavy gold and diamond earrings swung as she shook her head. "That fool girl, Dora Brown, has managed to fall into the conservatory fish pond."

The earl laughed, unfeelingly, to Daphne's mind, although her own lips twitched. "May I be of some help, Lady Silversby?" she asked. "The poor girl must be prodigiously overset."

"Overset? The lack-wit is probably laughing hard, and trying to catch all my fish into the bargain. No, child, you remain, and keep this rascal out of harm's way. Too many ladies here are as susceptible as Maryann Bisely, and are as like to fall easy prey to his blandishments. Take care you do not."

With a cackling laugh and a keen look from her snapping black eyes, Lady Silversby departed with the footman. In the little silence that followed, Daphne, having heard the earl's sharp intake of breath, glanced up at him. A frown had replaced his smile, and the look he sent after the marchioness chilled Daphne's blood.

"Who is Miss Bisely?" she heard herself ask.

"A friend." The earl bit the words out. "Lady Silversby enjoys making her little jokes at my expense."

Daphne suspected that Maryann Bisely must mean more to him than a mere friend. In the context of Lady Silversby's words, Miss Bisely was probably Lord Courtlea's mistress, or at least someone with whom he was emotionally entangled. A pit seemed to open in Daphne's stomach, and for a moment she felt quite ill.

Lord Courtlea looked away, a slight flush on his cheeks. "Pray think no more of it, Miss Summerhayes. The marchioness delights in causing dissention."

"Does she indeed?" Daphne said vaguely. She pretended to study the mythological scenes painted on her linen fan while she struggled to recapture her composure.

She could understand Miss Bisely, or any woman, losing her head over this arrogant lord. His attractiveness went far beyond his handsome features and magnificent form. Some power within him drew people as a magnet draws iron. Men seemed to respect, if not fear, him. Women, whatever their age or station, melted as if ready to relinquish their virtue at his merest whim.

As Flora, she had felt that power and had barely resisted it. However, too much stood between them for her to think of him as anything but an adversary; the emerald brooch, his callous treatment of her brother, his belittling of Sophie, his complete selfishness. Strangely, that thought did not bring comfort, but instead a twinge of something like regret.

With iron control, Courtlea subdued his fury at Lady Silversby's gibe. He had been discreet; how had she known about Maryann? He forced a smile. "The lady has a vicious tongue, but sometimes her words make perfect sense. You are ordered to have care of me, Miss Summerhayes."

She looked up, her face lacking some of its lovely color, and he knew with a sinking heart that she had made the connection between himself and Maryann Bisely. Courtlea bit his lip. He could not explain; one did not discuss one's mistresses, past or present, with ladies at a social gathering. And why, he asked himself in amazement, did he even consider explaining?

"If you find Lady Silversby so unkind, why do you come?"

He did not care for the distaste in her stiff tones and in the glance she slanted at him.

"Her ladyship is an old friend of my father," he said lightly. "She is also godmother to my brother Edgar. Now, Miss Summerhayes, I beg, what would amuse you? Cards? Music and dancing in the Green Saloon? Mayhap a stroll through Silversby's conservatory?"

Preferring the conservatory with its promise of seclusion, he gestured toward the wide glass and wrought-iron doors that showed inviting glimpses of foliage and flowers.

Her gaze followed his gesture, but she shook her head. "Sir, pray do not think of my amusement, nor consider Lady Silversby's suggestion as an order. You and I disagree on all matters, it seems. Indeed, I wonder you care to approach me, after our meeting at the Royal Academy yesterday."

He looked down into her serene, lovely face, and felt the challenge to stir her calm into something else. Not anger; he had had enough of her cutting tongue. Then he noticed the rigid set of her head and how her fingers twisted the tassel of her fan. Mayhap the lady was not as cool as she appeared. He decided on the truth.

"How could I help but approach?" He nodded toward a group of beaux boisterously steeplechasing over a row of chairs. "Almost all the gentlemen here are well known to me, and hardly a one is worth listening to. Courtesy prevents me from discussing the ladies' abilities for discourse. When I saw the belligerent Miss Summerhayes, I knew she alone, with her definite notions and stimulating conversation, could relieve my boredom."

He neglected to add that she stimulated him in other ways too intimate to discuss openly.

"Oh, what a gallant compliment, my lord," Miss Summerhayes retorted. "Clearly, you believe I exist only to satisfy your whims." She turned away to join the steady stream of guests edging toward the Green Saloon. Determinedly, he kept pace.

"Would you rather I said your beauty astounds me?" he drawled, enjoying her perfect profile. "Would you prefer to hear that your eyes threaten to drown me in pools of delight, and that your rosebud mouth promises sweets without number?"

She stopped stock-still, turned startled green eyes on him, and, to his complete surprise, burst out laughing.

"Why, my lord, I believe you have a sense of humor. I suspected it, and now you have confirmed my suspicion. Do you perceive me as a simpleton, whose head may be turned by such glib words? Fie, sir, I am not so easily won."

She looked a carefree girl, her perfect, white teeth flashing and her face bright with laughter. 'Twas the first time she had freely laughed in his company, and he smiled, charmed and pleasantly warmed. "Tell me, pray, if compliments to your intelligence and your beauty do not move you, except to amusement, what will win your regard?"

A shadow quenched the gay light dancing in her eyes. "I ask pardon, my lord, for my frivolity," she said coolly, turning away. "'Twas misplaced, and ill advised."

Her abrupt dismissal stung, but he held his place, silently cursing Lady Silversby and her malice. He considered revealing the truth to the forthright Miss Summerhayes, and then wondered if he had gone quite mad.

They reached the Green Saloon to find the chattering guests already seated on rows of gilt chairs facing a gleaming pianoforte. Only the back row was empty. Sophie Summerhayes sat well forward with a noisy group. Edgar would not be among them; he would not dare disobey Courtlea's order to avoid her.

"Pray be seated, Miss Summerhayes," the earl said, pulling out two chairs and setting them even farther back. "One should not be too close to the music."

She shook her head, looking toward Sophie and her group. "No, my lord, excuse me, I beg, but I must—"

"All the chairs are taken, I fear," he interrupted smoothly.

Without a further word but obviously reluctant, she sat down, her slim body stiffly erect. Courtlea took the other chair, turning it slightly toward her, the better to feast his eyes. He thought the character in her face heightened her beauty, adding an irresistible fascination. Her gown of some supple fabric delightfully molded her breasts and thighs. Desire stirred in him, tightening in his gut. He wanted her, and he cared not why.

Her cheeks had grown pink, her breathing more rapid, evidence that she was aware of his scrutiny. He realized he had bent close, almost touching her shoulder.

"Mr. and Mrs. Manley seem a most devoted couple," Miss Summerhayes said, a trifle breathlessly, wielding her fan hard enough to stir the curls atop her head.

"Indeed," he agreed, leaning back, delighted his closeness had affected her, "but they are young yet. Soon enough the bloom will fade, and they will begin to hate each other."

"Why, that is so cynical!" The fan paused, and she stared at him wide-eyed. "Surely one should expect more from marriage?"

He shrugged, wishing for more privacy to explore her reaction to him. "Did not you yourself categorize marriage as a union of incomes and bodies? Is that not cynical? Granted, the pleasure involved in the joining of bodies—"

"Sir!" Color flamed brighter in her face. "Lower your voice, I beg! Recollect where you are."

He glanced about indifferently. "No one is near enough to overhear, even if one could hear in this din."

"Nonetheless, 'tis not a proper subject for discussion." She turned her profile to him, chin lifted slightly, and again wielded the fan. "I may only add that I hope your own marriage may cure you of your skepticism."

"That unhappy event is far, far in the future, Miss Summerhayes," he murmured with a laugh. "I have neither the intention nor the need to marry for at least ten years."

"As to that, sir," she said crisply, shooting him a sharp glance, "it seems gentlemen, even husbands, may set up mist— alternatives—to serve their needs without shame. Avenues not open to ladies, or wives, unless they care not for utter ruin and loss of reputation. Is that just?"

"Naturally not, madam," he drawled, amused and impressed by her forthrightness. "Our young ladies are nurtured to find satisfaction only in the arms of their husbands."

"Satisfaction? And what of love, sir? Does not love—deep, true love—enter into your consideration?"

Leaning close again, he murmured in her ear, "I cannot say from personal experience, but I believe the charms of love to be grossly overrated. A woman is a woman. Supply her with a home and babies and she is content."

"Oh!" Her shocked exclamation rang out in a sudden silence. The crowd had quieted as a violinist and his accompanist entered, and now heads swiveled inquisitively toward the back row.

To her credit, Miss Summerhayes did not blush or look away in confusion. Her chin lifted a trifle more, and she smiled calmly into all the avidly curious eyes. The musicians began to play, and almost as one the heads turned to the front.

The look she gave Courtlea would have scorched a lesser man.

"Sir, you are more than severe," she all but hissed, snapping her fan closed. "'Twould be justice indeed if the lady who becomes your wife has the same cold, passionless notions of marriage as yourself. Good day, sir."

She rose, and ignoring a rustle of whispers, marched down the aisle. A young gentleman beside Sophie met her eye, turned crimson, and leapt to his feet. With a nod of acceptance, Miss Summerhayes sat down in his place and was lost from view.

The earl stretched out his legs and settled his large frame as comfortably as possible in the small chair. Yesterday he had decided to dismiss the sharp-tongued vixen from his mind. Today, without thought or design, he had gone to her side the moment his eye lit on her. Thank the gods that he had approached her, for he had discovered Miss Summerhayes was not as cold to him as she would have him believe. He was sure of it. He prided himself on his knowledge of women, even though this intriguing female did not conform to any he had known.

However, he sensed a struggle within her. One much as his own conflict; a push and pull between calculating brain and fleshly desires. Courtlea smiled, letting the music wash over him. He would not seek her out for dancing or for supper. No, let her wait, and wonder, and fret, until she came looking for him. Wisdom told him to avoid her; that red-headed saucebox was not really his taste. Yet, if she herself desired an affaire de coeur, he might consider it. Nay, he would bed her with the utmost speed.

* * *

"I pity the poor woman he marries," Daphne muttered.

"Pardon, Daphne, I beg. What did you say?"

Daphne started, realizing she and Sophie were nearly back at Upper Grosvenor Street. "Oh,—um—I pity those with a coachman who tarries," she said hastily. "Did you enjoy yourself today?"

"Oh, I vow I had the most delightful time. Why, Mrs. Manley is a dear, and she…"

While Sophie eagerly rattled on, Daphne smiled and nodded. Secretly she seethed. Though she had laughed and chatted as if enjoying herself prodigiously, Lord Courtlea had spoiled the party for her. How detestable of him to talk in such an outrageous manner!

Mistresses and marriage! Bodies and babies! 'Twas quite the outside of enough! She was annoyed with herself for listening, and totally furious that she had looked for him every minute afterwards. Several times she had glimpsed his tall, unmistakable form, but he had not so much as glanced her way.

As the carriage drew up to the door, she thought wryly that if she had known she would meet Lord Courtlea so often, she would have carried the boxed brooch in her reticule, ready to pop it into his pocket. Then let him puzzle that out!

CHAPTER 10

The morning promised fair, with spring in the gentian sky and soft airs. Daphne noticed only than it was not raining. She moved through the day in a daze. At morning calls and then at an afternoon concert she was oddly on edge without knowing why. Only when she returned home did she realize she had been expecting to meet the Earl of Courtlea at every turn. She was relieved of course, that she had not met him. Relieved, but unsettled.

Further, when she entered the drawing room before dinner she discovered her Uncle Valentine Burstone, Lord Wentford, standing by the pianoforte. He was beating time with a beefy hand while Sophie, nervously flushed, forged her way through a Haydn sonata.

Perfectly turned out, as always, his light brown hair hardly touched with gray, he presented a handsome, well-filled form. He nodded an indifferent greeting to Daphne, who took a seat beside her aunt.

"Is it not delightful to have your uncle join us?" Elizabeth queried, pink-cheeked, her eyes fixed adoringly on her husband.

"Indeed," responded Daphne, a touch dryly. Since her arrival in London, she had seen her uncle only twice. She knew he absented himself from choice, staying at his clubs, perhaps blaming his wife for their lack of children. Such selfish cruelty caused heartache to the wife who loved him, but he seemed not to care. For that, Daphne could not forgive him.

The music ended on a careful chord. "Delightful! Fine work, miss," said Lord Wentford, lightly clapping his hands. "Bang up to the mark, I must say."

"Thank you, sir," Sophie replied, with the relieved air of having survived a harrowing ordeal. "My touch is improving, I hope. My teacher at home complained that my fingering sounded as though I were wearing Papa's gloves."

The earl's heavy shoulders shook with laughter. "Capital! Another selection, I beg."

"Gladly, sir, but Cousin Daphne is much more able than I. Let me entreat her to play." Sophie smiled at Lord Wentford and managed a beseeching glance to Daphne at the same time.

"Eh?"

The earl's gaze switched to his niece. Once his light blue eyes would have warmed with affection, but he had ceased caring for too long. Mindful, perhaps, of his role of host, he gave a thin smile and crossed the room to her. "Indeed, many a gay tune have we heard from our Daphne. Come, lass, and play for us."

He extended his hand, and Daphne had no choice but to take it. As she exchanged seats with her cousin, Sophie whispered, "Daphne, what of tomorrow and Mr. Merritt? You have not said."

Searching through the sheets of music, Daphne shook her head and murmured, "Later, after dinner."

As she began to play a spirited piece by Johann Christian Bach, former music master to Queen Charlotte, Daphne's conscience pricked her. Edgar Merritt was without a feather to fly with, and totally dependent on his brother's generosity. Such lack of expectations made him a poor candidate as a provider. Was Daphne right to encourage him, or was she using the young man for her own ends?

Oh, fustian! Agitated, she finished the piece with extra vivacity as Clapham informed Lady Wentford that dinner awaited.

At the table, Daphne soon relaxed, drawn by Elizabeth's vivacity. The conversation grew gay and witty, and soon Daphne was laughing as heartily as anyone. Sophie sparkled charmingly, and Daphne noted that Lord Wentford's coolness eased during the sumptuous and merry meal.

"By Gad!" he exclaimed after the cheese had been passed, "I ain't enjoyed myself so much in a parson's age. Come, my three beauties, I intend to show you off tonight. What say you to a visit to the theatre?"

"Oh, the theatre, Lord Wentford!" Sophie burst out, clapping her hands. Daphne caught her eye, and she quickly collected herself and sat demurely as Lady Wentford accepted her husband's invitation. Daphne loved the theatre, and thought it a fitting end to a strained day.

After dinner, as Daphne changed into a gown of cream figured crepe, she pondered a puzzle. Despite Uncle Valentine's neglect and indifference, his wife still loved him. One had only to look into her glowing face to know the truth. Yet Elizabeth was a proud, strong-minded woman. How could she accept such treatment from her husband without returning coldness for coldness, indifference for indifference?

She, Daphne, could never act so. No, never could she imagine loving a man who did not love her.

She became aware of her abigail speaking. "Will you wear the emeralds?" asked Briggs, the brown case in her hand.

"No!"

Briggs stared in astonishment. "They are too grand for tonight," Daphne explained with a smile to soften her vehemence. "The amber will suit, I think."

"As you say, Miss Daphne."

As the abigail brought out the desired earrings and necklace, Daphne quietly slipped the case of emeralds into a drawer of her dressing table.

Barely had she drawn on her gloves when Sophie erupted into the room. "Oh, pardon, I should have knocked," she said airily, "but I am too excited to wait. Oh, I vow you are most elegant, Dee. And am I not a fashion plate?"

With a pleased laugh, Sophie spread her arms and spun about to show off her new gown of patterned white muslin. An undergown of yellow added warmth to the white, and a dainty tucker of lace edged the round neckline. Then, her laughter dying, she stopped at Daphne's side.

"Have you—that is, may I know your decision regarding Mr. Merritt? I vow not to be overset, but to accept your word as being in my best interest."

"My, how beautifully put, Sophie."

"Thank you. I practised it enough. Well?"

Daphne accepted her green velvet evening cloak from Briggs, and picked up her reticule and fan. "Should the weather prove fine, we shall take the air with Mr. Merritt. Now, go fetch your cloak. Uncle Valentine is doubtless waiting below."

Sophie gave her cousin a hug before bounding off. Lord Wentford was indeed waiting, but not impatiently, and, during the drive to Drury

Lane, entertained his ladies with the latest on dits being bandied about in the fashionable clubs. As they entered the theatre, he beckoned to two gentlemen standing at the foot of the stairs leading to the boxes.

"My dears, I have invited these gentlemen to join our party. Miss Daphne Summerhayes, Miss Sophie Summerhayes, may I present Samuel Coffidge, Earl of Tunney, and Thomas Copp, Viscount Launton."

Daphne thought Lord Tunney somewhat resembled his fishy namesake with his sloping forehead, eyes that goggled slightly, and a chin hardly worthy of the name. His dark hair was touched with gray, but his tall frame wore the stylish evening clothes with youthful dash. Daphne met his eyes as he bowed, and saw such a merry twinkle in their sky blue depths that she was immediately charmed.

"By Jove, Miss Summerhayes, I shall be the sinecure of all eyes tonight with such a beauty on my arm," he said in a surprisingly deep voice. "Had I but known of your presence in Town, I would have long ago presented myself at Wentford's door."

Daphne laughed, taking his proffered arm. Gallants often voiced extravagant compliments, usually in a bored, mechanical fashion that irritated rather than pleased her. This gentleman promised a sense of humor, perhaps even of the ridiculous. A welcome change from a certain earl's sarcasm and intensity.

"Tell me, pray, what occupies your lordship's time when you are not presenting yourself at ladies' doors?"

Lord Tunney grinned. "Nothing as daring as revolution, or as interesting as seduction. I am a harmless old fellow." With a flourish, he led her up the stairs behind Sophie and her escort, Lord Launton, a pleasantly attractive young man with brown hair and eyes. He appeared shy, but before the party was seated in their box, Sophie had him talking freely. For once, Daphne blessed her cousin's gift of conversation.

Daphne sat in front with Lady Wentford and Sophie, while the gentlemen behind to give the ladies the best opportunity to see and be seen. Daphne noted with pride and pleasure how Sophie sat, the picture of maidenly decorum, hardly raising her eyes to discreetly study the assemblage. The girl was learning.

The fan-shaped pit was noisy and crowded, the tiers of boxes slowly filling. The ladies' gowns bloomed and swayed like flowers in a summer garden, and a sound like a busy swarm of bees rose to the high curved ceiling.

"Are you familiar with the play the company is presenting?" asked Lord Tunney, leaning forward.

Daphne answered over her shoulder. "Not at all, sir, but it is such a treat to be here, I will enjoy the play no matter what its theme."

"By Jove, that's the ticket. Be sure to hiss the villain when he appears. I understand he is particularly dastardly."

He leaned back, and Daphne, with a chuckle, turned again to scan the crowd. Two boxes almost directly opposite were still empty, but even as she looked, a party entered one of them. The two gentlemen lingered in the back, but the young ladies moved to the rail, laughing and chattering.

One, in lilac satin, and with impossibly blond hair, threw off her swansdown boa, revealing almost all of her generous bosom. Jewels sparkled from her hair, throat and wrists as she bent forward and gaily waved to people below. Her friend, a more demure brunette, but equally revealing in blue, contented herself with sitting down and opening her fan.

"Ooh," whispered Sophie, "even Mama would balk at those gowns, last stare of fashion or no. Who are they?"

Daphne hesitated, considering her cousin's innocence. "Their names are unknown to me," she said at last, "but they are...ladies...who have lost their reputations. Their behavior both betrays and advertises that fact."

Sophie pursed her lips and nodded thoughtfully. "Then their escorts are not true gentlemen, is that so?"

A choked cough from behind warned Daphne that Lord Tunney, will he nil he, was overhearing the conversation. She lowered her voice. "That is as may be. You must know, even in Cornwall, that gentlemen have much more freedom than ladies."

"And a jolly sight more fun," added Sophie.

This time the cough was definitely a smothered chuckle. Daphne opened her fan to hide her own grin.

"Why, dear me!" Lady Wentford leaned forward slightly to peer across the theatre. "Is that not Victor Meritt in that box? The House cannot be sitting tonight."

Daphne's gaze immediately leaped to the box of the two demi-reps. How like the libertine to flaunt Miss Bisely, his light o' love, before all and sundry! But why should Daphne care?

He stood at ease, one white-gloved hand resting on the rail, the lamplight setting his dark hair gleaming, in the box next to the demi-reps. He ignored their loud chatter, did not even glance their way.

"Oh! He is not with—" Daphne flushed with chagrin mixed with an odd thankfulness. Again she had vaulted to a wrong conclusion, and never had she been so delighted to be in error.

The earl sat down, and now Daphne noticed his companion. She was young and beautiful, with a delicate complexion and hair as dark as the earl's own. Her gown of white embroidered silk revealed only the best of taste. A hollow feeling settled in Daphne's middle. Doubtless this was Maryann Bisely.

"I believe that is Prudence Abernathy, Lord Eggersly's daughter, with him," Lady Wentford murmured. "A charming girl."

"Indeed?" Daphne could not hide her surprise. "She is lovely," she murmured inanely, wondering rather bitterly how many paramours the earl had on his string. Somehow she doubted that Lady Prudence, as true a lady as Daphne had ever seen, knew of Miss Bisely. Or knew of his lordship's callous attitude toward marriage. But this lovely girl might change that attitude.

"Surely they are not alone," the countess continued, "unless, of course, their engagement is all but announced. Even so—ah!"

Two other couples, one quite elderly, entered the box. The ladies touched cheeks with each other in a sincere display of affection. Lord Courtlea immediately ceded his seat to one of the ladies, and moved back. As he did, he turned, as if drawn by an unseen force, and looked directly at Daphne. Her breath caught. Though she meant to turn disdainfully away, she could not. The earl's gaze held her spellbound. The buzz of noise faded, and people, the theatre, the world, ceased to exist.

Lord Tunney chose that moment to lean forward. "Miss Summerhayes, I hope you all will be my guests for a little supper after the performance."

"Why…" She blinked, as if awakened from a dream, then turned to glance at him. "Why, yes, if my aunt agrees, Lord Tunney."

Daphne did not hear his address to Lady Wentford. Against her will, her gaze had returned to the box across the way. Lord Courtlea still watched her. His brows rose slightly, perhaps in mute comment of her escort. In command of herself now, she sent him her coldest, most indifferent look, thinking that although he bested Lord Tunney in comely features, the latter outshone him in charm and manners. The earl's faint smile hinted he knew her thoughts, then he turned his handsome profile to her and began conversation with the other gentlemen.

The play started, a comedy depending on the mixing of two babies at birth. Daphne laughed at the humor, some of it quite broad, but, to her annoyance, she was always aware of Lord Courtlea across the way. It was the outside of enough to encounter him so soon after his outrageous performance at Lady Silversby's, and intolerable that she should be so affected. For the rest of the play, she refused to so much as glance in his direction.

The curtain dropped for the final time, the cast took their bows, the audience rose to leave, and Daphne could no longer resist a guarded look. Lord Courtlea's dark head was bent toward Lady Prudence while she smiled adoringly into his eyes. It was pleasant to see two people so enamoured of each other, Daphne assured herself while the gulf yawned within her. Rising, she hoped that Lord Eggersly's daughter might sweeten the earl's temperament as well as alter his opinion of marriage.

"Sophie, have a care for your reticule," warned Daphne, seeing the little purse balanced precariously on the rail. She reached for it, her eyes straying despite herself to the box opposite. At that instant, Lord Courtlea looked up, his gaze met hers, and Daphne knocked the reticule over the railing.

Laughter sprang into his face as the blood rushed to hers. A cry from below proved that the missile had found a human target. Daphne dared not look down, but the whole audience appeared to be staring up at her, and pointing. Her hands flew up to cover her flaming cheeks.

"Oh, dear!" exclaimed Lady Wentford, with a catch of laughter in her voice.

"What the deuce happened?" demanded Lord Wentford. "What happened, I say!"

Sophie attempted an answer, but had to press her fingers to her lips to stop a storm of giggles.

"Launton, go down and retrieve Miss Summerhayes's reticule," ordered Lord Tunney, rightly assessing the situation. Lord Wentford followed Launton to offer apologies and recompense should any be required, while Lord Tunney gently drew Daphne back to his own chair. "Sit down here, Miss Summerhayes, until you recover yourself. Do not be overly concerned, I beg; 'tis only a small mishap."

"Thank you, sir," said Daphne gratefully. "I do feel the worst gudgeon. And I am the one lecturing Sophie on deportment!"

She managed a smile, aware that, while normally she would easily dismiss such a mischance, her embarrassment was worsened a thousand fold because of Lord Courtlea's presence. She could almost hear his amused comments about clumsy country misses.

"You shall have a bite of supper, a glass of wine, and then a good laugh about this," Lord Tunney whispered in her ear. "Let us hope you have not brained a duke. Most have few brains to spare."

Lord Wentford met them in the lobby with word that Daphne's victim, a subaltern in the Lancers, had accepted an apology with a laugh and the hope nothing worse was ever thrown at him. The lobby was rapidly emptying, yet Daphne found herself searching for a certain tall, commanding form. Dismayed, she ceased at once, and allowed Lord Tunney to assist her with her cloak.

Then she saw him, strolling leisurely in their direction. She turned away, not wanting to meet his eyes, fighting down the rush of excitement he always caused in her.

"Good evening, Wentford. I trust the play was to your taste, Lady Wentford?"

"Indeed, yes, Victor. 'Twas light and amusing, which suited our mood to a nicety."

Despite herself, Daphne's head jerked around. Her aunt was smiling as she extended her hand to Lord Courtlea. He bowed, and straightening, sent Daphne a cool, casual glance.

She curtsied, rather automatically, a shiver of tension running along her spine.

"Ah, the Misses Summerhayes. Good evening." He gave the briefest of bows.

For a moment, Daphne had thought he had deliberately sought her out, as he had at the Academy and Lady Silversby's house. His coolness as he turned away persuaded her she was mistaken. Besides, why should he?

"Good evening, Tunney, Launten," he went on. "Had you heard the rumor that the Prince was to attend tonight?"

Lord Wentford merely grunted, but Lord Tunney laughed. "Yes, Courtlea, but I discounted it. I heard he was to be at three other places as well. We came tonight for our own amusement, and I must say, I am enjoying the evening prodigiously."

"As we all are," Daphne agreed warmly, with a smile for her escort. She wondered at the slight edge to his tone. Did some antagonism exist between him and Lord Courtlea?

"We are off for a bit of supper, Courtlea," put in Lord Wentford. "If you are free, come along and join us."

"Yes, do," urged Lady Wentford. Sophie, too, warmly added her voice to the invitation.

Daphne said nothing, hoping her fervent wish that he decline did not show in her expression. Nothing would kill her appetite more quickly than the earl's company.

"Many thanks, but I must beg to be excused," Lord Courtlea answered, with a regret that sounded genuine. "I am with another party."

He glanced over his shoulder to where the group from his box were in conversation with two other well-dressed couples. As Daphne looked, Lady Prudence Abernathy, elegant in a steel- gray peau de soie cloak trimmed with black velvet and silver lace, turned at the same time.

There was no impatience in Lady Prudence's large brown eyes, no annoyance that her escort lingered away from her side. Indeed, her sweet face showed no displeasure at all. Mayhap she was too sure of the earl's affections to be jealous of his absence. As she met Daphne's gaze, she smiled slightly in a reserved but friendly manner.

"Another time, then," Lord Wentford said cheerfully.

"I shall look forward to it, you may be sure," replied Lord Courtlea, smiling suavely.

He took his farewells, and strode away to his friends. There was a small silence, as every eye followed his handsome figure across the floor. Lord Wentford grunted again and reminded them their carriage awaited.

"Well, now, it was strange that he bothered to address us," murmured Lady Wentford as she moved to the door. "Victor rarely bothers with such civilities. He speaks only when there is a point to it."

"Truly, Aunt Elizabeth, I can offer no reason," replied Daphne as quietly. "'Twas not on my or Sophie's account, as he barely acknowledged our presence. But I am more than happy he declined Uncle's invitation. I cannot imagine a more disagreeable supper companion."

"Hmm. That is as may be, but 'tis puzzling."

Daphne silently agreed. Lord Courtlea's pleasant exchange, his smiling charm, seemed at outs with his arrogant, supercilious nature. Nor had he sent any barbs in her or Sophie's direction. Indeed, he had ignored them. What was his purpose, if indeed he had one?

Daphne gave up her speculations as Lord Tunney handed her into the carriage. Glumly she recollected how Lord Courtlea had drawn her awareness to him, and how she had reacted like a green girl, all thumbs and breathlessness. There was one saving grace; she had worn the amber necklace, not the emerald one.

Just as Daphne relaxed, an unpleasant thought struck her. Mayhap Mr. Merritt had invited his brother to join them for their drive on the morrow!

CHAPTER 11

"I vow, 'tis a glorious day," sang Sophie, bursting into Daphne's room and twirling across the carpet. She landed on the bed with a bounce and a laugh. "Do you not think today prodigiously fine, Dee?"

"Oh, prodigious." Despite her misgivings of the coming outing, Daphne could not help but smile. Sophie glowed, and not because her yellow spencer and yellow dotted muslin lent her color. "Is Lord Launton the source of your excessive joy today? He seemed a presentable fellow."

"Oh, I vow he is, and daft about fishing. He talked of little else." Sophie crossed her ankles, casting a sly look at her cousin. "And what of Lord Trout? He seemed quite taken with you, Coz." "Lord Tunney, you scamp," Daphne laughed as she donned the bonnet that matched her honey-gold serge carriage dress. "He is charmingly gallant and not a whit interested in me. In any case, my hands are full overseeing your Season. Did you enjoy your fittings with Madame Renee?"

"Oh, those." Sophie wrinkled her nose.

"Beg pardon?" Daphne paused in reaching for her reticule. "Sophie Summerhayes disdaining any matter of fashion? The girl who lives for the latest style, the newest rage? What has caused this dramatic change of heart?"

"Oh, pray do not tease. I still adore new things, but truly, Daphne, as one matures, other matters become more important." She delivered this wisdom as soberly as any grandmother.

"Why, well said, Cousin. I always knew there was more under your curls than—"

Briggs hurried in, a freshly pressed dress laid carefully over her arm. "A carriage is at the door, Miss Daphne."

Sophie squealed, leaped to her feet and fled. Daphne followed more sedately, breathing a prayer that Lord Courtlea had not accompanied his brother.

She was pleased and relieved that Edgar was quite alone in a gleaming landau. The coachman sat rigidly, large silver buttons glittering on his green, caped greatcoat, and a fine feather cockade to his hat. The groom beside him lacked a cape to his coat, made do with smaller buttons and a more modest cockade, but his posture was every bit as correct. Even the two magnificent horses maintained a rock-still pose, necks proudly curved, their coats with the sheen of ripe chestnuts, black tails and manes combed as fine as any lady's hair.

"Such beauties as the Misses Summerhayes make this fine day even finer," claimed Edgar, handsome in a cinnamon coat and buff breeches, his topboots rivalling a mirror's shine, as he gallantly handed Daphne and then Sophie into the carriage. He carefully spread a rug over their laps, and took the backward-facing seat, his eyes on Sophie.

The horses sprang off at a brisk trot. "What fine animals, Mr. Merritt," commented Daphne, as Edgar seemed content to spend the entire time gazing at her cousin. "Are they Cleveland Bays? I doubt I have seen a better matched pair, or with a finer gait."

"Your praise belongs to my brother, Miss Summerhayes," replied Edgar, sparing her the briefest glance. "Victor breeds these Yorkshire Coach cattle at Mordaine Knowe. I may say without boasting that there are no finer beasts bred anywhere. Should you wish an hour or three's lecture, simply ask Victor about his horses. You may safely nod off, and him none the wiser."

Daphne smiled, Sophie giggled, and a sudden high color suffused Edgar's cheeks. "Oh, I say, Miss Summerhayes, not that I meant you would, or that your company is not—not—that is to say—"

"I understand, Mr. Merritt," Daphne said quickly. Then, to lessen his embarrassment, as well as to satisfy her curiosity, she asked, "Does Lord Courtlea play an active role in raising the horses, or does he relay solely on his managers and trainers?"

"Egad, Miss Summerhayes, managers! Victor is the manager, and is not afraid to act the ostler. Why, when the mares are in season or ready to foal—" He stopped, blushing to a shade of scarlet Daphne had rarely seen in a human face, and turned miserable eyes to her.

"Pardon my language, I beg, Miss Summerhayes. Pray do not think me a bird-wit for dinning ladies' delicate ears with such subjects. If I have offended you—"

"I take no offense, sir, but agree such talk is better left in the stable."

Daphne sat back, letting Edgar and Sophie converse. How strange, this chaperon business! One felt intrusive, like extra baggage, and at the same time, an invisible nonentity. It was an unusual and not altogether pleasant position. She felt older than her twenty-three—almost twenty-four—years. How young Sophie and Edgar seemed!

She thought on Edgar's words. Could one really visualize that elegant, always immaculate lord mucking out a stall, or caring for a frightened mare in foal?

Yes.

Stripped to shirt and breeches, his cravat thrown aside, white linen shirt open over his broad, muscular chest, his arms cradling a laboring mare's head. Dark hair tousled, damp-curled; sweat beading, running sleekly down lean brow, cheek, and strong, columned throat; eyes smoke-gray and steady, lips softly murmuring endearments and pressing against her tingling skin; warm, powerful hands gently stroking, kneading, evoking—

Daphne gasped, her breath coming hard and fast, and firmly closed off her too-active imagination. Somehow her imagery had strayed from a foaling stall to that bedroom where she had been so close to yielding to Lord Courtlea's seduction. Her face flushed hot. Could she never forget that unnerving encounter?

Fortunately her companions had not noticed her agitation, and she saw with a start that the carriage had reached Hyde Park Corner.

"Of a certainty, Mr. Merritt," Sophie was saying, "dogs are a delight. Why, I have the sweetest little spaniel at home—"

Daphne breathed more freely as the carriage swung through the gates into the park. It was early, but other carriages were tooling along the Ring, their occupants eager to enjoy the fine day. The Broad Walk bore a fair traffic of strollers, many of the gentlemen in bright regimentals. Daphne hoped her red cheeks would be laid to the fresh breeze.

"Is the air too brisk for you, Miss Summerhayes?" asked Edgar. "Shall we return?"

"There is no need to be so solicitous, Mr. Merritt. I am hardly in my dotage." She immediately regretted her snappishness, knowing Mr.

Merritt was undeserving of it. "I ride every morning at home," she said, more easily, "in air much more wintry than this. Indeed, if I miss anything more than my family, 'tis my gelding, Golden Sovereign. As for returning," she added with a smile, "you well know that is the last thing you desire."

Edgar answered with a grin and a sheepish glance at Sophie. "You are a brick, Miss Summerhayes. May I suggest a solution, if you wish to ride and Lord Wentford keeps no mounts? My brother keeps several—"

"Oh, no, Mr. Merritt. I could not presume on his lordship's good nature—" Daphne bit her lip. "—on his kindness—" That was no better. "I could not presume on Lord Courtlea."

Edgar looked slightly taken aback at her stumbling refusal. "I assure you, my brother will in no way object. Egad, he will be pleased the cattle will be properly exercised."

"Oh, may we, Dee?" pleaded Sophie, clasping her hands and turning to Daphne. "I should so love a brisk canter. Of course, a carriage drive is splendid, and I am enjoying myself prodigiously, but may we, dearest cousin?"

"There, Miss Summerhayes, how can you refuse that plea?" demanded Edgar, his eager young face clearly showing that *he* could not.

"Well…" Oh, to ride again! To feel free and unworried, if only for a little time. Weakening, Daphne looked from one to the other. The temptation was irresistible.

"Done!" Edgar cried, striking his gloved hands together. "Shall we say tomorrow, and every morning thereafter?"

"I cannot agree for certain, as my aunt may have other plans for us." The fateful words sprang to her lips. "May I send word to you, Mr. Merritt, when we might accept your offer?"

She favored him with such a smile, such a radiant glance, that Edgar seemed quite dazzled, almost forgetting her question. He rallied, however, drew out a little gold pencil and one of his cards, and scribbled on the back.

Daphne could hardly restrain a cry of triumph as she slipped the precious card into her reticule. How very easy it had been! Now, she needed only the means to transport her little parcel to Number 41, Green Street.

* * *

Back in Grosvenor Street, slowly climbing the stairs to change before dinner, Daphne wished she could dash off at once, deliver the gem, and once more know a peaceful mind.

Light footsteps pattered up the stairs behind her. "What is it, Dee?" asked Sophie, slipping an arm about her cousin's waist. "You look most gloomy. Do you so long to ride that you cannot wait another day? I vow, I could go this minute."

The urge to confess was overwhelming. Accustomed to a clear mind and a quiet heart, Daphne had borne apprehension for several weeks. Finding sympathy in her cousin's trusting blue eyes, she burned to share her worry. But the secret was not hers alone; she must consider William.

"No, no, Coz, you are wide of the mark." Daphne forced a smile. "We must be patient, and not let our wants interfere with Aunt Elizabeth's plans. Recollect your presentation to the Queen in less than a fortnight away."

The hint diverted Sophie at once. Daphne was saved for the moment from telling her that they could not accept the loan of Lord Courtlea's horses. "How can I?" Daphne muttered, continuing on her way, "with all that is unresolved between us?"

She felt less than festive when she entered the drawing room. Her uncle was again present, stolid beside the hearth, while Lord Tunney, the Marquis of Silversby, and the Earl of Daly stood by. They bowed as Daphne curtsied. With a special grin, Lord Tunney lifted his hand slightly in salute. Daphne smiled, determined to be cheerful at any cost, then crossed the room to greet Lady Silversby and Lady Daly. Bosom-bows of Lady Wentford, the sumptuously gowned and jeweled ladies shared a sofa.

"Well, here is our chaperon, if a mere chit can deserve that designation," observed Lady Silversby, eyeing Daphne's simple but elegant yellow muslin and yellow net mittens. Her own gown of mauve tissue hung straight on her spare frame. "Do you intend to outshine your charge? Where is the miss—still primping for the fray?"

"Margaret, we know you to be tart-tongued," commented Lady Daly, who was, in her own words, "as plump as a Christmas goose" in rich mulberry satin. "Miss Summerhayes need not suffer a demonstration."

She smiled, shifting her position on the sofa, and nodded to where Lady Wentford and a young man stood before a cabinet displaying a fine collection of bisque figurines. Slightly above middle height, he appeared a thin, self-possessed gentleman of about twenty-five years, with sand-colored hair and eyes. "Lord Hamper is impatient to meet your cousin."

The marchioness snorted. "The fish swims toward the net, you mean, and we all await the coming of the bait."

Daphne could not help but laugh. "Such a harsh description of a come-out, Lady Silversby, but how apt!"

Sophie entered the room, looking entrancing enough to bait any man. The sprigged muslin was no whiter than her skin, the ribbon trim no bluer than her sparkling eyes. A buffont of lace shaded her bosom without concealing it entirely. She came forward quietly, but with a demurely confident air, and curtsied to all.

"Here is our dear Sophie," Aunt Elizabeth said, signalling her to her side. With a telling glance at Daphne, Sophie went.

"Now we may get on with dinner," murmured Lady Daly.

Despite her intention to remain cheerful, Daphne's spirits sagged. Had her come-out occasioned the same feelings and comments? She recalled her delight in the parties, balls, assemblies, picnics,—in short, all the activities offered during the Season. If the Season were nothing more than an excuse to furnish young ladies with husbands, what a disappointment she must have been!

The butler ushered in an elegantly dressed couple unknown to Daphne, yet she thought they seemed familiar. They were above middle age, and had the comfortable look of a long and happily married pair.

"Hah, Eggersly," boomed Lord Wentford. "Thought we'd have to start without you."

"Never!" retorted his lordship with a laugh. "Have you ever known me to miss a meal at one of the best tables in London?"

Everyone joined in the laughter, but the name pricked Daphne's recollection. Lord Eggersly? Was that not— A second couple entered the room. Daphne turned cold, and rose swiftly to her feet.

"Ah, dear Prudence." Lady Wentford kissed Lady Prudence Abernaty affectionately. "And Victor. How happy that you could join us. Allow me to present my niece, Miss Summerhayes. Oh, but you two have already met."

"Indeed, on several occasions," Lord Courtlea said smoothly, "and each more interesting than the last." He smiled, his eyes hooded as he bowed.

"To you, mayhap, my lord," Daphne murmured, shooting him a cool glance. She sketched the merest curtsy and turned to Lady Prudence, who looked lovely in a white gown heavily beaded with crystals.

She was young, about Sophie's age, and smiled shyly. "I understand that you are interested in painting, Miss Summerhayes, and are quite adept."

"Why, indeed," Daphne answered, surprised, "but I assure you my interest far outdistances my talent."

Daphne glanced wonderingly at Lord Courtlea, for only from him could have come such information. He looked down at her in absolute innocence.

He provided the perfect match for Lady Prudence in his immaculate dark coat and pantaloons. Daphne admitted, with a tightening around her heart, that they made a handsome pair, he so tall and dominant, she so dainty with the top of her fashionable ringlets barely reaching his shoulder.

As Clapham announced dinner, Daphne managed a blunt word with her aunt. "Aunt Elizabeth, how is it that Lord Courtlea is here?"

"'Twas your Uncle Valentine's notion. Does it distress you?"

"Of course not," she lied, not meeting her aunt's eyes.

Lady Wentford merely smiled and took the marquis's arm.

"Miss Summerhayes." Lord Tunney offered his arm. "I have the honor of escorting you in to dinner."

His blue eyes were serious, and she wondered if he had sensed something between herself and Lord Courtlea. Certainly, her face must have presented quite a picture when the earl entered the room and she shot to her feet.

"'Tis my pleasure, sir," she said quietly, and meant it.

At the table, however, her preoccupation returned. Lord Courtlea sat opposite and three places down—far enough away she need not converse with him, but too close to ignore. For the moment, he talked easily with the Eggerslys and Lady Silversby. He was far from the arrogant, sarcastic self Daphne recollected so clearly. In fact, he appeared utterly charming.

Daphne's eyes strayed to Lord Hamper, seated farther down the table. He had the habit of throwing back his head and staring down his considerable nose at whomever he addressed. He talked incessantly, while Sophie did little but smile and nod agreeably. She appeared quite captivated, and Daphne wondered if Edgar Merritt had already slipped from her mind.

If only Daphne could so easily rid her mind of his brother! Try as she might to shut him out, she was fully aware of him, hearing the low murmur of his voice and his occasional light laugh. She noted how he bent so deferentially to Lady Prudence sitting quietly at his side.

"Miss Summerhayes," murmured Lord Tunney, "I am using all my wit to win one sparkling look from your lovely eyes, and what I receive is an absent stare."

Daphne almost dropped her soup spoon. "Oh, do pardon me, I beg, my lord. I am somewhat…distracted this evening."

"Indeed? One could hardly guess." He gave a low laugh, and seeing her smile, he nodded toward Lord Hamper and Sophie. "Your pretty little cousin promises to cause a stir this Season, and if she is not enamored of this catch, why, there are always more fish in the sea."

Daphne laughed delightedly. Mayhap Lord Tunney had overheard Lady Silversby's remarks, or mayhap he poked sly fun at his own features. Whatever the cause, his warm humor immediately lightened Daphne's spirits. Why, she was allowing Lord Courtlea to control her as a puppet on a string! She gave the earl his sparkling glance, and a brilliant smile to go with it.

"Steady on, my dear Miss Summerhayes," he protested. "This old bachelor's heart can stand only so much stimulation."

Daphne chuckled, and then came one of those odd silences in general conversation. Lord Daly's words to his host rang clear.

"Demme, Wentford, will you not listen? The rumors grow stronger every day. We will be at war again before the year is ended. Bear me out, Courtlea; you are close to the War Office."

Everyone looked to Lord Courtlea. His eyes narrowed at the older earl's careless words, but he answered with a cool smile.

"I am not privy to confidential information, sir, and if I were, could hardly reveal it. In any case, do you not think such topics are better suited to the passing of the port, after the ladies have withdrawn?"

"Indeed, Courtlea," agreed Lord Tunney unexpectedly, bending forward, "but all of us know of your appointment to head the Prime Minister's committee. Your diligence is most admirable, considering how it must curtail your other…activities."

Daphne gasped. Lord Courtlea's head came up at Lord Tunney's insinuating tone. His expression froze. 'Twas as if the two lords faced each other over drawn swords instead of a dining table. Both wore tight little smiles as eye glared into eye.

Lord Courtlea relaxed first. He gestured airily, and his smile broadened. "Thank you for your concern, Tunney, but I do not find myself hindered in any way. However, sir, should you care to continue our discussion, I am gladly at your service."

The exchange was swift and low-voiced. Daphne doubted if anyone but she was aware that a challenge had just been issued.

Lord Tunney sat back with an expression of disgust. "This matter hardly requires further attention, sir. Not now."

His color still high in his fleshy countenance, Lord Daly cleared his throat and made an abashed gesture of apology. "Forgive me, I beg, Lady Wentford, for mentioning such a worrisome subject."

"Pray rest easy, dear sir," responded the countess. "One can understand your concern. Your son Rodney is home from his regiment, is he not? Such a dear boy. Do give him our warmest regards."

Thus smoothing the waters, Lady Wentford directed a remark to Lord Silversby, and the guests resumed their light chatter. Lord Courtlea, with a smile, turned to Lady Prudence. The Earl of Tunney, however, remained silent.

Daphne waited until the footman had removed her soup plate, then bent close to Lord Tunney's ear. "I have dear friends planning to travel soon to the continent," she murmured. "Do you think, sir, that these rumors of war have substance? Have they spread beyond London?" Lord Tunney helped himself to grilled turbot before he answered. "If you write to your friends soon, Miss Summerhayes, 'twould not go amiss if you mentioned the possibilities," he replied in his usual urbane tones. The incident with Lord Courtlea might not have happened. "I, myself, have no plans to leave our own shores."

Daphne smiled her thanks. "I shall speed a letter to Buckinghamshire tomorrow."

Her Aunt Elizabeth noted the smile, and was pleased. Samuel Coffidge, Lord Tunney, the youngest member of her and her husband's immediate circle, had been abroad for Daphne's Season, and so had not met her then. The lack seemed not to signify, if the earl's warm looks were believed. He would make the perfect husband for Daphne.

Elizabeth glanced to the other side of the table, where Lord Hamper held forth to Sophie. Oh, how much the countess wished for happiness for her two lovely girls! Happiness such as she had known the first years of her marriage.

Her gaze lingered on Courtlea's handsome profile. There was something between him and her niece. Did Daphne know how often her gaze strayed to him? And he, Elizabeth was sure, was aware of those glances. He was the prize of the Marriage Mart, save that he had shown not the slightest intent to marry. No, dear Samuel was the better choice for Daphne. Besides, there was Prudence.

"Indeed! Whatever did you do?" she said to Silversby. She had only the vaguest notion of his conversation, but that was the comfortable thing about the dear old marquis. One need not truly listen, but merely put in the odd word now and then.

She looked the length of the table, but the flowers, the epergne of fruit, the candles, blocked her view of her husband. Nonetheless, a thrill ran through her. Dear Valentine had looked at her with new eyes since the night of the theatre party. Indeed, he had become quite ardent. His words of the previous night, when he had come to her bed, were treasured in her heart.

"By Gad, Eliza," he had murmured, "have I been totally blind, or have you magically turned back the years? 'Tis like first we met, my love, save that I believe you more beautiful, more gracious, more charming than ever."

She knew the cause of her blooming. She had young people about her again, and she was happy. Did her dear Daphne know how much she brightened this old house? And Sophie, too, once she had outgrown her shyness.

The dinner had progressed smoothly, as did all functions at Wentford House. Now, with the pineapple cream, fruit, cheese, and nuts concluded, Elizabeth rose gracefully to her feet.

"Come, ladies, let us leave the gentlemen to their port and wicked stories. We shall await you, sirs, in the drawing room."

All the gentlemen rose, but Lord Wentford fairly sprang to his feet, and with great gallantry, escorted his wife to the door. "Eliza, my love," he murmured, pressing her hand, "we shall not keep you waiting long. You have my word on it."

"See to it, sir," she whispered in return, with a mischievous grin, "and your reward will be great."

He laughed, such a boyish chuckle that Daphne looked at him in amazement. Elizabeth merely smiled at her, and as the earl returned to the table with a decidedly jaunty step, led the ladies from the room.

"Dear Aunt," Daphne murmured in the passageway to the drawing room, "do my eyes deceive me? Do I see a reconcilement between you and Uncle Valentine? Believe me, were it so, nothing could delight me more."

"One might say there has been a reunion of sorts." Elizabeth blushed like any young bride. "Oh, my dear Daphne, only one thing might make my happiness complete; to see you suited with a life partner. Is there yet no one to whom you would give your heart, no gentleman who occupies your thoughts?"

"Come, come, Eliza," cried Lady Silversby, marching to the most comfortable chair. "My health and inclination demand a tot of brandy after my dinner."

Daphne welcomed the interruption, for she could hardly admit that the face of one man hovered constantly at the edge of her mind. Not while the girl rumor said was to be his wife smiled invitingly at her from across the drawing room.

Daphne answered the smile, sat down beside Lady Prudence on the brocade sofa, and mentioned the play they had seen.

"Oh, I enjoyed it," Lady Prudence answered eagerly, "though Mama thought it a bit broad. But one must make exceptions in the city, musn't one?"

"Do you not care for city life?" Daphne asked.

"'Tis fine for a short while, but I much prefer the country." She dipped her head shyly. "I like nothing better than to set up my water colors and sketch in the open air. I have yet to brave any attempt at oils."

"Oh, pray do not fear oils!" Daphne smiled. "They are much easier to handle and much more forgiving than water colors. When I make a mistake, I simply wipe it off."

"Indeed?" Lady Prudence regarded Daphne with shining eyes. "Oh, then I shall start tomorrow. Tell me, pray, have you attempted a portrait?"

While they talked as easily as old friends, Daphne found herself liking Lady Prudence immensely. Her sweet, pleasant nature matched her beauty. She was neither overproud nor condescending. In all, she was much too good for Lord Courtlea.

He opined a woman needed only babies and a home to be content. How cruel to treat this gentle creature so! Daphne bit her lip against the urge to warn Lady Prudence to take care.

Yet when the gentlemen rejoined their ladies, Lord Courtlea was still at his most charming. He fetched a cushion for Lady Daly's back, traded gibes with Lady Silversby, and had Aunt Elizabeth and Lady Prudence both laughing. Daphne watched and listened, almost captured by the magnetism of the man.

He did not speak directly to Daphne until he, Lady Prudence, and the Eggerslys took an early leave, pleading another engagement. To Daphne's annoyance, her heart speeded its beat and her breath quickened as he approached. She rose from her seat and absent-mindedly picked up a Sevres figurine from a rosewood table. The little figure, a blushing shepherdess, felt cool in her fingers.

"Miss Summerhayes," he murmured, bending his head toward her, "thank you for your attentions to Lady Prudence. She is often somewhat shy in company, but she tells me she has greatly enjoyed herself tonight. For that, pray accept my gratitude."

"Lady Prudence is delightful," Daphne answered, telling herself how fine it was to see a gentleman so concerned. The figurine rocked a little as she replaced it on the table.

"And as good as she is beautiful," he said, his eyes twinkling as though he knew her thoughts.

Was he mocking her? "Too good—" she blurted, and stopped.

"For the likes of me?" he finished.

He laughed gently, irresistibly, and despite her guard, Daphne's lips twitched in response. "You rogue," she murmured, and blushing, laughed with him. "You have learned flattery and compliments have no effect in winning my regard. Are you now bringing excellent manners into the fray?"

His smile turned irrepressibly wicked. "Ah, so there is still a battle between us. Recollect, I pray, that I am named Victor with good reason."

"Nay, sir, must you win every lady's approval? Seemingly you have already made a fair conquest." She looked meaningfully toward Lady Prudence.

Courtlea did not look around. Instead, he stood easily before Daphne, absently toying with the gold seal on his watch chain. The gesture reminded her of the emerald that had once hung there. Her heart guiltily skipped a beat.

"My blunt Miss Summerhayes," he murmured, his eyes glimmering with serious intent that his smile could not hide, "'tis not approval I hope to win from you."

Daphne caught her breath as the earl took her hand and raised it. Her net mitten was a frail barrier to the warmth of his hand. Ignoring the custom that the gentleman's lips stop short of the lady's hand, he deliberately kissed Daphne's bare fingers. Then, with a bow and a warm, caressing look, he turned away.

Daphne watched him leave with Lady Prudence and the Eggerslys. Her fingers tingled from the warm press of his lips, her mind swirled in confusion. Tonight she had seen a different side of Lord Courtlea; kind, entertaining, engaging and humorous. Only that brief exchange with Lord Tunney had called out his arrogance, and in fairness, the older earl had initiated it.

Had she been so wrong in her judgment of him? Had she leaped too quickly, and held too stubbornly, to her conclusions?

"What a charming fellow young Courtlea is."

She looked up. Lord Tunney stood by her side, smiling, but with a sharp edge to it. "All the ladies especially favor him."

"I have felt that you do not care for him, my lord."

"We have strongly differing political views, and more than once have been face to face on opposite sides. Still, that is of no account." He hesitated, as if uncertain, swirling the brandy in his glass. "May I speak freely, Miss Summerhayes?"

"Pray do, sir,"

"Pray believe 'tis generally known that Courtlea is a noted collector of hearts. He has great charm; few ladies can withstand it. He leads them on as long as they amuse him, and then they see him no more.

"I shock you," he added as she winced. "Believe me, Miss Summerhayes, I dislike talking so of another gentleman. It smacks of vicious gossip, which I deplore, but I speak from first-hand knowledge. I was abroad at the time, but heard the full tale from my family. He callously broke the heart of a relative of mine, a gentle, delicate girl. We feared for her life."

"Oh, how dreadful!" Daphne well believed how the handsome earl could possess a girl's mind. She sat down abruptly in her chair. "I trust she survived."

"Yes, but not until two years had passed."

"Two years!" Daphne gripped the chair arms and looked up at the earl. "Why do you tell me this sad story, my lord?"

His plain features showed his distress. "I have never spoken of it before, Miss Summerhayes. Pray believe I do not go about speaking against Courtlea. However, I felt compelled to reveal this unhappy occurrence to you, even though my cousin is now happily married."

Daphne sat silenced by this revelation of Lord Courtlea's character, and chagrined that Lord Tunney should think she had fallen under the earl's spell. What was she to believe? Was Lord Courtlea's manner this evening a mere sham? Did he want to win her heart, merely to prove that he could?

CHAPTER 12

As the hackney rattled toward Finsbury Square, Daphne mulled over her aunt's statements at breakfast that morning regarding Alice Coffidge, Lord Tunney's unfortunate relative, and the dashing Courtlea.

The Season before Daphne's come-out, Alice had developed a passion for the young earl, making, as Elizabeth said, a cake of herself. Finally she was hustled off to the country, reportedly suffering from brain fever. One rumor claimed Courtlea innocent of anything save being too handsome and too charming. Another alleged that he had indeed taken advantage of the besotted girl. Courtlea neither denied nor admitted the affair, and only a very brave man, or a very foolish one, would take him to task on it.

"So I must decide for myself," Daphne murmured. "Is he a blackguard, or not?" No one heard, as she was alone, having left Sophie to the modiste, and Briggs to her mending.

The hackney stopped. Daphne got out, bid the jarvey wait, and went into Lackington's book store. Some texts her papa had ordered were packaged and waiting at the circular counter. Never able to simply run in and out of a book store, Daphne left them there while she browsed in the travel section.

She was deep into a book on Tuscany when she became aware of a presence. She glanced up, and her breath caught in her throat. Lord Courtlea, immaculately turned out in mulberry coat and fawn pantaloons, negligently leaned on his gold-topped cane, studying her with an indulgent smile.

"La! You startled me, my lord. How long have you stood there?"

"Long enough to wonder if you intended to read that tome completely through," he replied with a laugh. Straightening, he gestured, palm up, at her book. "Pray allow me to purchase it for you to read in comfort at home."

Daphne jerked the volume beyond his reach and clasped it to her bosom. "Indeed not. I shall buy it myself if I want it."

Amused astonishment flashed across Lord Courtlea's features. He lowered his hand, and Daphne blushed at the vehemence of her reaction to a suggestion any mannered gentleman might have made.

"This one is not for me in any case," she added lamely, "but for a friend. She and her parents plan to travel through Italy soon, if war does not intervene."

Lord Courtlea nodded, and Daphne hoped he would leave. Or stay.

"'Tis an interesting country, Italy," he said, showing no sign of leaving, "if one enjoys ruins and scenery."

"Oh, indeed, 'tis noted for its beauty," Daphne quickly agreed, "and for music and art and sculpture and fine buildings and—and—" She bit her lip to stop herself from gibbering, and noticed his small smile. "My enthusiasm may amuse you, sir, but it is genuine. I was to accompany my friends to the Continent."

"And now you are not?"

Daphne could not repress a sigh as she ran her fingers over the book's green leather binding. "I was needed to oversee Sophie's come-out. Mayhap another time..."

Why was she explaining herself to him? She closed the book with a snap and added it to three others she had chosen for herself. "Now, sir, pray excuse me."

Lord Courtlea did not budge, but stood absently tapping his cane's gold top against one gloved palm. His wide shoulders almost filled the space between the rows of shelves and effectively blocked her escape.

"I cannot see you accepting such a change of plans without protest," he said easily. "Was no one else capable of the Herculean labor of chaperoning Miss Sophie? Or did you care whether you went to Italy or not?"

"Oh, I cared!" she assured him warmly. "In fact, I was so sunk in disappointment that I walked into the path of a speeding carriage. Had the driver not been so expert, I might well have lost all chance to see Italy, or indeed, to see another day."

"Thank God, then, for that skill." He looked down into her eyes, his own sober. "I shudder to think of you hurt, or worse, and it my fault."

His unexpected words and the quiet sincerity in which they were said took her breath away. He was as charming as he had been last evening, and, in her own defense, she distrusted that charm.

"'Twas my fault, too," she murmured at last. She glanced up, and despite her resolution to beware, her gaze locked with his. Swiftly came the sensation of being lost in their clear depths. She felt suddenly hollow, yet filled with a trembling warmth.

"Pardon, I beg, for disturbing you, sir and madam."

Daphne blinked, the trance broken. A plump gentleman in a raffish striped coat with its collar to his ears wanted past them to the shelves beyond.

Without a word, the earl stepped back, and Daphne read nothing in his schooled features. She looked away, reminding herself that the earl had no knowledge of her as Flora, no awareness of shared intimacies, and she must keep it that way.

"Your face betrays you, Miss Summerhayes," Lord Courtlea drawled when the portly book-seeker had passed.

Daphne tensed, but coolly raised her brows. "I do not understand you, sir."

"Knowing your opinion of young gentlemen, I can see the last place you would expect to find one is in a book store." He nodded in pretended earnestness, humor glimmering in his eyes. "I assure you," he went on, "I have been known to open a book rather more than once a year, although some persons of my acquaintance consider even once to be excessive."

He smiled charmingly, and Daphne found herself smiling back. "'Tis your fault, however, Miss Summerhayes, that I find myself thumbing through these stacks this morning. Last evening you recommended some books to Lady Prudence, and I was dragooned into searching them out."

"Oh, I see." Indeed, she saw much. He was so infatuated with Lord Eggersly's daughter that he ran errands for her that a servant with a list in his hand could as easily accomplish! With trembling fingers, and fiercely berating herself for weakening to his lordship's allure, Daphne picked up her books.

"Allow me, Miss Summerhayes," Lord Courtlea said, smoothly relieving her of her burden, and striding off through the crowd to the counter. Daphne could do nothing else but follow at his heels. She arrived to hear him order that all her purchases, including her papa's botanical text books, be put to his account.

"Really, sir, I cannot allow this," she protested, aghast at the thought of being in his debt. A gentleman might offer to buy one book simply to be courteous, but this was far over the mark. To the clerk, she added, "I shall pay for these now."

The middle-aged clerk, his pencil poised over his receipt book, blinked from one to the other through his thick spectacles. "Uh—well, of course, madam, if you wish. The sum is—"

"Madam wishes nothing of the sort," Lord Courtlea interrupted. "Do as I said, at once, and then have someone bring the books to my carriage. Now, Miss Summerhayes, if you please." He offered his arm.

"I do not in the least intend—" she began hotly, then realized she had an audience. All the customers at the counter were watching the little scene with interest, and the group was growing. Lord Courtlea stood with his arm still cocked, seeming oblivious to anyone but herself.

She glared at him, determined he should not again force her into meek obedience. He gazed back with that amused, slightly bored air that always caused Daphne's spine to stiffen. Leaning over the counter, she transferred her glare to the flustered clerk.

"Listen to me," she hissed. "On no account do you obey his lordship. Put my books to Lady Wentford's charge, and deliver them to Wentford House. Do you understand?" Her aunt would not mind, and Daphne would repay her later.

Without awaiting his answer, Daphne turned and faced Lord Courtlea. "Thank you, my lord, for your most generous offer," she said clearly for the benefit of her audience. "It grieves me most deeply that I must decline it. Good day, sir." She gave her brightest, sweetest smile to the earl's astounded face, and marched from the shop.

Barely had she reached the pavement when he was at her side. "Demme, Miss Summerhayes," he said, laughter mixing with frustration in his voice, "Why must you always present your back to me? 'Tis a charming back, I grant, but definitely daunting."

Daphne gazed straight ahead, not slowing her steps until she reached the hackney she had bid wait for her. "When a conversation is ended, one leaves, my lord." She slanted an irritated glance at the earl as the jarvey reached down and opened the carriage door. "Or must one beg permission to depart from your august presence?"

He let the barb pass with only a slight raising of his brows. "Not long ago you cried all town gentlemen rag-mannered nodcocks. Yet, when I courteously attempt to prove you wrong, you will have none of it. Is that how you prove your own superior manners, Miss Summerhayes?"

When she did not rise to that bait, he gestured with his cane toward a landau pulling up to the curb. "Allow me, I beg, since you are alone, to escort you home in my carriage. 'Tis far more comfortable than this hack."

Daphne drew a deep breath. Why did he not leave her in peace? Standing close, with that irresistible smile, a warm and caring expression on his handsome features—why, any woman would be enchanted to have him as an escort.

As Lady Prudence was doubtless enchanted, and mayhap young Alice Coffidge as well.

"Many thanks, my lord, but comfort is never my priority." Grimly, Daphne nodded to the jarvey, briskly gathered her skirts and stepped into the hackney.

The earl muttered something under his breath, and before she knew his intention, had followed her, slamming the door behind him. The hackney started off at an easy gait, and Daphne gaped as he settled on the backward seat, facing her. Her heart quivered with a sudden feeling of entrapment.

"My lord, I did not ask for your company," she began, swallowing an urge to leap from the carriage.

He raised a casual hand. "Let us leave off such petty fencing. You have some deeper resentment toward me, Miss Summerhayes, that prevents civility between us. Pray enlighten me, now that you cannot run off."

Deeper resentment? How could she reveal to him that she was a thief, tortured by conscience, agonizing over how to return the booty? Could she tell him how she trembled whenever he was near? That he roused fires in her; that she imagined herself in his arms, balanced on the knife-edge of surrender? All this, while confused as to his true character. And not least, while he was courting another lady.

"Sir, on the several times we have met, I have done my best to show that I did not wish to extend the acquaintance. Yet you persist in addressing me. Pray enlighten me as to your motives."

"Motives? I have none beyond the impulse of the moment."

Courtlea realized he had spoken impulsively, and worse, had acted on an unwise impulse when he saw her absorbed in that book. The light had reflected from the page into her face, lending it a creamy golden tint. In her yellow pelisse, matching hat with green feathers curling under its brim, she seemed Spring incarnate. He could no more help going to her than he could help drawing breath.

Her chin jerked up, and he automatically braced himself.

"Then, sir, I can only believe that either your pride blinds you to rejection or you enjoy suffering put-downs." Her voice was unusually harsh, and her eyes glittered with green fire. "Or, sir, mayhap you cannot believe a woman exists who does not yearn for a closer acquaintance with the notoriously eligible Lord Courtlea. I assure you, sir, I am that woman."

She stopped, paling suddenly, and caught her bottom lip between her teeth. He sat silent and still, as still as possible against the lurching of the carriage. He had pressed her too far, insisting on buying her books when she so obviously did not wish it. He had always used gifts to selfishly further his own aims, but this time he had merely wanted to please someone with presents she would enjoy.

Instead, his ham-handed action had forced yet another confrontation with her independent nature. He should have stayed with his plan of having her come to him. His miscalculation had simply strengthened her will to resist him.

She gazed past him, her hands tightly laced in her lap, as if bravely awaiting the fury a deeply insulted lord must rain on her. He let the seconds tick by, marked by the clip-clop of hooves.

"I vow, Miss Summerhayes," Courtlea said quietly, "you speak your mind more freely than any lady of my acquaintance. That was quite a facer you dealt me. Yet, if those are your sentiments, I cannot fault you for delivering them."

Miss Summerhayes, obviously amazed at such a mild response, slowly turned her eyes to him. Indeed, it had cost him to temper his anger, but what shocked him more was the deep hurt her words had caused. He cleared his throat.

"Are they indeed your sentiments?" he asked, almost forcing out the words. "Do you truly find me so reprehensible?"

A quiet "Yes" would have killed his desire for her in an instant. His pride could take only so much. There were other women than this one, as beautiful and far more open to his hand.

But Miss Summerhayes did not utter that fateful word. Her glance flew like a trapped bird—to her hands, the roof of the carriage, the clouded window—everywhere but to him. Her pale skin flushed rosily, and he read confusion and uncertainty in her expressive features. His hopes stirred and flared.

The hackney stopped before Wentford House. He moved to sit beside her, and dared to lightly turn her chin so she faced him. "Your answer, I beg. I know you too well to doubt it will be the truth."

She lifted her beautiful eyes to him, not denying his touch, but searching inwardly for her own truth. Her lips trembled, and he leaned forward, swept with a desire to kiss their sweet softness.

"My—my lord," she began haltingly, and he saw she was unaware of his intent to kiss her, so absorbed was she in finding the right words. "I fear my tongue sometimes has a mind of its own. It speaks more harshly than I intend. Too, I sometimes—I often—form opinions too quickly, and then cling to those opinions, rather stubbornly, mayhap, despite contrary evidence. In this case, your encounters with my brother—"

She stopped, flushing, and looked out the window as if only now realizing the coach had stopped.

Courtlea frowned, puzzled. "Surely that don't still rankle, Miss Summerhayes. 'Twas his boyish temper, and naught came of it, although I had the right to challenge him."

"Yes, and I thank you, sir, for your forbearance." Miss Summerhayes opened her reticule and fumblingly withdrew some coins. "My aunt will be concerned over my long absence," she said hurriedly. "Good day, Lord Courtlea."

"But wait a little, I beg!"

Before he could move to assist her, Miss Summerhayes bolted from the carriage and threw the fare to the jarvey. Courtlea was an instant behind her but she was too swift for him. Clapham opened the door as her foot touched the top step and she darted inside the house as though hounds of hell were at her heels.

As an impassive Clapham closed the door without a word, Daphne leaned against the wall, feeling thoroughly wrung out. Then, thinking the earl might follow her, she peered through the sidelight.

Lord Courtlea stood on the pavement, looking after her. He shook his head, but whether in anger, amusement, or futility, Daphne could not be certain. Then he climbed into his own carriage which had followed the hackney, and drove away.

He was no saint, she thought, and yet, was he too great a sinner? Pride and arrogance he had in plenty, but he had shown kindness at times, and gentleness. Certainly her hasty, flustered words had brought hurt, not simply wounded pride, to his clear eyes.

She felt like the trapeze artiste at Astley's circus, swinging from one extreme to the other. Hate or love. Never had she dreamed that the two could combine, and all for the same man.

CHAPTER 13

Daphne awoke to a storm howling in from the Channel that afternoon, with roaring winds and driving sleet. The wild weather continued all the next day, and no one stirred far from a blazing fireside. Sophie showed her sketches of a wardrobe fit for a princess, then taxed Tyson's patience by trying on every gown and bonnet she owned. Daphne caught up her letter writing and tried to banish the white, stricken face of Lord Courtlea from her mind. The hurt glimmering in his eyes haunted her. She did not know what to make of him, or of her own mixed feelings.

During the night the storm finally blew itself out. As Daphne sorted her mail after breakfast, the quiet was almost eerie. She opened a hand-delivered note first. Edgar Merritt desired to call on her that morning if it were convenient. Daphne thoughtfully tapped her fingers on the note. He wished to see her, not Sophie. Well, she would be in to him.

Mr. Merritt was very prompt. Daphne awaited him in the drawing room with her embroidery, not because she particulary enjoyed needlework, but because the dining room chairs at Weldern Manor needed new seats.

"Miss Summerhayes," Edgar began, a frown of great determination between his dark brows, "since our most enjoyable drive some days ago, I have come to realize why you chose not to favor me with your company on my morning rides."

Daphne's hands stilled on the piece of linen in her lap. "You have, sir? Pray sit down and tell me the reason."

"'Tis not dislike of my person, I humbly believe," he announced, gingerly settling on the edge of a sofa, "but the cowhanded way in which I extended the invitation. Ladies of your tender sensibilities cannot be treated so. Delicacy demands a reiteration, nay, many reiterations, until you are assured, Miss Summerhayes, that I desire your company above all things."

Daphne smiled and took several small stitches. How foolish of her to think this innocent boy suspected her involvement, if such a muddle could be called so, with his brother. "And my cousin's company as well, of course."

Edgar blushed and heaved a deep sigh. "'Pon my honor, madam, she is a cracking good sort. Why, one can actually talk to her."

Hardly an encomium, Daphne thought, repressing a broader smile, but indicative of friendship, not passion. "Time presses so, Mr. Merritt, what with our social duties, leaving little or no chance for riding. And too," she went on carefully, "we do not wish to inconvenience Lord Courtlea. Would he not want to—to oversee us, that we take due care of his beasts?"

Edgar's handsome face went blank, and Daphne feared he thought she slyly connived for his brother's presence. Doubtless many ladies schemed for Lord Courtlea's attentions, and she winced to be included in that throng.

"I had not thought to include him..." Edgar picked up a strand of colored floss and trailed it through his fingers.

"Just so," Daphne put in hurriedly. "As it is, we still keep country hours, and prefer to ride very early, well before breakfast. I doubt that would suit you."

Edgar's face lit like the sun. "Oh, no, indeed, Miss Summerhayes, but that is capital! Egad, quite the thing, in fact."

He had disposed of all her excuses, and now looked hopefully at her. Daphne bent to her stitching, finishing a pink rose while her mind worked as busily as her fingers. Mayhap Lord Courtlea was behind this invitation. He might think she would refuse him, but would accept from Edgar. Mayhap he intended to join them. A quick rush of pleasure took Daphne by surprise. A week ago she had not wanted to set eyes on that contentious lord again. Now, because of a few minutes in a hackney, she grew warm from head to heels at the notion of seeing him.

Daphne flung her embroidery into the work box on the small table at her elbow. "Your brother is very generous to us, Mr. Merritt. We shall be pleased to join you tomorrow morning."

"Oh, capital, Miss Summerhayes! Capital!"

Daphne laughed at Edgar's exuberance. One would think she had given him a priceless gift. She reflected that, although no great heiress, Sophie could expect a fair marriage portion, and several gentlemen, including Lord Launton, Lord Hamper, and Mr. Sutton, called frequently. Sophie was equally charming to all. Daphne had watched when Edgar Merritt happened to be one of the swarm, and had decided Sophie showed him no preference whatever. Sophie's heart was still her own.

That afternoon, at Lady Thornwold's reception, Daphne forged through the crush, frankly admitting to herself she looked for Lord Courtlea. He was not there, and Daphne's festive spirit dimmed a little. He was absent, too, from a rout that evening.

"I am being the worst fool," she muttered, as she lingered in the powder room. "He is doubtless escorting Lady Prudence somewhere."

Did he treat Lord Eggersly's daughter as he did the servant Flora? Did he kiss her, touch her, make love to her? And did the shy, reserved lady respond eagerly, receiving him with moans of pleasure?

Daphne closed her eyes and pressed her fingers to her temples. What madness possessed her to harbor such thoughts?

"Are you ill, madam?" asked a gentle voice.

Daphne opened her eyes. The maid tending the ladies in the powder room stood at her side. "No, I am well." Daphne managed a smile, and rejoined the party.

Then one of her whist partners mentioned that the new parliamentary commission headed by young Courtlea was doing a cracking job.

"Ah, so that is why he refused my invitation," said her hostess, trumping the trick. "He will be too busy for frivolity."

Daphne overtrumped, and her bright smile was not just for winning the hand. Busy or no, mayhap the earl would find time for an early ride in the park.

The next morning, Daphne was dressed and ready long before Sophie came to her room. "Mr. Merritt is here, Dee," she said excitedly. "I peeked out from a front window. I vow, he is an excessively handsome gentleman, yet not bumptious with it. Not like Lord Courtlea, who quite gives me a fit of the dismals with his stare. Am I presentable, do you think?" She twitched the skirt of her new chocolate brown habit.

Daphne laughed as they descended the stairs. "I doubt Mr. Merritt will find any flaw." She wanted to ask if Lord Courtlea were there too, but kept the words back. For all Sophie knew, Daphne still harbored only disdain and dislike for the earl.

In the hall, Edgar waited, crop in hand. In the dim light, clad in buff breeches and a dark green coat, he looked so much like his brother that Daphne caught her breath.

Another rider waited outside, but he was a groom, holding the reins of three other horses. Daphne scolded herself for building hopes on mere conjecture.

Her spirits lifted when she caught sight of the mounts Edgar had provided. Daphne never could resist a fine horse, and she loved her grey gelding, Emir, on sight. Its pretty face and huge brown eyes betrayed its Arabian blood. Sophie squealed her delight with her chestnut mare, which rolled its eye but stood patiently as the groom helped Sophie into the side-saddle.

Daphne chafed with impatience until they clattered into Hyde Park and reached Rotten Row. So few riders were about that Daphne ignored the custom of always walking one's horse on the Row, and let out her mount. Emir took off, as eager for a gallop as she. Daphne almost felt the cobwebs blow from her mind in the fresh spring air, and she laughed aloud.

"Oh, Mr. Merritt," Daphne cried, when at last she reined in, "what a goer it is! How wonderful to ride again! I am in your debt, sir."

"Oh, and I, Mr. Merritt," Sophie agreed, while Edgar beamed from astride his prancing black steed.

For the rest of the week, no matter how filled the days with assemblies, receptions, balls, and routs, Daphne made sure they never missed their morning ride. Lord Courtlea did not join the little group, and instead of growing indifferent, Daphne found herself becoming edgier, more impatient with every day. She did not try to explain her reasons, even to herself. She almost forgot about the emerald brooch that still waited to be returned. Only her morning rides offered perfect release.

One lovely morning, with grass and leaves burgeoning in the sunlight, they stayed later than usual. Despite Edgar's uneasy urging to leave, Daphne eyed the open ground and stands of trees away from the busy Row.

"Come, I must have one more good gallop," she decreed, setting off at once. Emir flew smoothly over the grass, driving deeper into the parkland. The Serpentine glimmered through trees clothed in soft green. Daphne lifted her face to drink in the wind. Oh, how she had missed this, galloping alone, no one near, all sight of the city obscured. She might be at home, these trees part of Howey Woods.

Hoofs pounded behind her, but she pressed on, riding easily, in no mood to stop or have Edgar pass her. His larger steed was gaining, however, its black head and flaring nostrils almost abreast of her. In a trice, it had surged past, and without so much as a cry of warning, Edgar leaned sideways and caught her bridle reins.

"Leave off!" Daphne shouted, surprised and outraged. "Leave off, I say!"

The horses jolted to a stop, and now Daphne realized Edgar's coat had changed color from corbeau to black. His shoulders appeared broader, his demeanour more aggressive.

"Oh, 'tis you!" she gasped, even before Lord Courtlea turned to face her. The earl's eyes widened as he recognized the rider in the bottle green habit. For a moment, he appeared as shocked as she. Then came the ironic glance she knew so well.

"Deuce take it! You seem to have an unfortunate way with horses, Miss Summerhayes." His mount pranced sideways, and Emir perforce followed, since its reins were clamped in Lord Courtlea's fist.

"How so?" Daphne demanded, vainly trying to free the bridle. "May not a lady ride at her own gait without being pulled down? Does some law determine the speed one may travel in this park? Release my reins at once, sir."

The earl stilled his steed, a twin of Edgar's. Emir stopped too, swinging close enough to bring Daphne's leg against that of Lord Courtlea. She started as the hard muscles of his thigh pressed against her before the horses moved apart. The touch was fleeting, but intolerably intimate.

"What! Bruising along over this broken ground, with no escort?" Lord Courtlea drawled. "Are you claiming you did not lose control of your animal?" His lips twisted into the cynical smile she recollected. "I swear, Miss Summerhayes, you go to any lengths to avoid responsibility! I have saved you from hurt, if not from death, for the second time, and instead of rendering thanks, you fly into a pet, and rail at me."

"Sir! I had no need of salvation. My mount was not running away, but enjoying a fine gallop." She stopped and bit her lip. He acted as though he had forgotten those tense moments in the hackney. Or was he simply wary, having revealed so much? He was too close, too handsome, too overpowering. She felt the familiar clench of her stomach, the excited thrill along her nerves.

A swift glance behind her showed no sign of Sophie or Edgar. She was quite alone, behind a screen of trees, with Lord Courtlea. His deliberate look, the concerned tilt of his head, mocked her protestations that she had been in no danger, and she would not add to his amusement by arguing further.

"Pardon me, I beg, my lord," she said stiffly, "for such an unseemly brangle. Whether I was in need or not, I must thank you for your good intentions."

The earl's smile widened as he studied her set mouth and uptilted chin. "I am leery of your apologies, Miss Summerhayes, but I am quite willing to accept your word. I regret if I interrupted your gallop without cause. May we cry a draw, and may I escort you back to your party?"

He released her reins, and at this gesture of good will, Daphne gave a little nod. "Yes, my lord, to both," she said, relaxing a little. She gave him a small careful smile.

"How is it, sir, that you are the one who comes to my rescue? Such a coincidence is remarkable." Had he watched Edgar, Sophie, and herself, unseen, all these mornings? Her body grew warm at the thought of his eyes studying her.

"Coincidences *are* remarkable." He made no move to ride on, but sat easily on his black, watching her with a keenness that stretched her nerves. "I always ride at this time, and my eye was drawn by your mount. I swear I have the blood brother of your gray in my stables. I followed, and when I saw no one attending you, I naturally assumed you to be in difficulty."

He shrugged as they turned their horses to walk back, although a grin tugged at his mouth and his eyes teased her. "Of course, had I recognized the redoubtable Miss Summerhayes, I would have gone about my business."

"I doubt that, sir. I think you would help any lady in distress." Daphne spoke without thinking, then wondered why she had. With his reputation, he was as likely to present as much danger as salvation to any lady.

Courtlea laughed. "Ah, but to what end, Miss Summerhayes?" And watched her blush. "No matter, you are quite safe with me."

He lied, of course. The familiar tightening in his gut told him that. He stifled a surge of impatience. Never had he spent such time or planning to win a woman. Not for worlds would he again live through her denunciations in that rackety old hackney, but now he knew she was softening to him.

"You ride well, Miss Summerhayes. Many ladies come here merely to be seen, and their poor mounts must content themselves with a walk."

Her face lit with enthusiasm. "Riding is one of my favourite activities, my lord. My mind is freed of worry and fret with a good gallop."

Perhaps she did not know how damnably attractive she looked, her cheeks gently flushed, her eyes brilliant, and a smile curving her lips. She sat her mount with practised ease, her slender body erect, yet moving as one with her horse. His eye had caught her at once. Had her bright hair not been hidden by that black snood affair, he would have known her immediately. What lucky chance had given him this golden opportunity? He eyed the small copse of trees ahead. His muscles tensed as though to sweep her from the saddle. Another few yards and he would suggest they dismount to rest the horses.

Daphne glanced at Lord Courtlea riding silently beside her, a slight smile on his lips. The only clear sounds were the thud of their horses' hooves and the raucous cries of a pair of rooks overhead. The hum of the city came faintly to Daphne's ears, reminding her of Sophie and Edgar waiting. All too soon she and the earl would not be alone. She wanted to stop time, to dismount under the trees. What then? His strong arms around her, his mouth hotly seeking— No, she must not! Think of something else!

Desperately, she opened her lips to thank him for lending his fine horses to her and Sophie. Surely that was a safe topic! Then she recollected Lord Courtlea's puzzling words regarding Emir. Did he not know that this was indeed his animal? Could he not know of his brother's arrangement? It was the outside of enough to think he had simply forgotten!

Dismayed, unsure of what to do, Daphne groped for words. "Um, my lord, do you have a special interest in horses?" she asked as casually as possible.

He looked startled, then shrugged indifferently. "I have a special interest in carriage horses, but keep several mounts in Town, mainly for my brother's use. When at Oxford, he often brought friends down with him. As I mentioned, there is a gray just like yours."

The suspicion that all was not right deepened in Daphne's mind. To gain time, she reached down and patted Emir's neck. "Mr. Merritt likes to ride, I gather," she said, off-handed. "Perchance he is with you this morning?"

Lord Courtlea laughed, but his laughter had an affectionate ring to it. "That slug-a-bed! He rarely stirs before noon. I vow he has yet to crack open an eyelid. How inviting the new grass looks under these trees."

It was shockingly clear to Daphne that he had no inkling that Edgar had lent out the earl's fine animals. Appalled, realizing the embarrassment of her position should Lord Courtlea claim her horse as his, Daphne abruptly pulled Emir to a stop. Lord Courtlea promptly followed suit.

"My lord," she said swiftly, "there is no need for your escort. My groom knows to await me, and will be near. Goodbye."

"What? No, wait!" He stretched out his arm to block her, and clasped her hands as they held the reins. "Do not be foolhardy, I beg," he said, in total seriousness. "Perhaps you are not aware that, until recently, footpads were common here. Some may still lurk in the wilder parts of the park. You must not go unattended."

She shook her head, tremblingly aware of the warm grip holding her hands prisoner. "I am not afraid, and I prefer to be alone." In her eagerness to have him gone, she spoke more brusquely than she intended.

The earl withdrew his arm, his features hardening. "Without my company, I think you to mean."

That was not at all her purpose, and her heart smote her for the unintentional cruelty of her words. She said nothing, however, miserably aware there was little she could say, until she had confronted Mr. Edgar Merritt.

"I had hoped—very well, Miss Summerhayes, you may go alone from here, safe from footpads and my attentions. I shall not trouble you further." In a sardonic salute, he raised his crop to the brim of his hat. Then he wheeled his horse and touched it into a canter.

With aching heart, Daphne watched him ride off, easily managing his powerful steed, back the way they had come. Oh, why must they part in anger and misunderstanding, just when she felt a closeness between them? Resentful, she spurred Emir on. Mr. Edgar Merritt had much for which to answer.

Daphne said nothing to him, however, until the party returned to Wentford House. Sending Sophie to change from her habit, Daphne invited Edgar into the small sitting room.

"Pray be seated, Mr. Merritt."

While he took an armchair near the door, Daphne chose a stance by the hearth. He bobbed up at once, seeing her still standing, but she impatiently waved him down.

"We have a serious matter to discuss, Mr. Merritt. This morning while riding I encountered your brother, Lord Courtlea. We had an interesting discussion, relating to certain horses."

Edgar, going from ruddy smiles to ashen grimace, gave a despairing gurgle.

Daphne nodded. "Well spoken, Mr. Merritt. You placed me in an intolerable situation, Mr. Merritt. Can you possibly comprehend my distress? Why, I faced arrest as a horse thief, Mr. Merritt!"

"Oh, Lord above!" the young man groaned, covering his face with his hand.

Resisting a twinge of pity, Daphne strode across the room, her boots soundless on the blue and cream carpet, to stand before him.

"Why?" she demanded sharply.

Slowly he removed the hand covering his stricken countenance. As he met her angry stare, he turned a deep crimson, but did not drop his gaze. "Miss Summerhayes, I did not mean to land you in such a pickle. Such a happenstance was furthest from my mind. You have every reason to be mad as hops, and to forbid me the house. I cannot apologize enough."

"No, you cannot. Now I await an explanation for your preposterous behaviour. I ask again. Why?"

He attempted a smile. "I wished to give you and your cousin some pleasure, and myself the pleasure of your company."

"Mr. Merritt, you know full well that is not what I mean. Why did you not inform Lord Courtlea of your plans?"

"I did not think it necessary, Miss Summerhayes. He has never objected to my use of the animals."

Daphne studied the earnest young face turned up to her, and was reminded of her brother, William, not much younger than Mr. Merritt, who could answer with the same apparent truth, yet keep something back. She crossed her arms, and assumed her "cold fish look," as William shudderingly described it.

"Pray do not attempt prevarication with me, Mr. Merritt. Your delight that we would ride very early, your reluctance to invite your brother to join us, your haste to get us away this morning—all these points are suspicious."

He nodded, with a shrug of resignation. "You have the right of it, but in honor, I cannot say more. Now, Miss Summerhayes, I must go and face my brother."

"A moment more, I beg."

Convinced she had not reached the end of the tangle, and determined to find it, Daphne began to pace, hands clasped behind her back. The earl showed no ill-will toward her; indeed, quite the opposite. Why would he object— Suddenly she recollected his belittlement of Sophie at Dunston Hall and at the Royal Academy. He had never hidden his poor opinion of her. Could it be— Daphne stopped pacing and whirled to face Edgar.

"Can it be that..." She paused, then continued deliberately, "that Lord Courtlea, your brother, has forbidden—" she choked on the word—"forbidden you to have contact with my cousin?"

Mr. Merritt sprang to his feet, and his shame-faced look provided her answer. Anger such as Daphne had seldom experienced burst within her. The arrogant, overweening, supercilious beast! And to think she had begun to warm toward him!

"I feel nothing for my own account," she said, her voice quivering despite her determination to speak calmly. "My indignation springs from the slight to my cousin, who has done nothing to warrant such contempt. How dare he be so high in the instep! My family lineage, while not attaining such titled heights, is no less worthy than his. Than yours, sir!"

Edgar winced and hung his head. The toe of one boot scuffed aimlessly at the carpet. "Miss Summerhayes—" Slowly he raised his head to meet her gaze. Then he gave a small, hopeless gesture, bowed slightly, and walked to the door.

"Mr. Merritt."

He paused on the threshold. "Miss Summerhayes," he responded tonelessly.

"You need not fear to face your brother," she said quietly. "He did not recognize Emir, and I told him nothing of your escapade."

He looked wonderingly at her. Then, with woeful dignity, gave her an elaborate bow. "You heap coals of fire on my head," he said softly.

"I will say nothing of this to my cousin. Perhaps, with all her other gentlemen callers, she will not notice your absence." With that last unkind cut, Daphne turned her back. After a moment, the door closed quietly.

With an outright lie, that Lord Courtlea needed the cattle for guests,

Daphne settled Sophie's curiosity about the abrupt stopping of their pleasurable rides. The same Banbury tale served to explain Mr. Merritt's absence from the drawing room. "He will doubtless be helping entertain the visitors, and can no longer spare the time for us."

Sophie accepted her cousin's word without expressing too much disappointment, but resentment burned in Daphne's breast. That Lord Courtlea should believe Sophie Summerhayes not good enough for his brother, who was without tuppence to his name, was the outside of enough.

Discreet inquiries had not revealed a reliable, untraceable way of ridding herself of the brooch. She might post it, and as Lord Courtlea would have to pay the postage, there was some justice in that. But sometimes small parcels went astray, pilfered as they passed through the mails. And what might prevent an urchin hired for a sixpence from keeping both money and parcel? For the hundredth time, Daphne retrieved the little package and glowered at it.

"You have caused me enough grief," she muttered. "If I can trust no one to do the deed, I must do it myself." She shuddered, imagining the earl's scathing words, his disgust, his triumph at discovering Daphne Summerhayes was no better than she should be.

'Twas not easy as Sophie's chaperon to absent herself. In two days, however, the Wentfords, Daphne, and Sophie were to attend an evening concert by a noted soprano. Since Aunt Elizabeth could chaperon Sophie, Daphne would beg off with the headache, a cold, or a broken limb if need be. Then, with everyone safely gone, she would slip away, find a hackney, and make her way to 41, Green Street.

Although, Daphne reflected bitterly as she replaced the brooch in its hiding place, what good was her care for secrecy? Lord Courtlea was not above bruiting the shameful episode to the whole of London!

CHAPTER 14

The night was well past its zenith when Lord Courtlea wearily entered his silent house. A night lamp on a table in the center of the hall cast a feeble glimmer. Shadows shrouded the corners, the statuary in niches, and the staircase rising into blackness. Rubbing his tired eyes, the earl went into his study. The fire was banked for the night, but, frowning, he stirred it into flame.

A key rattled in the front door lock, the door was thrown open, and heavy, stumbling footsteps echoed through the hall. Courtlea's frown deepened. "Edgar!" he called.

The footsteps paused, then lurched in the direction of the study. "Victor? Wha' th' deuce you doin' in the dark, at this time o' night?"

"What the deuce have you been doing, coming home at this time of night? And foxed, into the bargain." Courtlea thrust a spill into the fire and lit a branch of candles on the mantel. The rush of light revealed his brother standing unsteadily just inside the room, his cravat rumpled, his coat creased and stained, and a rather silly grin on his face.

"Jus' a bit of fun. Got bored at Lady—Lady Whoever's ball, so we—we left. More fun at Lady Bawd's accommodation house, in Covent Garden." Edgar winked broadly, then reeled to a chair. "Where did you get your night's entertainment, Victor?"

"Not in Covent Garden, in any case, and you would do well to avoid such houses." Victor eyed his brother sprawled awkwardly in the chair. He was puzzled by Edgar's riotous behaviour of the last few days. He wondered what had spurred him into debauchery, but Edgar refused any explanation. "Are you too bosky to listen? I have grave news, Edgar."

Yawning, Edgar rubbed his hand over the dark stubble on his chin. "I hear well enough. Say away."

Victor shrugged off his greatcoat and flung it carelessly onto his desk. "I have just come from the House. The Commons is still sitting, and the talk is of war. Napoleon refuses to honor the Amiens peace. He will not agree to a trade treaty with Britain, and he again eyes Egypt. If he does not relent, we may be at war by summer."

"Gad, that is a facer!" exclaimed Edgar, staring owlishly with pink-rimmed eyes. "I shall buy my colors at once. What think you? The lancers or the dragoons?"

Victor shook his head and kicked a loose coal into the fire. "I doubt you are sober enough to be sensible, but there is no need to get into a pelter. There will be time enough to consider such action. Now get to bed. You reek of drink."

Edgar got to his feet, swaying only slightly. "Drink was all I did tonight," he said, with an abashed dip of his head. "None of the canary-birds tempted me. Not one whit."

Despite the grave matters occupying his mind, Victor laughed aloud. "Does that relieve my worry, or simply replace one concern with another? Never mind," he went on, waving away his brother's uncomprehending gaze. "To bed, sir, and at once."

Edgar saluted, nearly putting out an eye, wheeled, and marched remarkably well from the room. The earl smiled, pulled a chair closer to the fire and propped his feet on a low stool. The fire snapped and flared, a cold wind howled among the chimney pots, and a lone carriage rattled past the house. He knew he should be abed, but still he sat, feet to the fire, alone with his thoughts. Not thoughts, precisely, but more of a melancholy, a restless dissatisfaction that had nothing to do with the rumors of war.

It had to do with that intriguing and elusive Daphne Summerhayes. His plan of having her come to him for a short, sweet affair had not worked. He had thought he could wait, concentrate on other matters, until she surrendered. Faugh! He was the one growing impatient. He was the one frustrated by his own desires, and unable to sleep soundly.

He should forget her and replace Maryann without further delay. Unfortunately, no form or face had taken his fancy. Except *that* one, of course. One who was far too independent, obstinate, and tart-tongued to meet his notion of a mistress. One who would either laugh in his face or box his ears if he even hinted at such an accommodation.

He thought of when he had last seen her—on the gray in the park, curtly sending him away. What had changed her warm friendliness so abruptly? He knew she was not insensitive to him; yet she had made it plain as a pikestaff she did not want his company. An emptiness yawned inside him when he thought never again to be near her, or parry words with her, or hear her laugh.

"Damnation!"

Rising, he kicked away the footstool, and stamped off to bed.

* * *

"Daphne, my dear, you are very pale. Are you feeling unwell?" Lady Wentford asked across the breakfast table. "Mayhap we should consult our medical doctor. You may be sickening for something."

Daphne forced a smile. "Oh, no. There is no need for a doctor, I assure you."

"Indeed? Then why is your breakfast only tea, and nothing else?" Lady Wentford demanded, indicating Daphne's empty plate. "You have enjoyed an excellent appetite until today."

"Perhaps I am a little tired," Daphne hastened to suggest. As the fateful hour crept closer, she could think of nothing else. Her stomach rose at the sight of food. "One cannot expect a country mouse like me to endure the mad whirl of London life without tiring somewhat. Why, look at Sophie. It's gone half ten, and she is not yet down. Of course, she danced until nearly two last night."

"As did you, miss, and my heart warmed to see it." Lady Wentford smiled over her teacup. "Although, I must say you favored no particular gallant. Lord Tunney took you in to supper, did he not?"

"Yes, with Sophie and Mr. Sutton." Daphne stirred her tea, watching the liquid swirl in the cup. "Lord Tunney is a kind, amusing gentleman, and I would be pleased to count him a friend, but that is all."

"Very well, my dear," said her aunt, heaving a sigh. "He will never win the blue ribbon for looks, but he is not niggardly, and has the wherewithal to keep a wife in fine style. Now, do you not fancy an egg, or a bit of fish with your tea?"

Daphne shook her head, but to please her aunt, took a square of toast from the rack and laid it on her plate.

"Perhaps you might have a nap this afternoon," suggested Lady Wentford, still keenly eyeing her niece. "Sophie has a fitting, and wants to shop, but Tyson can oversee her."

"Yes, Aunt, I shall. Tyson manages quite well, now that Sophie is less likely to kick over the traces. She knows now what is proper, and what is not."

"If you are still tired after your nap, perhaps you should cry off from the concert tonight. I know you want very much to go, but we do not want you ill. Recollect that Sophie's presentation is in a week."

Daphne stared into her cup. It was still half full, but she could not stomach another drop. Nor could she look into her aunt's concerned face without blurting the truth.

"Perhaps I will cry off, if you think it best," she said, giving up all pretence of eating. She rose, taking up her unopened mail. "Pray excuse me now, Aunt. I must answer these letters." On impulse, she went to Lady Wentford and kissed her. "That is for being the dearest, kindest aunt in the entire world."

"Why, thank you, dear." Lady Wentford smiled and patted her cheek. Daphne felt her aunt's thoughtful gaze on her back as she left the room. Her conscience squirmed uneasily; she had not lied, but had still deceived her aunt. She flew up to her room, banged the door, and began to pace.

Should she continue her course? If not, what choices remained? None!

Oh, blast! Her whole life circled around that damned brooch! Before she could waffle further, she jerked open the bottom dressser drawer, snatched up the small parcel, and thrust it deep into her reticule.

Daphne turned to her mail and eagerly broke the wafer of the first letter. As Daphne read Julia Todhunter's neat, round hand, she realized her letter and Julia's must have crossed in the mails. Fearing war's breakout, Squire Todhunter had postponed the trip to Italy.

"I am Delighted," Julia had written. "Can you guess why, dearest Friend?"

Daphne could, and the hope she might yet visit Italy with her friends almost offset her dread of the coming night.

Later, with her aunt receiving callers, and Sophie out in Tyson's care, Daphne lay in her darkened bedroom. Clucking in sympathy, Briggs wrung out a cloth in vinegar and laid it on her mistress's brow.

Daphne recollected the night she pretended the headache in order to slip out to Dunston Hall. This was worse, so much worse, that she dared not think on it. She feigned sleep, until, late in the afternoon, cracking and eye and seeing she was alone, she sat up and removed the vinegar cloth. It would not do to be too ill, or she would find herself fully abed and surrounded by doctors. Those gentlemen, scenting a fat fee, would undoubtedly find her suffering from some horrid, if not fatal, disease.

Nor could she recover too quickly and risk being deemed in fine twig to attend the concert. Therefore, when Briggs returned, she found her mistress propped up on pillows and allowing she felt a touch better.

"Oh, right glad am I to hear it, my pet," cried Briggs. "A cup of camomile tea to settle the stomach, a bit of supper, and you will be right as a trivet." As she left, she added, "Lady Wentford has been right worried, I can tell you."

Daphne groaned with guilt.

When Lady Wentford and Sophie quietly entered the sickroom, both agreed Daphne should remain at home and rest.

"In fact," added Sophie, "Do you not think we should stay with her, Aunt Elizabeth, lest she take a sudden turn?"

"Oh, no!" Daphne blurted. "That would not serve at all! You must go!"

Her cousin and aunt turned astonished faces to her. "I mean to say, I am so much better; just fatigued, not ill. Oh, I could never forgive myself if I kept you from the concert."

"Are you sure, Dee?" Sophie sat on the bed and took her cousin's hand. "I, for one, and I am sure I speak for Aunt Elizabeth too, could not possibly enjoy myself, knowing that you lay home, ill and alone."

"Indeed not," Lady Wentford agreed warmly. "We shall all stay home and play a game of Pope Joan."

Daphne repressed a scream of frustration and smiled brightly. "How sweet of you, but it is not necessary to disturb your plans. Why, I feel so much recovered, I may join you for dinner and simply retire early."

With a little more prompting, the countess and Sophie agreed to Daphne's wishes. When they finally left her room, Daphne collapsed into her pillows, totally drained. By the time this was over, she would be an actress even Mrs. Siddons might envy!

Dinner was not the ordeal she feared. Her uncle kept up a lively banter, capturing his lady's and Sophie's attention. Daphne ate little, forcing the food down on the butterflies in her stomach, but everyone expressed pleasure that she ate anything at all.

At last, after more protests and entreaties, Daphne was alone. Briggs readied her for bed, prepared a soothing posset, and pottered about the room while her mistress drank it. What with the posset and the strain of the day, Daphne was hard put to stay awake until her abigail finally left her. Five minutes later, Daphne flung back the covers and dressed herself.

Time was of the essence. The concert ended no later than eleven, and her caring relatives would doubtless hurry home to her side. With any luck, she would slip out, thrust the package at the earl's butler, and be back within an hour, ready to play the recovered invalid.

With the eerie sensation of repetition, she quietly slipped into the corridor. The servants should have been having their dinner, but Daphne's heart was in her mouth when she reached the first floor and peered over the railing. There was no sign of butler, porter, or footman. A sigh of satisfaction escaped her.

She slid the bolt, and in a trice was out on the pavement. The street was busy with carriages and sedan chairs as the inhabitants set out for their evening's entertainment, but there were no free hackneys. Daphne pulled her dark hood closer about her face, and hurried toward Grosvenor Square. It was not far, but to Daphne, on foot and alone, the hundred yards seemed a hundred miles. Turning the corner at last, she paused, her eyes darting anxiously. Tonight of all nights, not one hackney loitered, seeking a fare. She would have to wait.

Two gentlemen passing by on foot eyed her with unabashed curiosity. "I say, Pinky," said one, nudging his companion, "here's a pretty baggage, ready and waiting. She'd do for us, what?"

Daphne stalked off, disgusted and outraged. The gentlemen shouted for her to return, then laughed and went their way. Ahead, a hackney deposited a fare. The jarvey whipped up just as Daphne ran to the curb and signaled him. He pulled in, with some reluctance, regarding her with a doubtful frown.

"What're ye about, then?" he demanded. "I expec' brass, and naught else. 'Ave ye any blunt?"

"Naturally, I have money," Daphne retorted. "Why else would I expect to ride? Take me to Green Street."

"G'wan, ye can walk that far. It ain't but a mile or more from 'ere."

Daphne dug a coin from her reticule and held it up. "I want to ride. If you do not want this money, I shall find someone who does."

Her imperious tone, as much as her money, must have decided the man. Daphne gave directions and clambered into the decrepit vehicle. At last she was truly on her way. Any scandal would fall on her head alone. Lady Wentford's influence was strong enough so Sophie's presentation to Queen Charlotte would not be jeopardized.

The hackney, as ordered, stopped at the corner of Green Street. Bidding the driver wait, Daphne got out and walked down to Number 41. It was a large, but surprisingly unpretentious house, tastefully ornamented, with shining brasses and an imposing front door.

Daphne climbed the four steps to the door as though they led to the gallows. She had raised her hand to the lion's head knocker when she noticed a crack of light. The door was ajar. Daphne pushed gently, and the door swung open on oiled hinges. She glimpsed a square hall of rich, warm colors well lit with wall sconces, a staircase with a carved balustrade, and an empty porter's chair pushed back against the wainscotting. No one, servant or master, came to challenge her. All was still.

Daphne trembled on the doorstep, her heart racing. Then, holding her breath, she entered swiftly, pushed the door nearly closed and made for the central table. The servants would surely find her package there.

Footsteps rang on the steps outside. Frantic, Daphne looked about her, but nothing offered concealment. With no option, she darted into a darkened room off the hall. Barely had her skirts swished out of sight around the half-opened door when the front portal opened. A footman entered, rubbing his arms against the chill. Doubtless he had been sent on an errand nearby, improperly used the front entrance, and carelessly neglected to pull the door shut behind him.

With her packet clutched in her hand, Daphne watched from the shadows as the footman loitered in the hall. He was a tall, muscular fellow, very dashing in his livery, and with passing good looks. He stood admiring himself before a bevelled mirror. Minutes passed, and still he preened like a proud cockerel.

Daphne examined her refuge, hoping to discover another exit. The room served as a study or library, its walls lined with books. A dark mass must be a desk, and, as her eyes grew accustomed to the gloom, she discerned sofas and several chairs. There was a pleasant scent of leather book bindings, of ink, and a banked coal fire. The room was obviously well-used by its owner. The only window overlooked the street, and Daphne stood by the only door.

Holding her skirts to keep them from rustling, she moved to the desk. What better place to leave the brooch? Hah, what a dig for the noble earl! Daphne almost wished she would be present to see his face. As she dropped the little parcel on the desk, she heard the footman's scurrying steps. She froze, but he was only answering the front door. Someone entered, and Daphne, with a horrible sensation of inevitability, recognized Lord Courtlea's authoritative tones.

"Oh, dear God, let him go to his room, to his bed, or to Hades," she silently prayed, her heart hammering in her breast. "Let him go anywhere, but please do not let him come in here!"

CHAPTER 15

Courtlea had dined adequately at his club, and as he handed coat, hat, and cane to Robert, debated his choices for the evening. The theatre? A gaming house? Lady Flo's assembly? He made for the stairs, then paused, his hand on the carved newel post. None of those diversions suited his restless, ill-tempered mood. Indeed, little pleased him lately, from food to flirtation.

Altering course, he strode across the hall to his study. He could always lose himself in work for a few hours, he thought, and pushed open the door. Though dazzled by the hall's bright candlelight, he saw at once a form hovering at his desk in the darkened room.

A thief, by God!

"Robert!" he shouted, and threw himself at the intruder. The figure darted back, but stumbled over a chair and fell. The earl pounced, hearing a soft grunt as his weight drove the air from the miscreant's lungs.

Despite the thick, enveloping cloak, he knew at once his body covered that of a woman. The small frame might belong to a boy, but not the slender yet lush curves pressed against him. The sensation was distracting, but he concentrated on pinioning her arms lest the little cutpurse have a knife.

"Robert, a light, quickly."

A candle flared and wavered. Courtlea rose, keeping a firm grip, and dragged the girl to her feet. Mute, she struggled in his hold like a writhing cat.

"Stop that," he demanded, shaking her. "Now, let's have a look at you." He pulled back her hood and turned so the flickering light would fall full on her face—and received the shock of his life.

"Good God! You!"

Daphne Summerhayes glared up at him, her green eyes blazing, her bronze hair disheveled around a furiously white countenance. He released her and stepped back, too stunned to speak. 'Twas as if his dreams and desires had summoned her there.

"Shall I call the Watch, my lord?" asked Robert, staring goggle-eyed, the fireplace poker clutched in one hand and a candelabra with a single lit candle shaking in the other.

"No, Robert," Courtlea replied, his eyes on his visitor's white face, "that will not be necessary. You may go."

"But— Yes, my lord." Robert returned the poker, set the candelabra on the mantel, and with evident reluctance, withdrew.

"What the devil are you doing here?" Courtlea demanded. Despite her defiant stance and enshrouding cloak, he saw that she trembled. "At night and alone, slipping into my house like a common—"

"I am not a thief!" she flung at him. "That is..." Her shoulders, proudly braced back, suddenly drooped.

"I meant another occupation, not thievery, but one for which your obvious charms fit you well."

He spoke harshly, for his composure was wrecked. Had he not sat before this very fire, visualizing this woman as his mistress? Now here she stood. "Sit down, madam, before your limbs fail you."

She did not obey, but stared at him with lips parted and eyes rounded in horror. "You cannot think that I—" A crimson tide flooded her cheeks, and her trembling grew more pronounced. "How dare you speak such a vile notion to me! How dare you think of me as a light-skirt, angling for your favor! How dare—"

He grasped her by the shoulders and thrust her into a chair, then bent over her, his face inches from hers. She stared back with wide, stricken eyes, and he winced at the repugnance in them.

A delicate scent of wild flowers filled his nostrils as she raised a shaking hand to push back the heavy hair fallen over her brow. It was a totally feminine gesture, yet without coquetry, and, because it touched him, his confusion hardened into anger.

"Before you castigate me further, Miss Summerhayes, may I remind you that you sought me out, not the other way around. Whatever your motives, you are here, and alone. The facts speak for themselves."

His anger seemed a palpable force, a part of his powerful body. Daphne quailed before it, yet her traitor heart throbbed at his nearness. But how could she think with the man she most despised hovering close, his lips twisted in a sneer, his gaze like cold steel pinning her in place? She knew, as Flora knew, how helpless she was before his strength, should he choose to use it. Her knuckles whitened as she gripped the chair arm.

"Facts may be misinterpreted, my lord, or not tell the whole story," she said in a low voice, forcing the words through her tight throat. "I will ignore your scurrilous opinion of me—it is, after all, no more than I would expect from a person of your character—if you will allow me to explain why I am here."

His countenance darkened. Abruptly, he drew back, his fists clenched at his sides. "Deuce take it, but you and your insults try my patience to the limit!"

With an obvious effort to contain his rage, he wheeled away from her. Seizing the poker, he jabbed viciously at the glowing coals in the hearth. A small flame fluttered up.

Daphne nodded, although his back was turned. "Which I long ago found to be in short supply. As is your tolerance and compassion." She rose, drawing on her tattered bits of pride, hatred, and anger to lend her courage. Oh, how she ached to be done with him, and gone! "Now, then, my lord..."

She went to the desk, a handsome thing of carved rosewood, and picked up the little parcel. Without a further word, but with dread building inside her, she crossed to the fireplace and offered it to him. He took it, saw his name neatly inked on the wrapping, and glanced questioningly at her.

"Open it, pray," Daphne said tonelessly. "The contents will explain all."

She turned away, tensing, while he broke the string. The paper rustled loudly in the quiet room, and then there was a long, stretched silence. Daphne waited for his outburst, but heard only silence. When she could stand the quiet no longer, she whirled to face him. He stood fingering the emerald brooch, the paper and box on the carpet at his feet. He looked up at her, his expression blank as a graven image.

"How came you by this?" he demanded.

Swiftly, not sparing herself, Daphne related the whole tale. She spoke with her eyes down, too overset to meet his gaze. At last she stumbled to the end and raised her head, nerving herself for the contempt and derision he was sure to heap on it.

"You knew I had no memory of your brother," he said with surprising coolness, "and therefore no memory of the brooch's origin. Why did you not simply keep it, with no one the wiser?"

She drew in her breath at how calmly he offered that insult. Her chin lifted proudly. "My brother is young, and sometimes foolish, but he is no cheat. I could not allow a stain on his honor, even though no one else knew of it."

His brow rose a trifle, but otherwise his expression did not change. "If the young sir, your brother, is so tight to his honor, why did he not return the brooch himself, instead of heaping the responsibility on his sister?"

His question surprised her. "Why, William offered to do so, but I did not agree. Had I not interfered, I would not now be in such a pickle. Should I then cry for my brother to save me? Clearly, the responsibility was mine."

Lord Courtlea nodded but did not comment. Leaning his arm on the mantelpiece, he stared into the sullen flames that were once more lapsing into coals. Daphne bit her lip, wanting to scream at him to berate her how he would and have done with it.

"This is a fine stone, but not an irreplaceable one. How came you to risk so much for it?"

How maddeningly cool he was! Or was he aware how much his composed manner added to her torture? "It belongs—belonged to our mother. It may be worn as a brooch or as part of a necklace."

"I see. And so, to recover the bauble, you became Flora, who offered to stir my fire."

Daphne closed her eyes, feeling again that rush of heat, those conflicting desires that had so shocked her. "Yes," she whispered, "to my everlasting shame."

"Oh, I would not say that! Your performance was masterful." His voice lost its controlled smoothness and grated in her ears. "Why, you deceived me completely. I would swear I held a warm, willing maid in my arms, as eager for love-play as I."

Her eyes flew open. The earl had not moved except to turn his head and regard her with that same hard, blank stare. Angry words choked her, but she silenced them before they gained utterance. Let him say what he willed. What mercy or understanding could she expect from a man who considered his own wants and pleasures above all else?

Besides, part of what he said was true.

"What, no words of defense or protest?" The earl raised his brows in mock surprise. The light from the single candle left his eyes in shadow and barely touched his lips.

"Come, Miss Summerhayes, you were glib enough a scant minute ago, attacking my character. What of your character? You claimed to be no thief, yet I hold the proof of that falsehood in my hand." He held out the brooch that sparkled even in the faint light, then set it on the mantel.

"I told you why," Daphne protested. "I thought I was but reclaiming my own property. Had you been more of a gentleman—"

"Oh, 'tis my fault, is it, that you are a thief?"

He smiled, his eyes hooded, and a shiver ran down Daphne's back. Her breath seemed to stop in her throat. 'Twas the smile of the wolf at the helpless rabbit.

"As for not being a wanton—" he murmured with wicked promise.

Deliberately he walked toward her, and again fear touched her heart. Daphne took a quick step back, then stopped. She had never run from trouble, and would not run or cower now. He would not have the satisfaction of frightening her.

Lord Courtlea stopped a hand's breadth away. Daphne stared boldly up at him, realizing this was no time for the niceties of convention. His gaze locked with hers, beating at her determination, his masculine will attacking her feminine resolve. Still holding her gaze, he lightly trailed his fingertips along the curve of her jaw. She flinched at the sudden tremor that shot through her. His fingers stilled, and she saw he took her wince as revulsion.

"You forget, madam," he whispered, "how you melted to my touch, even offered your white throat for my kisses." Swiftly he unclasped her cloak and let it drop to the floor.

Daphne let out a strangled cry and crossed her hands on her breast. Although her gown covered her from neck to wrist to toe, she felt exposed and vulnerable. All the more, as the earl's hot words resurrected the wild desires she had strongly repressed. "You would not force me! You would not be so detestable!"

His hands slid about her waist. "But am I not detestable?" his low, insinuating whisper continued. "Do you not hold me in such low estimation that nothing I did, however base, would surprise you? Besides, Miss Summerhayes, Miss Daphne of the beckoning eyes, we are discussing your nature, not mine."

He moved his hands in slow, languorous strokes up to her shoulders and down over the fullness of her hips. The heat from his hands flowed through her body, fuelling passions to a height almost too fierce to withstand. When he cupped her hips and pulled her against him, she almost cried out in acceptance.

"Well, Daphne," he murmured, "most desirable of all the nymphs, what say you? Shall we begin with a kiss?"

"Never," she breathed. "Never from you!"

But she was lost, hopelessly lost in a flood that bore her beyond the reach of her will. Her eyes closed in surrender, her hands, trembling, moved from above her pounding heart to lie against his chest. They crept upward, past his coat's satin revers to his shoulders. She swayed forward, lifting her face to him, yearning to press against his whole strong body, to again feel the touch of his lips on her skin, and for the first time, on her eager mouth.

But instead of his kiss claiming her lips, soft, mocking words fell on her ears. "I see now, Miss Summerhayes, the truth of your statement to me, that day at the Royal Academy. Actions do betray our natures much more than words."

Daphne stared at him, shock holding her motionless. Even her heart seemed to cease beating, her lungs to refuse air. Then the enormity of his deceit exploded in her mind. Her hands leaped from him as though they touched something unclean. She jerked back, but he held her in an unbreakable grip. "Oh, you are contemptible! Nay, beneath contempt! Turn me loose, at once."

"When I am ready, I shall set you free, and not before," Lord Courtlea answered calmly. "I wished to prove that the passions which coursed through Flora's form also beat beneath that proper, cool facade Miss Summerhayes presents to the world. I succeeded beyond my hopes."

He smiled, but without amusement. "Some day I shall have that kiss, but with your full consent. Yes, some day you will give it to me willingly, and give me much more."

"Not as long as I draw breath!" Daphne cried, her cheeks hot with shame, for her blood still pounded a drumbeat of desire. She twisted furiously within his grasp, and this time he let her go. Scooping up her cloak, she threw it about her shoulders and fumbled with trembling fingers for the clasp. "You have your jewel, sir, and now we are quits."

"Perhaps."

Without answering, she whirled to leave, but he was first at the door. He laid his hand on it, blocking her escape. "How came you here?" he asked softly, as though avid ears listened from the hall. "In your aunt's carriage?"

She shot him a withering glare. "Do you think I would reveal aught of this—this degrading business to a living soul, much less my aunt? I have a hackney waiting."

He ignored her scathing contempt, saying merely, "The streets are not safe for a woman alone. I will return you to Wentford House in my carriage."

"Stand aside, sir. You are the last person to be concerned for my safety. My reputation would indeed be in ruins should I be conveyed about the town in the Earl of Courtlea's carriage!"

Daphne grimaced at her own words. When the earl finished entertaining his cronies with tonight's tale, her reputation would not be worth a bent farthing. As Lord Courtlea moved aside, she pulled her hood well down over her face, and without another word or look, swept from the room.

Courtlea watched through the open door as Robert, with a knowing leer, showed her out. Although he could hardly blame the footman for drawing the worst of conclusions, Courtlea itched to remove the fellow's smirk with the back of his hand.

"Robert," he called.

The man's features immediately resumed their usual subservient expression. He hurried across the hall. "My lord?"

"You do not know the lady who just left this house."

"No, my lord. Your lordship did not mention a name."

"Then, Robert, should any whisper reach my ears of a lady leaving this house tonight, you will be turned out without a recommendation. Do you understand me?"

The footman's face whitened. "Yes, my lord."

Courtlea waved him away, then crossed swiftly to the front door. Opening it, he peered cautiously up and down the street. At the corner, a cloaked figure was climbing into a rackety hackney. He drew back, lest he be seen, muttering, "At least you are safely on your way, stubborn, wilful nymph."

He closed the door and slowly returned to his study. Throwing himself into the desk chair, he propped his head in his hands. Never in all his life had he felt such confusion. He, so expert with women, had made a fine mess of things.

Why, when he sensed her surrender, did he not take her? Why, when every fibre throbbed with the need to crush her to him and savor the exquisite delight of her body, did he deny himself? The wench deserved such humbling, both for her superior airs and for the trick she had played as Flora.

Flora. He shook his head. What gall! When Daphne Summerhayes pulled a prank, she did it up brown. One had to admire her sauce. Then why, with this proud, infuriating, artful baggage trembling in his arms—and for the second time, by God!—did he not act? Yes, he might have earned her loathing. But, by refusing to play the lover, he had humiliated her and given her more reason to hate him. Faugh! He could not win!

And why did he sit now like a love-sick moon-calf, puzzling his brains over the feelings of a mere woman?

Courtlea swore, thumped the desk with his fist, and surged to his feet. He reached the door, then stopped short. Returning to the mantel, he picked up the emerald brooch. Thoughtfully, he studied it, turning it this way and that to catch its shimmer. The green stone sparkled no more brilliantly than a certain pair of eyes. The lone candle flickered, gone half its length, as Courtlea closed his fist over the brooch. The fire had died to ashes, but he felt the warmth that still lingered in the room. Warmth, and the faint scent of wild flowers.

CHAPTER 16

Daphne huddled into the cracked, stained squabs of the hackney, her face in her hands, reliving those terrible minutes with Lord Courtlea. What a rogue he was, what a thorough scoundrel! Treating her as a common— Deliberately mortifying her by suggesting the most disgraceful behavior. She could well imagine what a tale of this night's affair he would spread with knowing winks and nudges.

What was worse, he could say 'twas not her fault nothing dishonorable had occurred. Her face flamed again, recollecting those moments of weakness, of total abandonment, and of his scornful rejection. And such arrogance, his assumption that she would come to him willingly. Her pride would never allow such a thing.

The front door of Wentford House was firmly locked, but Daphne, past caring of minor problems, simply knocked. To the astonished Clapham, she explained that a sudden need for fresh air had driven her to take a stroll.

"But, miss," Clapham protested, blinking in agitation, "had you informed me of your intention, I would have accompanied you, or sent a footman. 'Tis not safe—"

"Yes, Clapham, but I did not think."

Anxious to reach her room, Daphne inched past him, but the portly butler, grown gray in Lady Wentford's service, followed her across the hall.

"Mayhap your illness, miss, addled your wits, if you pardon my saying," he said, peering closely at her. "You do not look in prime twig yet, begging your pardon, miss. Her ladyship will be most upset if she returns and finds you burning with brain fever."

Daphne paused at the foot of the staircase. "Indeed, you may have the right of it, Clapham. Truly, I am quite well, but may have tired myself overmuch. However, we do not wish to worry Lady Wentford, do we? If my aunt does not know of my—my impulsive stroll, she will not be concerned. Do you agree, Clapham?"

The butler's plump cheeks creased in a smile, and one eyelid fluttered in the merest suggestion of a wink. "I agree totally, miss. To my knowledge, you spent the evening in your room."

"Thank you, Clapham." Daphne sped on up to her room, knowing the butler would keep his counsel.

She fell into bed, expecting a long and sleepless night. However, exhausted in mind and body, Daphne dropped into a deep sleep almost at once. In the morning, when she realized she was indeed forever rid of brooch, earl, and guilt, she wanted to both laugh and cry.

"I am mad," she told her reflection as she washed. "Think of the scandal that rogue is about to spread."

Mayhap her heretofore pristine reputation might protect her from too much damage. Then too, one never knew how the ton accepted gossip—with censure, sympathy, or even laughter.

"Sufficient unto the day is the evil thereof," she reminded herself with a sigh as she went down to breakfast. "I shan't borrow trouble. Heaven knows, it always comes quickly enough."

Sophie was alone at table, bubbling with excitement. "Oh, Dee, what a pleasure to see you quite the thing again! You are yourself again, are you not? Oh, Aunt Elizabeth will be pleased! You were in a fine sleep when she and I peeked in on you last night. The concert was prodigiously good. Madame Davigne has a superb voice. And we met Mr. Edgar Merritt, of all people."

Still talking, Sophie rose to refill her plate from the silver dishes on the sideboard. "I vow, he mumbled a bit at first, apologizing for something or other with such a sad face, but he cheered up when I allowed him to sit with us. There was no sign of Lord Courtlea, though. Doubtless he was otherwise engaged."

Daphne almost choked. "Doubtless," she agreed, joining her cousin at the sideboard. How shocked Sophie would be if she knew just how the earl was otherwise engaged!

"Sophie, dear," she began tentatively, choosing a poached egg and a scone, "I think it unwise to encourage Mr. Merritt's company."

"How so?" Sophie stared at her in surprise. "I believed you favored Mr. Merritt."

Daphne went to the table and waited for Sophie to reseat herself. How she wished the entire Merritt family would suddenly decide to emigrate! "Except for his uncertain expectations, I find no great fault with him." Daphne did not mean to stress her final word, but she saw that Sophie caught the unintentional inflection.

She laid down her fork, her blue eyes suddenly serious. "I know you dislike Lord Courtlea, but is it fair to blame one gentleman for the nature of the other? I have seldom seen two brothers so like in appearance and so unlike in temperament."

"Indeed, that is true, but—" Daphne took a bite of egg, hardly tasting it. How could she hurt her cousin by telling her that the proud peer did not consider her a suitable acquaintance for his brother?

"Recollect that Mr. Merritt is dependent for his living on Lord Courtlea," Daphne stated. "That, aside from the normal authority an older brother has over a younger, strengthens Lord Courtlea's influence. Recollect too, that the earl thinks as little of me as I do of him. Any connection between his family and ours would overset him, the last thing Mr. Merritt would desire."

"Piffle, Coz! Piffle and balderdash." Sophie shook her head as she lavished plum jam on a scone. "Much as Mr. Merritt may respect his wealthy relative, I believe his nature is more constant than you credit him. Should his interest lie in a certain direction, he would not be so easily dissuaded. Not that I claim his affection," she added hastily, wiping her fingers on her napkin. "I merely express my opinion."

Daphne sighed. "I fear I must speak more bluntly. Consider, if the earl encountered his brother with you, as he might have last night at the concert, he would not scruple to embarrass you with his displeasure. Oh, subtly, I am sure, as he would not wish to offend Aunt Elizabeth, but you could not mistake his message."

"You may speak more bluntly still," Sophie said briskly, with a toss of her head that set the pink ribbons on her cap dancing. "Regardless of Lord Courtlea's opinion of you, he considers me a complete ninnyhammer. Oh, Daphne, what did you think? That I did not know?"

Sophie laughed at Daphne's round-eyed amazement, popped a largish piece of scone into her mouth, and smacked her lips appreciatively. "Mmm, I must get the receipt for these heavenly scones for Mama. Our cook is a dab hand at pastry, but her scones sit in the stomach like cannon balls. Now, Dee, when you are done breakfast, do come and see my court gown. It was delivered early this morning. Oh, I vow it prodigiously splendid!"

With a gay wave, Sophie bounced out of the dining room, leaving Daphne to finish her meal in thoughtful silence. Her cousin seemed to care not a fig for Lord Courtlea or his opinion of her. Indeed, the more Daphne thought on it, the more right it appeared that Sophie should not care. The earl had hovered like a dark shadow over Daphne's life, but in Sophie's clear vision, he was little more than a petty tyrant.

Daphne's heart lightened, and, smiling, she broke open another scone and reached for the plum jam.

* * *

The white silk gown for Sophie's court presentation was all a young girl might dream of. The petticoat was particularly fine, being embroidered with gold thread. Sophie held out her arms and turned slowly. "The train, Dee. Is it long enough? Too long? Oh, I vow I will trip on it and land in the queen's lap!"

"The train is perfect, and you will not fear tripping after you have practised a few turns and curtsies." Daphne settled on the chair before her cousin's dressing table and watched critically while Sophie inched slowly about the bedroom. "Do not be afraid to walk. One must move gracefully, as if accustomed to those infernal hoops. And for pity's sake, do not twist about to watch your train. It will follow—"

Daphne broke off as her Aunt Elizabeth entered the room. Sophie straightened, and, mindful of her train, turned in a wide circle for her courtesy aunt's inspection.

"How lovely you are, dear child!" the countess exclaimed with a broad smile, slipping an arm about Sophie's waist. "'Tis no wonder you gather admirers as treacle draws bees!"

"Or a dog fleas, as Papa says," said Sophie with a laugh.

Lady Wentford chuckled. She seemed in a high good humor.

"Aunt, I was about to offer my pearl and diamond necklace for Sophie to wear for her presentation and the ball. Will it be the thing, do you think?" Daphne asked.

"Oh, quite the thing, my dear. And you will wear your mother's emeralds, will you not? They match your eyes to a nicety."

Daphne's heart stopped, and then sank to her shoes. "Of a certainty, Aunt," she replied with a falsely cheerful air, "if you wish it."

Perhaps the countess would not notice the lack of the central stone. Oh, fustian! Her aunt would as like not notice Daphne appearing at the ball in her chemise, as not see the incomplete necklace.

The urge to confess was never greater. Surely confession was not only sensible, but necessary. Aunt Elizabeth and Uncle Valentine must be forewarned to confront gossip. How disappointed they would be in William, for foolishly losing an heirloom, and in her, for such wilful, brazen behavior!

"Aunt," she began.

A soft rap sounded at the door, and Clapham entered. "His lordship begs your attendance in the sitting room, my lady."

"Oh, I shall be there directly," Lady Wentford replied with a happy smile. A pink flush coloring her cheeks gave her a becoming girlish air. She moved with a light step to the door which the butler held open.

"May I attend you both shortly?" Daphne asked anxiously, following her aunt to the doorway.

"Indeed you may, child." The words floated over Lady Wentford's shoulder as she sailed out of the room. Clapham followed, closing the door behind him.

Daphne bit her lip, trying to marshal her thoughts in sensible order. Must she tell the whole tale? Yes, she miserably decided. She was through with lies and deceit.

"Dee, are you turned to stone that you stand and stare so?" asked Sophie, stepping from her gown. "No, no, Tyson, the dotted muslin and the blue sarcenet spencer. 'Tis warm as midsummer today."

"Oh, yes, miss. 'Tis one of your prettiest," Tyson cheerfully agreed. Daphne noted the abigail was less taciturn and withdrawn since her arrival in London, and actually smiled now and then. Perhaps her charge's improved behavior had sweetened her temper, or perhaps she basked in the glory of Miss Summerhayes' popularity.

With an effort, Daphne shook off her gloomy reflections. "Have we an engagement this morning?"

"I am in need of...um...stationery," Sophie answered casually, as Tyson fastened her bodice. "I shan't be long away."

"Why, Mitchell's will send some around, and save you the errand. Or, if you wait but a half hour, I may come with you."

"Oh, you are kindest, dear cousin, but there is no need to trouble yourself. I yearn merely to take some air, and shall return before you miss me." Sophie settled a straw gypsy hat carefully over her curls, brought the blue ribbon ends over the wide brim and tied them in a bow under her chin. "There. My gloves and reticule, pray. Do I pass muster, Dee?"

"Indeed, you are passing fine for a mere visit to a shop." Daphne surveyed her cousin more closely from top to toe. Sophie was dressed to the nines, and no mistake. "Are you certain you do not wish my company?"

"Oh, dear Coz, of course I wish your company!" Busy with her gloves, Sophie did not look in Daphne's direction. "Truly, though, this trifling errand is not worth your effort." Her gloves buttoned, she dropped a light kiss on Daphne's cheek and hurried out. Tyson, attempting to fasten her own cloak with one hand and tie her bonnet with the other, scurried out at her heels.

Daphne shrugged, returned to her room to tidy her hair, and then went in search of her aunt and uncle. The sitting room door was ajar, the room itself empty of her relatives. When the drawing room proved as deserted, Daphne tugged at the bell rope.

"Clapham, where may I find Lord and Lady Wentford?" she inquired when the butler answered the summons.

"His lordship and her ladyship are from home, miss."

Daphne stared. "They are gone out? Both? But they were here mere minutes ago. I was to speak with them."

"Yes, miss. They left rather speedily, miss." The butler's correct mien cracked slightly, and his brown eyes glimmered. "A picnic luncheon, I think. If I may make bold, miss, her ladyship was laughing."

"Thank you, Clapham."

He withdrew, leaving Daphne puzzling over what auspicious stars had collided in the heavens to spur her uncle to plan a romantic picnic. He spent more time at home, too, and seemed more his old self, much to his wife's delight. Daphne shrugged helplessly. At least his impetuousness had put off Daphne's confession, and she could not help feeling deep relief.

* * *

The Wentford carriage and pair spoken for by the master, Sophie engaged a hackney for Tyson and herself. "Direct the jarvey to Grafton's in New Bond Street," she ordered her abigail.

"But Grafton's is a draper's, Miss Sophie," Tyson demurred. "They don't have a fit selection of stationery, do they? And 'tis stationery you need, ain't it?"

Her answer was a quick, displeased frown. Tyson hastily gave directions, and the hackney moved off.

"I heard that Grafton House has a new shipment of silks," Sophie said in off-handed explanation.

"Another gown, Miss Sophie?" protested Tyson, pursing her lips. "I recollect Mr. Summerhayes, your Papa, reckoning your needs to four gowns and no more than three bonnets, besides other necessities. Why, you have more than that now, and that without mentioning your lovely court dress and ball gown."

"One may look without buying," stated Sophie, turning her face to the window.

"Miss Daphne might have enjoyed viewing the silks with you," observed Tyson, peering at her mistress. "'Tis passing strange, Miss Sophie, that you did not mention them to her."

Sophie gestured pettishly. "Oh, hush, Tyson. Miss Daphne had other matters to see to."

The journey was completed in silence, a rare occurrence for Miss Summerhayes, who usually commented on everything that caught her attention. In silence she entered Grafton's establishment, where an explosion of color dazzled the eye.

Bolts of muslin, wool, sarcenet, silk, velvet—in short, every fabric of warp and weft—lined the walls. Other bolts of delicate tulle, spangled net, and exquisite lace were piled on tables or hung from frames with a length of the cloth displayed. Ladies twittered like gay birds to the clerks and to each other. Gentlemen, escorting their ladies, or too fastidious to trust their tailor's selection, browsed among the superfines, twills, and fine linens.

Sophie moved slowly about the shop with Tyson at her elbow. A clerk offered his services, but she dismissed him with a smile. Pausing at the rainbow shades of a ribbon display, she glanced covertly about. From the corner of her eye, she glimpsed a tall, masculine form wending its way toward her.

With fast-beating heart Sophie pretended to examine the wares spread before her.

"Oh, I cannot decide on the blue, the pink, or the green," she murmured with a helpless shrug. "Poor Tyson, you must be weary while I debate such a heavy issue. Several chairs are set near the door for tired patrons; do go there and rest."

The abigail shook her head. "Oh, them chairs are for ladies, and not for the likes of me, Miss Sophie."

"Piffle. If a lady requires a seat, you will of course give up yours, but I see no need for the chairs to sit empty when I know your bunions are aching. Off with you now."

"Well, if you are sure, Miss Sophie..." Tyson sighed and shifted from one foot to the other.

"As sure as death, my suffering Tyson. And as I have yet to see the new silks, do not get in a pelter if you must wait for some time. I cannot leave without you seeing me."

Tyson gave her mistress a doubtful look, but the pain in her feet decided her. With a nod of thanks, she went off for a chair.

Sophie dimpled in satisfaction and, engrossed in finding the absolutely perfect ribbon, drifted to the end of the counter. There, behind a fall of lace, lurked the tall, masculine form.

"Egad, Miss Summerhayes," he murmured, "what luck for me that your watchdog should depart!"

Sophie raised startled, innocent eyes. "Why, Mr. Merritt! I vow, such a turn you gave me! What happy coincidence brings you here this morning?"

"No coincidence, I confess, Miss Summerhayes." Mr. Merritt's handsome face peered around the lacy curtain. "Last evening, at the concert, I overheard your intention to shop here. I have been here since the place opened, hoping to see you if only from a distance. I never dreamed of the chance to speak to you alone."

"Sir, you are overbold!" Sophie managed to express suitably shocked displeasure while maintaining a low tone. "Do you wish to endanger my reputation? What would Lord Courtlea, your noble brother, say should he learn of your addressing me like this?"

"I would give my life to protect you and your reputation, my dear Miss Summerhayes," Mr. Merritt avowed boldly, "but I don't give tuppence for my brother's opinion or his censure. He is kindness itself to me, but he does not understand the ways of the heart. He has never been in love, I am sure."

"Mr. Merritt!" Sophie raised one gloved hand, palm outward. "Pray do not speak here of such a tender emotion! My head is firmly fixed, and not easily turned like that of a Bath miss."

A light of desperation shone in Mr. Merritt's eyes. "Miss Summerhayes, could you—may I—is there hope you might look on me with more than tolerance?"

Sophie picked up a length of wide green ribbon and ran it through her fingers. "You ask much of me, sir, when others likewise demand my attention. Delicacy forbids naming these gentlemen, but all are earnest in their claims. Only one can be chosen, and, pray excuse my bluntness, I must choose soon."

He nodded reluctant agreement. "Launton and Sutton are two of the coves, I dare say. Faugh! One a beau and the other a prig! You cannot be buckled to either of those, Miss Summerhayes! You cannot!"

"Hush, sir!" Sophie cast surreptitious glances to each side, but discerned no one paying them attention. "If you attract notice, I must leave at once. As for making a choice...well, Mr. Merritt, both those gentlemen have much to offer a wife."

"I grant you that both are flush in the pocket, and will be well inlaid with brass when their sires pop off." He shook his head wretchedly. "I cannot match them in that."

Sophie hesitated only the briefest moment. "Since you have lit on that particular subject, Mr. Merritt, may one inquire as to the nature of your expectations in that quarter?"

"How much am I worth?" Edgar shrugged. "In truth, I cannot tell. I function on an allowance from my brother, and, in line with my father's wishes, Victor has promised a settlement when I marry. The amount of the settlement has yet to be named."

"Ah." Sophie fell silent. The green ribbon, unnoticed, rejoined its fellows. "And if you should marry against the earl's wishes...?"

He made a quick, anguished gesture. "Do not think that a hindrance for one moment, I beg! Only give me some hope, sweetest, kindest Miss Summerhayes, or I shall be past praying for."

"Indeed, sir, I should not wish you to fall into a decline for my sake!" She glanced full at him, giving him the benefit of her sparkling eyes and dimpled smile. "Oh, dear, this shopping business is tiresome, is it not? Tomorrow I must seek out some new stationery. At Mitchell's, perhaps, at about eleven o'clock."

Edgar's tormented countenance burgeoned into a sunrise of hope. When his lips parted in a smile of adoration, and he bent his glowing gray eyes on her, Sophie was hard put not to fling herself straightaway into his arms.

"Now, Mr. Merritt, you must leave me to my ribbons," she said breathlessly.

"Yes, dash it, I know, Miss Summerhayes, but I leave with the greatest reluctance. Dear Miss Summerhayes," he added, his voice deepening with a timbre that sent queer delicious shivers coursing through her.

Sophie covertly watched Mr. Merritt move deeper into the shop, to mingle with other patrons. When his proud dark head and straight back had disappeared from her sight, a long, quavering sigh escaped her lips. Her glance fell again on the ribbons, and she gasped in dismay. While she had talked, her fingers, all unknowing, had twined and twisted until the bright colored strands lay in tangled confusion.

She looked up, horrified, to meet the grimly patient stare of a senior clerk. Affecting an aplomb she did not feel, Miss Summerhayes caught up a silken handful, stared down her straight little nose, and ordered five yards of each.

CHAPTER 17

For the next few days Daphne was on tenterhooks waiting for gossip linking her, Lord Courtlea, and an emerald brooch. None was noised abroad, however. Had Lord Courtlea feared the story would recoil, making him a laughing-stock? Or was he waiting for some purpose of his own? When she thought of how much she was in his power, her blood ran cold.

She was thankful now she had not confessed to her aunt and uncle; they were inseparable, with Lady Wentford as bemused as a young bride. What had prompted Uncle Valentine's ardor Daphne dared not ask. Perhaps he had finally come to terms over his lack of family; perhaps he realized if he did not appreciate his wife's beauty and fine qualities, other gentlemen might. Whatever the cause, Daphne was happy for it.

The notice of Lord Courtlea's engagement to Lady Prudence Abernathy had not yet appeared in the Gazette. Was the noble lord playing cat's cradle with Lady Prudence's heart as once Sir George Sowerby had played with Daphne's tender feelings? If so, and if justice of any sort prevailed, the earl's callousness would rebound on him. Fair punishment indeed, should he fall in love with a lady who did not return his sentiments!

The great day of Sophie's presentation arrived in a downpour of rain. Fortunately, or perhaps in answer to many prayers, the sky cleared, and a watery sun turned puddles to mirrors. Sophie, dressing between anxious trips to the window, and driving poor Tyson frantic, was almost in tears when Daphne entered.

"Oh, Dee, I have practised my curtsy until my knees refuse to bend! Thank mercy the rain has stopped. Dodging a pelting rain while managing hoops and a train is the outside of enough! Oh, how I wish you were going with me! Do I look all right?" She touched the pearl and diamond necklace about her throat.

"I will be there in spirit, and Aunt Elizabeth will be at your side every minute. You look a treat." Daphne thought the necklace perfectly enhanced the slender white neck which wore it. Smiling, she lightly took Sophie's flushed face between her hands. "Recollect that no young lady, no matter how highly placed, will be lovelier or acquit herself better than Miss Summerhayes, from near Bodmin, in Cornwall."

"Oh, do you truly believe that?" Sophie whispered, her eyes glowing.

"Indeed I do, dear." Daphne kissed her cousin's cheek. "Come now. Loop your train over your arm. 'Twould not do to keep Queen Charlotte waiting."

Daphne followed Sophie out the door. She was not sorry to miss the Queen's Drawing Room. It promised to be a shocking crush, especially if the Prince of Wales chose to attend. Of a certainty, some of the royal dukes and duchesses would be there, as well as various ambassadors and ministers, but Prinny delighted in throwing a rub in the way of court occasions.

The Wentfords waited in the hall. Daphne thought her aunt had never looked lovlier. Her peach silk robe set off her fine complexion, and the cream-colored petticoat, embroidered with crystal bugle beads, shimmered as she turned to smile at her girls. Diamonds glittered at her throat, ears, and wrists. Daphne smiled as her uncle, elegant in blue satin coat, white knee breeches and stockings, held out his hands to his wife and Sophie.

"One rarely is privileged to see perfection itself," he said gallantly, kissing their hands in turn.

Tyson and Carter, Lady Wentford's abigail, had followed down the stairs, beaming with pride in their ladies. A smiling Briggs stood with them, doubtless recollecting Daphne's own presentation. At the door, under Clapham's stern eye, the servants, agog with excitement, were lined up in a row. They all broke into impulsive applause at the beauty of their mistress and Miss Summerhayes.

Sophie laughed. "Oh, thank you all." She turned slowly to show her finery to advantage, and then gave them a deep curtsy. Aglow, Sophie blew a final kiss to her cousin and then followed Lord and Lady Wentford out to the carriage.

With the carriage gone, a sensation of anti-climax engulfed Daphne. Needlework did not entice, nor did laying out a pattern for beading a new reticule. Restless, she wandered into the sitting room. She glanced at the small heap of books from the lending library. Usually she delighted in reading, but today she could not settle to open a book. It was not concern for Sophie's conduct that caused her unease. Truly, she had every confidence in her cousin. One was hard put to recognize the loud, heedless, impetuous girl who had arrived at Weldern Manor in the poised young lady who had just departed Wentford House.

Why, then, was she so disturbed? 'Twas more than anxiety over Lord Courtlea's intentions. She no longer enjoyed the parties, dances, and assemblies as she once did. Something was missing in her life, and its lack was driving her to distraction.

She fled up to her room. William was due a long-delayed letter regarding the brooch's return. He must inform their father soonest, if he had not already done so. Of course, he must only admit to losing the jewel at cards, and nothing more. Daphne could well imagine her Papa's reaction should he learn of his daughter's antics. Bread and water for her for a twelvemonth, and forbidden to set foot outside the Manor!

She had barely inscribed "My dear Brother William," when a quiet rap sounded at the door. Clapham entered, bearing a round silver tray on which reposed a single white card. "I informed the gentleman, miss, that Lady Wentford was from home, but his lordship insisted on asking that you receive him."

"How strange." Rising, Daphne took the card and read the name printed in neat, black lettering. "Oh, no! I cannot—" She read it again, disbelieving her senses, but the black letters refused to change into a different pattern.

"Shall I inform Lord Courtlea that you are not receiving, Miss Daphne?"

"Yes! No! That is... No, Clapham. I will see his lordship directly, in the drawing room."

The butler retreated, but Daphne stood frozen. She could not even speculate on the earl's reason for confronting her here. He must have known he faced rebuff, that after that horrible episode in his study she would not receive him. How could she, when the thought of that night still brought hot blushes to her cheek!

Yet he was here. Oh, one could never understand that man! With her heart beating fast, but determined not to show her trepidation, Daphne left the sanctuary of her room, and descended the stairs.

Lord Courtlea was standing at the window, looking out, his back to the room. When he heard the door open, he turned, his features coolly composed. As always, his attire was immaculate: claret-coloured coat fitting smoothly on his powerful shoulders, white, perfectly arranged neckcloth, buff pantaloons and gleaming boots, all without a trace of the mud occasioned by the recent rainfall. He was utterly handsome, compelling in his confidence, and totally unpredictable. Daphne's nerves tightened further.

Steeling herself, Daphne moved into the room, her hands clasped before her to still their trembling. For what seemed an eternity, the earl stood facing her, unsmiling.

At last Daphne could no longer stand the silence. "I believe you wished to see me, my lord."

He bowed slightly, and moved away from the window. "Wished is perhaps an inaccurate word, Miss Summerhayes, but it will serve. No matter my wants, I find it imperative that I speak with you."

"Indeed?" she retorted. "I cannot believe we have anything to speak about."

The notion sprang to her mind that he might be as ill at ease as she. But no, this coldly calculating gentleman was never uneasy. Having agreed to receive him, however, she was determined not to order him out until she learned the reason for his visit.

"Pray be seated, my lord, and explain." Daphne sat down thankfully, as her knees felt weak. The earl ignored her invitation and stood before her, hands clasped behind his back.

"Thank you for receiving me with no prior notice, Miss Summerhayes. I understand your family is out at the moment?"

"Yes." How formally he spoke, as though nothing had ever happened between them! "Lord and Lady Wentford are with my cousin at St. James's. Sophie is to be presented to Queen Charlotte."

"Ah, yes. The queen holds a Drawing Room today." He nodded and fell silent.

Daphne shifted slightly in her chair, bewildered and growing exasperated by his diffident manner. "Lord Courtlea, I cannot believe you are here merely to exchange civilities. Please comprehend I find this interview most trying. If you have come on a particular errand, my lord, perhaps I could hear it now?" A ghost of a smile touched his lips.

"Ever the brisk, straight-to-the-mark Miss Summerhayes! 'Tis simply this which brings me to you." He reached into a side pocket, withdrew a small, familiar box and handed it to her.

Daphne flushed, then grew cold as she turned it over in her hands. She looked up at the earl. "What is this, pray?"

"Open it, I beg, but I believe you know."

Her trembling fingers lifted the lid. From inside the box, the emerald brooch winked at her. Daphne surged to her feet. "What game is this, sir? Does it amuse you to taunt me, to flaunt my shame in my face? Oh, how cruel!"

Her fury drove him back a step. His features showed surprise, then a grim sort of humor. "Perhaps, madam, if you allowed an explanation before you shot off all your guns, you might have less to say! Devil take it, but your habit of always assuming the worst side is one of your less endearing qualities. Indeed, I am hard put to list any qualities to your favor!"

His blunt words took the wind from her sails with a vengeance, but there was little of meekness about Daphne's head as she resumed her seat. "Then pray begin, my lord, and for mercy's sake, let it be brief."

He gave a curt nod. "As brief as may be, I assure you. 'Twas not by choice—no matter, let us not outdo each other regarding our reluctance to speak together. The matter is simple: I cannot keep the brooch, and so I return it to you."

Daphne eyed him askance. "You do, sir? And the reason, pray?"

"'Twas unfairly won. Your brother is but a country lad, who has proven his lack of a cool head, and is doubtless less versed at cards than I. My honor will not tolerate the notion that my greater experience took advantage of the boy. Therefore, madam, the only possible solution agreeable to both parties is to return the bauble. Let William treat this matter as a lesson against gambling. Do you not agree?"

Daphne stared down at the brooch, not daring to trust a whisper of hope. The earl offered a perfect escape. No one, save William and herself, need ever know of the affair.

"Oh, how tempting to call an end to this," she said, looking up at Lord Courtlea. She wished he would sit down, or at least cease towering over her in that formidable manner. "You speak of honor, sir, but what of my brother's pride? Can you hope that he will accept this rebuke, like a master's caning at school? He may not, sir. His honor is every bit as important to him as yours is to you. Ah, you stare in disbelief that such could be so!"

"Your brother would kick up a dust at this easy solution? Madam, I find your family passing strange—"

"My family, sir, lacks neither honor, pride, nor lineage," she informed him coldly. "Pray recollect that fact." Before her resolve melted, Daphne rose to her feet and held out the little box.

"I cannot take it back, Miss Summerhayes," the earl protested, shaking his head. "It is not mine to keep."

"Then it is not yours to give."

Lord Courtlea's shoulders tensed as if he would seize and shake her. "Confound it!" He threw up his hands. "Then pretend, I beg, that the blessed thing never strayed from your hands! I wish only to be rid of it, and forget the whole sorry hubble-bubble."

"No more than I, sir!" Daphne heartily agreed. She wished to forget those moments in his arms, and those threatening words that she would some day surrender to him. How bizarre in the cool formality of this beautiful, serene room was the recollection of that ill-lit, emotional meeting! As her gaze challenged his, she saw a flicker of something in the gray depths. Was he recollecting too, and did he wish for the same forgetfulness?

"Miss Summerhayes," Lord Courtlea said in a calmer tone, "let us be sensible. Your brother is young, doubtless with a youth's quickness of temper. If his pride smarts a little over this, he will, I charge, wholly recover. The brooch has a meaning to your family it does not have for mine. It was your mother's, I believe."

She felt the earl's quiet, earnest reasoning weakening her resolution. "I am the third generation of my family to wear the emeralds," she admitted. "The sentiment attached to this brooch far outstrips its cost."

"Then, I beseech you, take it back. What is gained by refusing? Think on it, I beg."

As yet unconvinced, Daphne searched for sarcasm or condescension in his expression. There was none. "'Tis true my heart is lighter," she said quietly, "and doubtless my brother will agree when I explain the matter." Slowly her hand closed over the little box. A great flood of relief flowed through her. "Accept my thanks, Lord Courtlea, and that of my brother, for your great kindness..."

Daphne paused with the sudden realization that the proud lord had shown unwonted consideration when he chose to return the brooch, and by his own hand.

"Sir, I wonder if compassion for the loss of our heirloom and not an affront to your self-esteem has moved your lordship to make this gesture."

Lord Courtlea shrugged lightly. "Spare me your thanks or your surmises, Miss Summerhayes. I merely rectify a shadow on my honor, and you oblige me by allowing me to do so. Let no more be said."

So compassion had not motivated him. Daphne could not restrain a sigh as she set the little box on a side table. Whenever she attributed finer considerations to the earl, he had an uncanny ability to squash her.

"Then let me be grateful chance brought you here when my aunt and uncle were from home. At least I am spared further explanation to them."

Lord Courtlea's dark brows lifted ever so slightly, and the corners of his mouth quivered. The movements were scarce noticeable, but Daphne had come to read even the tiniest nuance of his expressions. She did not wish it so, but there it was.

Her fingers flew to her lips. "Why, you knew they would be out today! You deliberately planned your call for this time!"

He tipped his head in agreement, while a reluctant smile softened his mouth. "The Court Circular named those to be presented today. I protest, however, that I had already determined to attend you this morning. The fact of your relatives' absence was merely happenstance."

"Oh, sir!" Daphne clasped her hands and took an impulsive step forward. "Why do you deny your softer sentiments? Can you not admit you acted in kindness, without consideration of your own interests?"

For a long moment he looked into her eager face, while conflicting emotions warred in his own countenance. Arrogance, tenderness, pride, yearning—all struggled for supremacy, and pride won out. All warmth fled from his expression as if a curtain had fallen. "I never act against my own interests, madam," he said coldly.

Daphne drew back, bitterly chiding herself for looking again for gentler sentiments in the prideful lord. "Do not fear, Lord Courtlea. I shall never again lose sight of that fact. How foolish of me to doubt it, even for a moment."

He hesitated, then abruptly bowed. "Then I bid you good day. Your servant, madam!"

"Good day, sir." Daphne walked smartly to the bell rope, but paused with her fingers on the tasselled brocade. "One more thing needs to be said, my lord," she said softly without turning to face the earl. "Thank you for keeping this matter from common knowledge."

He did not answer. She glanced over her shoulder, and was

surprised to see him tight-lipped, his brow black as thunder.

"'Tis plain you have no notion—" he began, then broke off in an obvious effort to control his temper. "Your statement merits no response, madam. Again I bid you good day."

She had insulted him, completely unintentionally, implying he was no gentleman. Only a cad would spread the story of their encounters. "I am sorry—" She stopped, flustered, at his sharp glance, and feeling at a loss, rang for Clapham.

The butler entered the room so promptly he must have already been reaching for the doorknob. "Lord Courtlea is leaving, Clapham."

"Yes, miss." He extended his tray bearing another white card. "Lord Tunney awaits, Miss Summerhayes."

Lord Courtlea gave a crack of laughter. "Perhaps he too, is a reader of the Circular."

Daphne had been on the point of returning Lord Tunney's card, and not receiving him, but the earl's sardonic laughter changed her mind. She moved to the door, took the card and nodded to the butler. "You may show Lord Tunney up in a few minutes, Clapham."

"Yes, Miss." He hesitated, looking from Daphne to the earl, then quietly closed the door.

"Tunney has *entrée* here, then," Lord Courtlea muttered, his eyes hooded.

He stood too close, but Daphne could not step away. Her breath came faster. "All my friends are welcome here," she said faintly.

He continued to look down at her, not moving, seeming hardly to breathe. She thought suddenly that if he opened his arms to her now, she could not help but throw herself into them. Yes, and kiss that stern mouth a hundred times if he wished. Desire flowed through her until it seemed he must read it in her eyes.

Still, he did not move, although his breathing roughened. His gloved hands slowly closed into fists at his sides.

"My lord," she whispered.

"Miss Summerhayes," he said, his voice husky. A muscle quivered in his jaw.

Clapham opened the door. If he felt the tension in the air, he did not disclose it by so much as a glance. "Shall I show Lord Tunney up, miss?"

Daphne averted her too-revealing face and struggled for breath.

"Do, Clapham," she heard Lord Courtlea say. "I am leaving now. Good-bye, Miss Summerhayes."

Daphne swung to face him, but he was already striding from the room. He did not look back. Daphne sank into a chair with her hands pressed to her burning cheeks. She felt hollow, drained of all emotion. Had he not understood her readiness? Mayhap he waited for her to do or say something more.

Yes, of course, he waited for her open declaration, her humbling admission of surrender! She cringed at the thought that he had known perfectly well how she felt, but had not cared.

She looked up. Clapham still waited, the perfect servant, seeing nothing, knowing nothing. Courtesy demanded she admit Lord Tunney after accepting his card, but all she wanted at the moment was the peace and seclusion of her room.

"Clapham, please give Lord Tunney my regrets that I cannot at this time receive him, but assure him that I will be happy to welcome him tomorrow afternoon."

The butler nodded, his face unreadable, and quietly retreated. Daphne picked up the box containing the brooch, unconsciously gripping it until one corner of the box dug into her palm.

CHAPTER 18

Sophie returned in a calm glow of accomplishment. While Tyson helped her undress, Sophie enumerated to Daphne the exalted personages to whom she had been presented: the Duke and Duchess of York, the Dukes of Kent and Gloucester, the Duchess of Sussex, and innumerable earls and marquesses. The Italian Ambassador was charming, the Austrian Ambassador witty. The Prince of Wales, alas, did not favor the company with his presence.

"Oh, and Queen Charlotte was so kind, Dee!" Sophie added, slipping into a wrapper. "Such fine eyes she has, and the nicest smile! I could not be frightened of her. Oh, but waiting in the Long Gallery, I vow, I was in the worst quake! So many young ladies, all so beautifully dressed!

"Then the Lord Chamberlain flourished his great staff—oh, such a staff, half again as tall as I, and all carved and gilded, but you know that, having seen it—and called for Lady Wentford to present me. My knees shook, I can tell you! But then I recollected your words that I was as good as any, and I felt able to face dragons. But there were no dragons, and oh, I vow, life can offer no greater excitement than that I enjoyed today!"

She kicked off her white slippers, sadly stained with damp. Then, with a joyful squeal, she spread her arms and collapsed onto her bed.

"Did I not say things would go well?" Daphne forced a smile past her own distraction. "Now, why not rest until dinner?"

"No, indeed." Sophie sat up at once. "Here I have been babbling on without a word of how you spent your day. Was the time all too sadly flat?"

Flat! Daphne turned abruptly, pretending a loose pin in her hair. "No, Cousin," she said finally, "one can hardly say the time was as dull as ditchwater. Lord Tunney called."

"What? And you here alone? What a happy chance."

"Oh, I was resting at the time, and bade him return tomorrow," Daphne said easily, seating herself on the edge of the bed. "Why are you so set on matching me with Lord Tunney? Are you so very keen to have me caught in parson's mousetrap?"

"Why not?" Sophie tipped her head like a pert sparrow. "I intend to marry and set up my own household. Lord Trout is quite personable, except for his face, but he is kind, and you two appear to rub along well. Why then, do you not accept his suit?"

Daphne laughed. "Because, goose, he has not offered for me!"

"He will, given half a chance. Oh, Dee, anyone with half an eye can see he finds you pleasing. He is not young, but you like him well enough, do you not?"

Daphne shrugged impatiently. "Lord Tunney is a charming, considerate gentleman with fine sensibilities. Naturally, I enjoy his company. What lady would not?"

"There you are, then!" Sophie exclaimed with a triumphant bounce that made the gold brocade bed curtains swing.

"No, miss, I am not." How could one compare the turmoil Lord Courtlea excited in her with the pleasant ease she felt in Lord Tunney's presence? Daphne tweaked one of her cousin's curls and got to her feet. "Moreover, I am more concerned with your prospects than with mine. Have you chosen the fortunate man from among your suitors?"

Sophie shook her head. "Mama writes that I must choose the richest and most highly placed, but Mr. Sutton is the only one who shows any real keenness."

"Well, he will be a viscount one day, and wealthy." Frowning, Daphne eyed her cousin. "Has he indeed mentioned marriage?"

"No, no," Sophie protested airily, "but he has hinted, most strongly."

"Well, that may be a good sign." Daphne observed, carefully maintaining a neutral tone. "He hopes to be sure of your heart before risking a proposal."

Mr. Sutton was all together too cautious, too tied to his mother's leading strings to suit Daphne, but she would not air this opinion unless

Sophie asked for it. Sophie might see good qualities in him that were hidden to Daphne's eyes.

"And did you hint back, or freeze him for his forwardness?"

Sophie's smile was mischievous as she drew her knees up and wrapped her arms about them. "A little of both, I think. Mayhap he has run to his mama for direction." She shrugged, and then gave a prodigious yawn.

"You are more tired than you know," suggested Daphne. "Why do you not have a nap? Tyson will wake you in time to dress for dinner, will you not, Tyson?"

"Indeed I will, Miss Daphne." The abigail bustled forward, drawing up a blanket to cover her mistress. "A right good notion it is, to be sure, seeing as how we was too excited to sleep last night, and was up this morning before the crack of dawn."

Sophie pouted, but a second gaping yawn convinced her to snuggle into her pillows. Daphne and Tyson exchanged satisfied nods, and Daphne quietly left the room.

Frowning, Daphne moved toward her own room. Surely young Sophie was wide of the mark when she advanced Lord Tunney's suit! Daphne enjoyed his company, and she knew he enjoyed hers. Never had she invited his favor. Would he, as Sophie asserted, welcome encouragement?

Daphne paused at her bedroom door. Briggs was moving about inside, laying out a fresh gown for dinner as she had done thousands of times before.

And would continue to do so, Daphne thought despairingly, resting her forehead against the satin-smooth wood of the door, for thousands of nights to come. Later Briggs would lay out a plain nightgown, turn down the bed, and plump the single set of pillows for a single, lone head.

A vision flashed before Daphne of dark tousled hair against a white pillow, a handsome face open and vulnerable in the innocence of sleep. She shook her head to banish the sight, but the hot ache in her chest was not so easily defeated. Grimly she pressed a fist over her heart, recollecting that she gloried in her logical, factual mind attracted to character rather than mere good looks. Was it the good side of Lord Courtlea's character, admitting that he had one, that attracted her? Or was it what her vicar called the baser urges? The same urges had doubtless caused poor Alice's downfall. But whether or not the earl had seduced Alice and then cast her aside, as Lord Tunney claimed, Daphne had no intention of sharing her fate.

Would marriage to Lord Tunney prove so onerous? Daphne and he were well suited as to temperaments, and most marriages had not such a firm foundation. A meeting of minds, a joining of friends, a sharing of tastes—who might ask for more in wedlock? Almost half-convinced, Daphne went in to dress.

* * *

The invitation had arrived by hand, and, oddly enough, requested no reply. Courtlea had flung it on his desk, and now he unwillingly picked it up again. The invitation was no surprise; he knew the Wentfords well enough to expect one, but surely Daphne Summerhayes would have blocked it. As he idly flicked the card with his finger, he could not believe she wanted to face him ever again. Nor, he insisted, was he eager to see her.

Meeting with that miss was much like holding a hand over a burning candle: delightfully warm at first, then, before one is aware, the palm is scorched. Every encounter with her had left him slightly crisp around the edges. Even that last time, when he had nerved himself to return her jewel, she had stood close enough for him to take her into his arms, all the while looking up at him with such piercing openness, such melting trust.

Damnation! What he wanted from Daphne Summerhayes was not her trust! For his sanity's sake, he would do well to put her out of his mind once and for all.

A slamming door and a loud whistling in the hall interrupted his gloomy thoughts. In a moment Edgar's dark head appeared around the study door.

"What ho, Victor?" he demanded. "Why are you buried in here instead of enjoying this beautiful spring day outside?"

With a sour frown, Courtlea regarded his brother's beaming face. "Are you foxed, so early in the day?"

"I? You wound me." Edgar did not look the least offended as he came wholly into the study. "You know I have not been half seas over for…oh, for days and weeks. I vow, I cannot recollect the last time drink got the better of me. Can you, brother mine?"

"No." Courtlea folded his arms and leaned back against his desk, glad of something else to occupy his mind rather than the contentious Miss Summerhayes. "In truth, lately you have exhibited nothing but the most exemplary behavior. One deduces you are either ill or in love. I only hope it is the former."

"What?" Edgar's grin grew broader. "You would see me at death's door rather than at the church door? Shame, sir!"

Courtlea sighed and shook his head. "You are past talking to, but if your heart is engaged, I trust you have chosen sensibly."

"Hoo! You tie sense and love together? As well pair a mare with a pig, or an angel with a gargoyle. 'Tis simply not done."

Mention of the tender passion brought a sour taste to Courtlea's mouth. He would not be so afflicted, so moon-struck as to lose his head.

"Away with you! Such beef-witted philosophy quite defeats me." He gestured in disgust, and seeing the card still in his hand, threw it on the desk.

"What have you there?" Edgar asked, with an air of changing the subject.

Courtlea handed it to him, then dropped into the desk chair while Edgar read.

"Egad, Victor, I had no notion you were invited too. But this is prime! Now we may go together."

"My invitation is a surprise," Courtlea stated, his cold stare freezing Edgar's enthusiasm, "but I can find a reason for it. Why, pray, do you receive such consideration?"

Edgar flushed, shifted from one foot to the other, and looked fixedly at the card in his hand as though for inspiration. "Deuced if I know," he finally admitted, shrugging. "Sheer courtesy, I expect, letting me ride in on your coat-tails, as it were." Carefully, he laid the invitation on the desk.

"That could be so," Courtlea agreed, "but in any case, Lady Wentford's ball must progress without me. I shall not attend." For his peace of mind he must avoid that house as long as it sheltered the woman who had driven him almost to distraction.

Edgar shook his head, oblivious to his brother's grimness. "Oh, I say, Victor, you will miss a rousing good go! Lady Wentford's ball is the acme of the Season. The ton buzzes with it, and invitations are prized as gold. But if you insist on playing the hermit, I shall tender your regrets to our hostess."

"You shall not!" Courtlea leaped to his feet, sending his chair crashing over.

Edgar jumped back, open-mouthed. Then, with palms raised defensively, he edged toward the door. "Steady on, Victor, old man, steady on! You needn't glare or bite my head off. I shan't mention your name, if you prefer it."

"I do prefer it, but I strongly recommend you do not attend at all. You understand me, I trust."

After Edgar left, obviously puzzled by his brother's outburst, Courtlea tossed the card into a desk drawer. His eruption had shocked him too, but whatever the reasons for the invitation, he would not set foot inside Wentford House.

* * *

Wherever she went in the few days leading up to Sophie's ball, Daphne found herself looking for the dark-haired earl. Several times she felt his cool gray eyes upon her, but when she turned, her pulse racing, he was not there. Lord Courtlea might have vanished from London. Mayhap he had returned to Yorkshire. Daphne fervently wished it were so. His name was not on the invitation list, so she could relax and enjoy Sophie's ball.

But the earl leaped to mind with a vengeance as Daphne sat before her mirror, dressed for the ball. She loved her new gown of palest green shot silk. Blond lace and darker green ribbon edged the deep neckline and tiny puffed sleeves. The lace formed a deep hem, caught up here and there with green ribbon and rosebuds. Briggs had arranged her hair in soft curls over her forehead and at her temples, then swirled the back hair high in a graceful twist. The abigail had anchored the twist with a green and gold fillet, then nestled in it a small posy of flowers.

Then Briggs had proudly fastened the emerald necklace about Daphne's throat as the final, glorious touch. It lay heavily against her flesh, the brooch twinkling from its pride of place in the center. Repellent as the thought was, she owed the earl an immense debt.

Would that debt pick at her whenever she wore the emeralds? For how long would that strong, coolly mocking face hover at the edge of her vision? Slowly Daphne pulled on her long gloves and fastened the glittering bracelets. The earrings swung gaily as she rose to her feet. This was Sophie's night, and nothing should detract from its joy. Certainly not a cousin distracted by a will-o'-the-wisp earl who would not be present in body.

"There, Miss Daphne, you do look a treat." Briggs stepped back, her worn hands folded over her plump waist, her homely features alight with affection. "Why, you are more beautiful now than at your own come-out ball. Do you recollect that night? Oh, such a time! You danced all night, you did, then, without so much as a wink of sleep, and still in your finery, led the whole troop on a gallop through the park!

Oh, I nearly died of mortification, I can tell you!"

Daphne smiled as she hugged her faithful abigail. "Dear Briggs! Let us hope Miss Sophie does not hear of such madness. She has enough wild notions of her own without duplicating mine."

On her way downstairs, Daphne peeped into the ballroom, again blessing a previous Lord Wentford for building his London home on such generous lines.

Flowers and tubs of greenery gave a fresh, spring-like touch to the elegant room. Floor- length mirrors shimmered like water, reflecting the paintings between the pilasters of malachite repeated at intervals around the walls. Clapham was supervising the lighting of the candles in the wall sconces and the two great chandeliers. In a few minutes, the chandeliers would be winched back into place beneath the frescoed ceiling.

The sound of hurrying footsteps caught Daphne's ear as she closed the door, and Sophie, a vision in gold-spangled net over white silk, came skipping down the stairs. "Oh, Dee, wait a moment, pray!"

"Yes, but for pity's sake, have a care that you do not fall! This is not the time for a sprained ankle or a ruined gown."

Sophie laughed, but proceeded more sedately until she reached her cousin's side. "Oh, I vow that tonight I feel completely grown up! Hah, do I hear you add that it is not before time?" Her smile faded into an expression of unwonted seriousness. "Dearest Daphne, how may I thank you for all you have done for me? Why, without your guidance, I would yet be the raw, heedless girl who so blithely left home. More to the point, I would not have met…your aunt and uncle, and…and all the other wonderful…" She stumbled to a stop, catching her bottom lip between her teeth, her eyes glimmering.

"Why, Sophie, you must not cry!" Daphne slipped her arm about the girl's waist. "Rather I should thank you for freeing me from my comfortable country rut. What a time we have had together! Know, my dear, that I have loved every minute of it."

Sophie blinked, and gave her cousin such a skeptical look that Daphne laughed aloud. "Mayhap that is going a little far," Daphne admitted. "No matter, you catch my meaning. Come, Aunt Elizabeth is awaiting us."

Arm in arm, they entered the drawing room where Lord and Lady Wentford amused themselves with a game of piquet while awaiting their guests. Tables were set up, and packs of cards laid out for those who wished a change from dancing. At one end of the room, two liveried footmen presided over a large table laden with wines and fruit drinks, tiny sandwiches and cakes.

"Carte blanche again!" Lady Wentford cried. "You villain, I believe you read the backs of my cards!" She laughed, throwing her cards in a heap on the table. "Oh, see, my lord, how lovely are our two girls!"

"Our three," he averred with a telling look at his wife, who was elegant in azure satin. "Well, my pets," he went on, rising to his feet. "Are you ready for the fray?"

Daphne laughed and agreed, but Sophie went to her host and hostess and soberly thanked them for all their kindnesses. "I hope," she finished, "that no act of mine will ever make you think the less of me."

The countess looked startled. "Why, darling child, what an odd thing to say! Nothing will affect our regard for you. Oh, could we but keep you both with us forever!"

Clapham appeared, ruddy with importance, and announced the arrival of the first carriage. Lady Wentford rose, smiling, and extended a hand to her niece. "Daphne, you will help Sophie and me receive, will you not?"

Daphne was honored, and said so.

Barely had they taken their places when the first guest, all eagerness, bounded up the stairs. Daphne started, a thrilling shock coursing through her until she realized it was Mr. Merritt, and not Lord Courtlea.

"Because of the horses, you know," Sophie whispered to Daphne after Edgar had passed on. At Daphne's blank stare, Sophie explained further. "He was so kind to provide those darling mounts, I thought it only courtesy to invite him. Aunt Elizabeth quite agreed."

"Of course. But what of Lord Courtlea, the owner of the animals?" Daphne avoided meeting her cousin's eyes by carefully opening her fan. "Did your courtesy extend to him?"

"Why, Dee, such an odious man! Would you truly wish to see him here?"

A bevy of arrivals saved Daphne from replying. After that, a steady flow entered the front door, relinquished cloaks and hats, and then mounted the ornate staircase to the first floor.

Immaculate as ever, Lord Tunney bowed low over Daphne's hand, lingering much longer than necessary. "Miss Summerhayes," he began, smiling into her eyes, "may I say how much—"

"Charming, Eliza, and Sophie, m'dear, you acted a treat at St. James's. Heard the queen herself comment on how bang-up prime you were." Lady Silversby nudged Lord Tunney, none too gently, with her elbow. "Cut along, Samuel, the whole pack is panting at my heels."

"At once, dear lady." Lord Tunney relinquished Daphne's hand with a wry grimace, and strolled on down the wide corridor to the ballroom. The double doors were flung wide, with a footman standing rigidly on each side. Lord Tunney's assessing gaze flicked over them.

"Geminy! New liveries all around," exclaimed Lady Silversby, at his elbow. "Valentine is laying out a pretty packet for this little miss. One wonders why."

Lord Tunney smiled down into the sharp-featured face he once likened to a hatchet. The marchioness was loyal to her friends, but that trait in no way prevented her from digging out any possible gossip concerning them.

"Wentford and his lady are blessed with good, generous hearts. Recollect too, that whatever Elizabeth puts her hand to is always accomplished with the utmost style and good taste. Do you not find it so, Meggie?"

A reluctant grin tugged at Lady Silversby's thin lips. "You rogue, I have not heard that pet name in many a year. Are you softening me for some reason? We both know Valentine can pinch a penny with the best."

Lady Silversby glanced behind her. Her husband trailed along, utterly indifferent to his lady's conversation. Lowering her voice, the marchioness continued, "I lay his change of heart at the feet of that niece of Elizabeth's, Daphne Summerhayes. She has a way with her that can call the birds from the trees, should she set her mind to it. But mayhap you have not noticed, Samuel, although one has seen you paying her due attention."

"One must be blind to remain ignorant of Miss Summerhayes's fine attributes," Lord Tunney answered smoothly. "And deaf, into the bargain, for I have never heard her speak ill of anyone. Indeed, she is perhaps one of the few ladies of my acquaintance who choose not to indulge in gossip or idle speculation."

The marchioness gave a crow of laughter. "Hah! Do not attempt to put me in my place, sir. Many have tried, and none have succeeded." She took his arm, and they began to pace slowly around the room. Lord Silversby, abhorring even the slightest exercise, eased into a chair with a loud sigh.

"Come, Samuel," Lady Silversby coaxed, "you may safely confide in me. For many years you have avoided matrimony like the plague it is, but somehow one senses that you are weakening. Tell me, does Daphne Summerhayes hold your heart, or no?"

"Miss Summerhayes snares the heart of every man fortunate enough to spend even five minutes in her company. She is totally delightful. The wonder is that she is still unwed."

"You slippery rascal!" The marchioness lightly struck his arm with her fan. "I suppose I must read it in the Gazette, as must any clod curious about his betters. Fie, Samuel, to treat me so."

He said nothing as they came face-to-face with Lord and Lady Daly. "How now, what treatment is this?" asked the countess, her eyes brightening. "Tell me at once, Samuel."

Lord Tunney chuckled as he bowed over her hand. "I shall leave to my Lady Margaret the pleasure of recounting my vices, if the evening affords time enough to include them all. Until later, dear ladies. Daly."

He strolled away, apparently unperturbed, a slight smile on his lips. Inwardly, however, his thoughts churned. Evidently his attentions to Miss Summerhayes had been noted by others, and he did not enjoy having his conduct and intentions open to speculation. He was forty and two, and had managed admirably without a wife. Was he willing to consider a change for such a prize as Daphne Summerhayes?

He paused to scan the room. The ballroom had quickly filled, the ladies' white or colorful gowns brilliantly pointing up the darker garb of their escorts. Diamonds, rubies, sapphires— indeed, every gemstone fashionable into adornments—flashed and sparkled from wrist, throat, and head.

The murmur of voices grew more intense, and then, their welcoming duties done, Lord and Lady Wentford entered with the two Misses Summerhayes.

Lord Tunney had eyes only for Daphne Summerhayes. She stood, slim and lovely, framed by the green malachite pilasters flanking the doorway. Her face lit with laughter at some witticism, and his heart turned over. Then Lady Wentford was led out by a Royal duke for the first minuet, and the music began.

Daphne gave her hand to the dignified Marquis of Blendon, an old friend of her uncle, and followed Kent and Lady Wentford. Sophie, she noted, was eagerly claimed by Lord Launton. As the dance began, moving through one elegant figure to another, Daphne had ample time to heed her cousin and her partner. Lord Launton exhibited all the signs of infatuation: high, glowing color, earnestness in every line, gleaming eyes fixed in homage on his idol. Yet Sophie had claimed only Mr.

Sutton showed her serious attention. Daphne determined to have a chat with her cousin, and then forgot Sophie in her concentration on not putting a foot wrong in the more intricate figures of the dance.

Before the first hour was out, Daphne knew the ball had all the signs of success. The fine music invited dancing; the floor was always thronged. Talk and laughter rose freely, and Daphne saw smiles wherever she looked. A few of the older guests had retired to the drawing room for cards or refreshments, and were not missed by the younger folk.

Sophie, glowing with excitement and pleasure, was led out for every dance. Daphne danced as much, twice standing up with Lord Tunney. Each time, she thought him unnaturally quiet and totally lacking his usual wit and good temper.

"Sir," she said when the second dance ended, "pray do not take offense, but you seem distracted. Are you quite well?"

He smiled faintly, with a wryness seemingly directed at himself. "My affliction is a common one, and easily mended. Will you favor me with a few minutes talk, Miss Summerhayes? Would you care for refreshments? Or perhaps we may stroll in the corridor."

A sudden uneasiness made Daphne pause. "I freely grant the time, sir, but may we not make use of the chairs here? I am a poor chaperon at best, but I must remain for my cousin's sake."

He offered his arm, and led her to a sofa at the far end of the room. It was set a little apart, and with greenery arranged behind and on one side, offered a little privacy. Daphne sat down, touched by trepidation, and looked up at Lord Tunney as he stood before her.

CHAPTER 19

The ball was well started when Lord Courtlea ascended the stairs to the first floor. His hostess had long quitted her post, and a waltz was occupying most of the guests. For a moment he stood just inside the door of the ballroom, debating the urge which had drawn him to Wentford House.

He spied Daphne Summerhayes immediately, her hair burnished bronze in the candlelight. She was in the arms of a young viscount Courtlea knew to be married, but the look in his eye, Courtlea saw with a surge of temper, was decidedly lecherous. And devil take him, look how he clasped her trim waist with his hand spread possessively in the small of her back! And she merely laughed, obviously enjoying the situation, the brazen flirt!

Several acquaintances glanced at the earl, but his thunderous frown did not invite greetings. Indeed, as he turned to search out his hostess, people fell back before him.

"Where is Lady Wentford?" he inquired of a footman.

The man shrank from the earl's glare, and gulped audibly. "I b-believe m-my lady is in the drawing room, my lord. S-shall I announce you, sir?"

Lord Courtlea turned away without answering. He was of a mind to leave at once, yet he bent his steps toward the drawing room. This uncertainty was new and very strange; always he did as he pleased, when he pleased. This shilly-shallying was foreign to his nature, as if his mind decreed one course, but his body carried him in a completely different direction. He felt annoyed, frustrated, and totally baffled.

He exchanged courtesies with Lord and Lady Wentford, dodged several invitations to play at cards, and grimly returned to the ballroom and the rhythms of a vigorous galop. Courtlea sighted Sophie Summerhayes and Edgar bounding past, both grinning like a pair of idiots. Infernal cheek! Had he not warned the boy—? Then all thoughts were driven from his mind by the spectacle of Daphne Summerhayes whirling past with that ancient, fish-faced Tunney.

Miss Summerhayes smiled brilliantly at her partner, and he, Courtlea noted in distaste, regarded her no less lecherously than had the married viscount. Devil take it! Did she not realize how infernally tantalizing she looked? Or had she decided to stir up every man, young and old, in the entire company?

The music ended to much laughter. Courtlea started forward, not positive what he intended, but Lord Tunney, looking neither right nor left, whisked Miss Summerhayes to a seat among the chaperons at the end of the room. Courtlea ground his teeth in a rage at being so neatly, if unintentionally, thwarted, and retreated to a position along the wall. Folding his arms across his white waistcoat, he watched the two. He was oblivious to all else, and if his dour brow and aloof stance drew curious looks, he neither knew nor cared.

Tunney stood with his back to the room, but Courtlea saw Miss Summerhayes's face with complete clarity. The fresh color in her cheeks during the galop slowly faded as she listened soberly, eyes cast down, her head tilted slightly to one side. She glanced up at Tunney once, as if startled, then the dark copper lashes swept down again. He spoke earnestly, shoulders bent forward, his hands clasped behind his back.

Was the fellow tossing the handkerchief, actually declaring for her before the world's eyes? Courtlea was not sure he had guessed aright, even when Miss Summerhayes began to answer. She did not smile, but neither did she frown. Devil take the minx! Was any man sure where he stood with her?

At last she smiled and gave her hand to Tunney. A symbolic gesture? Tunney bowed, holding the hand an intolerably long time before releasing it and taking his leave. Courtlea studied his face, seeking signs of hurt, anger, or jubilation, but Tunney's expression betrayed nothing.

Giving Miss Summerhayes no chance of escape, and driven by an impulse he could not name, Courtlea strode swiftly to the spot recently vacated by the older earl. Miss Summerhayes gave a little jump at his sudden appearance, and while a variety of emotions sped across her features, delight was not one of them. "Why, Lord Courtlea!" She seemed unable to continue, even to voice the usual courtesies.

He stood equally dumb. Her face was tipped up to him, drawing his glance to the smooth, elegant line of her throat. A tiny pulse throbbed at its base, and he knew the strongest desire to lay his lips there. As he once had, he thought, burning with the recollection of the delectable Flora. He blinked, drawing back to sanity, and bowed as the orchestra struck up a tune.

"Will you honor me with this waltz, Miss Summerhayes?" he managed, a touch hoarsely. He extended his hand, and she, with the merest of pauses, put her hand in his. She rose, not looking at him, as cool and composed as a living marble statue, and allowed him to lead her on to the floor.

He commended with satisfaction Lady Wentford's daring in including waltzes at her ball; he could claim Miss Summerhayes's attention every moment. A strong urge prompted him to crush the little flirt in his arms, but his gloved hands held her with the utmost correctness. She followed his steps perfectly, gracefully moving with the music as light as a cloud within the curve of his arm. Yet if she were enjoying the dance, her cool features did not show it.

Her gaze never rose higher than his neckcloth, and he wished suddenly she would smile at him as she had smiled at her other partners. Just as quickly, he scoffed at such a ninnyhammer notion. He cared not a jot or tittle for her smiles.

An explanation seemed in order, lest she think interest in her had drawn him. "I do not share my brother's mindless pleasure with social functions," he drawled. "I find them invariably boring."

Her glance flew to his. "If such is your opinion, sir," she said evenly, "why torture yourself by coming? To find fault with Mr. Merritt, or to glower at me?"

"If I glower, Miss Summerhayes," he answered coolly, "and I protest I do not, it is occasioned by observing the flirtatious manner in which certain ladies conduct themselves."

"Certain ladies?" Her chin lifted and firmed, while her gaze turned a shade warmer. "Pray, sir, do not be coy in naming those who so offend you."

"Mayhap 'tis nothing more than country manners." What would she say if he told her what really occupied his mind? That is, if he himself were sure, which at the moment he was not. "I observed much of the same during my recent stay in Buckinghamshire."

"Indeed?" One dark copper brow cocked to a delightful, dangerous slant. "Then you refer to my cousin and me. I make no apology, for our conduct merits no reproach, and in any case, Lord Courtlea, you are hardly the one to offer it."

Ah, he might have expected attack rather than defensive protests! He must admire her contentiousness, even while he deplored it. "If I see someone heading for certain destruction," he said in quick riposte, "should I remain quiet, and allow the consequences to occur? No, Miss Summerhayes, I am not so indifferent to my duty."

"Your duty!" She stiffened in his hold, yet did not miss a step. He saw the flash of eye, the rosy tint that told of her rising temper. And the hotter she grew, the cooler he became. "Then," she cried, "by all means, Lord Courtlea, discharge your duty at once! Go to my aunt with your complaints, so she may rectify the matter and so relieve your mind."

"I have no wish to trouble Lady Wentford, when a word in one ear will serve as well." He noticed how well-formed and dainty was the ear in question. "You smile too much, Miss Summerhayes, and gaze coquettishly into the eyes of your partners. Such conduct leads a gentleman to certain expectations, as you well know. I say this not to offend, or to criticize, but to guide, especially as your aunt is absent from the room, and cannot observe your behavior."

"Oh, this is too much!" she fairly blazed. "'Tis outside of enough to be brought to task by someone whose own conduct leaves so much to be desired! Let us end this dance, sir, and you may retire, smugly confident you have discharged your duty."

"The waltz is not finished. We shall dance until the end."

Miss Summerhayes caught her breath, her eyes widening in disbelief. "Cease at once, sir, or I shall walk off and leave you. I swear I will do it!"

"And set tongues wagging, and so prove my point for me?" He smiled, stirred by the sight of her lovely white bosom heaving with indignation.

She glared at him, nibbling her luscious lower lip, but did not stop the dance. It pleased him to be in command, to hold the whip hand, as it were. Too often he had been the thwarted one, with Miss Summerhayes calling the tune. For the first time he noticed the necklace of emeralds that lay on that smooth, shapely bosom. The necklace was a beautiful piece, made even more magnificent by the clever addition of the brooch.

She saw his glance. "My aunt requested I wear the emeralds tonight." She swallowed, then continued with obvious reluctance, "The loss of the brooch would have overset her. My thanks again for returning it to me."

His gaze travelled to her hair, piled high on her proud head. He imagined green gems gleaming in those rich auburn tresses. He had supplied many such gifts to women, to appease or sweeten them. Again he felt moved by some urge other than self-interest: a simple wish to give pleasure. But if she would not accept books from him, she would never accept jewels.

"A tiara of emeralds is needed to finish the parure," he noted in an off-handed way.

She bridled, as color deepened in her cheeks. "And my gown, sir? Surely you wish to pass judgment on that."

He simply smiled as the music ended, not answering, although her gown was quite the most fetching in the room. Doubtless she had already received countless compliments from those gentlemen she had enchanted. He, thankfully, though admitting her charms, was immune to them.

"I notice Lord Tunney eyeing me with scant regard," Courtlea murmured as he led her from the floor. He could not resist asking, "Do I wish you happy, or must I await the announcement?"

If a look could smoulder and freeze at the same time, it was the one he received from Daphne Summerhayes. "Lord Courtlea, I am at a loss to know of what you speak. Your brain must be addled."

Nonetheless, when he guided her toward the door, Miss Summerhayes made no objection. With her hand barely resting on his arm, they strolled out to the corridor to join other guests perambulating there.

"Do you wish some refreshment, sir? Lady Wentford's butler mixes an excellent wine negus." Her words were polite, perhaps for the benefit of other ears, but her tone was distinctly chilly.

"I require no refreshment, merely enlightenment, Miss Summerhayes, but perhaps you have yet to give Tunney your answer. You did not blush with maidenly modesty or swoon from offended sensibility because a gentleman offered for you." He must know, and to hell with courtesy! "So, will you have him, or not?"

Her gasp was quite audible, and the fingers lying on his arm tightened. She did not answer at once, and when he looked down, her gaze had narrowed thoughtfully.

"My lord, at another ball, I attacked you for reasons you now know. Then, however, you were taken aback, disadvantaged, nonplussed as to my motives." She drew in her breath, seeming to gain more assurance. "Now, you employ similar tactics on me, hoping for the same end."

She smiled, but not in the fashion he had wished. This smile sent cold shivers down his back. "'Tis no use, sir. I reject your bait. In any case, my connection with Lord Tunney, or with anyone, is not a matter with which you need concern yourself."

"Tit for tat? Is that what I was about? Truly, you mistake my nature. 'Tis not so shallow and vindictive." He forced a smile, frustrated by her discernment, yet unable to do more to obtain an answer. "Excuse my amusement, I beg, but your surmise is so wide of the mark, a blind donkey would laugh."

"Why, then, did you come, my lord?" she asked with her usual directness.

"I did not want to," he admitted with commendable openness but poor tact. "Until the last minute, I had not the slightest notion of attending."

"Indeed?" Was her tone too carefully neutral? "Doubtless, however, it serves your best interests," she continued with a touch of bitterness, "since you never act against them."

"How astute of you to recollect that, Miss Summerhayes," he drawled, pressing her hand on his arm. Her hand jerked slightly, but she made no comment, continuing to walk silently at his side.

"Do I detect, sir, some enmity toward Lord Tunney?" Miss Summerhayes at last asked.

"Because he dares to desire you?" He smiled grimly, though her eyes were not on him. The thought of any man wanting her enraged him.

"Naturally not," she retorted, and he caught an upward flash from her green eyes. "But one could not help noticing a certain sharpness between you."

Courtlea shrugged, though Alice Coffidge's unwanted and unwarranted infatuation had greatly disturbed him at the time. "He thinks he has a grievance against me, and will neither drop it nor push it to a conclusion."

"And has he a grievance?" Miss Summerhayes asked, opening her fan and gently wielding it.

"In his mind only. But why your interest, Miss Summerhayes? Do you fear I may call out your lover?"

She shrugged her milky shoulders with a fine uncaring air. "You presume much, my lord. Surely a lady may indulge in simple curiosity about two gentlemen of her acquaintance."

As they strolled, the perfume of wild flowers drifted to him from her skin and hair. He would recognize that scent among a hundred others. It forcibly reminded him of the struggle in his study, and of his prophecy that the fiery Miss Summerhayes would some day freely come to him.

Faugh! No man is totally sensible with his passions aroused, but he had uttered that foolish boast like a foiled ravisher. Force would not move Miss Daphne; he knew that now. She would answer only to the prompting of her heart. She could never suit his inclination, or meet his taste, yet he felt an unexpected envy for the person who might win her love.

"Miss Summerhayes, pray do me the honor of the next dance." He had not intended to say that, and then he amazed himself even more. "And will you further favor me with your company at supper?"

Her surprised pause was hardly complimentary, nor was the long, searching look she gave him. "Indeed yes, my lord, with pleasure." The smile following her words warmed his soul.

Her sweet face, tipped up and lit with a tentative warmth, stirred thoughts of other pleasures, more interesting and satisfying, to share with a willing woman. Immediately he crushed such notions down, reminding himself of the reasons why such joys were impossible with Miss Summerhayes. That is, he tried to recollect the reasons he had so recently listed, but somehow nothing came to mind. Nothing except a possibility of affording her some slight happiness.

"I understand your uncle keeps no mounts in town," he said casually, and felt her slight start. "I can suggest a plan that may work to your advantage as well as my own."

"Yes, my lord?"

He admired her caution. Like himself, she was not one to commit rashly. "Did I mention that I keep horses for my brother's use? Well, they lack exercise. You enjoy riding. Both our interests may be served if I might stable two of them here for your use. And your cousin's use, of course." Then, recollecting Lord Wentford's reluctance to part with the brass unnecessarily, he hastened on. "At my expense, naturally."

She stopped walking, as they had again reached the ballroom

doorway, but she did not respond at once, possibly examining his offer from all angles. Her hand slipped from his arm, and he turned slightly, facing her. The smooth brow, the sweet curve of lip and eye were no lovelier on the marble bust of a Roman goddess on a nearby plinth than on Daphne Summerhayes's thoughtful countenance.

"Why do you make this generous offer, my lord? Pardon my bluntness, but you have never hidden your disapproval of my cousin and me. Not ten minutes ago, you upbraided us for shameless behavior. Indeed, can you recollect any meeting between us, other than that dinner here at Wentford House, that did not end in anger and hard words? I cannot, though I might wish…"

She paused, again catching her lower lip lightly between her teeth, a mannerism he found utterly charming. He thought he detected wistfulness in her tone, but she gave her head a little shake that was anything but pensive.

"In truth, sir," she continued, "surely you understand why I find your action puzzling, to say the least."

No more than he, but he was past questioning his motives. The cool, dispassionate brain that had served him well all these years had departed to regions unknown. He was helpless against a power he could not control.

"Can you not credit me with simple kindness?" he asked with a smile. "In any case, your recommendation to me has greatly changed from our first meeting. Do you not believe so?"

Her glance held wariness and hope in equal measure, and his heart gave a strange lurch. Then an alteration in those green depths dampened the hope. "Change does not necessarily mean improvement," she murmured, almost as if talking to herself.

Courtlea gave a choked little laugh. "Gad, Miss Summerhayes, you elude one's hold as easily as a will-o'-the wisp."

He saw a flash of surprise cross her features, then a glimmer of amusement brought a small smile to her lips. She tipped her head in a manner no man could resist. Suddenly, it was all he could do not to kiss her, here and now, and Devil take the consequences.

"My lord, your hold on ladies seems quite secure. There is, for instance, Lady Prudence, and—" Her gaze faltered, then steadied. "—and Miss Bisely."

He delighted in the challenge in her eyes and in the opportunity she presented. "Miss Summerhayes," he said swiftly, "pray believe that Miss Bisely and I parted company many months ago. Indeed, even before my visit to Buckinghamshire."

There, blunt and plain.

Her lips opened to answer, but her gaze flew past him, and she gasped.

He turned, following her look. The floor was quickly clearing from the last quadrille, the guests anticipating supper. Near at hand, however, stood a pale Sophie Summerhayes between two bristling young coxcombs.

"Of course, you meant it, Hamper! Egad, do you think I am such a gudgeon as not to know an insult when I hear one?"

Courtlea forwned as his brother Edgar clenched his fists and thrust out his jaw in a most pugnacious manner.

"You are a gudgeon of the first water if you think I spoke anything but the truth," retorted Lord Hamper, as angrily pale as Edgar was furiously pink.

"Come now, sirs!" said Sophie, looking apprehensively from one to the other. "Recollect where we are, I beg! Lord Hamper, doubtless you intended no insult, but mayhap you spoke hastily—"

"No, Miss Summerhayes, I never do so." Hamper threw back his head to look down his nose at his adversary. This occasioned a danger to his lordship's neck, as Edgar was the taller by several inches.

"Then, Mr. Merritt, surely you misheard Lord Hamper's words, or imagined a slur where none exists." Sophie clasped her hands and gazed imploringly at young Edgar.

"You side with him, against me?" he demanded with a hurt stare.

Courtlea had heard enough. With a muttered curse, he stepped forward. "What is amiss here, Edgar? Explain, if you please, sir."

Edgar started at his brother's command, and flushed an even darker shade when he beheld Daphne at Courtlea's side. He offered her a stiff bow, then drew himself up, the picture of offended pride.

"'Tis a matter which concerns Lord Hamper and myself, Victor. He has offered me a dire insult, and," he turned again to his antagonist, "I have a good mind to demand satisfaction!"

"Oh, Mr. Merritt!" gasped Daphne Summerhayes.

"Oh, no!" moaned Sophie Summerhayes.

"Oh, you have, have you?" queried Courtlea, furious with his bird-witted brother for landing in such a scrape. What chance now of his dance and supper and further talk with Miss Daphne! "May one inquire the form and manner of this perceived insult? No, not a word yet." He turned to the cousins and gave a short bow. "Pray excuse us, ladies, while we withdraw."

Gripping each combatant by an arm, Lord Courtlea marched them into the small salon opening off the ballroom. As the door banged shut behind them, Daphne, white-faced, drew her equally pale cousin out of the stream of guests intent on making their way down to the dining room. "Sophie, what in heaven's name occurred to cause such a fuss? Why, Mr. Merritt appeared set to tear at Lord Hamper's throat!"

"Oh, Dee," Sophie wailed, wringing her hands, "I hardly know, and I was there all the time! Mr. Merritt bespoke me to go down to supper with him. I agreed, thinking our second dance together ended then. I was wrong, oh, terribly wrong, for the last quadrille was with Lord Hamper. He, naturally enough, expected to escort me to supper, and when Edgar—Mr. Merritt appeared, he—Lord Hamper—said something about modern manners, which he—Mr. Merritt—took as a slur on *his* manners. Oh, it was all so silly! I thought Lord Hamper merely trying to extricate himself, but then Mr. Merritt bristled up, as much as accused Lord Hamper of being a sly dog, or a dog in the manger, I misremember which, and then insisted Lord Hamper had insulted him…But then, you heard the rest. Oh, Dee, what will happen?"

"Well, they dare not fight a duel, that is plain. King George is death against duels, and rightly so. Oh, such puffed-up masculine pride! Do not fret, Sophie, I am sure Lord Courtlea will settle the matter without bloodshed."

Daphne led her cousin to a chair, settled her in it, and began to chafe Sophie's cold hands, wishing her confidence was stronger regarding Lord Courtlea's peaceful inclinations. He would not hesitate to demand satisfaction for any insult to his own overweening pride. Why, then, did she think he would not encourage his brother to the same ends? Why, he was as like to provide the weapons!

Yes, at one time she would have thought so, but his behavior tonight was more than puzzling, it was out and out incredible. Teasing her, she realized now, and she, instead of laughing it off, had bridled into a fine rage. Then to walk beside him, every nerve alive to his presence! The offer of his horses—did he know of Edgar's generous but misguided act? If so, did he not care? And to so boldly explain Maryann Bisely! Yet had not she, Daphne, been overbold to ask after her?

Daphne shook her head, and although the conflict between Edgar and Lord Hamper was too serious to allow consideration of any other matter, in her heart a flicker of warmth grew into a flame.

The door to the salon remained closed. The ballroom was deserted; even the musicians had gone for their feed. Daphne paced back and forth, determined to wait all night if necessary to see Lord Courtlea again as much as to learn the outcome of the conference. Sophie sat, pale and miserable, her handkerchief pressed to her lips, more deeply affected than Daphne thought possible.

At last the door opened. Sophie rose and clung tightly to Daphne's arm. Lord Hamper exited first, then Edgar, followed by Lord Courtlea. Lord Hamper approached with nose so high in the air the wonder was he saw the cousins at all.

"My thanks for a delightful and eventful evening," he said, a touch stiffly. "Your servant, ladies." With a curt bow, he marched out.

"I doubt we shall see him again," Daphne murmured.

"Oh, Dee, how can you jest when we do not yet know what will happen?"

Lord Courtlea's expression gave nothing away, although Mr. Merritt's suggested satisfaction. "Well, sirs, what news?" asked Daphne.

"The fellow begged off," declared Mr. Merritt. "Too afraid of a facer on that claret-jug of his."

Daphne and Sophie looked blankly at each other. "I beg your pardon, Mr. Merritt?" Daphne queried.

"Indeed, yes, Miss Summerhayes. I'd darken his daylights soon enough, my word on it!"

Lord Courtlea clapped his brother on the shoulder. "Mayhap I should explain to the ladies, Edgar, as your vile jargon results only in confusion. The fact is, I defined the dire results of duelling—death or hideous wounds, and exile—and suggested instead another means of settling an argument. To wit, a match at Jackson's Boxing Saloon, tomorrow morning. Lord Hamper declined, insisting that he neither harbored nor intended any slight to Mr. Merritt's character. It was a bit short of an outright apology, but my brother, having cooled, opined he must have misheard, and so all is well."

"Oh, I am glad," said Daphne, smiling at Mr. Merritt, "but what of the facer, claret-jug and the dark daylights?"

"A blow to that pippin of a honker, his nose," answered Edgar with a hoot of laughter, "and two black eyes."

Sophie sighed and gave a shiver of relief. "Oh, I vow I have never been so worried. Indeed, I was all a-tremble with fright."

Lord Courtlea regarded her with a distinct coolness. "Part of the agreement to end hostilities relates to you, Miss Summerhayes. Since the difference between Lord Hamper and my brother arose over who was to conduct you to supper, it was decided that neither gentleman would have that pleasure. To be fair, both would withdraw from the house. In keeping with that agreement, we must wish you good-night."

Sophie, who had recovered a little color, promptly lost it, while Daphne's impulse was to protest Lord Courtlea's leaving with Mr. Merritt. She repressed the urge in time, however, recollecting the earl's admission he had not wished to come in the first place. Yet he had danced, and talked so strangely, and begged her company at supper!

"My regrets, Miss Summerhayes, at taking my leave so soon," Lord Courtlea murmured, raising her hand to his lips. His clear eyes did not mock or condescend, and Daphne believed he was truly sorry to depart. Indeed, his gaze rested on her face with a kind of wonderment. "I feel I must accompany this young jackanapes home, lest he rethink his position, and go in search of Lord Hamper."

His words sounded mechanical to Daphne, as though his thoughts were distracted, and not on what he uttered. Daphne nodded, her smile tremulous with disappointment at his abrupt but necessary departure. "I understand fully, my lord."

There was a small silence as he looked steadily at her, and she held her breath, waiting for him to say more. He merely bowed again, released her hand and moved aside for his brother. Daphne hardly heard Mr. Merritt's leave-taking, but murmured the appropriate responses.

Then, her senses awhirl, she watched Lord Courtlea exit, propelling a reluctant Mr. Merritt before him with more vigor than seemed required. At the door, the earl hesitated before swiftly looking back over his shoulder.

The glance was fleeting, and then he was gone. Daphne stood breathless, flushed and thrilled, for it seemed he had reached the length of the room and gently touched her cheek.

CHAPTER 20

"He blames me." Sophie whispered, her cornflower eyes bedewed with tears. "Oh, I know he blames me, but truly, Dee, I could not help it. I vow, I tried my best to avoid a confrontation. Oh, Lord Courtlea thinks me the worst flirt, I know he does."

"Fustian, Sophie!" Daphne murmured, and shook her head to clear her thoughts of that same bewildering, confusing earl. "Do not vex yourself with what he may think, dear. Why, he would find fault with a fat goose! Come now, you have done nothing to merit reproach. Dash away those tears."

Sophie allowed a weak smile when Daphne offered her own handkerchief and an encouraging hug. She turned away, damping her eyes, as the musicians strolled in with the red faces and complacent manner of those who have dined and drunk very well indeed.

"Sophie, dear," Daphne whispered in her ear, "you must not let two foolishly contentious young men spoil this evening for you. No fault may be laid at your door." In truth, her own enjoyment of the ball had faded with Lord Courtlea's departure, but Sophie must not know of it.

"Think of Aunt Elizabeth," she urged with a smile. "Think of me, if you will. Here I stand, starving for supper, but how may I leave you in this state?"

Sophie laughed then, and as they left the ballroom, linked arms with Daphne. "I vow, I am blessed with the most considerate cousin ever! You have the right of it, as usual. On to supper! But wait, why is not Lord Trout standing by as your escort?"

Daphne gave a little shrug, but had no mind to explain further. "I do not expect Lord Tunney to dance attendance at my elbow every moment. Indeed, we may not be as favored with his company henceforth as we were previous."

"Oh? And why not, pray tell? Oh, Daphne!" Sophie drew her aside though they were alone in the corridor. "Do you mean—?" she whispered, her eyes gleaming. "Did he? Did you? Oh, tell me. I must know at once!"

Daphne smiled, a trifle wryly. "This has been a most interesting evening, Coz." She glanced over Sophie's shoulder, and gave an amused grimace. "Oh, dear! Lord Launton is bounding toward us, closely followed by Mr. Sutton. Seize Lord Launton with all speed, I beg, while I intercept Mr. Sutton. We do not wish another squabble over your company, do we?"

* * *

At three o'clock the last guest departed, the weary musicians packed their instruments, and even Sophie was ready for bed. Daphne stared out her bedroom window at the black night, too restless for sleep as she recollected every word, every gesture, every expression of Lord Courtlea. Why had he come? Had gentleness and warmth truly shone in his eyes, or was it her own wishful thinking?

As to Alice Coffidge, Daphne strongly suspected the earl innocent of wrong. But, in the cold night before dawn, as she tried to assess her feelings, did Alice matter? Or Maryann Bisely?

Daphne shivered in the chill and quickly climbed into bed. Sleep eluded her tightly-wound mind until the birds in the garden started their dawn chorus and the darkness dissolved. At last she dozed off. Minutes later, it seemed, Briggs had bustled with a clink of china and silver.

"What time is it?" Daphne asked, yawning.

"'Tis gone twelve, Miss Daphne. I brought a breakfast tray for you, and Miss Sophie asks you to join her in a walk as soon as you feel fit." The abigail set the tray across her mistress's lap and pulled back the curtains to the new day.

Daphne's head felt filled with cotton wool, and after breakfast, she agreed to set out for some fresh air with her cousin, with Briggs and Tyson following. The day was warm and fair, with fat white clouds playing follow-my-leader across a periwinkle sky when the four moved briskly down Upper Grosvenor Street toward the Square. An errant breeze tugged at the brim of Sophie's gypsy hat and belled the sleeves of Daphne's yellow pelisse.

Daphne wasted no time. "Sophie, I fear you were less than truthful as to Lord Courtlea's invitation to the ball. Why did you not tell me he was expected? 'Twas a shock, I can tell you, when he popped up before me, hard on Lord Tunney's heels." How much a shock she could hardly explain.

"Oh, I am sorry, Dee, truly, but one could hardly ask Mr. Merritt and not Lord Courtlea." Sophie made a little helpless gesture. "Why, you said as much yourself, did you not? In any case, one never dreamed he would attend."

Yes, Daphne had said as much, but she was yet unsatisfied. "Still, I should have been warn—that is, informed of the invitation. For what reason was I not told?"

"Why, for no reason in the world, Cousin, save that since you dislike the earl so strongly, you would have been overset, and apprehensive of his coming. Recollect how Mr. Merritt's appearance so startled you."

Daphne admitted that truth with a wry nod. "I thank you for such delicate consideration of my feelings."

Sophie gestured airily, then threw a calculating glance over her shoulder. "Now, Daphne, pray tell me of Lord Trout, ere I burst from curiosity," she begged, lowering her voice.

"I will oblige," Daphne said gently, "if you oblige me in never using that nickname for Lord Tunney again. Oh, I know you are just funning, and I must admit the name is apt, and decidedly clever, but do you not think it cruel? Consider his feelings, should you slip and say it to his face. He does not deserve to be mocked in such a fashion, Sophie."

"Oh, I vow I did not think!" Sophie stopped short and turned a stricken face to her cousin. "I have been excessively unkind. But truly, I never, never used the name to any soul but our two selves."

"I believe you, dear, but you will be careful, will you not?" Daphne walked on a little, then gave a little sigh. "As to Lord Tunney's attentions, last night he offered matrimony to me."

"Oh, Dee, how exciting! You accepted him, of course."

"There was no 'of course' about it."

"You-you refused him? But why?"

They had reached Grosvenor Square. Soberly-clad governesses walked or wheeled their charges sedately along the pavement in front of the imposing residences. One little boy carried a hoop for rolling in the park. The usual carriages and sedan-chairs bore ladies on their calls or to the shops. Daphne walked on through the pleasant bustle, unseeing and unheeding, as she recollected her emotions when Lord Tunney uttered the fateful words every miss hoped to hear.

"I very nearly plunged in," she admitted. "Indeed, my mouth opened to agree he should approach Papa, yet quite different words emerged. I was as surprised as he."

Sophie was aghast. "But surely he will not be put off with one refusal? Surely any gentleman worth his salt will ask again?"

Daphne shook her head impatiently. "Sophie, I will be twenty-four in a month. Hardly an age for coyness, expecting such an offer would be repeated. Lord Tunney is well enough acquainted with my nature, I think, to know exactly that my refusal is just that. No, although I strove to couch my words gently, so we might continue as friends, I doubt he will present himself again."

Sophie gestured helplessly, her face a study in confusion. "Dee, I still do not understand what made you refuse him. You said you liked him well enough."

"Mayhap you have hit on it," replied Daphne with a considering frown. "I do like him, and I half-believed fondness was enough for a marriage. I suppose I realized at the last moment that it was not enough. The thing is, I do not love him, and I would rather remain unwed, than marry where my heart is not engaged."

"Oh, Cousin," Sophie cried, "I know not whether to weep, or cheer, or stamp my foot in exasperation. Tell me, how do you know you do not love him? Indeed, how does anyone know when one is in love?"

Daphne could not answer at once, for she dared not give a name to her feelings for Lord Courtlea. Quickly, she thought back to the days of her infatuation with Sir George Sowerby. She scarce recollected his face, her hurt was long passed, but memory of her emotions was still clear. "Why, one is always happy, and—and thrilled. Excited, and eager to see the loved one."

Sophie looked askance at her. "That is all? And you did not ever eagerly anticipate Lord Tunney's visits, or laugh with him, or be happy in his company? Have you ever been in love with anyone?"

Daphne bridled defensively. "Naturally, when I was young, but nothing came of it. I was soon cured, I assure you, so do not think I pine from unrequited love." No, she was far too sensible to imagine affection where none could possibly exist.

"Hmm, this love business seems rather mild, then," Sophie observed. "Not at all what poets lead one to believe. Burning kisses, the agony of separation, overwhelming passion—"

"Sophie, where on earth have you learned such things?"

"Well, Shakespeare's sonnets, and Papa has some translations of Greek poets, like Sappho, and she was a woman and should know of what she speaks..."

"Indeed." Daphne walked on in silence, feeling as though she waded in waters beyond her depth. Passion. That burning, melting, loosening power that made one lose one's head, and had nothing to do with love. Oh, yes, she well knew of that!

But what of the thrilling warmth she felt last night at Lord Courtlea's final glance? Could that not be an awakening?

"Authors and poets allow their sensibilities to be overcome by their imaginations," she said at last, with some firmness. "They do not write of what is, but of what they think the thing should be. Their own words carry them off to some fantastic cloud land. We must keep our feet firmly on the ground."

Her last words, though of sound advice, might be considered indelicate for a young miss. Daphne did not retract them, but hurried on. "While we speak on the subject, I think Lord Launton is quite as infatuated with you as Mr. Sutton. You may soon have a choice to make."

"Yes." Sophie nodded, her brow creased in a little frown.

Their perambulations had brought the cousins twice around the Square. Now, as they turned their steps into Upper Grosvenor Street, Daphne noted a carriage drawn up before Lord Wentford's residence. Before they reached the spot, however, a groom came from the house, mounted to his seat, and the carriage moved off.

"I surmise another invitation," Daphne observed, "though heaven knows where we will fit in another engagement."

She discovered on entering the hall that she was wrong. A note, folded and sealed, awaited her. A similar missive was for Sophie, as well as a most beautiful posy.

"What heavenly flowers!" cried Sophie, burying her pert nose in the blossoms. "Oh, and such a scent! Daphne, do look."

"Yes, lovely," said Daphne absently, perusing her note. The writing marched across the page, bold and clear, in a fine, educated hand. The signature, "Courtlea," was bolder still, and underlined with an impatient slash.

"Lord Courtlea sends his regards," she told her cousin, "and apologizes in a fashion for his brother's behavior last night. He also states, very definitely, that such behavior has no chance of being repeated." Daphne refolded the note and slipped it into her reticule. "Perhaps that means he has forbidden Mr. Merritt our company." Again, she thought. She hoped not; the one thing she could not forgive was the earl's slight to Sophie.

Sophie glanced up. "Oh, how gracious of him!" With an ironic grimace, she returned to her note. "Mr. Merritt also sends apologies with the flowers," she said, a pleased smile curving her lips.

"And that is all?" Daphne queried, forcing a lightness she did not feel. "No words of sad farewell, of regret your paths will never again cross?"

"Do not tease, Daphne." With dignity, Sophie slipped the note into her glove, and caught up her flowers. "I might twit you that Lord Courtlea did not see fit to send you flowers, but I shan't. Tyson, fetch up some water for these. I want them in my room."

Daphne had to laugh as she started up the stairs. "Thank you, Cousin, for your graciousness in not pointing out my lack of a posy. Many another would have mentioned it."

Once in her bedroom, she waited impatiently until Briggs had helped her change and had left the room. Then Daphne withdrew Lord Courtlea's note, sat down in a little slipper chair near the window, and once again read the earl's words. Very crisp and clear, they were, and cool. No reference to his talk with her, or to his odd admission of his reluctance to be there in the first place. Yet he had come, though late, and she could not help but wonder what might have occurred had he stayed longer.

Her hands tightened on the note and fell to her lap as she closed her eyes, recollecting that one waltz they had shared. She loved to dance, and every waltz was enjoyable, but oh, what a difference when Lord Courtlea partnered her! His arms possessed her, she anticipated every movement of his body. How her heart had pounded! How she had floated on the music, content to continue without end, without thought.

That is, until he had taken her to task over her behavior and her relationship with Lord Tunney. How quickly his arrogance had brought her to earth! Or was it, as she had surmised, merely his way of giving sauce to the goose? He had denied it, yet she had sensed a change in him—a tentative reaching-out, a new warmth and sensitivity—that touched and thrilled her, as if... Oh, why did she dwell on such silly and unproductive thoughts? She was far too old and sensible for such nonsense.

Impatient with herself, she rose and went to Sophie's room. Neither her cousin nor Tyson was there, and further search gained the information from Clapham that Miss Sophie had gone out.

"How strange. Did Miss Sophie indicate where she was going?" Daphne inquired.

"Yes, miss, she did. Evidently Miss Sophie had an urgent need for stationery, and wished to purchase some. Mrs. Tyson accompanied her. In a hackney, miss."

"Stationery? Dear me, Miss Sophie must be writing a torrent of letters to have gone through so much paper. You are certain it was stationery of which she spoke?"

A pained expression crossed the butler's august features.

"Yes," said Daphne, hurriedly, "of course you are. Will you inform me, pray, when Miss Sophie returns? Thank you, Clapham."

The butler bowed and withdrew, leaving Daphne puzzled. Sophie had said nothing of an errand, yet within minutes of returning from their walk, had left the house without even asking Daphne to accompany her. Sophie seemed to prefer Tyson's company, and now that Daphne thought on it, the two set off nearly every day. As Daphne strolled into the library in search of a book, a vague unease persisted that she had grown lax in her responsibility as a chaperon.

* * *

Sophie had to visit two shops on Oxford Street before accidentally encountering Mr. Edgar Merritt outside the third.

"Why, good day, Mr. Merritt," she said, dimpling prettily. "Imagine meeting you here! May I thank you, sir, for your kindness in sending the delightful posy?"

Edgar doffed his hat, and since no gentleman kept a lady standing talking in the street, immediately turned and walked beside her. "My pleasure, I do assure you, Miss Summerhayes. May I repeat my abject apologies for leaving the ball so early last night?"

All this was said in fairly clear tones, audible to Tyson, who had dropped behind as Mr. Merritt usurped her place at Miss Summerhayes's side. Tyson shifted the parcels in her arms and sighed, praying the conversation would be short, and she could return home to soothe her tired feet.

"You were very wrong to cause such a fuss," Sophie said, lowering her tone. "I vow, all you accomplished was to be banished, and I had to eat supper with Lord Launton."

Mr. Merritt also spoke quietly. "That I regret, more than I can say, but I could not help it, Miss Summerhayes. 'Twas not so much Hamper's words, nor even his insufferable tone, but the way he regarded your sweet person. Egad, the bounder positively oozed proprietorship, and I swear that was more than a fellow could bear. I should have fetched him a facer right there and then."

"Had you done that, we would not now be conversing, I assure you. How could I? 'Twould seem I condoned an action that would have totally ruined Lady Wentford's party. No, sir, I could never forgive that!"

He nodded soberly, before offering a shy smile. "But you are here, as I begged in my note, and by your smiling greeting, I judge you are not angry with me now, and nothing else signifies."

Sophie was wearing her new "conversation" hat, with silk flowers clustered around the crown and the brim turned up above one ear. Edgar believed she had never looked more adorable, especially when she favored him with a forgiving smile and a brilliant glance. Those eyes, so pure and fine, seemed to him as snippets of heaven itself.

"What does signify, Mr. Merritt, is the fact that your brother, Lord Courtlea, prefers us to remain as strangers. I wonder that you dare defy him."

Edgar shrugged. "Oh, Victor thinks to punish me, and in truth, Miss Summerhayes, never to set eyes on you again would be dire punishment indeed. Think nothing of his strictures, I beg; they mean nothing to me."

Craftily, he slowed his steps, hoping she would not notice such a delaying tactic. The pavement was crowded with shoppers and the wide road jammed with tony carriages. Sooner or later some nosy acquaintance would come along, and then he must take his leave, when what he wished to do more than any thing was to take the delectable Miss Summerhayes into his arms. Egad, but one embrace would be worth all the ensuing fuss!

"I must talk with you, Miss Summerhayes, and not merely for fleeting seconds in the street or in busy shops. If only I could bowl up in the carriage and whisk you off for a drive in the country," he said wistfully. "We could talk to our heart's content."

Miss Summerhayes shook her head. "With my cousin or Tyson as chaperon? Oh, sir, pray think again!" She strolled on a few more steps. "Do you read much, Mr. Merritt? Lady Wentford and my cousin Daphne both read a prodigious amount. I have offered to return their books to Hatchard's lending library on Piccadilly tomorrow. Mayhap you make use of the library too, Mr. Merritt?"

"I shall tomorrow, Miss Summerhayes. Indeed, I shall haunt the place for an eternity, if need be." Edgar paused, cleared his throat, and then continued off-handedly, "I may be leaving England soon."

Her expression of dismay quite gratified him, though it wrung his heart to cause her even a moment's unhappiness. "'Tis all this talk of war," he hastened to explain. "Naturally, I shall want to get bunged in at the start. So, you see, my time may be limited."

Her cheeks, the most delicately rose-tinted alabaster, grew pale. "Oh, Mr. Merritt, pray do not speak so. Oh, I know how handsome the officers are in their regimentals, and they do make a brave show parading their men, but I vow, the mere thought of more fighting puts me in the worst quake."

"Then may I believe that you would think of me, should I go off to war? Dare I believe you might even worry, or shed a tear if I should fall?" He had a splendid vision of Miss Summerhayes weeping over his broken, mayhap lifeless body, and he nearly cried out with joy.

Miss Summerhayes stopped in her tracks and looked full at him, as if the busy street had disappeared, and Tyson with it, and they two were alone in a vast meadow or deep forest. Something in her look made his heart swell within his bosom, and hope spring up green in his soul.

"I—I should be most unhappy should any such calamity befall you, Mr. Merritt. Most unhappy, as would be all your friends. Good day, Mr. Merritt."

She entered a draper's shop, and he stood blissfully and watched Her go. How could Victor, the chuckle-headed flat, believe that She, the adored, lacked both good sense and fine sensibilities? Why, she embodied every feminine virtue, every fine quality one sought for in a woman. Any man on this earth would be blessed to win Her affection, save that no man on earth was worthy of Miss Sophie Summerhayes. But mayhap even the most unworthy might dare to hope.

CHAPTER 21

Daphne folded the letter from William and then sat staring into space. Busy with his activities at Oxford, William had long ago relegated the incident of the emerald brooch to history. Daphne sighed. Her brother did not know how much that green bauble had affected her life. Which all brought her rather dreamily around to the Earl of Courtlea.

"Clapham said you wished to see me."

Daphne started. Sophie had come into the sitting room unheard as she daydreamed. Daphne nodded hurriedly and turned in her chair to face her cousin. "I do not mean to take you to task, Sophie, or find fault, but I must ask why you left the house so suddenly and where you went."

Sophie slowly removed her hat and smoothed its ribbons. "Dear me," she said, raising her brows, "if that is not finding fault, or questioning my behavior, I vow I do not know what is! Did not Clapham tell you?"

"He mentioned a sudden need for stationery."

"Well, then." Sophie tossed her hat to the sofa, and strolled to the window overlooking the garden.

"That is all?" Daphne waited, but Sophie neither answered nor turned. "Sophie, I do not want to quiz you, but I cannot help wonder why you said nothing of your errand to me."

Sophie gave a dainty shrug. "I decided all at once to go, and reckoned to return in such a short time, it seemed unnecessary to trouble you."

Daphne glanced at the little ormolu clock on the mantel. "Two hours is hardly a short time," she said crisply. "You are nearly late for dinner."

"I shopped for a few more things—handkerchiefs and gloves. Oh, and some ribbons."

"I see. Did you happen to meet any friends?"

Sophie shrugged again, but did not turn from the window. "One always meets acquaintances. Sometimes 'tis difficult to avoid them."

"Sophie, this is not like you. I sense evasion in your answers, and your manner is too cool by half. Is something troubling you? You would tell me, would you not, if you worried over some problem?"

"Yes, Dee, I would." Sophie turned at last, her expression thoughtful, a ghost of a smile touching her lips. "But I doubt you—"

She broke off as Lord and Lady Wentford entered, smiling as with some delightful secret. "Ah, here you are, girls," Lord Wentford boomed. "Your aunt and I have a surprise for you. No, Sophie, I shan't answer any questions. Come along at once, my dears, at once, I say, just as you are. Pray do not forget your shawl, Daphne, and follow us."

In high good humor, rubbing his hands in satisfaction, he led the way to the front door. In the street, golden in the late afternoon sun, two mounted grooms each held a side-saddled horse. One, a gray with a pretty, dished face, pricked its ears toward Daphne and whickered. Daphne sucked in her breath.

"Ain't they prime?" exclaimed Lord Wentford.

At sight of the second horse, Sophie clasped her hands together and gave an excited jump. "Oh, Dee, 'tis my own Bramble," she cried. The tall chestnut mare snorted and rolled its eye.

As Daphne hurried down the steps, she realized Lord Courtlea had acted in his usual arrogant manner. A helpless resentment that he had not waited for her aye or nay quickly died. The high-handed action was so typical of the earl. Gently she stroked Emir's velvet nose. "Oh, you beauty," she murmured. "So you did not forget me?"

The animal whickered again and nudged her shoulder. She turned to her uncle, who rocked complacently on his heels, his thumbs tucked into his fob pockets.

"Well, now, will they serve?" he demanded. Assured that no finer animals existed, he launched into his explanation.

"I did not know until recently that you two were such eager horsewomen, and how much you missed your morning rides. My dear lady wife made mention of it only a few days ago, and I resolved at once to purchase some mounts for you. Then, last evening, I mentioned my plan to Courtlea, asking his advice as he is known to have a prodigious fine eye for horseflesh."

Daphne made no comment, but wondered how Lord Courtlea had brought the conversation around so her uncle would believe the notion to be his.

"Well," resumed Lord Wentford, "imagine my surprise when he begged a favor instead. He had several mounts on his hands, he said, lazing about in the stables and growing fat. Would I make use of them, stabling them in the mews here at his expense, for as long as I had need of them? He guaranteed their fitness and good manners, which Tattersall's cannot do, had I purchased a pair. Now, is that not fine?"

Daphne allowed it was prodigiously fine, as well as excessively kind of Lord Courtlea. "Can you think why he was so considerate of your needs, Uncle?" she asked. "Lord Courtlea did not strike me as one too concerned about another's problem."

Her uncle raised his brows and shrugged. "Mayhap he is growing out of his wild ways and over-proud manner. He was dashed respectful last night, though he left before the duke. But, dash it all, never mind Courtlea. Are you happy with my surprise?"

"Oh, Uncle, you are kindness itself!" Laughing, Daphne ran to throw her arms about Lord Wentford's neck, knowing that she could not thank the giver in the same fashion. She wondered, somewhat skeptically, she admitted, what lay behind Lord Courtlea's offer.

Although she fervently wished to believe his generosity was prompted only by kindness, Daphne's scepticism still nudged her when after dinner she slipped out the rear door with a carrot and a piece of sugar cadged from the cook.

The evening sky of indigo blue held a pale sliver of moon in the east and a tinge of apricot in the west. Daphne skirted the garden, keeping to the cobbled path leading to the rear wall. There, a high, barred gate led to the mews which served that block of the street. Daphne pulled her thick woolen shawl closer against the cool air, which was heavy with scents of the garden, dinner fires, and as she swung open the gate, the stables. She was quite at home in the stables, and gave no thought to going there unaccompanied. More of her country manners, she thought with a wry smile.

The mews was quiet as ostlers and grooms, having seen to the feeding of their masters' horses, sought their own meal. A few carriages stood out, ready for a hitch to be put-to, and a small, dirty stable-boy sat cross-legged against a wall while he polished a pile of harness.

Halfway down, a groom sat slackly on his mount, holding the reins of a second saddled animal. Lanterns spaced the length of the area flared like pale orange suns, and Daphne easily found the correct door. It was unbolted, and on entering, she heard the contented crunching of jaws and the rustle of bedding straw.

A lantern hung from a post, its light revealing a row of stalls and the shadowy hind ends of horses. She could not quickly see Bramble, but the gray was easy to locate in the second stall. Speaking softly, she patted its rump and moved into the stall beside it.

"There, good Emir," she crooned, stroking its neck. "See what I have for you?" The horse nuzzled her as she broke the carrot in two. "Half for you and half for Bramble. Shan't show favorites, although we both know who is the smarter, the braver, and the handsomer. But you, my pet, shall have all the sugar."

The horse nodded, still munching its carrot, and Daphne laughed.

A sudden, startled exclamation came from a stall farther down the way. Daphne drew in her breath and went still. A groom, finishing his work late, or an intruder?

"Who is there?" a deep voice demanded. "Quirn, is that you?"

Daphne's heart gave a queer little jump. She did not need to see the speaker, for she would know that voice among any number.

"No, Lord Courtlea," she said, "'tis I—Daphne Summerhayes."

"What the devil—"

She heard his rapid strides down the aisle, and in a trice he was staring at her over Emir's manger.

"Miss Summerhayes!" His exclamation mixed surprise, consternation, and, she decided, pleasure. "How did you know it was I? And why are you here?"

"As to the former, sir, I have a good ear for voices," she answered lightly. "For the latter, I might ask the same question. Have you so soon repented of your offer to my uncle, and come to reclaim your horses?"

His hat brim shadowed his eyes as he slowly shook his head. "I do not renege on my word, Miss Summerhayes," he drawled. "I merely intended to satisfy myself as to their care."

Daphne laughed breathlessly. "And are you satisfied, sir? Have they been rubbed down, and grained, and is the bedding clean and sweet?"

"Yes, on all counts. Are you here on the same mission?"

His warm tone, touched with amusement, created a bubble of intimacy around them. He had removed his gloves, and his strong, eloquent hands rested on the edge of the wooden manger.

"Very nearly the same, my lord. I brought a treat— Oh, naughty Emir! You have eaten all, even poor Bramble's share!"

Lord Courtlea laughed. "What Bramble don't know, Bramble won't miss. How clever of you to discover their names, Miss Summerhayes! Doubtless one of the grooms so informed you."

A lie refused to leave her lips, and he laughed gently at her confusion. "I recognized Emir at once," he said, smiling, "and soon discovered the truth of the matter from my rascal brother. But after that day, you no longer rode. Why did you stop? Because of our meeting in the park?"

Daphne nodded. "You had ordered your brother to avoid our company, sir. How could I do other than refuse to ride? Even so, I doubt you would have given me much choice. Am I wrong?"

He gestured, half in defense, half in protest. "May we not forget the past, Miss Summerhayes?"

"Indeed, I would like nothing better, sir, but..." She drew breath and thought of Sophie. "Is Mr. Merritt forgiven too? My cousin and I both miss his cheerful company."

"You ask much of me, Miss Summerhayes." He paused, his hands tensing on the manger. "I admit my considerations, my judgments, were too severe, and too hasty, though meant for the best. I am sorry for any pain I caused you or your cousin."

Daphne guessed what that earnest declaration had cost him. Pride and temper he had in plenty, but not, she believed, cruelty or deceit. Recollecting his former reserve, however, his quick retreat when he showed his softer sentiments, she warned herself to take care. But how, when more and more she glimpsed a fine character behind his prideful arrogance? A person she could love.

"What, have I rendered the formidable Miss Summerhayes speechless? Does the lady yet harbor ill-will toward me?" He laughed, but she heard uncertainty in the sound, and he had stiffened.

"Not speechless, sir," Daphne said with a smile, "but pleased we may begin afresh, as friends." On impulse, she extended her hand to him.

The tight set of his shoulders relaxed, and he grasped her bare hand in both of his. He smiled, and even boyish Edgar could not equal the warmth, the guilelessness, of that smile. Her heart lifted, suspending time and place. The heat from his hands flowed through her with a pleasurable tingle.

Then Emir poked her arm for attention, bringing her back to reality. She wondered how long they had stood thus, hands tightly clasped, smiling at each other. Forever, she thought, would not be long enough.

The earl released her hand and cleared his throat. "Now come out of there and I will see you safely home."

Daphne shook her head in automatic resistance to his authoritative tone. "That is not necessary, my lord, as Uncle's gate is only a few steps away." She retreated swiftly from the stall, but the earl met her at the door, and swung it open for her.

"Miss Summerhayes, you are, without a doubt, the most contentious female I have had the delight to meet." His mild, playful tone made his words an observation, not an accusation, and she could not resist answering in the same vein.

"Have you never considered, my lord, that you and your actions stir up contention? I offer that as a suggestion, a guide, as it were." She stepped out, and the earl closed the door behind them.

"My thanks, madam, for the advice."

She eyed him teasingly. "What is this, my lord? Why do you not stalk off in the highest dudgeon, as you have done before when I dared to criticize?"

The groom slouched on his mount had straightened at the sight of his master. He started forward, leading the earl's black steed. Lord Courtlea signalled him to wait before answering Daphne's question with one of his own.

"Why do you harp so at me, Miss Summerhayes?" He pushed open the gate to Wentford House, and as Daphne passed by him, whispered the last of his question in her ear. "Do you find as much to criticize in other gentlemen, Lord Tunney, for instance?" He stepped in after her, let the gate swing closed, and stood looking down at her, one hand resting on the gate.

Clouds had ambushed the sickle moon. In the deepening darkness, Daphne saw the flash of the earl's smile, the dark shadow of his brows. She knew she should depart at once, but not for the life of her would she leave.

"Pray do not mention Lord Tunney, or any other." Her voice came breathlessly. She wrapped her shawl more tightly about her as if to cloak her agitation. "In any case, sir, you do not model your behaviour upon anyone I recognize. You go your own way, I think."

The earl moved closer, nearer than any waltz required. "I do, so why find fault?"

"I—I hardly know," she admitted. Her heart pounded, but not in fear. She was shiveringly aware of Lord Courtlea's hands settling lightly on her shoulders. "Unless it is my urge to always set things to rights," she went on, scarcely knowing what she said. "My brother often derides my tendency to manage."

"He may have the right of it." Slowly, he pulled the shawl away from her throat until it looped uselessly from her arms. "Managing, forcing your way on others, often earns dislike."

"Oh, yes," she whispered, her breath catching when one of those large hands slid down her back to grasp her waist. "B-but what of duty. Last night, did not you mention duty?"

"Sometimes duty calls one to leave matters alone, and let the individual work out his own affairs." His soft, deep murmur throbbed through her being. He touched her hair, and then, shockingly, drew his fingers gently down her cheek. "Even affairs of the heart, my stern Miss Summerhayes."

"S-Sir, you forget yourself..."

"And I know the proper Miss Summerhayes has forgotten herself on several occasions," he whispered, his breath warm on her cheek.

Both hands gripped her waist, but lightly. With no effort at all, Daphne could have won her freedom. The notion never crossed her mind.

"Lovely Daphne, can you not, for once, admit to the stirring of your heart? It beats so swiftly, I see its flutter here..."

His head bent low and lower until his lips touched the little hollow in her throat. Pure sensation flooded through her, and her eyes closed in delight. She bent her head back to allow his lips freer rein, and knew she was lost.

"...and here..."

His kisses moved higher, to the sensitive spot below her ear. Daphne moaned softly, her blood aflame. Her hands crept to his shoulders as she swayed against him. She lifted her face, pressing herself against his body, all thoughts of decorum consumed in the fire roaring through her veins. She looked up and saw his shapely head framed against the darkening sky, the diamond flash of his eyes. All she yearned for, burned for, was that he hold her tightly in his arms and crush his mouth against hers.

Daphne reached higher, boldly framing his face between her palms, feeling his skin warm, his cheeks smoothly barbered. Slowly she drew his head down until their lips met—gently at first, lightly, as if he tested her sweetness. Then his mouth grew more demanding, his arms tightened around her, pulling her even closer, until their bodies seemed fused into one. She clung to him in complete surrender, responding to his kisses with all the fervor her inexperience allowed.

When at last he drew back, she was trembling, exhilarated and yet drained. "Oh, my lord Courtlea..."

"Victor, you goose." He gave a soft laugh and nodded toward a wooden garden bench. "Sit there with me, for a little. I cannot let you go so soon."

She gave no thought of refusing, but went eagerly.

"Sweetheart," he murmured, gathering her close again, "you have bedeviled and beguiled me since first we met. You haunt my dreams and every waking moment until I am good for naught. My enchantress."

He sought her lips again, and she gave them freely. "Oh, Victor," she sighed when she could speak, "how I have struggled against you! You were all I deplored in a man, and I would not look beyond my first harsh opinions."

"And now, sweet nymph?" he whispered, running his thumb lightly over her lips. "What think you now?"

She chuckled wickedly, then kissed his stroking thumb. "I think, sir, you are a gentleman worthy of my consideration at some future time."

"Minx! Vixen! Must you always just elude me?" He laughed softly, then again found her lips.

His kiss deepened, with an intensity Daphne met with equal eagerness, without shame or outraged sensibilities. She felt only need, and only one man, the one in whose arms she lay, could fulfil that need.

When he pushed the gown from her shoulders and his fingers brushed the top of her breasts, she knew no fear, just a breathless expectancy.

"Soft as satin," he murmured hoarsely, "sweet as violets."

Daphne caught her lip between her teeth, near bursting with a desire for him to touch her, to kiss and caress her breasts to his heart's content. When he hesitated, she arched her back to give his hand freer play.

"Yes, my love, do what you will," she whispered with a pounding heart.

He hesitated no longer. Slowly, achingly, his hand slipped into her bodice. Daphne gasped as his hand gently enclosed her breast. She leaned back against the bench's arm and closed her eyes, desire running through her like liquid fire. His lips had followed his hand, kissing, nuzzling, teasing, until she moaned with delight. Her fingers dug into his thick hair, then slid down to knead his shoulders.

He raised his head, all too soon for her, and she opened her eyes. "My God, but you are honey and wine," he whispered brokenly, "and so lovely!"

He tensed suddenly, his head turning sharply toward the house. "Damnation!"

Dazedly, Daphne saw that a door had opened from the house, sending a shaft of light into the garden. She hardly cared that someone might discover them, with her body throbbing so with desire.

"I must leave you, my sweet."

She nodded reluctant agreement. "Yes," she murmured, hastily putting her clothing to rights, "though I hate the thought of parting."

"As I do, sweetheart," Victor murmured.

He paused only for one swift kiss, then slipped noiselessly out the gate. Daphne barred it, and turned to meet Briggs coming in search for her. She scarce heard the abigail's grumbling scold over her long absence, but went quietly into the house and up to her room. That is, her body went there, but her mind still dwelt on the magic happenings beside the garden wall.

Of all the men in the world, why had she fallen in love with Victor Merritt, Lord Courtlea? For a fall it was, a plunging from great heights into a sea of joy and delight. And was it love? She laughed aloud, recollecting her description of love to Sophie. That insipid emotion felt for Sir George paled miserably at this rapture, this desire not only for the body, but for the mind and the soul. Oh, how long the hours until tomorrow, when she would again see Victor, her love!

* * *

Daphne and Sophie, accompanied by a groom, rode out early the next morning. Sophie commented on her cousin's cheerful spirits despite the heavy, threatening clouds.

"Why, I am happy to be riding again, Coz," Daphne answered with a brilliant smile. Indeed, she had not noticed the dour weather, warmed as she was by inner sunshine.

Sophie allowed to her pleasure in having Bramble again, but she was hardly ecstatic, as Daphne appeared to be. "'Tis a pity Mr. Merritt cannot accompany us this morning," she observed. "Do you not think we might invite him? Oh, no, we cannot; I vow, I had forgot Lord Courtlea's objection."

Daphne smiled again, or had she simply not stopped? "Mayhap we can, and soon. I feel that Lord Courtlea will not enforce his decision, and we may count Mr. Merritt among our friends once more."

"I do hope you have the right of it," Sophie sighed, not at all convinced.

Daphne tremendously enjoyed the ride. The Arabian responded as though it knew her every intention as soon as she did. It was almost like riding her dear Golden Sovereign. When Sophie inquired why they kept decorously to Rotten Row, Daphne laughed and passed off an answer, but she knew she looked for Lord Courtlea. No, now she must think of him as Victor.

He did not come, although they stayed later than usual, and Daphne's cheer was somewhat dimmed on the journey home. Of course, an earl active in the House had certain duties, and Daphne must not expect him to dance attendance on her.

Yet she did expect it. Did he not feel the same urgent need? Last night he had not declared his intentions, but surely that was because of Briggs's interruption. He had not wished to compromise Daphne, but now there was no reason not to present himself.

She stayed home all day, expecting some word—a note, at least, if not a personal call. As the threatened rain had not materialized, Lady Wentford departed for some charity work. Sophie left with Tyson to return some library books, and Daphne let her go without a qualm. Time dragged past, and Daphne waited in mounting apprehension. She was loitering in the drawing room, pretending to read a book, when Sophie returned.

"Oh, Dee, you should have come with me," claimed Sophie, dropping into the nearest chair with a groan of happy exhaustion. "Everyone and his aunt was shopping today, and I vow, every shop had new goods on display. Oh, the fabrics! I bought some dotted muslin, white with pink spots for the gown, and some pink with white dots for a spencer. Oh, it will look prime! I know I should have resisted, and not bought, but the combination seemed so perfect, and even Tyson agreed I must have it!"

She laughed and stripped off her gloves. "By the by, I met Lord Tunney, looking a bit down, I thought, and he asked me to tender his regards to you. The fire is not out there, I dare to think. Oh, yes, and on our way to Oxford Street, whom should I see but Lord Courtlea. He nodded to me in that cool manner of his, but as we were both in carriages, we did not speak. Not that I regret not speaking, far from it, but should we send notes to him, thanking him for the loan of Emir and Bramble? Would that be the thing, do you think?"

Daphne, who up to the mention of Lord Courtlea, had paid scant attention to Sophie's chatter, grew cold. "In Oxford Street, you say, in a carriage?"

"Who? Oh, Lord Courtlea. Yes, with that lady...oh, you know the one. We met at the theatre, and she was here to dinner."

"Lady Prudence Abernathy."

"You have it. I say, Dee, are you quite all right? You have gone all pale."

"Nonsense, 'tis but a trick of the light." With a great effort, Daphne summoned a smile. Closing her book, she rose to her feet. "I do feel a touch tired, though, Sophie. I will lie down for a few minutes, and will soon be right as rain."

"Well, if you are certain. Oh, do you think we should send notes?"

"What? Oh, yes, if you wish. Doubtless Lord Courtlea would appreciate your consideration."

"'Tis odd, though," Sophie mused, "that he lent Uncle Valentine those horses, and yet he forbids his brother to even speak to us."

"Who knows what is in that gentleman's mind? I, for one, refuse to speculate."

Sophie looked up as if in wonder at the bitterness in Daphne's tone, but Daphne, striving for a serene countenance and steady step, left for her room. She wanted no questions from Sophie, no concerned inquiries over her unsettled state. She wanted only to be left alone.

Yet her thoughts circled around and about in her head, driving her to distraction without settling to any conclusion. She stood staring blankly out her bedroom window, her arms wrapped around her waist, and called herself the worst of fools. Oh, but that odious lord was a clever beast! She lacked experience in dissembling, and doubtless he had sensed her warming attraction to him, her wish to think well of him. Attending the ball, dancing, smiling, yes, and teasing her, all to allay her suspicions and engage her affection. Then, the final, appeasing touch—the horses.

He had intended from the first to humiliate her. "Some day you will give your kiss freely to me." He had said that, or something like, that frightful night in his study. He had never forgotten, and like the beast he was, stalked her until he claimed the victory.

What a magnificent opportunity she had presented him, when she walked into the stable last night, all alone, without even a groom standing by! 'Twas easy now to understand his puzzling mildness, his gentle friendliness as an attack on her innocence. And he had succeeded, oh, so completely! Had Briggs not interrupted, he could have taken more from her than kisses. Daphne covered her burning face with her hands as she recollected her complete surrender. She had even given him permission, no, urged him to touch her, to fondle her until she moaned with pleasure.

Worst of all, she had wanted him, and he knew it.

How he must have laughed. How he must yet be laughing!

CHAPTER 22

Her wound was deep, almost past bearing. Distraught and ashamed, Daphne stayed late abed the next morning, claiming the headache. Before noon, however, knowing she could not hide forever, and although she felt like death, Daphne dressed and went downstairs. In the sitting room, she found her aunt with her needlework and Sophie sorting her colored floss.

"Daphne, my dear," Lady Wentford exclaimed, laying down her work, "Are you feeling better?"

"Yes, thank you, Aunt."

"May I say you do not look all that fine," commented Sophie, her head tipped to one side as she critically studied her cousin. "You are much too pale, with dreadful dark marks under your eyes. Witch hazel, then wheat powder; that will do the trick. You want to look your best at Almack's tonight."

"I want to go home."

The simple statement shocked Lady Wentford and Sophie into gaping amazement, and startled Daphne herself. Until the words escaped her mouth, she had not realized how she yearned for the peace and safety of Weldern Manor.

"Home?" echoed Sophie in dismay. "We must go home?"

Daphne instantly regretted her impulsive outburst as a torrent of exclamations, questions, and expostulations rained on her head. Since she could not bring herself to reveal her reason for such a retreat, her relatives were more confused than ever.

Aunt Elizabeth insisted she sit down. Sophie used the latest ladies' fashion magazine to fan her.

"Ah, pay me no mind, I beg!" she said at last, forcing a smile. "You shan't miss your Season, dear Coz, just because I am blue-deviled this morning. No, Aunt, I am not sickening for something, nor is there trouble at home. 'Twas but a whim of the moment, and I spoke without thought."

So calm was restored, but not in Daphne's heart. She hated London, detested the mad social crush of the Season, despised the vain, shallow gallants mouthing insincere compliments. Most of all she loathed the villainous Earl of Courtlea.

Dressed that evening in her cream-coloured crepe, Daphne sought for some way to thaw the coldness within her. She stared into her mirror, and was shocked at the white face and hollowed eyes that looked back. Where was her pride, her self-esteem? Was she so easily vanquished?

Her wound was all the deeper because she was too ashamed to share her hurt with anyone. Bitterly she recollected all the comforting sayings for a broken heart: one man is like another; marry and forget him; time heals.

She would never forget. In time, mayhap, the sore might grow over, but it would never heal. She saw of a sudden that running off home was the wrong thing to do, as was withdrawing to mope in her room. Such retirement would only give Lord Courtlea more satisfaction. How he would gloat at breaking her spirit! Well, she would not be such a rabbit. She was not Alice Coffidge.

She turned to her abigail, who stood by holding Daphne's cloak. "Briggs, I shall wear the emeralds after all, but without the additional piece in the necklace. And my new fan, I think; the one of ivory and painted silk."

Now let anyone believe her heart was broken, she thought. Why, even her color had improved.

* * *

Almack's was crowded and growing stuffy when the party from Wentford House arrived. Daphne had wondered why everyone considered Almack's so important, but had soon realized the immense influence of its patronesses on Society. Without *entree* to Almack's, one was simply not in with the ton.

A hasty scan of the floor and the galleries above revealed many familiar faces, but not, Daphne noted with relief, the one she most feared to see. Lord Tunney, urbane and poised as always, first greeted the Wentfords. He bowed over Daphne's hand as if they had parted the best of friends.

"Will you grant me the favor of this dance, Miss Summerhayes?" he asked with perfect equanimity.

Daphne had intended to sit quietly with the chaperons, but Lord Tunney would misunderstand her refusal to dance, seeing it a further rejection of himself. And if she must dance, who better than with Lord Tunney?

Daphne summoned a smile. "With pleasure, sir."

Lord Launton claimed Sophie at the same moment, and they moved out on the floor together. Lord Tunney leaned close to murmur in Daphne's ear.

"Your words of refusal have rung in my head without cessation for two days. In the normal case, I would hold myself aloof from you, but I discovered that I prize your friendship too highly for such a drastic action. May I still claim that accord which you so generously offered?"

"Indeed you may, my lord," Daphne assured him, "and know that I, too, value that friendship highly."

"I am delighted that it is so, Miss Summerhayes." He smiled, his eyes twinkling in the wry manner that never failed to bring an answering smile to Daphne's lips. "I shall warn you, however," he continued, "that hope dies hard in a Tunney breast. Pray do not think ill of me for yet harboring the most tender affection for your lovely self."

His gentle consideration threatened to bring tears to her eyes. Why could she not love this fine gentleman who offered her everything her heart could desire? Except, of course, her heart's desire.

"What lady can despise such affection, even though she may not condone or return it? Certainly not I, sir. Such regard comes when and where it will, with or without our permission."

She dropped her gaze, fearing he might discern the sadness behind her forced smile.

"Well said, my dear. You express an understanding beyond your years." He said no more, but after the dance he stayed at her side, and Daphne was grateful for his company. She could talk or not, and he accepted both her conversation and her silence with equal content.

Surprisingly soon, Sophie expressed boredom, weariness, and a sudden concern over keeping Aunt Elizabeth from her bed. Although Lady Wentford was not in the least tired, she recognized the reluctance of her charges to stay, and so agreed to an early departure. The tallcase clock in the hall chimed half twelve as they entered Wentford House.

Sophie yawned prodigiously, barely covering her mouth with her fingers. "Oh, I vow I have never felt so tired. I expect to sleep all day tomorrow, so do not be distressed if I do not appear for breakfast." She gave a high, nervous giggle. "I may even be absent for luncheon."

Daphne said goodnight, as she wanted nothing more than to get to bed. Briggs awaited, and in a satisfyingly short time, Daphne was snuggled in bed, hoping for the oblivion of sleep.

He was with her the moment she closed her eyes. She saw his handsome face, his eyes smouldering with desire, his smile beguiling and assured. He bent close, seeking her mouth. His kiss teased her lips, arousing fierce desires and needs. His arms locked her body close to his, yet never close enough to satisfy her wants. His hands moved warmly, seductively, over her tingling body, weakening her will to resist, while strengthening her desire to surrender.

Daphne groaned, tossing and turning, until, in despair, she lay wide awake, staring overhead through welling tears at the embroidered medallion centered in the bed canopy. Oh, how she despised him for his betrayal! How she loathed him for causing all her tears and pain! Yet, she realized bitterly, she knew his over-proud nature, and should have expected such treatment. He was what he was.

Gradually she became aware of a soft tapping on the bedroom door. "Who is there?" she called, hastily wiping at her wet cheeks.

The door opened just enough, and Tyson crept in, biting her lips and wringing her hands. Strangely, at this late hour, she was still fully dressed.

"Tyson, what is the matter? You look frightened to death." As she spoke, Daphne threw off her covers, almost blessing this interruption of her torment. "Has Miss Sophie taken ill?"

The abigail shook her head, swaying back and forward as she wrung her hands. "No, she ain't ill, though I swear she is out of her mind. Oh, miss, please come at once. Please come and stop Miss Sophie before it is too late. Oh, the master and mistress will blame me, I know they will!" She began to moan.

Daphne caught the distraught woman by the shoulders. "Stop this noise at once, Tyson. Calm yourself. Where is Miss Sophie now?"

The abigail's lips writhed in terror. Her head jerked in the direction of the corridor. "In her room, miss," she gasped, "almost ready to go. She don't know I came to you, miss, and she will be put out about it, but what could I do?" She moaned again and hung her head.

"You did well, Tyson. Wait here until you collect yourself, and then come to Miss Sophie's room." Daphne ran out into the corridor. All was dark, except for a crack of light below her cousin's door. She pushed the door open and stepped inside.

Sophie, fully dressed, bent to her mirror, tying the ribbons of her hat. "Tyson, where did you go? Try to cram that dotted muslin into the valise."

Receiving no answer, Sophie jerked upright and swung around. Her eyes widened at the sight of Daphne bearing down on her.

"What do you mean by this, you foolish girl?" demanded Daphne. "Where can you possibly intend to go at this time of night?"

Sophie sank down on her dressing chair, her face white as paper. "Oh, Daphne, why did you not stay asleep? I will be gone in a minute, and you could truthfully say you knew nothing of it. Now you have spoiled everything."

"Knew nothing of what? Spoiled what? Certainly, I intend to prevent you from leaving this house, as I intend to get an explanation of this outlandish prank."

"'Tis no prank," Sophie protested with some pride. "We are eloping. To Gretna Green."

Daphne stared in horror at her cousin. "Have you quite lost your senses? To elope! Why, that would kill your mama!"

"Oh, Mama will survive the shock, and although Papa will be furious, I can talk him around, given time. I know they both will love Edgar as much as I do."

"Edgar Merritt! But how?" Daphne gestured helplessly. "Oh, no matter—you are insane, both of you. Well, 'tis all off now, naturally."

"Daphne! You cannot mean to stop me!"

"Indeed, I do and I shall." Despite her firm words, Daphne's heart ached at the misery in her cousin's face. "Where were you to meet?"

"A post-chaise is waiting in the mews," Sophie whispered. "I am—was to come as soon as the house was asleep."

"Well, Mr. Merritt will wait for you in vain." Daphne gestured toward a bulging valise on the bed. "When Tyson returns, she can unpack that, and get you into bed. I will say nothing of this disgraceful affair to Aunt Elizabeth or Uncle Valentine if you promise you will never again attempt such a thing."

"Oh, Daphne, I must go to him." Sophie's features crumpled into tears. "I cannot bear to think of my dearest Edgar waiting, waiting, all through the night, and thinking I have deserted him. Oh, let me go and tell him we have been discovered! Just a moment with him is all I ask. You do not know what it is to love!"

Oh, did she not? "Oh, Sophie, dear!"

Daphne opened her arms and her cousin flew into them. She held the sobbing girl tight, sharing the keen ache of Sophie's distress, while tears stung her own eyes. She knew, however, the folly of letting her cousin meet with Mr. Merritt, even for a moment.

"Hush, now," she whispered. "We cannot have him found loitering behind the house, but you must stay here. I shall go and send him packing."

Sophie's sobs lessened, and she raised a face stained with tears. "Oh, Dee, how good of you, but do not scold him, I beg. I vow, I could not bear to have him scolded."

Daphne allowed a glimmer of a smile as she untied the ribbons, now sadly crushed, of Sophie's hat. "I promise to treat your impetuous Mr. Merritt with the greatest gentleness. I must leave you, but promise me that you will not set foot outside this room."

With trembling lips, Sophie gave her word, and Daphne hurried back to her own room. Hastily donning dressing gown and slippers, and tying back her heavy fall of hair with a ribbon, she berated herself for giving even the slightest consideration to Edgar Merritt. Yet, as she quietly quit the house, wrapped in a hooded cloak against a light rain that had started to fall, Daphne suspected that the headstrong Sophie was doubtless as much to blame as he.

Every step to the mews gate stabbed Daphne with memory. She could almost see Lord Courtlea waiting in the shadows, smiling at her. Angrily, she shook her head to banish the vision, drew her hood forward to keep the rain from her eyes, and concentrated on lifting the wet, slippery bar as silently as possible. The gate opened easily, and she saw the post-chaise a few yards away. The interior was dark, but the outside lanterns showed a short, broadly built post-boy standing at the door, hunched against the cold drizzle. He opened the door as Daphne neared. With an impudent grin, he seized her arm, and lifted her to the step.

She drew back, resisting his urging. "I do not—"

"'S'awright, milady. We 'ave our orders, we 'ave. In ye go." An adroit shove, and Daphne stumbled into the carriage, barely saving herself from falling to her knees. The door slammed to behind her, and Daphne had time only to note that she was quite alone before the carriage started off at a brisk pace.

"Stop!" she called. "Stop at once and let me out." Her cries went unheeded. If anything, the carriage speeded up, swinging wildly around a corner and sending Daphne sprawling into the opposite seat.

She hammered on the carriage ceiling. "Coachman, can you not hear? I demand you halt this carriage at once, at once!"

Again there was no response, save for the cracking of a whip urging on the horses. "Coachman! Stop, I beg," Daphne shouted desperately. "'Tis all a mistake, I tell you! Stop!"

When the carriage continued on, Daphne sank back on the seat, feeling furiously and utterly helpless. 'Twas not a pleasant sensation. "Oh, let me get my hands on you, Edgar Merritt," she muttered. "I shall make you cry 'enough,' I warrant you."

She noticed suddenly something white shoved between the squabs and the carriage wall. She pounced on it, and drew out what appeared to be a letter. The light was poor, so she held it near the window and the flare of the outside lanterns. The carriage jounced her unmercifully, but she discerned the initials S. S. written on the front. Daphne immediately broke the wafer and opened the single sheet.

"My dearest, darling S.," she read. "A thousand thousand Apologies, my Love, for not being with you at this Moment, but I shall Meet with you Soonest at our trysting Place. Fear not, the Driver will Conduct you safely to me. Forgive me, dearest Heart, I beg. You cannot Know how I long to Hold you in my Arms!"

It was signed with an E. The writing was not of the neatest, indicating Edgar had dashed it off with some speed. "Oh, blast and double blast!" Daphne exploded. She crumpled the letter and threw it across the carriage.

Determined to end this farce, she let down the window and leaned out her head. The wind of their passing took her breath away. Rain dashed into her face, mixed with the spray thrown up by the six galloping horses. The clatter of their hooves echoed and re-echoed against the close, grimy buildings in the narrow street. Obviously the driver was keeping to the back streets, avoiding the main thoroughfares which were busy with traffic even at this late hour. Daphne had no notion as to her location, but knew at this speed they would soon quit London. Hurriedly she retrieved Edgar's letter.

"Coachman!" she called in her firmest voice, waving the letter out the window, "this letter from the gentleman who hired you directs you to return me at once to my home. Do you hear, Coachman?"

"Aye, miss, that I do." His words floated down to her, and hope rose in her heart. "But I 'ave me orders, miss, and beggin' yer pardon, I know how young misses might 'ave second thoughts, if you get me meanin'. Yo, there, you Ginger! Settle, now! Just you sit back, miss, and rest easy."

"But 'tis a mistake! Can you not understand?" Daphne shrieked, leaning her head out again. "I am not the person Mr.—the gentleman who hired you expects. Oh!" The fetid spray from a deep puddle splashed high. Daphne was forced to retreat or be soaked. "Coachman!"

"Sit back, miss. Pull up the winder and keep out the night air."

'Twas futile to argue further, as 'twas sheer lunacy to consider throwing herself from the racing vehicle. Daphne jerked the window shut, and, fuming, could do little else but try to make herself comfortable in the swaying, bumping carriage. She huddled in her cloak, wearily rubbing her burning eyes. She was exhausted by the events of the last two days and by her lack of sleep, but she must stay awake until they reached the first toll-gate on the Great North Road. Surely someone there would come to her aid.

But sober reflection showed that she dare not cry out for help. Miss Summerhayes, in nightgown and wrapper, rescued from an abduction, or rethinking a planned elopement? The ton would indeed enjoy such a juicy on dit! Better to meet Edgar, and, with good fortune, slip without notice back to Grosvenor Street.

With a tired sigh, Daphne wrapped her cloak tightly about her, settled into a corner and closed her eyes.

*   *   *

"'Ere we be, miss."

Daphne sat up, blinking and disoriented. The carriage had stopped and the post-boy stood at the opened door, stifling a yawn. 'Twas still night, and the rain had all but stopped.

"And just where is 'here'?" she demanded. "I shall not set foot to ground until I know to what place you have brought me."

The post-boy grimaced with all the impatience of his seventeen or so summers. "'Tis t'inn yer gennulmun chose. Out ye come, now, if ye please."

He looked as determined to drag a reluctant passenger bodily from the coach as he had cheerfully shoved one in. "Very well, I shall descend, but you must wait until I see that all is right."

"Oh, aye, miss," he assured her, all seriousness.

Reluctantly she gave him her hand and alit from the coach. Hardly had she stepped away when he leaped to the box, the driver swung his horses, and despite Daphne's shout, the carriage clattered away.

"Oh, Edgar, you have much to answer for," she muttered, shivering apprehensively as she squelched in her damp house slippers across the shadowy inn yard. A lantern shone by the door, illuminating a sign proclaiming the inn to be "The Beef and Bone." A faint light glimmered inside, and as Daphne hammered on the door, the light came nearer. The door opened.

"Are you the landlord?" Daphne demanded of the rotund personage who stood there, a flickering candle in his hand.

"Aye, that I am, miss. Potley's the name, at your service." He yawned and scratched his thinning mouse-coloured locks. Though fully dressed, there was a frowzy look about him that hinted he had been asleep.

"I am searching for Mr.—" The necessity of not naming names stopped her. Edgar might well be known here as Smith or Brown or a dozen other names. "That is, I was to meet a—a gentleman."

"Oh, aye. A gentleman, to be sure. Come this way, miss." He stepped aside with such a knowing leer and raking look that Daphne was glad of the protection of her thick cloak and its shadowing hood.

He led her through the common room where a fire smouldered smokily on the hearth, and up a narrow flight of stairs to where several doors opened from a short corridor. He threw open one door, going in first to light a candle.

"Why, where is—the gentleman?" Daphne asked after a swift look about the room.

"Oh, he be along, I've no doubt, miss," Potley assured her with another suggestive leer. "Make yourself comfy, miss, and would ye be wantin' food or drink?"

"No, landlord, but notify me at once when the gentleman arrives. Oh, and what is the time, pray?"

"'Tis just after three, miss. You won't be disturbed, you and your gentleman, as only one other room is bespoke for the night." He backed out, taking his bawdy grin with him.

The room, though cold with early morning chill, seemed clean enough and not too mean. The bed looked solid, its linens fresh. The bed curtains even had tassels to them, and a table flanked with chairs sported some carving. The hearth held only cold ashes, but Daphne dreaded calling the landlord back to build a fire. Hoping her wait would be short, she wrapped her cloak well around her for warmth and settled into one of the chairs, listening to every creak and groan in the old building.

Time dragged on, and Daphne grew more apprehensive by the minute. What would she do if Edgar did not arrive? "The Beef and Bone" appeared reasonably respectable, but it could be, like many inns, a den for footpads and other felons. She had no money to pay for the room or for passage to London. And what if Sophie, alarmed by her long absence, roused Aunt Elizabeth and Uncle Valentine? They would be frantic! Oh, what a mare's nest!

A floorboard creaked on the stairs. Daphne held her breath. Then came the welcome sound of booted feet striding purposefully along the corridor. Daphne stood, gathering all her outraged dignity to read Edgar a fine scold the moment he walked through the doorway.

The door flew open, but 'twas not Edgar Merritt who entered the room.

CHAPTER 23

The Earl of Courtlea violently swung the door shut, sending drops of water flying from his caped, white drab driving-coat. The sweet scent of fresh, rain-washed air swirled into the room with him, but his tight-lipped glower denied any sweetness of temper. His presence seemed to fill the little room.

Daphne gave a startled cry, and stared open-mouthed, too shocked and horrified to do anything more.

He gave the room one swift, disgusted glance, then rivetted his glare on the cloaked figure before him. "Your wait is over, Miss Summerhayes." Despite the rage crackling from him, his voice was deadly quiet. "That insolent pup, my brother, will not be with you to continue this mad scheme. He is safely locked in his room, and I guarantee he will remain so. I know not how much this affair was at your insistence, but I shall return you to your home, and for all our sakes, pray stay there."

"At my insistence?" Daphne demanded, taken aback. "You cannot seriously consider that I—I should en-encourage—"

She stumbled to a stop as his head suddenly lifted, a puzzled frown contracting his brows. He took a step forward, peering closer in the light from the single candle on the mantel behind her, and she realized he did not recognize her. Slowly she raised her hands and pulled back her hood.

He started, then stared while the color drained from his features. "Daphne! Devil take me," he whispered, "what means this?"

Words stuck in Daphne's throat. She longed to scream, to fly at him like a harpy, striking hard with her fists, until he felt some of the pain she had endured. Here he was, this man who had deceived her and deserved her hate. The notion of being near him, the sound of his voice and the sight of his handsome face, should fill her with revulsion.

Yet, God help her, she knew she still loved him.

"What means this?" he repeated, near shouting, closing the distance between them with a single stride. He seized her by the upper arms. "I thought to find Sophie. It can't be that you and Edgar—" His countenance crimsoned; a small vein throbbed at his temple. "Explain yourself, Daphne, for God's sake," he snarled. "I demand that much."

"I explain!" she gasped. "You dare, sir, to demand an explanation from *me*?"

His look—mouth thinned in fury, gray eyes blazing beneath the brim of his beaver hat—was exactly like her first glimpse of him. If only it had been her last! Her temper roused at all she had suffered through this man. The pain of his fingers gripping her arms only added to her anger.

"How is it, madam," he insisted through gritted teeth, "how is it I find you eloping with my clodpole of a brother?"

Daphne could not believe her hearing. "You cannot possibly believe that Mr. Merritt and I were eloping!" she exclaimed. "Good God! Not I, you chub, you utter fool! Sophie was indeed your brother's intended bride." In hurt and despair, she tried to strike his arms aside. "Now release me, sir, at once."

His anger swiftly changed to dawning realization as he stared down at her. "But how came you here? And where is your cousin?"

Daphne stood rigidly, struggling to retain her grim expression. 'Twas difficult, with him so close. "Let me go, my lord," she said through stiff lips, "and although you hardly deserve the courtesy, I shall tell you why you find me here in Sophie's stead."

"Of course," he said at once, releasing his grip on her arms, "but pray do not frown so at me."

Without answering, she quickly sat down, putting the width of the table between them.

The earl relaxed, letting out his breath in a soft laugh. "Forgive me for getting the wrong end of it, Daphne. Blame my quick temper, if you will." While he spoke, he removed his hat and shrugged out of his driving-coat. "I knew nothing of this elopement until I came home and all but tripped over Edgar's valises in the entry." He grimaced, tossing hat and coat over a chest at the foot of the bed. "Suspecting some devilment, I sent for him to come and explain himself to me. After some delay,—"

"Doubtless to write this note," Daphne put in, taking the letter from her pocket. He scanned it quickly, then nodded.

"'Twould seem so," he agreed, handing the note back to her. "His man Blount was missing for an hour or so; he probably delivered it. In any case, when Edgar saw he was my prisoner, he confessed all. Naturally I could not trust him to fetch Miss Summerhayes back, so I hurried here to retrieve Miss Sophie, as I thought, and take her smartly home."

He lifted the candle from the mantel and set it on the table, already marked with tallow drippings. "The better to see your fair face, sweet Daphne," he explained lightly. Taking the opposite chair, he leaned forward as though to grasp her hands. Deliberately, she slid them into her lap. Her heart twisted inside her; he looked so touchingly handsome, a small smile on his lips and the candleglow lighting his eyes and dark hair. He did not seem to notice her withdrawal; his mind was evidently on his story.

"Edgar was so furious to come that three footmen barely subdued him," he said in wonderment. "My placid, easy brother. He swore that money did not signify; he would marry on nothing, he loved his darling so much. Then he accused me of never knowing what love is."

"If that is so, you are to be congratulated, sir," Daphne declared, recollecting Sophie's same words to her, "for love can be most painful."

His brows rose at her tart tone. "To whom do you refer? Lord Tunney, who must surely be suffering a broken heart?"

"'Tis odd, how gentlemen differ so widely," she retorted with an exasperated toss of her head. "One has all the pleasant traits, while another is arrogant, over-proud, and cruel. Pity the woman who is fond of one, yet loves the other!"

His hand lay stretched out on the table toward her, the long fingers and short square nails on the edge of her vision. She dared not think of how that hand had touched her throbbing, hungry body.

In as few words as possible, her eyes fixed on a wine stain on the table, she told of how she came to be at the inn. Lord Courtlea listened in silence except for one or two comments muttered under his breath.

"Sophie is not the thoughtless child you believe her to be," she finished briskly. "She loves Edgar as much as he loves her. This elopement was an act of desperation, as they were forbidden to meet as a natural course, and I have Sophie's word it will not be repeated."

She forced herself to look up at him. "Their fate lies in your hands, my lord, though I shudder to say so. Will you not consider their position with an open mind?"

He was narrowly watching her beneath dark brows drawn in a frown. "They are young yet. Edgar is barely twenty. How can he be so certain of his heart's desire?"

"How old must one be to know love?" Daphne asked bitterly. "Or do you plan to choose his wife for him?"

"Naturally not. What do you take me for? He will marry whom he pleases..."

"Indeed?" she mocked.

He fell silent, frowning and stroking his jaw. "Edgar will come into a fortune when he marries, though he knows it not," he mused. "Very well, Advocate, I will let him court Sophie in the usual manner, and see the result. If 'tis merely a case of forbidden fruit being the sweeter, we shall soon discover it. Does that please you?"

Daphne gave a brief nod, thankful that at least two lovers would come happily from this confused piece of work.

Lord Courtlea continued to frown. "Demme, but my blood boils! 'Tis no wonder you are angry, and sharp with me. I will have that coachman by the heels, and the boy too, for their treatment of you."

"Pray do not spend your indignation for my sake," Daphne rejoined coldly. "Doubtless they were well paid to follow Edgar's orders."

"That don't signify in the slightest. The hounds! I shall—"

"—do nothing further, I beg," Daphne snapped, glaring. "Indeed, had you minded your own affairs and not come charging in like an outraged father, all would have come well. Edgar would have been in the coach, and I could have sent him on his way with a flea in his ear and no one the wiser. Instead I have been kept from my bed, bounced for hours in a rackety coach, and left alone and unprotected in a public inn."

Daphne bit her lip, fighting hysteria and tears of hurt and frustration. She would not cry. Though exhausted, her nerves stretched thin, torn with love and loathing, she would not cry.

"But how was I to know that?" the earl demanded. "I thought to find Sophie. Good God, Daphne, when I saw your face instead of the other—" He went white, and passed a shaking hand over his brow. "Such a turn you gave me! I cannot describe it. I know only that I wish never to endure its like again. Confound it, Daphne! Promise me at once, sweetheart, that you will never do the like to me again."

Daphne bit back an anguished cry at his mocking endearment. "How dare you," she cried, leaping to her feet. "How dare you call me so? Do you wish to wreak more revenge on my poor pride?"

The earl made no move, but sat staring at her as if stunned. The candle, almost a stub, flared bright as a draft caught it. Daphne knew the light must reveal her stormy eyes and trembling mouth, her hair, barely restrained by its ribbon, wildly curling about her face and falling down her back. She did not care; her heart was too heavy for vanities.

"Whatever is sadly amiss here," Lord Courtlea stated, his voice dangerously soft, "I mean to get to the bottom of it." He sat back in the chair, the hand on the table curling into a fist. "One night past, in a garden, I held a warm, beautiful woman in my arms and made love to her. She answered me in the sweetest of kisses. Did those kisses after all mean nothing to her?"

"Nothing," Daphne answered in a low voice, looking down at her trembling hands grimly clasped together, "other than 'twas she who first kissed you, and—and offered herself. You had promised to humble her so, and she cannot deny you your victory."

"What the deuce are you saying? My victory? Oh, good Lord!" His fist banged the table. "You mean that vain, boastful nonsense in my study? No, I swear, I had long ago rejected that foolish notion."

"Then what notion occupied your mind in Lady Prudence Abernathy's company the very next day?" Daphne cried, smacking her palm down beside his fist. "Had you dismissed me so casually from your head, or did you consider me such a one as dispenses kisses and liberties as freely as tuppences?"

He stared at her, looking as puzzled as though she spoke an unknown language. "But you know better! Did you not read my note? True, I dashed it off with all speed—"

Daphne straightened with a bitter little laugh. "A note, is it? I know of no note, sir. Do not attempt to paste a prettier face over your behavior with such a flimsy excuse. You sent me no message."

The earl uttered a short, sharp curse. He shot to his feet, captured both her hands in a tight grip, and drew her from behind the table.

"Listen to me, Daphne, and listen without interrupting. Lady Prudence is a close friend—"

"Extremely close, I would say." Although his touch warmed her to her toes, Daphne jerked her hands away. "She dotes on you, my lord, if the looks she gives you are any indication."

"Hush, you vixen! Not one more word, or I vow I will throttle you where you stand." Glowering, he waited until he had her stiff-necked, tight-lipped agreement.

"Lady Prudence is secretly married to a gentleman of whom her family disapproves. I, who have known Prudence since childhood, promised to help them and act as her escort to allay her family's suspicion. With her husband's full agreement, I might add. If you saw any look of love from her, it was only because she spoke of her husband."

As he paused, she lifted her head and gave him a straight look. "Do not try to cozen me, my lord, with such an improbable story," she warned. "I have had enough of lies and deception."

"Listen to me! I have never lied to you, and I do not lie now!" He raised his hand as if to touch her. She sent him such a scorching look that he sighed and let it drop to his side.

"Enright hopes to make his fortune in Jamaica," he went on, holding her gaze with his, "and he is the sort to do it. This morning—no, yesterday morning now, Prudence sent a note, saying he had booked passage to Jamaica, and now awaited her in Bristol. I had promised to take her to him the moment her word came, and although I had planned to come to you, I could not let down my friends. I left at once, after scribbling that note to you."

"Which did not arrive." She searched his face for the truth, desperately wanting to believe, but not daring to trust.

He nodded, and anger sparked in his clear gray eyes. "Doubtless Robert, that fool of a footman, misheard my instructions. He leaves my service today; this is one lapse too many. Oh, sweetheart, what you must have thought of me! But truly, I did not betray you. Fortunately, Enright, impatient for his wife, met us on the road, or I could not have arrived back in London so soon."

He smiled crookedly, and again captured her hands. This time, though she still hesitated to believe, she did not protest. Gently he kissed her fingers, one by one. "I came from one elopement, for so we must call it, to another." He released one of her hands to cup her cheek in his palm. "Only my given word could have kept me from you today. You must believe me, most beautiful nymph, that my absence from you wrenched my heart more with every mile."

His eyes glowed with such ardor and truth that her heart turned over in her breast. "Oh, can it be so? I—I doubted you, but indeed, considering all, can you fault me for that, my lord?"

"Victor, dash it! No, sweetheart, I cannot blame you, and your only fault is to drive me to distraction." He drew her into his arms, and with a deep sigh, Daphne rested her head against his shoulder. He kissed her brow, gathering her tightly against him.

"My sweet," he murmured, his deep voice like warm honey, "do you know how I burned with jealousy, watching you dance in other men's arms? And why? Because I wanted you for my own and did not realize it."

"What, with my off-putting nature?" Daphne smiled, happy but uncertain, rubbing her cheek against the firm weave of his coat. Victor had said nothing about loving her. Wanting, yes, but not loving. He wanted her for his own. Not his wife; he had made clear to her his attitude toward marriage. As his mistress? Her upbringing scorned any accommodation other than wedlock, but her heart was already committed, and love knows only its own rules.

He laughed softly, kissing the top of her head. "You, Daphne, are all I decry in a woman; headstrong—" he lifted her chin and kissed her lightly on the lips— "opinionated, overly-intelligent, stubborn—" with each word he kissed her more deeply and possessively.

"And managing?" she whispered huskily as he finally raised his head. "Do not forget managing."

"To be sure," he breathed, seeking her lips again.

Daphne melted against him. Her arms crept about his neck, and she rose on tiptoe to meet his kiss with all the passion she possessed. She cared for nothing but the safe haven of his arms and the glorious demand of his mouth on hers. Nothing mattered; not father, aunt, uncle, cousin, or the possibility of scandal.

"I must return you home, sweetheart," he murmured, "though I burn with wanting you. I would hold you here forever, but there are certain arrangements…"

"Arrangements?" she repeated, knowing she was his under any circumstances. She must not think of the shock and hurt to her family.

He smiled and loosened her hair ribbon so her thick, wavy tresses fell freely about her shoulders. "This is what I dreamed of," he murmured. Gently he ran his hands through the thick mass, letting the silky strands flow through his fingers.

"What—what arrangements must be made, pray?" She must hear him say it.

He straightened, the better to see her face clearly. "What, managing me already? Well, Miss Summerhayes, I must speak to your father, then see to a special license so we may be married as soon—"

"Married?" cried Daphne. "You said nothing of marriage."

Courtlea smiled, much as a cat having caught the mouse far from its bolthole. "Why, my dear, what other arrangement might you have considered? Mayhap we should discuss the options you offer."

Daphne flushed more deeply than she thought possible. "You arrant, impossible rogue," she muttered.

He threw back his head and laughed. "You scorn my offer of respectability, madam, after meeting me at this inn and passing most of the night with me? Your reputation is ruined. And in any case, what if I refuse to accept you in any manner save as my wife?"

She did not join in his banter, and his smile quickly faded at her serious expression. "Are you certain, sir," she asked calmly, though she had to force the words, "that marriage is what you wish? You are not merely saving my reputation at the expense of your freedom? I can face scandal more readily than a loveless marriage."

Looking deep into his eyes, she searched for indecision, confusion, or regret, but found none. Those clear crystal pools held only depths of tenderness and love.

"My lovely, beloved one," he murmured, brushing back the hair curling at her temples, "my mind was early set in a cynical, selfish view of marriage. Though such an outlook was kindly meant, I see now how wrong, and sad, was that advice."

Daphne did not understand the reference, but she heard the pain in his voice. Gently she laid her fingertips on his lips. "Then say no more of it. I cannot bear to see you distressed."

He smiled, kissing her fingers. "Bless you, my love. From that first telling look across that ballroom floor, you have lived in my heart, though I knew it not. I want you, my Daphne, for I cannot face any future without you. A lifetime as my wife, dearest one, will not be long enough to prove the depth or constancy of my devotion."

A shadow crossed his features, and his arms tightened. "Tell me you are of the same thought."

Daphne did not answer in words, sealing her love with all the ardor her kiss could show. His passion answered hers. She pressed against the long length of his body, aching to be closer still. Then his lips found that tender place below her ear.

"Ooh," she moaned, arching back her head as he trailed kisses down her neck, "that gives me shivers, delicious ones, right down to my toes."

"Does it so?" he murmured, his lips at the hollow of her throat, "and did Flora find it as delicious?"

"Aye, my lord," she gasped, "though it shames me to confess it."

"No, dearest heart, there is no shame."

Victor unclasped her cloak, and when it dropped to her feet, gave a slight start at sight of her loose wrapper. "There was no time to dress," Daphne murmured, flushing hotly. "I had no thought for anything but to stop the elopement."

"Indeed." He smiled seductively. "I understand their impatience."

His fingers toyed with the ties of her wrapper. It fell open, revealing the white swell of her breasts through the thin cambric of her nightgown.

"My love, you well know how to drive me to the edge," he whispered.

Daphne smiled, loving the passion in his eyes, the warmth of his hands on her shoulders. "My love, no more than you know how to tempt me," she whispered.

He caught her to him and kissed her. Then his hands fell and he stepped back, breathing heavily. A muscle jerked in his tight-clenched jaw.

"No. I want you too much, but I vowed our loving would not be a rushed thing and certainly not in such a poor place as this." Victor shook his head as she would have spoken, and held up his hand. "I know too, that you believe in the sanctity of marriage. I do not wish you to act against that belief, although I—" He broke off, his eyes gleaming.

"Daphne, my carriage is below. 'Tis outrageous, and scandalous, and asking a deal of you, but will you come to Scotland with me?"

"Do you mean we should elope?" Daphne gasped. "Now?"

"When better?"

"But—but I have no clothes, not even a comb." Of all the reasons against elopement, why should that silly drawback be the only thing to come to her mind?

He gestured as if nakedness was not a concern. "All may be bought on the way. Is lack of apparel your only stumbling block? What say you, my love?"

Excitement pounded in her veins. 'Twas indeed outrageous, mad, and totally beyond the pale for the proper Miss Summerhayes. But not beyond the scope of Flora. She gave a delicious gurgle of laughter.

A VERY PROPER THIEF

"'Tis a prodigious disgraceful proposal, my lord Rascal, and I accept it with great delight. Let us finish what Edgar and Sophie began."

He laughed, looking so boyishly eager Daphne had to kiss him again. When he could next breathe, he reluctantly let her go. "We must change horses before we leave. My poor brutes fairly flew over the road and need to rest. You, my love, may sleep in the carriage, wrapped securely in my arms."

"But—but Victor," Daphne whispered, not daring to raise her eyes above the perfect knot in his immaculate neckcloth, "'tis yet two hours before dawn. You must be prodigious tired too, what with driving Lady Prudence so far, and then rushing off here. Would you not care to—to rest until daylight?"

She heard his in-drawn breath. "This is no palace," she went on, resting her hands on his chest, "but the room is clean, the linen fresh. Besides, no place is too mean where love is."

Tenderly he raised her chin, and she, blushing furiously, but with a wicked glint in her eye, met his gaze. "I once asked Flora to share my bed," he said unsteadily, "thinking only of a casual pleasure. What you offer me is a thousand times more precious. Do you indeed mean what you say?"

For answer, she slowly shrugged off her wrapper, then stepped out of her nightgown. She quailed at her boldness, but made no move to cover herself. Standing proudly, she faced Victor, and saw her reward in her lover's eyes. He looked at her slim white body in the candle's flickering light as at a miracle, a miracle for him alone.

"My beautiful one," he whispered hoarsely, "you are sure?"

With her heart full to overflowing, Daphne reached up to frame his face with her hands. Drawing his head down, she whispered: "Yes, Victor, my love. Oh, yes!" and kissed him.

With an exultant laugh, he swept her up in his arms.

PATRICIA HARRISON

"Words, language, books—all have held a life-long fascination for me," says Patricia, "ever since learning to read at age four. English is such a rich language, and part of the challenge of writing is in choosing the right word to portray the desired picture, or to achieve the desired effect."

Patricia enjoys reading any good book, but especially likes mysteries, sagas, and historical fiction of any era. She became interested in England's Regency period (early 1800s), and this led to her first book, *A Very Proper Thief*. Her next book, *Lord Compton's Folly*, adds adventure and suspense to Regency manners.

Her first ambition was to become a librarian, as she enjoyed working in the Public Library after school and during the summers. Then, in midstream, so to speak, she was drawn to teaching, graduating from Hamilton Teachers' College and from courses in Primary Education from the University of Toronto. "Teaching the primary grades is a real high. The children are so receptive, like little sponges. I hope I passed on to them my own love of reading and language."

After ten years, Patricia left teaching, and with husband Bill moved to the country to raise daughters Stephanie and Valerie, several Quarter horses, a German Shepherd named Zenta, and Serendipity, a Siamese cat. Next, the family (minus the animals) moved to Australia for several wonderful years before returning to Canada. Now empty-nesters, Bill and Patricia split their time between their home in Southern Ontario and their cottage "up north." Traveling is on the agenda, too. They have visited the U.K., especially Scotland, home of Patricia's parents, Hawaii, Singapore, Southern U. S., and of course, Australia.

Patricia's interests besides writing? Their granddaughter, oil painting, forests and everything in them, gardens, people, learning stuff, and anything Scottish. Oh, yes, and singing in the church choir.

Since writing "for real" Patricia has twice been a finalist in the Golden Heart contest of the Romance Writers of America. She is a member of The Beau Monde and The Golden Horseshoe Writers' Group.

AMBER QUILL PRESS, LLC
THE GOLD STANDARD IN PUBLISHING

QUALITY BOOKS
IN BOTH PRINT AND ELECTRONIC FORMATS

ACTION/ADVENTURE	SUSPENSE/THRILLER
SCIENCE FICTION	PARANORMAL
MAINSTREAM	MYSTERY
FANTASY	EROTICA
ROMANCE	HORROR
HISTORICAL	WESTERN
YOUNG ADULT	NON-FICTION

AMBER QUILL PRESS, LLC
http://www.amberquill.com